LOVE AND HATE

DREDA SAY MITCHELL

Love and Hate Series Book 1

Print ISBN 978-1-0685091-1-7

Editing and formatting: https://studioenp.com
Additional editing: Christine Dunlop
Cover design: Mitchell and Joseph Ltd/ Book Brush
Cover Photographers: Iniraswork, Eyecan and Feedough

Praise for Dreda Say Mitchell & Ryan Carter

'As good as it gets.' **Lee Child**

'Great book by a great girl.' **Martina Cole**

'A truly original voice.' **Peter James**

'A fast-paced thriller that will keep you guessing until the very last page.' **Paula Hawkins**

'Sharply observed and a moving story of conflicting loyalties and unfinished business.' ***Guardian***

'Zippy, twisty plot...a bevy of memorable supporting goodies and baddies.' ***Sunday Times***

'Thrilling.' **Sunday Express Books of the Year**

'Awesome tale from a talented writer.' ***Sun***

'Fast paced and full of twists and turns.' ***Crime Scene Magazine***

Acknowledgements

Big thanks to the guys at the legendary Repton Boxing Club.

Wendell, Dave, Andy and all the other trainers, coaches and boxers thank you!

Without your welcome, your time and expertise this book could not have been written.

Free Novella

Join Our Exclusive Book Club

If you haven't already, plunge into the gangland world where the Steele and Watson Crime Family Drama started.

DANGEROUS

A LOVE & HATE SERIES PREQUEL

Fate throws them together. The streets try to tear them apart.

Bertram Watson, aka Brother Bertie, newly arrived from Jamaica, finds himself on the run in London's gritty streets. Jimmy Steele, son of a feared gangster, is bleeding out in a warehouse after a botched heist. Their paths cross in a twist of fate that will change their lives forever.

As Bertie's Jamaican street smarts clash with Jimmy's East End savvy, they form an unlikely alliance. But with rival gangs closing in and dangerous secrets coming to light, their newfound friendship is put to the ultimate test.

In this thrilling novella, loyalties are tested, blood is spilled, and love is pushed to its limits in the unforgiving world of London's underworld.

Visit www.dredamitchell.com

Prologue

The East End Docks

Hoods were shoved over Jimmy's and Brother Bertie's heads, plunging them into darkness. Hands grabbed their ankles, hauling them backwards. They were dragged across the ground, every stone, every loose brick tearing into them. The cold night air knifed through their clothes. Brother Bertie's shoulder smashed against something solid. A wall maybe. His grunt of pain echoed along with Jimmy's.

'Keep your mouths shut,' a harsh voice warned from above.

Jimmy tried to twist free. A boot slammed into his ribs, driving the air from his lungs. The hood trapped his gasps, the fabric sucking across his mouth with each desperate breath. The cloth tasted of oil and something metallic, probably blood. His pulse thundered in his ears.

'That was just a tap.' His tormentor's tone promised more to come. 'Next one breaks something.'

Brother Bertie's heart jack-hammered violently in his chest. The rough hands started moving again, yanking them onwards. Pebbles and broken glass bit through their clothes. The air grew danker, heavier. His stomach turned to lead because he knew where they were heading.

The Executioner's Steps.

The ancient stone stairs where the tide washed up bodies.

The first step cracked against Brother Bertie's skull, stars exploding behind his eyes. Then another impact, and another. Each edge battered into his spine, his shoulders, his legs. The steps were merciless, each one feeling like it was ripping strips from his flesh. Beside him, Jimmy's muffled groans told him his friend was getting the same battering from the stone.

'Bertie!' Jimmy's muffled shout earned him another kick.

'I'm all right,' Brother Bertie called back, although the tightness and pain in his voice told a different story. 'What's happening?'

The only answer was the sound of the River Thames slapping along the shore below, each wet smack, a promise of what was to come. The dragging stopped, rough hands hoisted them upright, bashing them into something cold and solid. The old timber wharf piles, driven deep into the riverbank that supported the warehouses. Rope bound and bit into their wrists, tight enough to restrict the blood flowing to their hands. More rope tied them to the wooden piles.

Abruptly, their hoods were yanked off.

The night exploded around them. Their eyes couldn't make sense of what they were seeing at first. Then the shock of where they were crashed into them. On the shore of the river, the vast, dark, scary expanse of water stretched before them, an endless black void of darkness. The river was alive, a writhing, ancient beast eager to feed. The terrifying sight stole the air from their lungs.

Nothing stood between them and the dangerous water. No buildings. No barriers. Nothing.

Jimmy shouted, 'Who are you? Show your face.'

The only answer he received was the chilled wind howling in the night.

The incoming tide surged towards them, a nightmare made real. Jimmy thrashed against his bonds, the rope slicing into his wrists until warm blood trickled down his arms. The water rose, a wall towering over them. There was nowhere to run, nowhere to hide.

The wave struck with the brutal force of a sledgehammer. First against their legs and surging up to their waists. The water tortured their flesh with ice-sharp cuts that burned like acid. The stench was revolting, waste and decay gagging them. The current pulled back, trying to sweep their feet out from under them. The greedy fingers of the river tried to haul them under. If not for the ropes holding them, Jimmy and Brother Bertie would've been ripped away instantly.

The water was stronger than anything they'd imagined.

Again and again it hit them, getting higher and higher.

'Where is it?' The question came from the shadows above, nearly lost in the roar of the river.

Brother Bertie's teeth chattered violently, his whole body shaking. 'Where is what?' he bellowed back. 'We don't know what you're talking about! Let us go!'

'Who are you?' Jimmy roared into the darkness, straining against his bonds until fresh blood flowed.

Another wave crashed into them, harder this time, carrying the weight of the whole river behind it. The filthy water climbed past their waists, its rotten stench of death and decay filling their nostrils. Each surge tried to knock them sideways, the current wrapping around them, a python slowly squeezing.

'Tell me where it is,' the voice demanded. 'Or the Thames gets two more secrets tonight.'

Brother Bertie caught Jimmy's eye. In all their years running the streets together, they'd never faced death like this. The freezing water crept higher, past their chests now, stealing their body heat. A deadly numbness crept through their muscles, turning their bodies to stone.

'Last chance!' the voice warned. 'Where is it?'

The black water rose to their necks, ice-cold tendrils seeking their mouths. The foulness of the river kissed their lips. Back and forward, back and forward. This time when it came back, a black wall of death closed over their heads. Brother Bertie's and Jimmy's screams bubbled into watery silence.

They knew they were about to die.

Chapter One

The East End
1967
Months Earlier

Twenty-six-year-old Jimmy 'Southpaw' Steele's fists itched for blood. His feet danced and bounced on the sweat-stained canvas of the boxing ring. This was it, his shot at the big time. If he won this, the next stop was fighting for the East London heavyweight crown. The smoke-filled hall buzzed with bloodthirsty excitement and anticipation. Jimmy barely noticed the baying crowd because his world had narrowed to the other boxer and beating the living shit out of him.

Jimmy's presence dominated the entire room. Body slick with sweat, bare-chested, he was six foot plus of bulging, toned muscle and raw manhood. His arms, particularly his left, promised annihilation with every swing. A colossus in the ring, he prowled the canvas with the sleek grace and power of a caged predator. He exuded a masculine energy that commanded attention.

Simply put, Jimmy Steele was a fucking masterpiece of destruction.

The other fighter resembled a brute, with a face resembling one that had been put through a mince grinder. He lunged forward, throwing a wild hammer-like blow which Jimmy easily ducked, years of training kicking in. He countered, landing a stiff jab to the solar plexus, feeling the satisfying thud as it connected.

'That's it, Jimmy!' His sister, Sin's, voice cut through the din. 'Clobber the bloody bollocks off him!'

Jimmy's silver-grey eyes flickered to where she stood in the crowd. Right next to her sat their father, Danny Steele, face impassive save for the slight twitch of the long scar running the length of his cheek.

The momentary distraction cost Jimmy. His opponent landed a glancing blow to the ribs. Red-hot pain burst in his side, but he pushed it down. He'd endured plenty worse. He retaliated, unleashing a flurry of jabs, his left hand a blur. 'Southpaw' had become his nick on account of his explosive left because it was the name given to fighters who favoured their left hands. He was determined to have as lethal a left as Henry Cooper. Get in the way of that and you were a goner.

The crowd went wild, the chant starting low and building to a roar.

'Southpaw! Southpaw! Southpaw!'

The support skyrocketed Jimmy's determination. He pressed forward, forcing his opponent onto the back foot. A right cross grazed Jimmy's jaw, snapping his head back, but he shook it off. He'd tasted his own blood before, and it only made him hungrier for victory.

The bell rang, ending the round. Jimmy retreated to his corner, where his cornerman and sparring partner, twenty-five-year-old Brother Bertie, waited. He wore his trademark porkpie hat tilted at a jaunty angle. The men were best mates, thick as thieves in a world where their friendship stuck out like a sore thumb. In 1960s Britain, a white East End bruiser and a black Jamaican immigrant being mucker and mate was rare as hen's teeth. But these two couldn't care less about what anyone thought. Jimmy would sooner knock a bloke's teeth down his throat than hear a bad word about his friend. And Brother Bertie? He'd walk through fire for Jimmy, no questions asked.

'You're doing great, bruv.' Brother Bertie's Jamaican accent was still solid after arriving in Britain back in '63, though a good dose of Cockney patter was creeping in these days.

He continued. 'But it's time to end this, yeah? Knock him on his arse. Give the punters what they came here for!'

The bell sounded.

Jimmy surged forward, but the other boxer came barrelling towards him. Before Jimmy could get his guard up, a solid punch connected with his upper face. Searing pain erupted in his eyes. He blinked rapidly, trying to clear his stinging vision, but it only got worse. His eyes shouldn't be hurting this much. Instinctively, Jimmy sensed something was off. It was the stink that alerted him first. It invaded his nose and mouth, each breath bringing a chemical taste to the back of his throat, making him want to gag. The acrid smell in his nostrils, adding to his disorientation.

Realisation suddenly dawned.

This could only mean one thing.

His opponent was fighting dirty. Jimmy would bet his life that while in his corner, the other fighter's cornerman had smeared some type of ointment on the boxer's gloves so when they connected with Jimmy's eyes it would interfere with Jimmy's vision.

Through the haze of white-hot pain behind his eyelids, Jimmy could make out his opponent's smug grin.

The cheating rat!

The other fighter came at him with all he had. The impact of the blows were devastating, rocking Jimmy back on his heels. Air whooshed explosively out of his gaping mouth, leaving him gagging for oxygen. Burning pain sliced through him with the sensation of a blade gutting him from belly to chest. Fighting the retching sensation choking him, he managed to right himself, just in time to elude a deadly uppercut gunning squarely at his jaw.

Jimmy's chances at getting one step closer to that heavyweight title fight were slipping away. Panic threatened to overwhelm him. Everything he'd worked for was on the line. The early morning runs, the bruised knuckles, the countless hours he'd gone without seeing his kids to train down by the river.

'Jimmy!' Sin once again belted through the fog of pain. 'Don't you DARE give up now!'

Her words ignited something in his belly. Nothing else mattered but this fight. He was an East Ender through and through and East Enders never quit.

With a roar of defiance, Jimmy's retaliation was swift and merciless. Popping up, an unholy jack-in-the-box, he launched a ferocious punch, the two front knuckles of his fist twisting into the other man's washboard stomach. Sweat dripping in his already blurry eyes, Jimmy proceeded to annihilate the other boxer. His jab landed with the power of ten men against his opponent's jaw.

Watching the dirty fighter reel back, Jimmy grinned through the taste of blood, knowing he had him bang to rights. He was on his opponent, a raging lion with the other man literally on the ropes. He let loose a one-two jab combination against both sides of the other man's ribs.

'That's it, Jimmy! Murder him!' Brother Bertie breathlessly shouted. 'Smash him! Crucify him!'

The crowd's chants grew louder, becoming a wall of sound that propelled Jimmy on.

'Southpaw! Southpaw! Southpaw!'

Summoning every ounce of strength he had left, Jimmy unleashed his signature left hook. It connected with a sickening crunch. The other man's eyes rolled back before he toppled to the canvas.

The ref didn't even bother to count. It was lights out.

For a moment, Jimmy stood still, his chest heaving. Then the reality of what he'd just accomplished hit him. He'd done it. He'd won. He was heading to East London's heavyweight championship.

The crowd erupted. Brother Bertie vaulted into the ring, almost losing his hat. He hoisted Jimmy's arm high in the air, proclaiming his victory.

'Ladies and gents!' Bertie bellowed, his grin wide enough to split his face. 'Listen up:

'I've got a tale to tell about Jimmy 'The Southpaw' Steele.

A couple of months from now, the heavyweight crown he'll steal.

His fists are fast, his spirit's free.

The new champ of the East End, just you wait and see!'

The crowd went mental at Brother Bertie's Muhammed Ali style rhyme.

The unnatural sting in Jimmy's eyes returned with a vengeance. He blinked rapidly, trying to focus on the blurry figures surrounding him.

Through the haze, he could just about make out his father's face. He tapped his glove meaningfully near his eye, indicating to his father the dirty play that had gone on, but his dad's attention was elsewhere. His gaze was fixed on something else in the crowd. Two newcomers.

Eric 'Batters' Rogers and his hulking son, Lucas. Jimmy's stomach dropped. Batters was his dad's bitter rival, and his presence here could only mean trouble with a capital T.

His father and Batters locked stares. The air between them crackled with barely contained violence.

The chants of 'Southpaw! Southpaw!' faded into the background as Jimmy watched the silent confrontation unfold. He'd won the fight, but he couldn't shake the feeling that a bigger battle was just beginning.

Chapter Two

Rage, thick and hot, rushed through Danny's veins when he clapped eyes on Batters and that fuckwit son of his.

The King of the Docks, that's what one and all called Danny Steele. It was a title he'd carved into the flesh of East London with blood, sweat, and a mind sharper than a docker's hook. At forty-eight, he cut an imposing figure, leaner and rangier than his powerhouse son, with a presence that had geezers and ladies alike hanging off his every word. He oozed old-style charm, a razor-sharp wicked grin and tough guy swagger accompanied by a jagged scar cut deep into his cheek that the women went nuts over. That silver tongue of his could sweet-talk the Devil himself, which he used to wrap the dock management around his little pinkie whenever he had to talk with them on behalf of the dockers.

But don't let that slick exterior fool you. Underneath lurked a power-hungry, dangerous bastard gagging for control. He'd built his gangland firm from scratch, using his legitimate position at the docks as his personal playground for a criminal empire that was growing faster than clap in a knocking shop. To Danny, showing mercy was for mugs and suckers. Anyone who didn't play ball was just a river rat waiting to be squashed under his hobnail boots. In Danny's world, you either toed the line or ended up face down in the Thames. He didn't just run the docks – he bloody well owned them, lock, stock, and barrel. And heaven help any stupid fucker who tried to nick what was his.

Batters was the only man with the bottle to give Danny grief, challenging his authority. They'd been enemies for as long as anyone could remember. Danny's suspicious gaze eyeballed his enemy, son, and accompanying nearby muscle as they slithered through the crowd.

'What's that tosser up to?' His scarred cheek twisted into a scowl.

Pushing through the throng, Danny made his way towards Batters, closely followed by some of his men who were also in attendance. The crowd scrambled aside when they clocked the murderous gleam in the King of the Docks' eye. Smart move. You didn't hang about when Danny Steele was on the warpath.

'Oi, Batters!' Danny's gritted shout rose above the noise. 'What the fuck you playing at?'

The other man slowly turned, like he didn't have a care in the world, a sly grin spreading across his face. 'Lovely night for a fight, innit?'

Danny's fists clenched at his sides. 'Cut the dogshit. Why would your ugly mug turn up at my boy's fight?'

The other man feigned innocence, but his eyes were a dead giveaway, glinting with malice. 'I'm just here for the entertainment, same as most of the good folk of the East End here tonight.'

Just then, Danny was distracted by a shout from Jimmy in the ring. Urgently turning, he saw his son jabbing his glove to his eye. 'Tried to bloody blind me! The fucker's fighting dirty!'

The crowd's excitement turned ugly in an instant.

It didn't take a genius to figure out that Batters was behind the match fixing.

'You best order your headstone now because you're fucking dead,' Danny roared, lunging at his enemy.

His fist connected with the other man's jaw, sending his arch-enemy staggering back. An outraged and wild Lucas moved to defend his old man, but Danny just managed to duck in time to miss his meaty punch. The ring erupted into chaos, Jimmy and Brother Bertie jumped the ropes, diving straight into the thick of it. They fought side by side like brothers. Because that's what they were. You didn't need to be blood to be family. Fists flew in every direction, the once-orderly boxing match had spiralled into brass knuckle mayhem.

Danny caught a glimpse of Brother Bertie's porkpie hat as the lad weaved through the melee, laying out Batters' goons left and right. Jimmy was a blur of controlled violence, his years of training evident in every precise strike.

It was all-out war between the Steele and Rogers gangs. The fight spilled out onto the East End street.

Danny found himself face to face with his arch-enemy. And grinned.

Fucking bring it on!

Both men snarled and circled each other, sharks scenting blood in the water. The years of rivalry and hatred burned bright in their eyes.

'You've been a thorn in my side for too long,' Danny growled, feinting left before landing a solid right hook.

Batters stumbled but didn't go down. Blood trickled from his lip, but he hardly noticed. In the East End you learned how to spit blood from an early age. 'And you've been living on borrowed time, you greedy wank job.'

They clashed in a flurry of punches and grunts. Danny felt a rib bruise under Batters' power punch, but the pain only ratcheted up his determination and red-hot rage. He drove his knee into his enemy's gut, followed up by a vicious uppercut that sent the man reeling.

Nearby, Jimmy was holding his own against two of Batters' crew when Lucas barrelled into him from behind. The giant's arms locked around Jimmy's throat in a crushing headlock.

'Not so tough now, are ya?' His voice was thick with hate in Jimmy's ear.

Face turning purple, Jimmy struggled for air. Black dots danced before his eyes, his lungs burning for much-needed oxygen. His vision blurred at the edges. The other man's grip surprisingly suddenly loosened.

'Tell Mini I love her,' Lucas rasped, low enough for their ears only.

Jimmy's features froze in shock. Before he could respond, Lucas glanced over at Batters, making sure his old man hadn't heard. Satisfied, he shoved Jimmy away and roared back into the fight.

Meanwhile, Danny had his opponent just where he wanted him. Years of pent-up aggression poured out while he rained blows down on his rival. Batters' face was a mess of blood and bruises, but still he wouldn't stay down.

'Is that all you've fucking got, Steele?' Batters taunted, followed by an ugly laugh.

Danny hesitated for a split second, and Batters seized the opportunity, landing a haymaker that sent Danny sprawling. He hit the ground. He rolled, narrowly avoiding Batters' stomping boot. Gritting his teeth against the pain, Danny swept Batters' legs out from under him, sending the big man crashing down.

Both men struggled to their feet, bloodied and battered but neither willing to concede. The fight sounds died around them. They locked eyes, years of hatred condensed into this one moment.

'You cocky little cunt,' Batters hissed. 'You think you're untouchable, don't you? Big man Danny, lording it over the docks.'

'You're nothing but a bad memory around here,' Danny sneered.

They came together in a final, brutal exchange. Fists flew, each blow carrying the weight of their long-standing feud. With a roar of pain and triumph, Danny unleashed a devastating combination, fists unleashed into Batters' face, once, twice, three times. He crumpled, hitting the ground hard. Chest heaving, Danny stood over him, his knuckles raw and bleeding.

'COME ON THEN!' Danny dared, teeth bared, his challenge carrying over the suddenly quiet street. 'Anyone else fancy taking a potshot?'

Batters' remaining men glanced nervously at each other, then at their fallen leader. As one, they began to back away, dragging their unconscious mates with them.

Bloody cowards! That's it, run off to hide behind your mum's skirt!

Danny watched them retreat, grim triumph twisting his features. He found Jimmy and Brother Bertie, both appearing worse for wear but still standing.

Batters stirred at his feet.

The beaten man stared up at Danny. Far from broken, his one good eye burned with murderous promise. 'One of these days I'm going to put you in the ground for good.'

Chapter Three

Iris Steele knocked back another glass of Distilled Dry Gin as the kitchen clock chimed eleven at night. The harsh liquid scorched the back of her quivering throat, a familiar sensation that both comforted and condemned her.

At forty-nine, she barely recognised the woman staring back in the reflection of the streaky kitchen window. Her mane of once lush chestnut hair was long gone, replaced by an all-over iron-grey that matched the colour of her eyes, twisted into a matronly bun at the nape of her neck. She wore a face full of such sadness, telling the silent story of years spent turning a blind eye to her husband dipping his wick in any obliging piece of muff from here to Mile End.

Hand trembling, Iris reached for the bottle once more, seeking solace in the only companion that never judged her, had never done the dirty on her, and never asked for more than she could give.

Then she put on a smile as plastic as Tupperware, got her trusty tin of potions and plasters in hand, and stepped into the sitting room to tend to the walking wounded. The room was scented with oranges because she loved putting orange peel into the blazing fire. One of the perks of living on the docks was you got your hands on all types of exotic things from around the world.

Her Danny sat in his armchair like a king on his throne, while Jimmy sprawled on the settee. Mini, his wife, tenderly fussed over him. Both Iris' children, Jimmy and Sin, still lived under her roof which warmed her heart. Even with her boy married with two young 'uns, he'd stayed put. Their house on Sugar Cane Wharf, the area nestled between Wapping and Shadwell, was one of the few rows of terraces Hitler's bombs had spared. Sometimes Iris reckoned it was pure stubbornness that kept their home standing.

She clucked her tongue at the sorry sight before her. By rights they should've been toasting Jimmy's win in the ring, his golden ticket to a shot at the local heavyweight championship. Instead, this lot had stumbled home after a proper tear-up with Batters in the streets. Sighing heavily, she wished for the umpteenth time that Danny and Batters would knock it on the head and bury the bloody hatchet. She hated seeing her darling Jimmy caught in the crossfire. Mind you, truth was Jimmy had put himself smack bang in the middle of proceedings when he'd run off with Mini, Batters' daughter.

Iris watched twenty-four-year-old Mini tend to Jimmy's wounds, and her heart squeezed with love. Her daughter-in-law's gentle hands moved expertly, cleaning cuts and applying salve, her tenderness speaking volumes. Mini might be tiny – hence the nickname – but she was strong with a right set of brains on her. Just the sort of missus her Jimmy needed. Marrying Batters' daughter might've stirred up more aggro than a hornet's nest, but Iris never regretted a day of Mini becoming part of the family.

Those two shared a passion that made Iris' heart ache with both joy and a touch of envy. The way Jimmy's swollen and bruised eyes softened when he gazed at Mini reminded Iris of the love she'd once held for Danny.

That had withered away that terrible day nine years ago.

'All right, let's see the damage,' she announced with gusto, approaching her husband. His face might be a right mess, but he wore a boyish grin as wide as the Thames.

'It's nuthin',' he insisted.

'Course it isn't, love. Now hold still.'

She opened a bottle of TCP, its eye-watering medicinal scent overpowering the room. Danny winced while she dabbed and cleaned his wounds. Iris was known far and wide for her quiet, gentle nature.

The door opened, and in stormed twenty-four-year-old Sin, with Brother Bertie hot on her heels. Cynthia was her girl's given name, but no one called her that. She'd been Sin as far back as Iris could remember.

The tension between her daughter and Jimmy's best mate crackled and hissed. Iris shook her head. These two were always at each other's throats.

'This is all down to you!' Sin stabbed an irate finger at him. 'Your fault. Aren't you supposed to be keeping Jimmy focused on boxing? Not getting him into scraps with every Tom, Dick, and Herbert on the docks!'

Brother Bertie, cool as you like with his porkpie hat perched on his head, just flashed her one of his cheeky grins. 'Now, now, sweet ting.' He was having fun deliberately underscoring the Jamaican pronunciation of 'thing'. 'After his win, Jimmy deserved to let off some steam.'

'Don't you "sweet ting" me, you cocky git.' Sin looked about ready to clock him one. 'And take that ridiculous hat off indoors.'

'Sin, shut your noise,' her father growled, all signs of his earlier boyishness gone. 'You're doing my nut in.'

The heated stare Sin shot her father was filled with barely concealed hate. Iris flinched. Watching the toxic dance between father and daughter tore at her, as it had done for these last nine years. Then again, was it so surprising after what had gone on? Some wounds run too deep to ever heal.

Danny turned his attention back to Jimmy, his face a portrait of pride tinged with something else. Something that made Iris' skin crawl.

'You done good, son. Showed that dickhead, Batters, and that shower he touts about as a gang what for. 'Course, what you did, it's not quite the same as me keeping the peace on the docks, but it's a start, eh?'

Iris watched her beloved son's face fall ever so slightly at his father's barbed praise. Her poor boy, always chasing his dad's approval and never quite catching it. She wished Danny could be like other dads down the boozer, thumbs hooked in their braces, chests puffed out while they boasted about their boy's achievements. But who was she bloody kidding? Danny Steele would sooner cut off his right arm than let anyone else share the spotlight. The only person Danny truly gave a toss about was Danny.

Mini must have sensed it, too, because Iris noticed a quick hardening of her daughter-in-law's expression.

'Come on, love,' Mini coaxed Jimmy. 'Let's get you upstairs and into bed. You need your rest.'

***

The moment the door shut on their room on the first floor, Jimmy gathered his adored wife into his arms. Despite his battered body screaming in protest, he crushed her against him. She breathed in that uniquely Jimmy smell, something indefinably masculine that always made her feel safe.

Mini Steele was a spitfire wrapped in a pint-sized package. Barely reaching five feet tall but with enough fire in her soul to light up the Christmas Lights up at Oxford Street. Quick witted and savvy, she was more than a match for any docker or gangster who dared cross her path. But beneath all that grit and intelligence beat a heart of pure gold, especially when it came to her Jimmy and their kids.

'We did it, Mini! One step closer to the heavyweight crown.' Jimmy celebrated quietly so that he didn't disturb their children.

Five-year-old Violet and four-year-old Robbie shared a bed in the corner of the room, their soft breaths a gentle counterpoint to the harsh realities of life in the East End.

Careful of his bruises, Mini slid slowly down his body to the floor, relishing the feel of his hard muscles against her. 'I'm so proud of you. I just wish the night hadn't ended with…'

Her shoulders sagged, her features clouding over, flushed with upset.

'You hate that I was fighting with your father and Lucas.'

Mini swallowed hard at the mention of her dad and big brother. The familiar bitterness knotted around her ribs, squeezing until each breath came short. 'When's it going to end? This hatred between our families?'

Batters had disowned her when she'd secretly married his arch-enemy's son. Even after all these years, a part of her still hoped to mend fences with her father. Being cut off from her blood family was the price she'd paid for choosing love over family loyalty.

That's when Jimmy remembered. 'Your brother gave me a message on the quiet for you. Said to tell you he loves you.'

Mini's eyes welled up at that. Her big brother, still protecting for her even though he was under strict instructions from their father to turn his back on her, too. He'd been protecting her since their mother – God rest her soul – had passed when Mini was a little girl.

'You're not seeing Lucas behind my back, are you?' Emotion suddenly thickened his words. 'I don't want you anywhere near trouble or in harm's way. You're so precious to me.'

Despite the pain, Mini's love for Jimmy burned fierce and true, a flame that not even her father's rejection could extinguish.

'You know that pair of Georgian houses down by the river?' she told Jimmy, changing the subject. 'The ones on Molasses Quay. Number one has come up for sale.'

Jimmy raised an eyebrow, wincing as the movement pulled at a fresh cut. 'Yeah? What of it?'

Mini took a deep breath, carefully considering what she was about to say. 'I think it's time we got our own place. Somewhere just for me, you, and the kids.'

Her husband's gaze wavered, trying to hide his inner struggle. She knew Jimmy's heart better than he did himself. Deep down, he craved the same future she did, but his father's voice echoed in Jimmy's head, demanding loyalty with every breath. It was a noose disguised as family ties, slowly choking the life out of her husband's dreams. She longed to grab those invisible strings and snap them, freeing Jimmy to be the man she knew he could be.

Staying under her father-in-law's roof wasn't good for Jimmy or their young family. So she told him the news she'd been keeping literarily tucked away inside until his fight was over.

'Jimmy, I'm expecting.' Her small hand slipped to her tummy, a protective gesture as old as time.

His jaw hit the floor. For a moment, he was lost for words. Then, a one-hundred-watt grin transformed his features. He swept her up in his arms again, twirling her around, his own pain forgotten in the rush of euphoria.

'Bloody hell, Mini!' He whooped and threw his head back with joyful laughter.

He delicately set her down, his mind racing. Another kid on the way. His gaze swept the room. It was cramped, a space that four of them shared and most days felt like they were squeezed in like sardines in a Billingsgate tin. When the baby came that would be five of them chock-a-block in here.

'You're right,' he finally agreed. 'The kids need their own space. And so do we. We can't go on living in one room together.'

'Oh, Jimmy!' With giddy abandon, Mini clapped her hands together, her eyes jumping with hope.

Jimmy's face fell, reality crashing back in. 'But we don't have much money put aside to buy a house.'

'Where there's a will, there's a way.' Mini's voice was razor wire threaded through silk.

Hand in hand, they walked over to where their children were snuggled up in bed. Bending down, Jimmy kissed each gently in turn.

'Sweet dreams, my precious angels,' he whispered.

As they stood there in the dim light, watching their little ones sleep, Jimmy turned to Mini.

'I'm going to ask Dad if he can loan us the money for the house.'

Mini's heart dropped like a stone. The thought of her proud, strong husband going cap in hand to that old man of his left her fighting the rising acid in her throat.

So she told him straight. 'I don't think that's such a good idea—'

Jimmy pulled her close and kissed her on the forehead. 'Don't you worry about a thing. You just focus on taking care of yourself and our bundle of joy you're carrying. Leave handling dad and getting the money for the house to me.'

Mini bit her lip, a chill running down her spine. She knew all too well the price of Danny Steele's 'generosity'. But for now, she held her tongue, praying that this time, just this once, Jimmy's father did the right thing.

Chapter Four

Jimmy prowled Sugar Cane Wharf, a man on a mission. He pushed down the anxious knot in his gut that screamed this was a bad idea. He'd been putting off asking his dad for going on a week now, but that pokey room at his parents' wasn't getting any bigger.

The dock sat in a sharp bend of the Thames, a stone's throw from Wapping's London Docks and downriver from Shadwell Basin. Unlike most of the capital's docks, this slice of docklands was privately owned by an aristocratic family who'd once been a big noise in shipping.

The familiar pungent cocktail hit him – tarred rope, diesel fumes, and that rank stink drifting over from the Bermondsey tanneries. Music to his ears was the racket of dockers yelling, boats tooting, cranes groaning. This was his manor. Every nook and cranny as familiar as his callused hands.

Officially, he was on the books here as a stevedore, but all those in the know understood the score: it was a cover for his real purpose, helping his father run his various illegal rackets that kept Danny Steele flush with cash.

Cash.

That's what Jimmy desperately needed a cut of now, and his father was the man to dish it out.

Sure enough, there was his father, holding court, a bunch of dockers hanging off his every word near the wharf edge. Danny Steele wore the same rough work trousers and heavy boots as his men, topped with a plain button-up shirt and donkey jacket. His dark hair was slicked back and glossy with Brylcreem. No working man's cloth cap for him. He understood the power of standing out just enough to remind the dockers who was really in charge.

Danny worked the docks the same as any other man but he also served as an unofficial mouthpiece for the workers. He fought their corner with one hand while the other was busy lining his pockets and growing his gangland criminal empire.

Sugar Cane Wharf was a goldmine for a man like Danny who wasn't afraid to get his hands dirty. Every day, ships from around the world docked, their bellies full of cargo ripe for the picking. Contraband flowed through the docks faster than blood from a knife fight. Tobacco, booze, the illegal pills that kept the swinging sixties swinging, dirty books and blue movies slipped past customs. You name it, the docks had it, and if you wanted something a bit iffy, something that had 'fallen off the back of a ship', Danny Steele was your man.

He spotted his son, and broke into a broad grin. 'Jimmy boy! To what do I owe the pleasure?'

The gathered dockers suddenly found urgent business elsewhere. They knew when the boss wanted privacy.

'Need a word, Dad.' Jimmy wished his voice didn't sound so tight.

His uneasy manner caused his father to pin him with an intent stare, though his smile stayed fixed. 'Something's eating you, son? You look like you've just read your death notice in the East End Advertiser.'

Jimmy was nervous. His rehearsed speech vanished quicker than morning mist off the Thames. Fuck it. Straight out with it. 'I need a sub.'

'That right?' His dad's look narrowed. 'What's got you coming to the Bank of Dad?'

'A house.' The words hung heavy in the air.

'A house?' Danny's squinting gaze cooled scouring his son's face. 'Now why would you be wanting one of them?'

'Me and Mini reckon it's time we had our own place. Set up our nest somewhere else.' Jimmy forced the words past the tightness in his throat.

His dad's head tilted, cold assessment in every line of his face. 'What's wrong with living under my roof? It's been good enough these past years.'

'Nothing, Dad.' His answer was emphatic because the last thing he wanted was his dad thinking him and Mini weren't grateful and obliging for being given a helping hand.

Nevertheless… 'But that room—'

'That room's been yours since you was knee-high to a grasshopper.'

'It's cramped with four of us.' Jimmy sucked in a breath. 'Well, five soon enough.'

'Five?'

Pride swelled Jimmy's chest despite everything. 'Mini's expecting.'

For a moment, Danny grinned for all he was worth, happiness lighting up his face. 'Another grandkid? Your mum will be proper over the moon. Nothing she loves more than having little ones running about the place.'

He clapped a heavy hand on Jimmy's shoulder, spinning him to face the sprawling river. 'This is what you should have your eye on. Gonna be all yours one of these days.'

Jimmy surveyed the expanse before him. 'The way I hear it, the docks aren't going on forever.'

'You ain't seeing it son. Really seeing it.'

Jimmy peered hard, genuinely confused about what his dad was getting at.

'See past the docks to the river, the land. One of these days it's gonna be worth a king's ransom.'

Jimmy couldn't see it himself. Who in their right mind would pay over the odds to live in a grimy place like this? The familiar heavy weight of expectation settled on his shoulders. His father had always wanted him to follow in his footsteps, running the docks and the rackets. But truth was, all Jimmy dreamed about was being a boxing champ, of making his own way in the world.

Fighting to keep the frustration out of his voice, he held his ground. 'Mini's been dreaming of her own place. I want to give her that.'

Danny gave his son a quelling look. 'Your mum never wanted her own gaff. A proper East End wife knows her place.' His father stabbed a finger in Jimmy's taut chest. 'What's really going on here? Your bird wants to spread her wings, does she? Next thing you know, she'll be taking my grandkids over to the enemy's camp.'

You what?

Nah, Jimmy wasn't having that. Bad-mouthing Mini was bang out of order. Memories of his wife standing by him through thick and thin, birthing his babies, making their room a home despite the limited space, flashed through his mind. His father had never forgiven Mini for being Batters' daughter – Jimmy saw that clear as day now. But he'd be fucked if he'd stand here and let the old man run her down.

'Mini's loyal to the bone,' Jimmy ground out. He squared up to his father. 'She's a Steele now, has been since the day she took my name. She'd cut out her tongue before she'd betray this family.'

Danny was quiet for a long moment. His response was soft, almost gentle. 'Your mum has grown to love that girl. She'll be heartbroken if you move out. You know how she dotes on her grandbabies. She loves taking Violet and Robbie up the convent to see Sister Bernadette.'

The anger withered inside Jimmy. 'And me and Mini are grateful for all that Mum does for the kids. But we can't stay there forever.'

Danny rubbed his fingers along his chin. 'Money, you say? A loan? 'Course I'd love to help you out, son…'

Hope bloomed strong inside Jimmy.

'…But money's a bit tight right now.'

All Jimmy's hopes crashed and died.

'Maybe next year, eh?' his dad continued. 'We'll see how things pan out then.'

His dad's explanation sounded like a load of old cockle, as far as Jimmy was concerned. Danny Steele always had a pocket full of readies, was always flush. Then again, maybe the uncertainty about the docks and the future was making his father hold tight to his cash?

'Dad, please,' Jimmy pressed, hating that it felt like he was on his knees. 'I can pay you back. I've been saving up, and I can take on extra work here—'

A cutting wave of his dad's hand stopped him dead. 'I said maybe next year. That's final.'

A surge of blistering anger rushed through Jimmy, quickly followed by a wave of guilt. This was his father, after all. The man who'd raised him up, taught him everything he knew. He loved him with everything he had. Still, the anger wouldn't quite go away. He opened his mouth to argue further, but before he could speak, a commotion erupted nearby.

Both men turned to see a docker hanging precariously from a cargo crane high above the docks.

'Fuck me!' Danny exclaimed. 'That's Stevie up there. What the bloody hell's going on?'

Stevie was a member of Danny's firm, part of his inner gangland circle. Stevie's fingers slipped. They watched in helpless horror while he plummeted towards the ground. At the last second, Stevie managed to grab on to a lower section of the crane, slowing his fall.

He hit the ground hard.

For a second there was silence. Then everyone moved, including Jimmy and Danny who raced over.

Stevie was writhing and groaning in agony, his leg bent at an unnatural angle.

'Thank God, he's alive. Give him some space,' Danny shouted, waving the others back. 'And someone call an ambulance.'

'Christ almighty, Stevie,' Danny went on, kneeling beside him, quickly followed by Jimmy. 'What happened up there?'

Stevie's features were twisted, a picture of pure torment. Sweat poured down his pasty skin, and his eyes bulged, wild and desperate. 'Dunno, boss! One minute I was securing the load, next thing I know the winch gave way. Must've been faulty or something.'

Abruptly, Danny's whole demeanour and face changed, his expression contorting. 'Here's a word to the wise. It wasn't faulty. I took the pin out of the winch myself.'

Jimmy shook his head, convinced that he'd heard wrong.

Stevie's eyes widened in shock, fear creeping into them. 'What?'

'Don't act the innocent with me, you thieving toerag,' Danny snarled, voice low enough for none of the gathered dockers to hear. 'I know you've been skimming gear from my warehouse.'

'Nah, boss. I swear on my sons' lives—'

Danny brutally ploughed on, ignoring Stevie's desperate protests. 'It ain't your sons you've been thinking about when you're dipping your wick in that doxy you've got tucked up East Ham way. Giving her things that belong to me.'

Stevie's face went ghostly white. 'Someone's been feeding you a load of bollocks.'

'Don't lie to me!' Danny's voice was controlled but filled with menace. His face pushed close to Stevie's. To the onlookers it appeared like concern. 'You know the penalty for anyone who tries to fuck me over.'

Stevie's whole face crumbled. 'I never meant it, Danny. I swear, I'll never do it again.'

Ignoring him, Danny casually turned to Jimmy. 'You know, son, sometimes you gotta make an example. Our Stevie here thought he could make a mug outta me.'

Part of Jimmy wanted to feel sorry for the docker, but Jimmy hardened his heart to the man's whimpers of pain. In their world, loyalty was everything. If you stole from the King of the Docks, you paid the terrible price. That's how things worked in the East End.

You can't go betraying your criminal family and expect to walk away scot-free.

The wail of an approaching ambulance filled the air.

After one contemptuous glance in Stevie's direction, Danny got up and pulled Jimmy aside.

'Loyalty's what keeps us breathing.' He paused, letting his words sink in. A warning entered his words. 'You start looking elsewhere for the money for that house, well… that'd be a real shame, wouldn't it? Might give me the wrong idea.' His lips curled into a cold smile. 'And you've seen what happens to them that betray me. Nasty business, that.'

Before Jimmy could answer, Pete, the youngest member of Danny's gang appeared, breathing ragged and harsh. He whispered in his boss's ear, 'Rita said you need to come lively like. There's trouble at The Sing-Song.'

Jimmy watched his dad urgently head off, a chill slithering down his spine. Cross Danny Steele, and you'll wish you'd never been born. Turmoil tightened and churned in Jimmy's guts. Mini was his world, his rock, the mother of his kids. She deserved her own home, especially with another baby on the way. But going behind his old man's back?

That thought made him feel physically sick.

Torn between his love for his wife and his loyalty to his father, Jimmy felt like he was being ripped in two.

His work boots crunched on broken glass as he turned away. The jagged pieces glinted in weak sunlight, as sharp as the choice tearing him apart.

Chapter Five

The blood was everywhere.

'Shit-fuck!' Rita Lawless cursed a blue streak surveying the room on The Sing-Song Lady.

The boat bobbed in its usual spot, a shadowy corner of Sugar Cane Wharf where the Thames kept its dirtiest secrets. From the opposite bank, she cut a fine figure, gold lettering proclaiming her name with tarnished elegance. Up close, though, the cracks showed exactly what she was: a floating knocking shop masquerading as a pleasure boat. Coloured lights winked along her railings like tired old tarts, half the bulbs burnt out. Below decks, narrow corridors led to private cabins reeking of river damp, vice and sex.

Rita might run the place, but never call her a madam. You'd end up with a thick lip for that. She was Danny's fifty-fifty partner in this flesh trade venture.

So as far as she was concerned, that put her in the bracket of being a businesswoman. And a bloody cracking one at that in her eyes!

Rita could be a right hard bitch, make no mistake. Twenty-five going on fifty, with a square jaw and eyes that'd cut you faster than the flick knife she carried everywhere. She'd been walking the streets and working her arse off since she was sweet sixteen. It was either that or end up like her old man and her brothers, breaking her back down the docks, or her mum, pissing away her life in some two-bit factory. Fuck that for the way to live a life. Rita had bigger plans.

She was six foot plus in her heels, with a face that was more handsome than pretty. Mind you, beauty was for mugs anyway, she'd learned early on in life. It was all going to fade in the end. But a bit of grit and graft? That'd see you through. Especially in the East End.

Rita was done with turning tricks, though. Well, almost. These days, she had her sights set higher. She was moving on up in the world, bit by bit. But it wasn't just the money she was after. Nah, Rita Lawless wanted a proper piece of the action. A slice of the brutal gangland pie.

Livid to the max, she surveyed the carnage in the cabin. It was a dead ringer for something out of a horror film. The silk sheets on the bed were torn and stained, hanging off the mattress in tatters. Shards of a shattered champagne bottle glittered across on the floor. A pool of sticky crimson was slowly spreading across the polished wooden floor, seeping into the grain. The ornate gilt mirror was cracked, flecks of red marring its surface. A heavy brass lamp lay on its side, its base sticky with blood.

There were two other people in the cabin.

One was alive, the other dead.

Joanie, one of her girls, was huddled in a corner sobbing her heart out. The girl was catatonic, shaking with inky scars of mascara running down her face. Her dress was ripped, revealing nasty bruises on her pale flesh. Rita felt a pang of sympathy but quickly doused its flame. Soft feelings had no place in this game.

The sounds of grunting and moaning drifted through the thin walls. Business as usual in the other cabins, Rita had made damn sure of that. No way could anyone get wind of what had gone on here. The Sing-Song Lady's reputation was built on discretion, and Rita would be fucked if she'd let one hysterical tart and a dead punter bring it all crashing down.

She moved closer to the body, her cream leather block heels softly tapping against the wooden floor. The man lay face up, his expensive suit now ruined with blood. A jagged piece of the broken mirror protruded from his neck, explaining the horrific amount of blood.

The door flew open and Danny burst in, his expression thunderous. He quickly noted Joanie hunched in the corner, and then his eyes widened in disbelief at the lifeless body sprawled on the floor.

'Fuck's sake!' His face turned an alarming shade of red. 'They come here for a shag, not to star in their own murder mystery.'

Danny let his temper simmer down when he clocked the daggers Rita was shooting his way. He knew better than to get on her bad side – he'd seen what happened to the poor sods who did. She wasn't some two-bit tom down on her luck like the other girls here. She was a proper East End scrapper who could lay a bloke out flat before he knew what had hit him. Truth was, she was the only woman Danny truly respected. He'd learned early on that Rita wouldn't stand for any old bollocks from anyone, not even the King of the Docks himself. Funny thing was, that's exactly why they worked so well together running the floating brothel.

Danny Steele and Rita Lawless made the perfect criminal partnership.

Rita opened her mouth to explain, but Joanie's anguished wail cut her off.

'He... he tried to kill my baby! Our baby!' she sobbed, her words barely intelligible.

Rita couldn't believe what she was hearing. The girl had allowed herself to not only fall for the guy but fall pregnant to him. Rule number one: Let the punters into your knickers but never into your heart.

'Said he didn't want it,' Joanie continued between ragged breaths, her chest heaving. 'He started hurting me... I had to get away... I loved him! I didn't mean to hurt him! But he wanted to murder me and our baby!'

Danny crouched next to her, compassion melting his usual gruffness into something tender.

'There, there, Princess. It's all right now. Whatcha mean, he didn't want it?'

Rita watched, bemused. She'd never seen the hard-as-nails Danny go soft as rice pudding like this before. But then his next words made her blood run cold.

He took a longer look at the dead man and exploded. 'That's Mark Harrison. One of my key shipping contacts.'

Standing abruptly, he wiped the back of his hand across his mouth.

'We need to get him out of here,' Rita told him.

When Tiny, the mountain of muscle who guarded the boat, entered, Rita jerked her thumb at the corpse. 'Sort it. Make it seem he got tanked and stumbled onto the East London line tracks.'

Danny turned to the distraught girl. 'Come on, gorgeous, let's take care of you.

Palm in the small of her back, he guided her outside the room and towards another cabin that acted as Rita's office. Rita watched them go, a niggling feeling of unease in her gut.

***

Smile glued to his lips, Danny shut the door behind him and the terrified seventeen-year-old. Instead of sitting her down, he guided her towards the other side of the cabin. When her back was against the wall, he tipped her chin up and smiled.

Joanie trembled something chronic while Danny Steele tenderly wiped a trail of tears from her cheek. The shakes weren't on account of her having just stabbed a punter to death. Nah, it was being this close to the bossman that had her bricking it. Ever since she'd started working on The Sing-Song, she'd made it her business to be scarce whenever Danny put in an appearance. Stories about Danny Steele kept Joanie awake at night. Sure, he played the big-hearted hero, helping those in need. But whispers in dark corners told different tales - of a man who'd skin you alive soon as look at you.

Yet, here he was in the flesh and Joanie couldn't believe it. The King of the Docks hisself treating her like she was made of fragile china. Where was the monster everyone banged on about? This fella had a heart of gold. They'd got him all wrong. Dead wrong. He was a proper gent underneath all that flash. Patient. Caring.

'Now! Now! There's no need for all that.' The sympathy in his words wrapped around her with the comforting security of a warm blanket. 'We are going to get this sorted out.'

Joanie relaxed, more at ease now. 'I never knew he was a good friend of yours, Mister Steele. I would never—'

He stopped her nervous chatter with a firm finger across her lips.

Without warning, he balled his other hand and punched her hard in the stomach, taking her totally by surprise. Joanie's eyes bulged in shock. Her strangled cry rang across her office.

Poor Joanie had been too busy being sucked into Danny's legendary, slick charm to notice how his eyes stayed glacial while he smiled. How his fingers lingered just a fraction too long on her throat.

Danny's smile vanished in a heartbeat. Low and menacing, he spat at her, 'Thought you'd cause trouble for me, did ya? You stupid slag.'

He punched her again in the same place. This time she doubled over.

He continued, 'We've got a problem here all right, and I'm going to get rid of it.'

Joanie screamed. Grabbing her by the hair so she wouldn't fall, he brutally yanked her head back. He delivered two more cold-blooded blows before shoving her away. Gasping, Joanie staggered and collapsed to her knees and then tumbled onto her side. That's when the pain in her belly came, the most terrible pain she had experienced in her life. Moaning and withering on the floor, she wrapped her arms around her middle. But it was too late. Blood started seeping from between her legs. Her baby was lost to her.

Abruptly, the door thrust open. Rita stood fixed in the doorway, her masked gaze taking in the dreadful scene. She took a deep breath and squared her shoulders. This was the world she'd chosen, and there was no room for weakness. She'd known from the start that running a floating brothel for one of London's most notorious gangsters wouldn't be all champagne and roses. But this was a whole new level of cruelty that turned her stomach.

Joanie's body was curled in on itself, blood pooling between her legs, staining the cheap carpet. Her eyes were open but vacant, staring at nothing.

Cutting her eyes at Danny, Rita bit out, 'You can be a right bastard sometimes. Besides which we agreed that any sorting out to do with the ladies was to be done by me.'

His seething response was a twist of his mouth and, 'Well, you need to go back to sorting-out school because you've done a piss-poor job where this is concerned.'

With scathing contempt, he stared at the young woman he had attacked.

'Don't do it! Don't take him!' Suddenly it was his mum's screams Danny heard echoing through time. He was no longer on the boat but in a house. That house. He was so young. His mum shrieking with the fear of a wounded animal.

Blinking hard, air trapped in his throat, Danny fought hard to throw the past off and come back to the present. The cabin tilted sideways for a moment. Sweat trickled down his spine, his shirt sticking to his back. That's why he never thought about that fucking house. Ever.

Shit, he needed a bloody knock back of rum, badly.

Steeling himself, Danny stared down at the bleeding Joanie and felt nothing. Not a bloody thing. That house had taught him early – there was no place for being soft in the East End.

Dispassionately he informed Rita, 'She doesn't work here anymore. Got it?'

***

After the doctor – the same one who checked the girls remained disease-free – had arrived to see to Joanie, Rita found Danny on deck. She clocked straight away something wasn't right with him. Without a word, she got a large glass of Docker's Courage, the local name given to the unmarked bottles kept behind the bar. The vodka-whisky blend was lethal stuff, known to put dockers on their arse, but Danny knocked it back like mother's milk.

Rita watched him, careful-like, while she topped up his glass. She needed him back on point, sharpish, because there was a subject she wanted to broach with him. Rita was a master at judging the right moment. Knew exactly when to push and when to pour another drink. It was why she was still standing while others were six feet under or sleeping with the fishes in the Thames.

'The Sing-Song Lady has seen better days,' she started with practiced ease. 'We should move our operation to solid ground. That way we can pull in a better class of girl.'

Rita filled him up again, then honey-coated whispered, 'And I know the exact right place.'

'Oh yeah?'

'One of those houses on Molasses Quay is up for sale—'

'You fucking what?'

The venom in his voice rocked Rita back on her heels. 'You all right, Danny?'

He looked peaky, like someone had slapped him silly. He stared back at her, features pale and blotchy.

'Find out whose organising the sale. No one else gets that house. It's mine.'

For once Danny let red-hot anger take the reins, blinding him to everything but getting that house. If he'd been thinking with his usual ice-cold brain, he'd have twigged it was the same property his son was going after.

The difference was, Danny would spill blood to own it.

Chapter Six

'Bertram! I know you've got a white woman in there! Open this blasted door! Right now!'

The resounding voice of his sister, Gertie, outside his room nearly made Brother Bertie jump out of his skin. Her bellowing rattled the walls of her boarding house in Whitechapel.

Brother Bertie, born Bertram Watson in the parish of St Ann, Jamaica, had 'rascal' written over him from day one. He was a born flirt who couldn't help himself. Women loved him and he loved them right back. His porkpie hat was as much a part of him as his quick wit and quicker tongue. Legend had it he'd sooner part with a limb than that hat. The name 'Brother' had stuck with him from Jamaica to London because he had that way about him, always throwing an arm around someone's shoulder, flashing that million-quid smile like you were family.

But make no mistake, Jamaica had taught him some hard lessons early on. Cross him and you'd find out just how dangerous this 'brother' could be. Especially if you messed with his nearest and dearest. Loyalty was more than a word to him; it was the heartbeat of how he lived his life.

Quickly, he glanced at the woman in his room.

The white woman.

Ruddy. Although she was not the type of white woman his sister was getting upset about. Gertie was referring to the type who wanted romance and a happy ever after. Which was never going to happen with Ruddy because since his arrival back in '63 a strong friendship had grown between them, as thick as thieves, they were. Plus, Ruddy had been living under Gertie's roof long before he'd come to England and was a close friend of hers, too.

Still, if Gertie got wind of what the two of them were up to inside her God-fearing boarding house…

Ruddy quivered in surprise, making her towering dyed-red beehive wobble.

Nora Baxter, known to one and all as Ruddy because when some saw her coming they'd mutter, 'Ruddy Nora,' was about Brother Bertie's age. What that exact age was she never revealed. Ever! Ruddy was a crafty woman about town, known from the East to the West End, with more tricks up her sleeve than a magician. Despite her knobbly knees, which she flaunted with gleeful abandon, she was always decked out in outfits above the knee. Today's frock of choice was a sleeveless number with swirling oranges, electric blues, and shocking pink psychedelic patterns. To top off the look, a pair of large, round sunglasses perched on her nose, despite being indoors.

Ruddy and Brother Bertie's astonished gazes caught and then shot down to the bottles of alcohol at their feet. Brother Bertie did a roaring trade in his homemade brew called Lord Have Mercy Rum Punch, high-proof white Wray and Nephew Rum with marijuana leaves soaked in it.

'Quick!' he hissed. 'Scram outta the window.'

Ruddy snatched up a bottle – cheeky chancer that she was – and made for the balcony on the other side of the window. But her dress caught on a loose nail.

'Bollocks.' Her eyes rolled in aggravation. 'Just got this off a contact at Petticoat Lane who does a brisk below the table business in knockoffs from Bond Street.' She tugged and tugged, the fabric tearing just as Gertie's pounding hand struck the door again.

'Bertram! You open this door right now because, let me tell you, if you don't I'm going to mash it up with my bare fists!'

With one last desperate yank, Ruddy managed to free herself. Blowing her friend a saucy kiss, she disappeared over the balcony into her own room next door. Bertie hastily shoved the remaining bottles of his homemade booze under his bed and smoothed his shirt before opening the door.

Gertie stood there, hands on ample hips, her suspicious stare spearing him to the spot. At nearly forty, short and stout as she was, Gertie held a commanding presence in every space she was in along with her red, gold, and green paisley headwrap. Her keen eyes missed none of the goings-on in the little kingdom of her boarding house, which was why her gaze now lifted over her brother's shoulder and swept the room.

Brother Bertie worshipped his larger-than-life sister. He was in awe of the empire she had created for herself in England. Not only did she own this boarding house in Whitechapel, she owned two others, in the Roman Road end of Bow and Stepney. He'd move heaven and earth for her. They would always be Gertie and Bertie. No matter what mischief he got into, no matter how many times he stumbled, his big sister was always there, ready to pick him up, dust him off, followed by a swift lick around his head, if necessary. He'd promised her he would stop his criminal ways and go straight.

Easier said than done.

Still giving him the eye, she pressed, 'I could swear on the Good Book I heard voices.'

'Just me.' He flashed his most innocent and winning smile. 'Talking to myself, you know how tings go.'

Concern still creased her brow. 'You know I worry. And you know I have nothing against the colour of anyone's skin.' A quiver of apprehension shook her lip. 'Still, these streets, sometimes they're not kind to our people, especially when it comes to black men mixing with the white ladies.'

Bertie's smile faded. He knew all too well the dangers that lurked in 1960s London for a black man.

Gertie had come over in '57, part of what would later be called the Windrush Generation. She'd faced discrimination, closed doors, and suspicious glares. Her fears for him weren't unfounded.

'I know, big sis,' he said softly. 'But tings different now. Us young ones, we don't care where people come from no more. We're mixing it up.'

Body stiffening, she considered his optimism. 'Maybe so, but be careful. Promise me.'

She loved her brother more than anything in this world. Since she'd arrived in London, Gertie had gone all out to create a good foundation for Bertram to thrive.

But stepping out with a white girl… No, that shook her to the core. Gertie wasn't prejudiced. She'd box down the first person who suggested she had a racist bone in her body. Her boarding house, which had originally been a place of refuge for people from the Caribbean who had found doors slammed in their faces when they went looking for a home, had become a haven for all sorts, regardless of colour.

'I promise.' Catching the fear flickering on her face, he pulled her solid body into a hug, breathing in the homely scent of coconut oil and spices that always clung to her.

When they parted, Gertie's brows sharply dipped together. 'The real reason I came up is Claudette's downstairs with Precious.'

Claudette, his former lady, and Precious? What were they doing there? He'd met Claudette on the ship coming over to England, and the result was his gorgeous four-year-old daughter, Precious.

'Precious? Is everything all right?' he asked his sister with alarm.

'Best you get yourself down there now and find out.'

***

He found them in Gertie's immaculately kept prized private parlour. Located at the front of the house, it was only used for special guests. It was filled with ornamental knick-knacks, red, pink and white crochet covers across the tops of the settee suite still covered in the plastic it had arrived in. A huge walnut-coloured radiogram was set against the wall below a 3D painting of the Last Supper.

Claudette, beautiful and with her nose in the air as per usual, held the hand of his daughter. When he found nothing physically wrong with Precious, relief flooded through him, quickly followed by that special daddy-ache whenever he saw his little girl.

'Daddy!' Precious launched herself into his arms.

Holding her close, Brother Bertie inhaled her innocent sweetness. His biggest regret was that his child didn't live with him. He met Claudette's gaze, searching for answers. She cut her eyes at him increasing his unease.

'What's going on, Claudette?'

She arched her brow. 'We need to talk. In private.'

Setting Precious gently down, he whispered with a wicked smile, 'Go see Auntie Gertie in the kitchen. Daddy needs to talk to Mummy.'

After his daughter had scampered off, Bertie got into it straight away with her mother. 'Out with it, then.'

There was always some drama going on with Claudette. She had more storylines that that show, *Coronation Street,* that had everyone glued to their telly.

Her lips curved into a smile that didn't reach her eyes. 'I'm getting married. To a good man. A settled man. Everything you never managed to be.'

She couldn't resist having a dig at him. Besides, what a bloody nerve she had! By day, Claudette played the sanctified church sister, all buttoned in her Sunday best. But come the night she'd be winding her waist low enough to smell hell's fire at a blues party. Grinding up against some man in the darkness. The woman was as two-faced as a bent penny and twice as cheap.

'Congratulations,' he said, ignoring her taunting. 'May you live happily ever after.' He meant every word of it.

She smacked her lips at that. 'My feeee-on-say.' She stretched out each syllable like she was the bleedin' Queen of England, although everyone knew she was as common as chip paper. 'He wants to adopt Precious. Give her his name.'

A shattering, loud buzzing erupted in Brother Bertie's head because he couldn't believe what he was hearing. His baby-gal with some other man's name? You'd have to kill him first.

Boiling hot, he faced her off. 'Over my dead body. She's my daughter. My blood. My name.'

In a gesture of complete contempt for him, Claudette kissed her teeth long and hard. 'If you'd wanted her to have your name, you should've put a gold band on my finger.'

Oh, now they were getting to the heart of the matter. She was still hacked off that he'd never proposed marriage to her during their time together. Truth was, he'd never hidden the type of man he was from Claudette. Free as a bird, that was Bertram Watson. He'd given it a go playing the dutiful boyfriend, but it hadn't taken him five minutes to suss that Claudette wasn't his Miss Right.

'Blood don't pay the damn bills or put shoes on her feet,' she continued to rail at him.

Brother Bertie wasn't having that. 'Hold up, one raasclaat minute. I pay you money, regular as clockwork, for the upkeep of my child. Never missed one payment. I see my daughter every chance I get. Buy her nice things. Take her places. And now you want to take her away from me?' He ended on a strangle of words.

Folding her arms, Claudette jeered, 'Think about her future. The opportunities she could have with a father who's established, who isn't busy running around with that gangster, Jimmy Steele.'

'Leave Jimmy out of this.'

'A father who actually wants to be part of a family.'

She'd touched a raw nerve. Brother Bertie had to hold himself back. 'Don't you dare. Don't you dare act like I don't want my family. You're the one who walked away, Claudette.'

Bracing one foot forward, she leaned into him, her stare cold. 'Walked away? You practically shoved me out the door. Always chasing the next thrill, the next scheme. Batting your deceitful lashes at every loose woman who walked by.'

'And this is your revenge, is it?' Bertie felt robbed of breath at the catastrophic turn of events. 'Taking my daughter away?'

Claudette's eyes glittered with malice. 'It's not revenge. It's justice. For me, and for Precious. We deserve better than the part-time shit you sling our way.'

Spinning on her heels, she marched out of the room. 'Precious!'

For a moment Brother Bertie was too stunned to move. Then a wave of outrage gripped him so strong it propelled him into the hallway where he found a worried Gertie guiding his daughter towards her mother. He got there first and grabbed up his precious baby into his arms.

In a broken hush, he promised her, 'Daddy loves you. Always and forever.'

The words tore something loose in Precious because she began sobbing, great heaving cries that shook her tiny frame like she was coming apart at the seams.

Claudette ripped their bawling child from her father's arms, her withering gaze dripping with the kind of venom that could stop a man's heart.

Then she was gone with his beloved child, leaving Brother Bertie gutted, feeling like someone had taken a butcher's knife to him. The thought of never seeing his Precious again nearly brought him to his knees.

Gertie moved close to him, mama-bear fierce like she'd been doing since the day he was born. Hadn't she warned him about Claudette from the start? That the girl was trouble from her fancy head down to her high-heeled toes?

'I heard every word,' she said. 'You can't let her take away our beautiful Precious.'

'But what can I do?'

'You have to get a solicitor. Make it legal and binding that you are the child's father.'

Helpless and heartbroken, Brother Bertie answered, 'But that's going to take money. Money I don't have.'

Chapter Seven

Fists raised, Brother Bertie and Jimmy circled each other. They were on the river's foreshore practising for Jimmy's upcoming shot at the local heavyweight crown in a month's time. Thick mud squelched beneath their boots while they sparred. Jimmy's muscles screamed with exhaustion, but he pushed through. He had to, his family's future depended on winning the Big Fight.

Brother Bertie danced back, his hat somehow staying firmly in place despite the fancy footwork. His movements lacked their usual fluid grace, his mind clearly elsewhere.

'Watch your left guard,' he barked, his instructions carrying an edge that wrong-footed Jimmy. 'You drop it again, your next opponent will scatter your teeth across the ring.'

That put Jimmy's back up, his frustration mounting. For hours they'd been at it, and his timing was still off. The weight of everything – the new baby, the house they couldn't afford, his father's iron grip – it all pressed down, making his punches wild, desperate.

His best mate circled, trying to spark some of their usual fire. 'Thought you wanted to be like Ali. The guy's turned boxing into a master class in dancing.' He demonstrated with a shuffle that should've had them both grinning. 'Fast and slick, forward and backward, on the balls of his feet, dancing around his opponent and then – BAMMM! – knockout punch landed.'

The Ali Shuffle everyone was calling it. Well, the boxing world had better watch out for the Southpaw Swing that was going to rule the ring. If he could just get everything else sorted first.

Brother Bertie's glove connected with Jimmy's ribs, harder than intended. The pain shot through him, lightning fast and fierce.

'Chrissakes!' Jimmy sucked in a sharp breath, doubling over.

Brother Bertie dropped his hands immediately, worry creasing his face. 'Sorry, mate. My head's all over the place today.'

Jimmy straightened slowly, studying his friend properly for the first time. The usual sparkle was gone, replaced by something darker and haunted. 'You've been wound tighter than a docker's fist all day. What's going on?'

Exhaustion gripping him, Brother Bertie's shoulders slumped. He mournfully stared out at the Thames. 'It's Claudette,' he finally managed. 'She's getting married.'

'Good riddance then—' Jimmy started; he'd never liked her sly ways, but Brother Bertie cut him short.

'She wants to give Precious her new bloke's name.' The confession tore from his throat. 'My baby-gal, Jimmy. My flesh and blood. My princess who runs to me yelling "Daddy". That bitch wants to wipe me out of my girl's life, y'know, like I never existed.'

His best mates' choking anguish hit Jimmy harder than any punch. They'd been through hell and high water together since that fateful night they'd met back in '63. Seeing his friend hurting made his blood boil.

'There's got to be something you can do,' Jimmy pressed. 'Some legal way to stop her.'

Brother Bertie bitterly scoffed. 'Need money for a lawyer, don't I? And you know where every spare penny goes. Keeping clothes on Precious' back and making sure she never goes hungry.'

Jimmy nodded, understanding the weight of a father's pride and responsibilities. His own chest tightened thinking about Mini at home, carrying their third child. Another mouth to feed, another soul to shelter from the harshness of the world beyond their front door.

'Speaking of kids,' he said, trying to lighten the mood. 'Looks like there's gonna be another Steele running around soon.'

Brother Bertie's face transformed, a beaming grin breaking through his gloom. He playfully punched Jimmy's arm. 'You old dog! Congratulations!'

After taking off his gloves, he jogged over to their bags, returning with a bottle of his infamous Lord Have Mercy Rum Punch. They settled onto a relatively dry patch of ground, passing the bottle between them as the tide crept in.

The fiery liquid loosened Jimmy's tongue. 'It's mad, ain't it? Being a dad. Love my kids more than anything, but sometimes…' He trailed off, the enormity of being a parent overwhelming him.

'Sometimes you wonder if you're doing right by them?' Brother Bertie finished softly.

'There's this house Mini's got her eye on. When it's done up it will be a proper little palace down by the riverfront.' Jimmy gestured further down the river. 'I want to give them something better than what we had. Something that's ours.'

'So what's stopping you?' Brother Bertie licked a drop of the pungent rum mix from his lips.

Jimmy's face darkened. 'I asked dad to help with a loan. He shut me down flat. Said maybe next year, and warned me not to go anywhere else for it.' The familiar resentment bubbled up. 'I'm not a kid anymore, dancing to his tune. Got my own family to think about.'

'Strange timing,' Brother Bertie mused. 'Both of us needing money like this.'

They passed the bottle back and forth in silence, each lost in thought. Then Jimmy sat up straighter, an idea taking hold.

'Bertie.' A dangerous, reckless gleam deepened the grey of his eyes. 'What if we did a job?'

His friend scowled hard with bafflement, but when he finally caught Jimmy's meaning his eyes widened. 'A job? Like a robbery—'

'Not a blag. Nothing that risky.' Jimmy laid the bottle down, shifting his body so he had his mate's full attention. 'Something low-key. Clean and quick. But it will net us enough to sort out both our problems.' His words grew more excited. 'You get money for a brief to fight for your Precious, and I get that house for Mini and the kids.'

Conflict warred across Brother Bertie's face. 'Your father specifically warned you not to—'

'Does that sound right to you?' Jimmy's bitter resentment was in full flow. 'That a grown man has to put his life on hold, watching his kids suffer, waiting for someone else's permission? Fuck that!'

The liquor was giving Jimmy the bravery to talk his truth.

The dockyard sounds seemed to grow louder while Brother Bertie wrestled with the choice. Finally, he made his decision, determination replacing doubt.

'All right,' he said quietly. 'But we do this carefully. No room for mistakes.'

''Course,' Jimmy agreed. 'We ain't amateurs.'

'Blood brothers?'

They made fists and touched knuckles, copying that pre-fight ritual that had become their sacred gesture over the years. More binding than a handshake, deeper than words. In the rough-and-tumble world of the East End, where loyalty was rarer than gold, their knuckle touch was a promise – they had each other's backs, no matter what.

'You got any ideas of a low-risk type of job we can do?' Brother Bertie asked.

Jimmy nodded, a plan already forming. 'I know just the person to get the ball rolling.'

Gathering their gear and heading for solid ground, the same chilling thought went through both their minds:

The King of the Docks could never find out what they were about to do.

Chapter Eight

Sin Steele flashed her million-quid smile at the camera, striking pose after pose as Diego's lens clicked away inside. They were inside the Voodoo Lounge, a club in Soho. Lean and leggy like her idol, Twiggy, Sin was the epitome of swinging sixties chic. Her chestnut pixie cut, a perfect copy of Mia Farrow's famous Vidal Sassoon creation, framed a face that could stop traffic. Those enormous eyes, lined with thick black Max Factor eyeliner, could melt hearts or freeze them solid, depending on her mood.

She smoothed her hands over her waif-like figure, appreciating how the latest Mary Quant number hugged what little curves she had. This girl was going places, mark her words. Sin was destined for the glossy pages of the magazine, Queen, for catwalks in Paris and New York and Milan. Sin didn't look down on the East End, far from it, she was proud of her

Cockney roots. But that father of hers… It wasn't just his criminality she wanted shot of as quickly as possible, it was him.

Sin hated her father to the core.

The Voodoo Lounge's plush red velvet booths and polished brass railings gleamed under the studio lights, a far cry from its nighttime dark side where toffs rubbed shoulders with gangsters and those with money ordered drinks alongside the lower classes. The high-stakes gambling, the high-class tarts, the shady geezers cutting deals in even shadier corners. In the soft daylight, though, it resembled something straight out of a Hollywood film, perfect for a photo shoot.

'That's it, love! You're a natural!' Diego's enthusiasm was infectious.

Diego was all revolutionary chic in his black leather jacket, military-style cap tilted just so, and that perfectly trimmed goatee screaming Che Guevara does the King's Road. His neck was always draped in silk scarves, wrists jangling with copper bangles, and he rocked those Cuban-heeled boots like he'd been born in them.

Sin adored working with him. Unlike the other snappers, too many of whom were always trying to get into her knickers, his warm smile and kind eyes put her at ease. She'd clocked early on that he preferred blokes to birds, not that he ever said it straight out. Even with that new law passed this year, a gay colleague who she worked with explained it was still dangerous out there. Still in danger of receiving a kicking from thugs and a legal booting from the coppers and the limits of the law.

'Blimey, Sin! You look like you just stepped off the cover of Nova!' a pleased-as-punch voice rang out from behind Diego.

It belonged to Kath Docherty, Sin's best mate since they were in school. Well, except for that period when Sin was sent away to that other school which she never talked about. Red-haired and chatty, with a heart of gold, Kath was a rare soul who tried to see good in everyone, including Sin's father. Her best mate was a puzzle. Folk wrote her off as thick as two short planks, but she had an uncanny knack for reading people that Sin envied.

And beside her was her constant shadow, her eighteen-year-old sister, Dilly. The sisters were joined at the hip. Where you saw one you saw the other. Dilly was never the same after some bastard had ploughed into her with his motor back in '57, then done a runner. The accident had left it hard for her to communicate, often seeming trapped in her own world, her soft brown eyes mostly holding a faraway expression. She moved slow and careful-like, never speaking, but Kath had learned to read every tiny change in her expression. A slight furrow of her brow, the ghost of a smile, that was how Dilly talked now.

When Kath made it clear to men she went out with that her and Dilly came as a pair, meaning if marriage was on the cards her sister came, too, most dropped Kath like a hot potato.

Sin beamed at her best friend. 'Thanks, Kath.' She switched her attention to Kath's sister. 'You all right there, Dilly, hun?'

Dilly didn't answer, but her eyes lit up at Sin's words. There were moments when her gaze would sharpen, and Sin could see the spark of understanding there.

Sin blew Dilly a kiss before Diego called her attention back to the shoot. As she worked through another series of poses, Sin's mind wandered to her family back in the East End. She was tight with her big bruv, Jimmy. He was her protector, her rock, the one person she could turn to if she had a problem. Watching him with his own kids made Sin's heart swell. Mind you, they still had their ding-dongs, especially over his involvement in their dad's dodgy dealings. Sin might be the family rebel, running around with her fashion crowd and modern ideas, but Jimmy was her world. The thought of ever losing his love or respect gutted her.

As for that best mate of his? Sin's lips pursed at the thought of Bertie Watson. That mouthy git with his tilted hat and cheeky grin. She'd be well shot of him and his nonsense when she finally escaped the East End and her father's shady empire.

'Right, that's a wrap!' Diego's voice snapped Sin back to the present. 'Sin, honey-bun, come here a tick. Got some news for you.'

She couldn't get over to him quickly enough, her heart racing with anticipation.

Diego's eyes were twinkling. 'Listen, sweetheart, I've only gone and got you an invite to an exclusive party happening next week.' He was preening, very pleased with himself indeed. 'Do you want to know where?'

Barely able to contain herself, she punched him playfully on the arm. 'Stop mucking me about.'

A smirk of pure satisfaction curved his lips. 'Carnaby Street.'

He jaw dropped. 'You're having me on! Carnaby Bleedin' Street?'

'Cross my heart.' Diego grinned. 'Someone very important in the bizz will be there. One in particular wants to chat about your future. This could be your ticket out of the East End, gorgeous. Sky's the limit for a stunner like you.'

Currently she worked in a hair salon around the corner while doing a bit of modelling on the side. All Sin had ever wanted was to be a model full time.

Squealing with delight, she threw her arms around the photographer's neck. 'Oh, Diego! I could bloody kiss you!'

'Save it for the bigwigs, darling.' Diego laughed, gently disentangling himself. 'Make sure you get yourself dolled up to the nines. First impressions stick. Heaven forbid you waltz in there like you've been dragged through Brick Lane backwards. This is Carnaby Street, not Cable Street.'

This was it. Her big break. She could feel it in her bones. Her chance to leave the grimy streets and her family's reputation behind. To reinvent herself as the face of swinging London.

Mind already racing with possibilities, she hurried over to Kath and Dilly with her news.

Her best friend's face lit up, but Sin caught the flash of concern beneath her smile. 'Cor, Sin! That's proper exciting, that is!'

Sin twirled, her excitement bubbling over. 'This is my chance, Kath. My chance to be somebody.'

Kath paused, her teeth worrying her bottom lip. 'Just be careful, yeah? Them toff types…' She glanced around the club, lowering her voice. 'I heard things, Sin. About girls who go to these fancy parties. Girls whose families never see hide nor hair of them again.'

That properly ruffled Sin's feathers. Her enthusiasm dimmed. 'Don't be such a ninny. The men in that business are sophisticated, real gents. Dead ringers for Warren Beatty.'

That made them fall into loud giggles. Despite the laughter, Sin could see her mate wasn't convinced. It was moments like these when Sin was reminded of the gulf between them. Kath, rooted in the East End, while she was desperate to fly free.

Sin glanced around the Voodoo Lounge every part of her glowing. Soon, places like this would be her stomping ground.

She'd be Sin the model.

Not Sin the gangster's daughter.

As they packed up to leave, Sin caught her reflection in one of the club's long mirrors and froze. It wasn't the transformed, sparky, super-confident Sin who was going to take the modelling world by storm she saw. The person who stared back was her fifteen-year-old self, nine years ago. Wilful and scared, with rage burning so hot it had blinded her. That brutal afternoon rushed back, ripping through her. The blood, her mother's face gone chalk-white with horror, her dad's expression of pure hatred. Sometimes Sin still woke up with the metallic taste of fear in her mouth.

Nine years had passed, but the darkness still haunted her, lurking beneath the glossy new Sin she'd worked so hard to become.

Outside, she tried to shrug off the bad feelings by linking her arms through Kath's and Dilly's and skipping, at Dilly's pace, to the hair salon. By rights their carefreeness should've driven the demons of the past away.

It did not.

Chapter Nine

Jimmy walked right into a major league punch-up in the heaving River Rat pub. A bunch of sailors on shore leave were kicking off, flexing their muscles and mouthing off to anyone within earshot. They were obviously not from around these parts because they would've known better than to start creating in this particular boozer. It was owned by Jimmy's dad and was Danny's HQ in Sugar Cane Wharf where he held court, conducting his below-the-counter deals.

'Oi! Watch where you're fucking going!' one of the sailors bellowed, shoving a regular so hard the poor bollocks nearly went arse over tit.

Jimmy's hand instinctively clenched into a fist, but he forced himself to stay near the door. This wasn't his fight – not today, anyway. Watching the out-of-order sailors, Jonesy, the barman's usual chipper and jolly manner disappeared with his normally twinkling eyes blazing with retribution.

'Think you can come in here and tear my gaff apart? Think again!' His growl shook the place.

He rounded the bar quickly for a man with a belly that spoke of a lifelong love affair with countless pints. His grizzled beard couldn't hide the scar running along his jaw, a souvenir from his merchant navy days. The gentle giant who'd share a laugh and slip you an extra whisky was gone. In his place stood an old sea dog ready to unleash hell. Right on cue, a few of the strapping lads in the pub were soon by his side.

'Out!' he roared at the sailors, cracking his knuckles.

The sailors, pissed out of their skulls, didn't take kindly to being told to sling their hook. One of them, a great lump with more muscles than brains, took a swing at Jonesy. Big mistake.

In the blink of an eye, the pub erupted. Fists flew, chairs toppled, and the air filled with curses that would make a docker blush. Jimmy watched the barman and his men make short work of the sailors.

It was over in minutes. The barman's massive hands latched on to the first sailor's collar, hoisting the man off his feet like a rag doll. Knowing what was coming, Jimmy obliged by opening the door. With a practiced swing, the barman hurled the sailor outside. The man sailed into the night, landing with a thud on the cobblestones. One by one, Jonesy dispatched the fighting sailors, tossing them out onto the street as easily as emptying a dustbin. The last one, a burly bloke with a split lip, tried to stand his ground. Jonesy didn't break stride. He yanked the man by his belt and scruff, lifted him bodily over his head, and pitched him out to join his fallen mates.

Dusting off his hands, Jonesy surveyed the wreckage of his pub.

'Right then.' Jonesy lengthened his neck and straightened his apron. 'Who's for another round?'

Jimmy used the rush towards the bar to head towards the back of the pub. The least people who remembered seeing him here tonight the better. His contact wasn't inside. The last thing Jimmy needed was his father finding out what he was up to so he'd instructed the contact to meet him away from prying eyes and ears.

Jimmy stopped at a battered wooden door which opened with a groan of ancient hinges. A blast of chilled night air hit him square in the face, carrying with it the familiar scents of the Thames. Stepping out onto a small landing, the pub's warmth fell away. The landing gave way to fifteen worn stone stairs that descended into the darkness of the river. Not many people came here if they could help it on account of the name of the stairs.

The Executioner's Steps.

'Keep your front to the river and your back to the wall.' That's what his old man had drummed into him about the Executioner's Steps.

Even in summer, a chill hung over them. Jimmy had grown up hearing tales about these stairs. Back in the day, condemned men from the Tower took their final walk down them to waiting execution barges. Later, the press gangs worked here, snatching drunks for His Majesty's navy. These days, the steps had a different reputation. More than one grass had taken an unfortunate tumble down them on a moonless night - Danny Steele had made sure of that.

A match flared halfway down, briefly illuminating an older man's face as he lit up a pipe. Carefully, Jimmy made his way forward because the steps were treacherous, slick with river scum and irregular edges from centuries of use.

'The way I hear it, you're a bloke who knows his way around a ship's manifest,' Jimmy began.

The man's shrewd gaze narrowed, then he nodded. 'That I do. Jan van der Meer. You must be Jimmy.'

Jan was all rough edges and sharp angles. Face weatherbeaten from years at sea, but Christ, those eyes – like a bloody hawk's, missing nothing. His peacoat had done the rounds, same as the chunky jumper underneath. That old sailor's briarwood pipe might as well have been welded to his teeth. His English was spot on, only a hint of his Dutch accent giving him away.

'Heard you might have a proposition for a fella looking to earn some extra readies,' Jimmy resumed.

Jan leisurely puffed before putting to Jimmy, 'How d'you feel about high-end cars?'

The docks were well known for smuggling all types of goods including stolen cars. The right word in the right ear, a stuffed brown envelope, and valuable motors could disappear into ship's holds bound for eager buyers across the Channel.

Jimmy's pulse quickened. 'I'm listening.'

A searchlight from one of Wapping Police's Marine Unit boats swept across the river, causing both men to instinctively press deeper into the shadows until it passed. As they talked, Jan pulled out a leather pouch and began packing his pipe with sweet-smelling baccy. His movements were practiced, almost meditative. He struck a match, puffed till the tobacco glowed, then shook out the flame with a practiced flick.

'Now then,' Jan said, wreathed in aromatic smoke. 'Let's talk business.'

'What's hot these days?'

Jan's eyes gleamed. 'Jaguars are always popular. The E-Type, sleek as sin and faster than the Devil himself. Aston Martins fetch a pretty penny, too. The DB5 drives the continental crowd wild. Something about that James Bond connection, I reckon.'

'Here's how it works,' he continued settled against the damp wall. 'You produce the car. How you do it, that's your business. Bring it to me, and I'll see it onto the right ship. My contacts on the other side handle the rest. Simple as that.'

Jimmy nodded slowly. 'And the split?'

'Fifty-fifty,' Jan said. 'Fair's fair.'

That meant twenty-five for him, twenty-five for Brother Bertie.

Still, Jimmy knew it was best to be cautious. 'How do I know you're the right man for the job?'

Jan chuckled, low and rumbling. 'You need connections to shift these cars once they're on the continent. Connections I've spent years building. Plus, you need someone who can get them on ships without raising eyebrows. That's where I come in.'

He had a point, Jimmy had to admit. 'All right. When would you need it?'

Jan tapped out his pipe against the ancient stone. 'Once you've got one in your possession, call me. You give me the car and you get paid. Job done.'

Jimmy almost punched the air in triumph. The money was within reach to buy the house on Molasses Quay and give his darling Mini her dream home. He started back up the steps, careful to keep one hand on the slimy wall.

Behind him, Jan's pipe glowed like a malevolent eye in the darkness, watching him go.

***

Back home, Jimmy got straight on the blower to Brother Bertie.

'We're on! Just need to find a motor now.'

'You sure this is the right type of job?'

'It's perfect. Who's gonna come after us for stealing a set of wheels?'

Jimmy had no idea how his cocksure words would come back to haunt him.

Chapter Ten

Heart beating like the clappers, Mini gripped her children's hands tightly and crept down the narrow alley off Sugar Cane Wharf. The terrace house loomed ahead, its dark windows watching her every move. She shouldn't be here. If Jimmy got wind that she'd brought Violet and Robbie he'd go fucking mental.

Glancing furtively up and down the empty street, she ushered the kids around to the back of the house. The soft click of the door opening sent her pulse racing. A massive figure filled the doorway, blocking out the light.

'Love,' he crooned thickly, enveloping Mini in a bear hug. 'It's so good to see you.'

Mini melted into her brother's embrace, feeling like a little girl again in his protective arms. 'I've missed you, Lukey,' she murmured gruffly, almost overwhelmed by fierce joy.

After they pulled apart, he knelt to greet his niece and nephew, his usually hard features gentled into a lively grin. 'Growing like weeds, the both of ya.' Chuckling, he ruffled their hair affectionately.

Mini watched the tender interaction, her heart swelling with love and gratitude. Despite the rift with their father, she was determined that her children would know the warmth and devotion of their uncle. Jimmy was clueless about her secretly meeting Lucas for the last couple of years.

He had warned her a thousand times to stay away from her family. And as for Danny? Christ. Her father-in-law would be quick to point the accusing finger of disloyalty at her. After all, her father was his sworn enemy. In her heart, Mini wasn't fooled: Danny had never approved of her marrying his son, no matter how much he pretended otherwise.

Lucas ushered them inside, closing the door softly behind them. The kitchen was exactly as Mini remembered, the worn oak table, the faded floral curtains, the ancient kettle that had survived decades of use. It was as if time had stood still within these walls.

Memories flooding back, a lump formed in her throat. Her dear ole mum, Fleur's laughter, the heavenly aroma of her mum's fresh-baked crusty baguettes and croissants. Her parents embracing with so much love. All at once, more heartbreaking memories made her face fall slightly. This was also where her mother had taken her last breath when Mini was just a little girl. The weight of that loss still pressed heavily on her heart after all these years.

Lucas' voice brought her back to the present. 'Remember how Mum used to let us lick the spoon when she made cakes?' His eyes misted over with nostalgia.

A bittersweet smile played on her lips. 'She'd always save the biggest dollop for you, you greedy sod.'

They shared a quiet laugh, the sound mingling with the ghosts of happier times that still lingered in the air.

'You know.' His words came slow and heavy. 'I made a promise to Mum before she died. Told her I'd always see after my baby sister.' He reached out, gently tucking a stray strand of hair behind her ear. 'You're so like her, you know. Small and strong, just like our Fleur.'

Mini blinked back tears, overcome by the depth of her brother's love and loyalty. Despite everything that had happened, despite their father's rejection, Lucas had kept his word. He'd been her lifeline, her secret connection to the family she'd left behind.

While the children explored the kitchen, wide-eyed and curious, Mini said, attempting to sound casual, 'Lukey, I was wondering, is Gazza Brown still around? Still running the bar in that flash hotel Up West?'

He frowned, the skin on his forehead creasing, clearly surprised by the sudden change in topic. 'Yeah, he is. Still with his missus, too. Why d'you ask?'

Mini shrugged, all airy-fairy like she couldn't care less. 'Oh, I thought I saw him last week. Just been on my mind, I suppose.'

Before Lucas could press further, Mini shifted their chat to safer ground. She playfully nudged her brother's arm. 'So, when are you going to settle down and give these two some cousins, eh? You're not getting any younger, you know.'

Lucas gave a shy grin that didn't quite mask a hint of sadness. 'Ah, you know me, sis. I'm married to the job. Besides, who'd want to take on this ugly mug?'

The words had barely left his mouth when heavy footsteps thundered outside the front door. Mini's blood turned to ice. The familiar sound of her father's heavy tread sent terror shooting through her.

'Bloody hell,' Lucas hissed, his face draining of colour. 'Quick!'

'We have to go,' Mini urgently whispered, gathering her children close. Her hands shook so badly she could hardly grab their coats.

The little ones, sensing her fear, stayed deadly quiet.

Lucas nodded, his face etched with panic. Urgently, he ushered them towards the back door, pausing only to press a desperate kiss to Mini's forehead. 'Take care. I'll be in touch soon.'

The front door opened with enough force to rattle the windows. Their father's gruff voice boomed through the house like a thunderclap. 'Lucas? You here?'

Mini's heart slammed against her ribs. She pushed her children through the door, praying they'd stay silent. Lucas stood frozen, torn between protecting his sister and facing their father.

'Go!' he mouthed, giving Mini a hard shove. 'Now!'

Mini hesitated for a split second, her eyes locked with her brother's. In that moment, she saw all the love, fear, and regret that words could never express.

The floorboards in the hallway creaked under their father's heavy boots. Any second now, he'd be in the kitchen. Mini's muscles coiled, ready to run.

'Lucas?' Their father's voice came again, closer this time. Much too close. 'Who's here? I heard voices.'

For a few precious seconds, Mini stopped to soak up her father's voice. It had been so long since she'd heard him. Sure, he was gruff and tough, but he was still her dad, and she missed him so much.

Mini's trembling fingers fumbled with the back door's latch, panic making her clumsy. The metal seemed to scrape impossibly loud in the silent yard. Finally, it gave way, and she ushered her children through. Pulling the gate behind her, she caught one last glimpse of Lucas, standing in the doorway, his broad shoulders set in a protective stance.

Heart breaking, Mini hurried her children down the alley, praying they hadn't been seen. The sound of raised voices drifted after them, her father's curious questions and Lucas' muffled responses.

It wasn't until they were several streets away that Mini allowed herself to breathe. She huddled Robbie and Violet close, hugging them with a mother's love.

But she ached for her blood family she'd left behind.

They made their way home, and Mini's mind raced. She'd come so close to being discovered. But it had all been worth it.

She now had the information about Gazza Brown.

Jimmy had no idea that she'd heard him talking to Brother Bertie on the phone about needing to steal a fancy car.

Chapter Eleven

A day later, Mini watched Iris fuss over the children, straightening collars and smoothing down wayward curls. Furniture polish scented the air and the unfortunate sour whiff of gin that followed her mother-in-law like a bloody curse. Mini observed the slight tremor in Iris' hands, and a pang of sympathy twisted her gut because it couldn't be easy being married to Danny Steele. The man was all charm and danger cloaked in a docker's donkey jacket.

'There now, don't you both look smart,' Iris cooed, with warm grandmotherly pride. 'Sister Bernadette will be ever so pleased to see you.'

Stepping forward, Mini gently adjusted Violet's ribbon. 'Bless you for always taking them to visit the good Sister.'

Iris dismissed her thanks with a wave, genuine warmth lighting up her careworn face. 'It's no bother, love. The old girl's been good to me over the years. Least I can do is bring her some cheer. Besides, the little ones always brighten up her day.'

Mini nodded, knowing how much Violet and Robbie loved going. For years Iris had given up her free time to help clean the convent and church, telling her husband it was her Catholic duty. But Mini suspected Sister Bernadette was more than just some nun to her mother-in-law. Their bond went deeper than prayers and Hail Marys.

'Now, you two be good for your Nana Iris,' Mini instructed, kneeling to kiss her children goodbye. 'And mind your manners.'

The moment the door clicked shut behind them, Mini sprang into action. She hurried to the tiny storeroom she'd claimed as her sewing sanctuary, heart hammering against her ribs with a mix of anticipation and raw fear.

Mini Steele had built up quite the reputation with her Singer sewing machine. While the fancy ladies Up West flashed their Bond Street finery, the East End girls came knocking at Mini's door. For a fraction of the price, she'd rustle up spot-on copies that would make the latest hotshot fashion designer herself do a double-take. Word was, even a few of the West End dolly birds had started sneaking east for her services, drawn by whispers of the docker's wife who could turn cheap fabric into pure fashion gold.

In the corner hung a vision in midnight-blue silk. A 1950s style dress that would make Grace Kelly weep with envy. It had a nipped-in waist that flared out into a full, sweeping skirt with tiny seed pearls adorning the sweetheart neckline, twinkling in the light with a star-like quality. Mini traced her fingers over the fabric, pride swelling in her chest at the countless hours of work she'd poured into every stitch and pleat.

With reverent care, she lifted the dress from its hanger and wrapped it in layer after layer of crisp pink tissue paper. The final touch was a perfectly tied bow around the sturdy box she'd placed it in. Clutching the box to her chest with precious care, Mini began her journey on the Tube at Wapping station and ended it on the elegant streets of West London.

Her thoughts raced, replaying the phone conversation she'd overheard between Jimmy and Brother Bertie about their hunt for a car to nick. Day after day, watching Jimmy trudge about with his shoulders hunched, it hit her that he was having zero luck finding a set of wheels. That's when Mini decided to step in. She knew in her bones he was doing the job to get money for that house. If Jimmy was willing to risk everything for them, how could she do any less?

The hotel she was after dominated the street in all its gleaming Art Deco glory. Squaring her shoulders, she strode through the polished brass revolving doors and approached the solid mahogany reception desk.

'Excuse me,' she ventured. 'I'm looking for Gary Brown. He works in the bar?'

The impeccably groomed receptionist arched a perfectly plucked brow. 'Mr Brown is currently on duty in the Starlight Lounge. Straight through those doors and to your left, madam.'

And there, holding court behind a sparkling glass bar, was Gazza Brown. His impressive girth strained against a crisp white shirt and black waistcoat. A carefully waxed tash adorned his upper lip. Gazza was always extra when it came to his appearance.

'Well, well, if it ain't little Miss Mini Rogers,' he bellowed, spotting her. 'Or should I say, Steele now?'

Walking over, Mini flashing her brightest grin. 'Gazza, hun. Good to see you.'

He eyed her with naked suspicion. 'What brings your East End self to my neck of the woods, darlin'?'

'Got a little something for Claire.' Mini patted the box. 'Thought I'd drop it by, seeing as I was in the area.'

His eyes narrowed further. 'For my Claire? I didn't know she had you working on something special for her.'

Mini shot him a knowing wink. 'I remember how much she loved ballroom dancing, and I recall how she always kept her waistline trim, so I got to thinking…'

Understanding her message that she wanted to talk private-like, he called out to a young man polishing glasses. 'Reggie! Take over for a tick, will ya? Got to attend to my unexpected guest.'

He led her to a quiet alcove, away from prying eyes. 'Come on then, let's have a butcher's.'

Mini carefully unwrapped the dress, letting the silk shimmer in the soft light.

Gazza let out a low whistle. 'That's a bit of all right. Our Claire will be over the bleedin' moon.'

His expression hardened, a hint of the street-smart tough guy peeking through his polished exterior. 'What you really after, girlie?'

Taking a steadying breath, she confessed, 'I need you to keep an ear out for a set of wheels.'

Gazza was what some in the business called 'a tea leaf's eye', someone who watches and cases places and people for criminals planning jobs. Batters had spotted Gazza's talent when he was fourteen, barely more than a bag of bones scavenging around Mayfair's pristine streets.

'Your dad knew what he was doing when he picked me.' Pride crept into his voice. 'I could spot a Roller's routine from fifty yards. Which posh git left their motor running while picking up his mistress. Which fancy madam kept her car keys in her coat pocket instead of her handbag. Their routines, their habits, I logged the bloody lot.'

'That's why I need you on this one,' Mini insisted. 'You're the best spotter in the business.'

'Was,' he butted in, slicing through her words. 'I haven't done that stuff in years.'

Mini noticed the shadow that darkened his face. 'Gazza, is something wrong?'

'Claire.' His voice trembled. 'A few years back she was a touch poorly. I give up my bad ways to see after her.'

Mini's hand flew to her mouth. 'I'm so sorry, I didn't know.'

His face brightened. 'Now, there's no need for that. She's all tickety-boo now. Mind you, when I told her she was looking better than a fresh cod at Billingsgate, she clipped me round the earhole.'

With gentle fingers, Mini touched the opened box. 'You give this to her with all my blessing and love.' She pressed a tender kiss to his cheek. 'Gazza, you're a good man. I'll be seeing you.'

Then she turned away, bitter disappointment eating her up. Sure, there were others she could ask, but she didn't trust any of them. In the Life, you learned quick who not to trust your secrets to.

'Hold up!'

Mini froze at Gazza's sharp command and turned back.

'What kind of jam jar you after?'

Hurrying back to him, Mini couldn't give him the information quick enough. 'Something flash. Tasty. Enough money to get me and my old man a house.'

'Ahh!' His brows shot up, his eyes suddenly sparking with a knowing combination of admiration and mischief.

'As it happens,' he drawled, 'I think I might have the perfect motor for you. Practically begging to be taken for a spin, if you catch my drift.'

Chapter Twelve

'You did WHAT!?'

For the first time ever, Jimmy raised his voice to his wife. They were in their bedroom, the kids tucked up, sleeping in bed. Mini wasn't surprised at Jimmy's reaction because she'd known full well he was going to hit the effing roof.

Minutes earlier, Mini had been pacing their room, heart banging like crazy, knowing there were going to be ructions. Finally her husband had appeared, his broad shoulders filling the doorframe, his piercing silver-grey eyes quickly taking in her tense posture. Mini's resolve faltered when she studied him because he seemed done in. Exhausted. He'd been pushing himself hard lately, training for the Big Fight, grafting down the dock and for his father and then waiting for word on a car ripe for the taking.

'What's wrong?' Concern etched into his weary features. Then he'd gone ashen. 'It's not the baby?'

Her waved hand dismissed this. Mini hesitated, worried by what her revelation would trigger. Finally she managed to push out, 'I've found it, Jimmy. The perfect car.'

For a moment, confusion clouded his features. 'Motor? What you going on about?'

'I overheard you.' Her words were steady despite her racing pulse. 'You and Bertie on the blower. I know you need a jam jar, I'm assuming to sell on. Something to help us get the house.'

Understanding dawning, he lost it. 'You did WHAT!?'

Mini held her ground, lifting her chin defiantly. 'I went to see Gazza Brown Up West.'

Jimmy's face darkened, the fatigue momentarily chased away by a flash of fury. 'Christ, Mini! You're pregnant! What were you thinking, getting mixed up in this? Are you out of your fucking mind?'

'I was careful,' Mini shot back, her own temper flaring. 'I'm not some helpless little chick, Jimmy. I knew what I was doing.'

Jimmy ran a hand through his hair, frustration radiating from every pore. 'That's not the point! You're carrying our child. You can't be taking risks like this!'

If he thought she was taking any of his bollocks lying down he had another think coming.

'For Christ's sake!' She thrust her face up close to him. 'You think I don't know what goes on in our world? My father is Eric "Batters" Rogers. Ring any bells?'

The rage burning in Jimmy's eyes didn't faze her one bit. Mini might only stand five foot nothing in her stockinged feet, but she knew how to hold her own.

'I grew up watching Face after Face come through our door.' She planted fists firmly on her hips. 'While other kids were learning their times tables, I was learning who could be trusted and who'd stab you in the back quick as look at ya. I watched my dad run his rackets, saw the bruises on his knuckles, heard the hush-hush chats.'

Jimmy softened slightly. 'This ain't about trust, baby. I'm trying to protect you.'

'Protect me?' Mini let out a harsh laugh. 'I've been around villains since I could walk. My dad didn't get his nickname for his baking skills.'

Tutting, hurriedly taking his arm, she drew Jimmy to sit next to her on the bed. 'Listen to me, you handsome idiot. I might be happy playing house, cooking your dinner, and raising our kids, but don't ever think I'm some innocent who doesn't understand the score.'

His hands covered hers, warm and rough. 'Mini—
'

'No!' She bristled over him. 'You need that motor because we need our own house.'

Jimmy's resistance was crumbling. 'It's dangerous.'

'Life's dangerous,' Mini replied emphatically. 'But we're in this together. Partners, right? Through thick and thin, that's what we promised.' She smoothed down his collar with practiced tenderness. 'I'm not letting you do this alone. Not when I can help.'

He crushed her close, burying his face in her neck. 'What did I do to deserve you, eh?'

Mini smiled against his chest. 'You were worth turning my back on my old man for, weren't you? Worth getting cut off from my family.' Easing back, she stared up at him. 'So don't you dare try cutting me out now.'

A ghost of a smile played across Jimmy's mouth. 'Wouldn't dare, darlin'.'

Their mouths met in a searing, hot, lingering kiss. Mini couldn't get enough of this wonderful man she had walked down the aisle with.

'You really found a car, didn't you?'

Mini nodded, relief washing over her. 'An Aston Martin D4 or 5, something or other. Gazza says it's perfect. Barely moved in days.'

As Mini began to detail the information about the vehicle, Jimmy abruptly scowled, his lips twisting. 'Mini, how exactly did you get in touch with Gazza?'

She bit her lip, realising her mistake too late. 'I asked around.'

Jimmy's eyes narrowed. 'Asked who?'

Mini's shoulders slumped. There was no point in lying now. 'Lucas,' she gently rasped. 'I asked my brother.'

The silence that followed was deafening. Jimmy's face went through a kaleidoscope of emotions – confusion, realisation, and finally, fucked off.

'You went to your dad's house?' he exploded, leaping to his feet. 'Are you off your rocker, Mini? Do you have any idea how risky that was?'

Mini flinched at his tone but refused to budge from her position. 'I was careful. No one saw me—'

'That's not the point!' Jimmy gritted out, wanting to roar but mindful of disturbing the children from their sleep. He paced the small room like a caged animal. 'You put yourself in danger. You put our unborn baby in danger! If your dad had caught you…'

The dam inside Mini finally broke. Tears welled up in her eyes, spilling over onto her cheeks. 'I miss them, Jimmy,' she sobbed, her voice cracking. 'I miss my family so much. Miss my dad.'

Jimmy's anger evaporated in an instant. In all their years together, he'd rarely seen Mini cry. She was always so strong, so composed. To see her break down like this, it tore at his heart.

He dropped back on the bed and gathered her into his arms. Mini buried her face in the safety of his warm chest, her small frame shaking with sobs.

'Shh, it's all right.' He stroked her hair with a soothing that belied his size. 'I didn't mean to have a go. I just don't want you to have to go through all that pain again.'

Mini clung to him, years of pent-up emotion pouring out. 'I see Lucas. Every couple of months. I can't let him go, he's the only connection I have left.'

Jimmy held her tighter, guilt washing over him. This gorgeous, amazing woman had given up everything for him.

'We'll figure it out,' he promised gently. 'Somehow, we'll make it right. And soon, we'll have our own place. A proper home for our family.'

Sobs eventually subsiding, Mini raised her head. Jimmy wiped her tears away.

'Do you want me to tell you more about the car?'

Jimmy nodded. 'Tell me everything.'

'Gazza says this is the best day to do the job…'

Chapter Thirteen

Rita's heels clanged against the iron steps as she climbed one of the overhead walkways connecting Sugar Cane Wharf's warehouses. These walk-bridges, or walk-acrosses as the locals called them, suspended high above the cobbled streets, were built so dockers could shift cargo between buildings without having to navigate the busy streets below. In her mink fur coat, Rita was a flash of glamour against the grimy industrial backdrop.

At the top, two blokes lounged near the entrance to the warehouse, to the uninitiated appearing as nothing more than idle dockers. But Rita knew better. These were Danny's men, lookouts standing guard over the treasures inside.

One of them had the audacity to wolf-whistle. 'Hello, darlin'! Fancy a bit of how's your father?'

Wanker!

In a flash, Rita was on him. Her wicked flick knife appeared like magic, pressing firmly against his family jewels. His eyes bugged out in terror.

'Listen here, you piece of undiagnosed venereal disease,' Rita hissed, her voice dripping with venom. 'You want to learn some respect and stop being a dickhead.' She increased the pressure, eliciting a whimper. 'Or I'll slice that tiny dick of yours clean off and have your balls for earrings. Got it?'

The guard nodded frantically.

She stepped back, her lips curled into a snarl. 'I run a respectable business, darling. Just because it ain't the kind you tell your mother about don't mean you can treat me like some two-bit street walker.'

With a killer glare, she swept past and entered the warehouse. As always, it was the delicious aroma of spices that hit her first. Cinnamon and nutmeg quickly followed by oranges and limes and then came the booze, brandy and rum and wines. These were just a sample of the many different types of cargo that passed through the docks daily. The difference with this particular warehouse was it served as Danny's personal Aladdin's cave. Every crate, every barrel, every box had been nicked straight off the ships that docked at Sugar Cane Wharf. The King of the Docks made sure his firm got their cut of everything valuable that came through the port. The place overflowed with the spoils of his criminal empire.

Rita heard a low giggle followed by a man's husky chuckle. Rounding a stack of crates, she came face to face with Danny emerging from his office, his arm wrapped around the waist of a young brunette.

The woman couldn't have been more than twenty, all legs and tits, a face full of makeup that didn't quite hide the fact she'd seen too much of life for her age. She gazed up at Danny with adoration and lust that made Rita want to gag. Just because her bread-and-butter business was her ladies servicing the needs of men didn't mean she had to like it.

Her thoughts turned to Danny's old girl, Iris. Poor cow!

Danny grinned when he saw his business partner, not a shred of shame on his face. The dirty sod! He pulled his bit on the side close and planted a sloppy kiss on her lips.

'Run along now, plum sugar.' He finished with a firm slap on her bum to see her on her way.

Rita raised an eyebrow, unimpressed. 'Enjoying the perks of being King of the Cocks… Oops, I meant Docks.'

Her smart-mouthed comment was rewarded with a sarky twist of his mouth. He straightened his collar. 'I hope this visit means you've got news on the house because you've been taking your sweet time about getting me the info I asked for.'

'Had to make sure I got it right,' she responded, perching herself on a nearby crate. She crossed her legs, letting her fur coat fall open to reveal a glimpse of thigh.

He leaned against a stack of crates, arms crossed, staring at Rita from under hooded eyes. 'What have you found out?' he drawled a touch too casually.

Danny's reaction was subtle, but to Rita's trained eye, it spoke volumes. She'd known him for years, had seen him in all sorts of states. But this was different. There was an undercurrent of something she couldn't quite put her finger on. It made her skin prickle with unease. His shoulders tensed, almost imperceptibly, and for a split second, something sparked behind his eyes.

Bloody hell, was that fear? Before Rita could confirm her suspicions it was gone as quickly as it had arrived, replaced by the usual indifferent mask he wore.

She took her time responding, pretending to adjust her coat while she studied him. Danny was good at hiding his feelings, you had to be in their line of work. But Rita hadn't survived this long in the game by taking things at face value.

'I'm assuming you know that both number one and two Molasses Quay are owned by the Blacklock family, the same toffs who own the Wharf.'

It was a stupid statement really because Danny, of all people, would know who the owners of Sugar Cane Wharf were. The dock was privately owned by the aristocratic Blacklock family whose current head was Viscount Alexander Blacklock. The twin Georgian houses on Molasses Quay had been built by the family at the height of the sugar trade. They had once been the administration offices for the dock, similar to the original job of the Pierhead houses in neighbouring Wapping.

Never taking her canny gaze off her business partner, she continued. 'The agent selling the houses for the family goes by the name of Mortimer Stiffington.'

There it was again, that flare-up behind his eyes. He was trying so hard to appear unaffected, but Rita could see the tension radiating through his body.

What the bloody hell is it about this house?

There was a story here, something big. Something that had the almighty Danny Steele practically quaking in his boots.

'Stiffington?' Danny scoffed, his voice gruff. 'Sounds like a right jobsworth.'

'You've got it in one,' she agreed. 'A right proper stick up the arse. He's a by-the-book man all the way. If he doesn't play ball, it won't be easy to grease his palm, if you catch my drift.'

Danny's fretful gaze darted around the warehouse, looking anywhere but at her. To Rita, it might as well have been a neon sign flashing:

'THIS IS PERSONAL'.

And if there was one thing she'd learned in her years in the flesh trade, it was that 'personal' always meant trouble.

'You think that will stop me?' Danny growled, his voice low and dangerous. 'What I want, I get. And I want that bloody house.'

Uncrossing her long legs, Rita stood and moved closer to him. Placing a hand on his arm, she felt the taut tension in his muscles. 'The way I hear it, he's been tasked with selling it to someone respectable. And…' She nervously cut off saying more.

Danny looked about ready to blow his top. 'And what? Spit it out?'

Rita drew in a deep breath. 'Thing is, Danny, Stiffington's been given strict instructions not to sell to any known not rights under any circumstances. Dodgy geezers need not apply, you get me?'

Danny's face drained of colour. For a split second, raw pain contorted his features before his expression turned to granite again.

After stepping back, Rita tentatively offered, 'I could buy the house on your behalf.'

'They might get wind of your connection to me.' He rubbed his hand over his face. 'Bollocks!'

Heaving himself forward, he found and yanked a bottle of expensive South American dark rum from a dusty wooden crate. He knocked it back straight from the bottle.

Rita continued, 'Or I could set something up at The Sing-Song Lady. Get one of the girls – or some, depending on his tastes – to pleasure him nice and sweet until he'd even agree for Jack the Ripper to buy the house.'

Danny shook his head, his expression knowing and crafty. 'Nah! If he's one of them squeaky-clean choirboy types, we'll need something different. Shoving a quality piece of juicy muff in his face isn't going to cut it.'

Just then, Rita's face lit up. 'I've got an idea. I'll need a bit of time to set it up but I'm thinking of something very special for Mortimer Stiffington up at the Voodoo Lounge.'

Chapter Fourteen

Sin was on the point of tearing her hair out. She stood, frustrated, in front of her wardrobe, staring at the clothes, not sure what to put on. Tonight's party in Carnaby Street wasn't just another piss-up, it was her big shot at clawing her way out of the East End and into the glamorous world of modelling.

'Make sure you get yourself dolled up. First impressions stick.' That's what Diego had drummed into her.

Her trembling hands rifled through the hangers, a mix of gear from the rag trade on Commercial Street and Petticoat Lane, knockoffs that came via the docks and Mini's homespun creations. Nothing seemed right. Nothing screamed 'notice me' loud enough.

'Ruddy hell,' Sin cursed, yanking out a white shift dress with a bold print. She held it against herself, considering. It was dead trendy, no doubt about it, the kind of clobber Jean Shrimpton might wear, but was it too much? Not enough? Groaning through gritted teeth, she tossed it on the growing pile of rejects on her bed.

The pressure was building inside her like a ship's foghorn about to blow. This party wasn't just about impressing some poncy photographers or landing a few modelling gigs, it was about proving to everyone, especially that bastard father of hers, that she was more than just another East End bird destined for a life of babies and bacon sarnies.

Sin's gaze landed on a pale-pink minidress tucked away in the back of her wardrobe. It was the kind of thing that'd make heads turn and jaws drop. Perfect. She slipped it on, studied her reflection, and allowed herself a small smile. The dress was short enough to show off her legs but not so short it screamed desperation. The high neckline and long sleeves kept it classy, while the colour turned her fresh and youthful.

Deciding she needed a cuppa after all that drama, she headed downstairs for the kitchen. To her surprise, Jimmy was there, leaning against the counter with a mug of tea already in hand. His eyes widened as he took in her appearance.

'Bloody hell, sis, you scrub up all right, don't ya?'

He wolf-whistled playfully, which earned him an eye roll from her, but she couldn't help the pleased flush that crept up her neck. 'Cheers for that, you berk. Think it'll do for the party in a couple of hours?'

Jimmy's expression softened while he made her a brew. 'It'll more than do. You're a proper star, Sin. Some top modelling agency would be mad not to snap you up on the spot.'

'Yeah?' She hated the hint of vulnerability in her voice. 'You really think I've got a shot at this?'

''Course you do,' Jimmy replied firmly, handing her a steaming mug of tea.

They sat down facing each other at the table.

'You've got more talent in your little pinkie than half of them stuck-up models put together. Don't let no one tell you otherwise.'

An emotional lump formed in her throat. 'Ta, bruv. That means a lot, coming from you.'

Their father's frame suddenly filled the doorway. Sin immediately stiffened. His cold glance flickered between his children, lingering on Sin's dress with obvious disapproval.

'What's all this, then?' he grunted. 'Having a nice little chinwag, are we?'

The mood in the room turned sour in a heartbeat.

Jimmy carefully responded. 'Just talking about Sin's party tonight. The one with all them high-kicking fashion types.'

The corners of their father's mouth drooped in disgust. 'Modelling? That what you call it these days?' His stern gaze on his daughter turned into a withering glare. 'Listen here, girl, a woman's place is in the kitchen and the nursery. Not prancing about in your knickers for a bunch of perverts.'

Shame and anger burned Sin's cheeks.

'Leave it out, Dad,' Jimmy said, a warning edge to his voice. 'Sin's got real talent. She could make something of herself.'

But their dad was on a roll now. 'The girl thinks she's too good for the likes of us now, don't she? All high and mighty 'cause she went to that poncy convent school. Well, let me tell you something, my girl—'

Sin's chair shrieked against the floor as she sprang up, every inch of her vibrating with white-hot fury. 'I didn't ask to go to that school! I was sent there, remember? After—'

She broke off, chest heaving, her throat closing with the tightness of a fist. For a moment, memories of that terrible day, nine years back flooded back. The day that had changed everything between them. They never spoke of it, but it hung over their family, a cloud of suffocating poison, seeping into every Sunday dinner, every birthday, every Christmas. And Jimmy… Sin didn't need to see his face to know it would be pale, waxy, and sick with his own memories.

'Make something of herself?' Danny's voice dripped acid. He carried on like she wasn't in the room. 'That fucking princess thinks she's better than us. Well, she ain't nothing but gutter trash in fancy clothes. And she'll learn that lesson the hard way. Mark my words.'

He left them, stomping out of the kitchen. Sin shook with an emotion she still couldn't control after all these years.

'I fucking hate him!' The fury tore from somewhere deep and broken within her. 'I'll bloody show him. Who does he think he is? King of the whole sodding world, that's what he thinks. Well, I ain't some doormat he can wipe his boots on anymore. I'm done playing the dutiful little daughter, done tiptoeing round his precious feelings. I'm gonna make something of myself, and when I do, I won't need his permission to breathe. And won't that just stick in his craw? His daughter living life on her own terms. Bet that'll have him choke on his bloody criminal money.'

Jimmy enveloped her in a tight hug, the fierceness of it betraying the depth of his love and protectiveness. Sin clung to him, tears burning behind her eyes, her body still trembling. Sin loved her brother so much. What would she do without him? No matter what, she'd always have Jimmy in her corner.

'You listen to me.' Rough emotion was evident in his every word. 'You're meant for bigger things than this. Don't you ever let anyone make you think different, you hear? Not even Dad.'

Sin nodded, not trusting herself to speak.

Pulling back, her adored brother stared her firmly in the eye. 'You're going to walk into that party and knock 'em dead. Show 'em what us Steeles are made of. And when you're living it up in Paris or New York or wherever the hell it is models go, you remember this: you did it all on your own. No one gave you nuthin'. You earned it.'

A watery smile tugged at Sin's lips. She suddenly realised Jimmy was dressed to go out. 'Where are you off to, then?'

His expression became guarded. 'Just some business I need to take care of.'

Sin's heart sank because she knew what that meant.

Criminal business.

Probably with that gallivanting best mate of his. Annoyance flattened her lips at the thought of Brother Bertie.

'You be careful, yeah?'

Jimmy threw his head back and winked. 'Always am. Don't you worry about me. You just focus on your big night.'

He took a step towards the door, then paused, looking back at her with an intensity that made Sin's breath catch. 'You're not the only one whose life's going to change tonight. Me and Mini, we're on our way up, too. Things are going to be different for all of us, you'll see.'

With that cryptic statement, he was gone. Sin desperately wanted to believe him, to imagine a future where they were all free of the shadows that haunted their family. But deep down, she feared that the iron grip of gangland would always be too strong for Jimmy to resist.

Pushing those dark thoughts aside, Sin headed upstairs again. In her room, she couldn't wait to strip off the minidress because it now felt splattered with her father's ugly words. Besides which, she knew exactly how to stand out from the crowd at the party.

Two hours later, she took in her reflection in the mirror, a leisurely grin transforming her features. The fashion crowd at the party would never know what hit them. Because Sin Steele was done playing by anyone's rules but her own.

Chapter Fifteen

The black cab glided to a halt by the side of Whitechapel Road, and Jimmy and Brother Bertie climbed in the back. They were wearing black overalls they'd borrowed from the docks. Their pockets were full of the tools of their trade, and their trade that evening was car theft. They both wore flat caps tugged low over their eyes.

'Grosvenor Square, mate.'

The cabbie eased away and headed down towards Aldgate. Jimmy noticed their driver was eyeing them in the rearview mirror which made him yank his cap down even lower. The guy was still at it with the eyeballing before finally he cackled.

'It's Jimmy, isn't it? Jimmy Steele?'

'Who wants to know?'

The menace in Jimmy's voice didn't appear to register with the cabbie. 'I know your old fella, Danny.

Top geezer, he takes a ride with me some times. Very good tipper, your dad. Everyone in the East End knows Danny Steele.'

'Yeah.'

Even though it was clear Jimmy wasn't in the mood for a chat, the guy kept at it. 'What you up to in Mayfair then? Wouldn't have thought that was your neck of the woods. 'Ere, you're not going to that demos up at the American Embassy, are you? Protesting against the war in Vietnam?'

Jimmy leaned forward. 'What's your name, mate?'

'Bobby.'

'All right Bobby, let me ask you a question. Are you familiar with this rhyme – mind your own business and don't mind mine, kiss your own sweetheart and don't kiss mine?'

The driver slowly nodded. 'Yeah.'

'Why don't you repeat it to yourself for the rest of journey?'

'All right, mate, just trying to be friendly.'

The glass slat that divided Bobby from his passengers was shoved across to stop him listening.

Brother Bertie shook his head. 'I said we should have caught the Tube. Now we've got a witness and we ain't even there yet.'

'If we'd taken the Tube we'd bound to have been spotted by more people we know,' Jimmy flashed back quickly. 'And anyway, if this Herbert knows my old man, he'll know better than to go gobbing to any and anyone about who he's been giving a lift to. He's going to keep it schtum.'

'Unless that "anyone" is your old dad.'

Jimmy said nothing because it was true.

The cab dropped them in Grosvenor Square, and the two men made their way down a side street towards New Bond Street. Kept going until they came across a swanky townhouse on a quiet street. Outside the townhouse, there it sat.

An Aston Martin DB4.

Even from here they could see it was a thing of beauty. British Racing Green, all elegant curves and pure class sitting there bold as brass under the streetlights. The body, beautifully handcrafted, was sleek, its paintwork shimmering even in the dark, all topped off by the distinctive winged Aston Martin badge.

'Fuck me!' Brother Bertie breathed reverently. 'Will you get a butchers at that set of wheels.'

Jimmy had to agree. He'd seen plenty of flash motors in his time, especially being delivered through the docks, but this was different. This was James Bond territory. Everything about it screamed power and privilege.

Suddenly, Brother Bertie brought them both back down to earth with: 'That motor is too special. Someone is going to miss it and want it back. The whole point of doing this is it should be low risk.'

'Whoever owns it has got more money than sense leaving it parked on a London street. They're loaded, which means they'll just buy a new one.'

They went on with the next step of their plan. Bertie walked slowly up the road on one side, keeping his eye open for anyone who might interfere, and then back down the other side to check there. Jimmy made his move towards the car. When he reached it he fished around in one of the long pockets of his overalls and took out a massive chain with about fifty car keys on it. The guy who'd sold it to him had promised him one of these keys would open any Aston that had ever been made, even if it took fifty goes to find out which one it was.

Jimmy hunched down low by the door and began to go through the keys. On the eighth, he heard a clunk on the door. He was in. Opening it, he ran his hand over the seats and dashboard. It was perfectly finished. Lush. A work of art. He bobbed up to signal for Brother Bertie when a shout split the air.

'Oi! You there!'

Jimmy nearly died on the spot. It was a bobby on the beat. The copper's voice shattered the night's silence. Jimmy's blood ran cold. He froze, half in the Aston, watching Brother Bertie's shadow stretch long across the pavement as the bobby's torch beam caught him.

His friend didn't miss a beat. Brother Bertie's demeanour changed to staggering dramatically, grabbing a lamppost, and launching into Lord Kitchener's famous calypso tune, 'London Is the Place for Me'. His rendition and the wobble and vibration of a man totally plastered.

'Keep it down!' The copper advanced, truncheon tapping against his leg. 'This is a respectable neighbourhood.'

Through fretful eyes, Jimmy watched Brother Bertie weave down the street, leading the law away from the car. His mate was putting on a masterclass in drunk dancing, one step forward, two steps sideways.

'Evening, Offisher!' Brother Bertie's words were pure slur. 'Just sharing some Caribbean cheer with these fine folks of May… Mayflower… I mean, Mayfair.'

The officer wasn't having any of it. 'Name and address.'

'I only wanted…' Bertie stumbled, catching himself. 'Only wanted to bring some island sunshine to this cold English night.'

'You're going to share a nice cell at the station if you don't clear off.'

Jimmy's fingers tightened on the car door in horror. If Brother Bertie got nicked, the whole job would go tits up. Worse, his dad would hear about it with his corrupt connections in the force.

The copper grabbed Brother Bertie's arm. 'Right, you're coming with me.'

'Now hang on…' His act slipped for just a second.

Jimmy's heart hammered. He had to do something. But moving now would blow the whole thing.

A police whistle pierced the air a few streets over. Sharp. Urgent. The kind that meant serious trouble.

The police officer's head snapped around. He hesitated, still gripping Bertie's arm.

Another whistle. Closer this time. More insistent.

'Must be those long-haired students back up at the US Embassy,' the bobby muttered. He gave Brother

Bertie a hard shove. 'Get yourself home before I change my mind.'

Bertie stumbled backward, maintaining his drunk act. 'You're a proper gentleman, Offisher.' He saluted. 'God save the Queen.'

The cop was already moving, his footsteps quick on the cobbles heading towards the whistles. Once he'd rounded the corner, Brother Bertie swung back into action, straightening up and sprinted back to the car.

'Blood fire!' He jumped into the passenger seat, breathing hard. 'That was close.'

Jimmy's hands were shaking so bad he almost dropped the keys. 'You had me worried there.'

'Had myself worried.' Bertie wiped sweat from his forehead. 'Thought I was going to be spending the night at Her Majesty's Hotel for sure.'

The Aston's engine purred to life. Keeping the lights off, Jimmy rolled away from the kerb. Neither man spoke until they were three streets clear.

'A calypso in Mayfair?' Jimmy finally sarcastically quizzed. 'That was your plan?'

Bertie grinned. 'Should've gone with classical. More their style round here.'

'You're one lucky bastard. If those whistles hadn't…'

'Luck's got nothing to do with it. That was the ole Bertie Watson magic.'

They'd got the car, and now for the next step.

Finding somewhere to stash it away.

Chapter Sixteen

Just over an hour later, they parked the Aston outside a set of shutters of a garage under a railway arch in Mile End. On the way, they'd made a detour to a quiet side street in Camden where Jimmy had left two new registration plates in a bin outside a disused factory. Then they were off again to see Dabs, Jimmy's associate who owned the East End garage.

Jimmy sounded his horn to alert Dabs of his arrival.

Bertie was curious. 'Why is he called Dabs?'

'Because he's a dab-hand with cars. Dad would use him, but he's got his own wheel man near Sugar Wharf. Him and Dabs go way back, though. His real name is Percival Gross.' Seeing the look of astonishment on his friend's face, he added, 'Yeah, you'd want people to call you something else, too.'

'Do you know him well?'

Jimmy nodded. 'I wouldn't be trusting him with a job like this if I didn't.'

The shutters on the workshop went up, the signal for Jimmy to drive into the brightly lit and cavernous space inside where cars in various states of repair were parked. Dabs was short and round, a man who had learned how to have his ears and eyes to the ground. He shook Jimmy's hand warmly but squinted at Brother Bertie, who he didn't know, with some suspicion. That was one of the things Jimmy liked about Dabs, he didn't trust anyone, a useful skill in a trade like his. He did the introductions and promised Dabs that his friend was sound. Dabs still didn't seem convinced, but he knew better than to ask questions of Jimmy Southpaw.

The three men stood and admired the Aston.

Dabs circled it like a wolf sizing up its prey. Opening the doors, bonnet, and boot, he let out a low whistle. 'This motor is sex on wheels.' He slid into the driver's seat, running his hands over the leather. 'Some cars you drive. This beauty?' He shook his head. 'You just worship her.'

Jimmy shifted his weight, nervous energy rolling off him. 'Can you sort it? Full respray, file off the numbers, maybe add a few custom touches?'

''Course I bloody can.' Dabs' eyes narrowed. 'My fee goes to your dad, yeah?'

The word 'dad' hit Jimmy like a punch to the gut. 'Nah, mate. Give me a decent price and I'll settle up.'

'Hold up!' Dabs unfolded himself from the car, his expression hardening. 'Danny don't know about this little acquisition, does he?'

Jimmy tried throwing an arm around the garage owner's shoulders, voice dropping low. 'Look, there's good reasons my old man ain't in the picture on this one. The less you know, the better off you are, get me?'

Dabs shrugged him off. 'Your dad's made it crystal clear – anything dodgy comes through my doors, he wants to know about it. Far as he's concerned, this garage is his manor.' He jabbed a finger at Jimmy's chest. 'And you think I'm gonna risk everything just because you're playing at being the big man?'

'Only three people know about this car,' Jimmy pressed. 'Me, you, and my mate. We keep our gobs shut, no one's the wiser.'

Dabs barked out a laugh. 'Your old fella? He's got X-ray vision when it comes to bullshit. I've watched harder men than you try pulling the wool over Danny Steele's eyes. Know what happens?' He drew a finger dramatically across his throat. 'And here's his own flesh and blood, asking me to help him take the piss.'

'Come on, Dabs. After everything I've done for you and your boy?' Jimmy's voice took on an edge. 'Even if you tell me to drive this motor straight out of here, I'd still have your back.'

'Don't.' Dabs' face darkened. 'Don't you dare bring my lad into this.'

'All I'm saying is—'

'Nah, all you're saying is you want me to stick my neck out because you've nicked some flash motor and don't want Daddy finding out.' Dabs snorted. 'I may be a grease monkey but I ain't thick. Your father finds out, I'll be lucky if all I lose is the garage.'

Dabs caught Jimmy's eye before turning on his heels and going back to his office without another word.

Brother Bertie said, 'He ain't going to help us out.'

Frustrated, Jimmy bit his lip and cursed under his breath. There were other garages in the East End, but none of them were as good as Dabs'. And if any of them thought they were treading on Danny's toes they would not hesitate to slam the door in Jimmy's face.

'Where are we taking the Aston now then?' Brother Bertie continued.

Jimmy rattled the car keys in frustration. 'Fuck knows. I've half a mind to drive it back to Mayfair and dump it there.'

The two men got in the car, and Jimmy started the engine. As they gently rolled forward, Dabs emerged from his office and stood in front of the car with his hand raised like a cop making a stop. Then he beckoned for Jimmy to follow him to his office.

Inside, Dabs settled behind his desk. 'All right, mate, I'll do it. I'm not happy but I will do it. You're right, I do owe you.'

His palm in the air signalled he was not finished having his say. 'I don't want any money. We'll be quits after this. But I need to make one thing clear. If your dad comes round and starts asking questions, I'm not covering for you. I'm going to admit you brought the car here but I'll say I assumed that he was in the picture. That will be because, no one, not even his own son, would dare mess him around like that on his own turf. It's up to you what you want to tell him, but I'll be sticking to my story.'

'Don't worry, he won't find out.' Jimmy thought about it for a moment before saying, 'But if he does, I'll take the cop. There'll be no dropping you in it. How long do you want?'

'Call back in a couple of days.' Suddenly he squinted at Jimmy. 'This motor ain't going to turn up on Police 5 with Shaw Taylor telling the kids to keep 'em peeled?'

'No one is coming after this. Believe me.'

Dabs finally looked satisfied. 'Check back with me tomorrow in the morning.'

Business concluded, for now, Brother Bertie and Jimmy headed towards Mile End Tube.

Brother Bertie asked, 'Are you worried about Danny?'

Jimmy didn't answer. He carried on silently walking into the chilly night.

Chapter Seventeen

The party was in full swing by the time Sin got there. The flat sat above one of Carnaby Street's trendiest boutiques, not far from the super trendy Lord John and Lady Jane. Sin's absolute fave shop was I Was Lord Kitchener's Valet because of its military-style clothing. Even in the darkness, the street pulsed with life. Shop windows sparkled with the latest mod fashion, their psychedelic frontages splashed with eye-popping colourful designs. A lone coffee bar was still open where Sin spotted young women in minidresses dancing to the latest hits while their guys watched on, decked out in paisley shirts and tight trousers. People paraded in their latest purchases, undeterred by the late hour, their laughter echoing off the buildings and night.

Her heart was beating like mad with the excitement of being here. This was where London Cool hung out, and now she was part of that in-crowd, too.

Sin had pulled out all the stops to stand out at the party. She radiated pure East End swagger. Instead of trying to run away from who she was, Sin had embraced it.

Her style was a bold declaration of her roots, a defiant middle finger to anyone who dared judge her because of where she came from. She was decked out in a showstopper, a micro-mini shift in brilliant white vinyl, adorned with oversized silver discs that caught the light with every movement. The hemline was short enough to make a vicar blush, but not so much that she'd flash her knickers to all and sundry. White go-go boots made her pins seem like they went on for bloody miles. With jet-black liner, she'd created an exaggerated cat-eye. She'd applied three pairs of false eyelashes, building them up to outrageous proportions. Her lips, in stark contrast to her dramatic eyes, were painted a pale, frosted pink, slightly overdrawn to create a perfect bow shape.

To finish the ensemble, Sin had backcombed her short hair, securing it with enough hairspray to withstand a hurricane.

She walked down the alley where the door to the flat was tucked away. Now she was here, an attack of the wobbles, scared silly she was going to make a right cake of herself by putting her size fours right in it.

Her fierce inner voice psyched her up: 'You were born for this, Cynthia Steele. This is your moment!'

Confidence bolstered, Sin quickly pulled out her enamel blue Stratton compact and used the plump puff to freshen up her cheeks. Not too much, mind; entering the image of a ghoul was not a good look.

The door was unexpectedly flung wide open, making her gasp and stumble back.

A very anxious Diego stood there.

'Darling!' He dragged the word out in his usual flamboyant sing-song style. 'Thought I was going to have to send out a search party for you.'

Giving her no chance to respond, he clasped her hand and tugged her into a long, narrow passage, kicked the door back with his heel, and then, with a critical eye, brow arched, he checked her over.

Sin held her breath.

Finally, his face lit up with a dazzling smile. 'You're absolutely divine, my queen. Pure Carnaby Street gold. You're going to eat this place alive.' He ended with a mock imitation of a lion growling, which made her giggle.

Ahh, bless his soul for putting me at ease. She was thankful to have someone of his calibre on her side.

The main room was jam-packed with people. Couples were getting on down and grooving to Sly and The Family Stone's 'Dance to the Music'. Ciggy smoke hung thick like a London fog. Sin's wide, excited gaze drank in every detail. This was it! What she'd always bloody dreamed it would be. The people who had it all in the flesh, dripping Biba and Mary Quant from every perfect pore. Women with razor-cut fringes mixing with posh boys in velvet jackets. Black faces, white faces, everyone moving to the same beat. Crystal glasses clinked, ice cubes tinkled, champagne fizzed.

The room was massive white walls covered in artwork that made her heart stop. Paintings and pop art that probably cost more than she could earn in a lifetime. Bloody hell, was that a real Andy Warhol?

'Get that down you.' Diego shoved a glass of Bolly in her hand.

Knocking it back, Sin savoured the taste of it – very dry with an aftertaste she wasn't sure she liked that much. Then again, the truth was she found champagne overrated. Give her a glass of Babycham over it any day of the week. But she kept this to herself, not wanting to come across as uncultured.

Sin laughed her head off. This was a million miles away from the trouble and strife of Sugar Cane Wharf. The photographer introduced her to this person, that person, all major players in the fashion industry. When she met a guy who she recognised as an actor off the telly, she thought she'd gone to Heaven and back. However, something was niggling at the back of her mind. Why were there more men here than women? Why were most of the men middle-aged or older? Then again, the fashion industry was dominated by men. Wasn't it?

'And who might this pretty kitty be?'

Hearing the deep tones of a man's voice, Sin spun around. He was both older and much smaller than her, round with a comb-over to conceal his bald patch. His Italian suit and shoes screamed money and class.

He smelled good, too. He appeared supremely confident, his palm casually cupping the round bottom of a brandy tumbler.

Sin boldly shot back, 'This kitty doesn't meow, but she does possess very sharp claws.'

He roared with laughter. Sin couldn't help but join in. There was something about him she liked. Or maybe it was the booze, because the strangest thing was, she was getting way tipsier than she usually did. Plus, the room was starting to look weird, sort of blurry.

The man leaned in and spoke for her ears only. 'I like my kitties to scratch. And bite.'

Through the blur, Diego seemed to appear out of nowhere and thrust more booze in her hand. The man pulled him aside and whispered in Diego's ear, eyeing up Sin at the same time. What was said between the men, Sin couldn't hear.

Instead of drinking, Sin merely held the glass because she really couldn't stomach the champagne. Plus, her temples were throbbing. And things were going in and out of focus. Despite the importance of the party to her career, Sin began to think the unthinkable – maybe she should go home.

Go home? Stop being such a ninny. Tough it out!

But before she could make any decisions, Diego was back, holding her hand, this time with more force than he had previously.

'Do you know who you've just been speaking to?' he gushed with feverish anticipation close to her ear. Typical Diego, he didn't give her any time to respond.

'He's one of the owners of Sterling Design and Fashion.'

No way! Sterling Design & Fashion was one of the leading fashion brands. Sin sucked in her breath, barely able to contain her delight.

'That short, fat man?'

'You better believe he's fat, nice and plump in the pocket, m'girl.' He ended with a dramatic wink.

Somehow he was guiding her up a narrow staircase. How had they got here? Sin didn't recall them leaving the party room.

She couldn't shake off that strange, muddled sensation. Why did it feel like she was floating up the stairs? She blinked repeatedly in an attempt to clear it up, but it only seemed to get worse.

'You play your cards right and you're going to score big time, secure your future. Have a shot at becoming the next "It" girl.' Diego's voice seemed so far away, a hollow echo in the distance.

Then they were in a large bedroom dominated by a round bed covered with shiny, scarlet sheets.

The room was bathed in a seedy red light.

'What's going on?' she asked.

Well, at least that's what she thought she'd said, because her voice sounded slow and slurred. All she got back from the photographer was a smile. Why did his mouth appear so twisted and ugly?

'You lie back and think of England.'

It came as an almighty shock to Sin when she realised she was flat on her back on the bed, her bag flopped by her side.

How did that happen?

The erratic sound of her heartbeat thundered in her ears. A terrible weight pushed down on her chest, her limbs so heavy. Sin tried to shout at Diego to help her, but her tongue was stuck to the bottom of her mouth.

Terror suffocated her, increasing when the door opened and the short, fat man from downstairs walked in.

Diego told him, 'She knows the score. And I get that shoot in Monaco as promised.'

Through the fuzzy, foggy brain, things became clear to Sin. That arsehole, Diego, had spiked her drink and was now offering her on a plate to this bastard.

The man approached the bed and stared down at her. 'Let's see how sharp your claws are now, little kitty.' The tip of his filthy tongue licked his foul, greedy lips in anticipation of what he was going to do to her. He undid his belt and trousers.

No fucking way! No! No! That creep wasn't putting his diseased prick inside her.

Desperately, Sin tried to move but collapsed back. She flinched when his pudgy, sweaty hands touched her legs and worked their way up her naked thigh. His heavy, nasty breathing filled the air. His hands were near her knickers.

Help me! Someone help me!

HELP ME!

He pressed his gross body on her, his erection digging deep into her belly. Tears slid down her face. His revolting body rocked deep on her. His breath stank of garlic and red wine. He fumbled with her knickers and managed to jerk them down to her ankles. Then he got between her legs.

And that's when Sin's vision cleared a little, her body coming back to partial life. Thank God she hadn't drunk that last glass of drugged champagne.

Her hand scrambled by her side, frantically hunting for her bag. The tip of his wet penis touched her inner thigh. With both hands, and with all her might she shoved him off. He crashed onto his back, surprised. Sin rummaged in her bag for her Charlie perfume and blasted his eyes. He screamed, clawing at his face.

Frantically, she crawled off the bed and tipped onto the floor.

'You bitch!' A face full of fury, he came at her and caught her by the hair and dragged her across the room. 'I'm going to teach you a lesson you're never going to forget.'

He punched her in the stomach. Sin cried out in gut-wrenching pain. His hand went up again, ready to do more damage, and that's when Sin remembered who she was.

A Steele.

And Steeles didn't take shit from anyone

Her hand yanked his balls into the tightest fist she could form. And twisted. His mouth gaped in a silent scream. She twisted again. He crashed to his knees. Sin forced herself up, legs shaking. A bronze statue of a woman stood on the sideboard. She lunged for it and smashed it against his skull. Rage drove her boots into his ribs - once, twice. Her head spun but she didn't care.

She snatched her bag, ripped open the window. The rusty drainpipe tore into her palms on the way down. Sin bolted into the darkness, black mascara running wildly down her face.

Chapter Eighteen

The vicious banging on the front door downstairs jolted Gertie awake. Her eyes flew open, heart pounding like Judgement Day before the Lord had arrived. She'd been dreaming Satan and his minions were chasing her, and for a moment, she thought they'd finally tracked her down. But as awareness crept in, she realised she was safe in her bedroom. The Devil was just a dream. The banging, however, was all too real.

There it went again.

Who the backside? At this ungodly hour.

Gertie took a sip from the glass on her bedside cabinet, her secret tipple of Lord Have Mercy Rum Punch. Her brother thought she didn't know what he and Ruddy were up to in his room. Gertie was aware of everything that happened inside her boarding house. She'd 'liberated' a bottle from its hiding place.

Making sure her nighttime head wrap, a silk stocking, was still in place, she slipped out of bed, popped her feet into her well-worn slippers, and cinched her dressing gown around her waist.

The banging continued, more insistent now. Whoever was out there wasn't going away.

'I'm coming! I'm coming!' she grumbled, then kissed her teeth. 'It's the middle of the night.'

After flicking on the hallway light, Gertie cautiously approached the door and opened. She let out an audible gasp at the sight that greeted her.

'Lord have mercy!'

It was Jimmy's sister, Cynthia. But not as Gertie had ever seen her before. The girl was barely recognisable. Gertie had never seen her without a hair out of place, she always took such pride in her appearance. Sin's clothes were in disarray, hanging off her slender frame like she'd been involved in a fight. But it was her face that made Gertie's suck in a sharp intake of breath. In the harsh light from the hallway, she could see a few angry bruise on Sin's face and neck.

Urgently, Gertie drew her inside and shut the door. In disbelieving shock she asked, 'What happened, darlin'?'

Sin managed, her voice quivering and thin, 'I need to see Bertie.'

'He's not here. Him and your brother had to collect something.'

Sin swayed on her feet, and Gertie reached out to steady her. As she did, she noticed more bruises on the girl's arms, stark against her pale skin. Those bruises were clearly the brutal marks left by another person's hand.

Oh no! The terrible realisation finally hit Gertie. Some man had attacked this poor child. Gertie's protective, maternal nature kicked in.

'Please,' Sin whimpered, 'I need to see him.'

The rattle of a key in the lock shattered the silence, startling them both. Brother Bertie's slight frame and porkpie hat filled the doorway. He stopped dead, shock and disbelief slamming into him at the sight before him. A strangled sound escaped his throat before his dark eyes hardened, taking in the purple-black bruises that snaked up her neck. Gone was the firecracker who'd trade insults with him quick as lightning. In her place stood a hollow shell of a woman, terror etched into every line of her beautiful face. The woman who'd face down the Devil himself with a smartarse comeback stood there, all her fierce spirit drained away.

'What happened?'

Sin's composure crumbled at the sight of him. She stumbled forward, flinging herself into his arms, rattling sobs racking her body.

Brother Bertie held her tight, comforting her as best he could while doing his best to hold on to his anger.

'Who did this to you?' It was there in the menace laced in his voice that whoever it was had better watch out.

Gertie watched as Sin tried to speak, her words muffled against Brother Bertie's chest. She couldn't make out what the girl was saying, but she saw her brother's expression darken further.

'Gertie.' Bertram's blistering stare meet hers over Sin's head. 'Get the medicine box. And put the kettle on.'

'No!' Sin reared back with an adamant shake of her head. 'I need to freshen up.'

Gertie's wise head understood exactly what 'freshen up' meant. That desperate need to scrub away the memory of her violator's hands. Sadly, Gertie had seen this too many times before. And the awful truth was Sin would learn, even after the bruises yellowed and faded, no amount of soap could cleanse the memory from her skin. Some scars, Gertie knew, carved themselves deep into a woman's soul.

She placed her hand on Sin's trembling shoulder. In that simple gesture, Gertie became more than just a witness to the girl's trauma, she became a silent guardian who understood the long road ahead. Without a word, she guided Sin to the downstairs bathroom. Some hurts went beyond words, and right now what this poor child needed wasn't talk, but understanding and a safe place to fall apart.

Leaving her to her privacy, Gertie returned to the kitchen where she found her brother pacing.

He stopped dead, his face ravaged. 'Do you think…?' The rest of the words wouldn't come.

Gertie wasn't one to hold the truth back from her brother. 'Those bruises on her arm are from a hand. A cruel hand.' When Bertie's responded by balling his hand, Gertie warningly added, 'The last thing that girl needs is another man using his fists.'

'She's right.'

They turned at the sound of Sin's voice to find her in the doorway.

She looked washed out, weary circles under her eyes in a face that was ashen and bloodless. Her arms were folded protectively around her middle, almost like she was holding back a scream clawing at her throat. 'Can I spend the night? I can't go home like…like this.'

Sorrow whelmed up inside Gertie because the poor girl felt too ashamed to face her family. The shame wasn't hers, it was the bastard who had perpetrated such an evil act.

Before Gertie could offer her a room, Brother Bertie stepped in. 'You can stay in my room. I'll sleep on the floor.'

For a moment, Sin closed her eyes in relief. Her legs trembled so badly under her, she thought she was about to fall over. She was still trying to process what had happened. The drinks making her head fuzzy. Brutal grabbing hands burning every inch of her body where he'd touched her. Her head and heart pounded together. Her stomach heaved from fear and disgust. The taste of panic stayed bitter in her mouth. She'd walked into that posh party proud, certain this was her chance to make her dreams come true. Now she felt small. Dirty. Stupid.

Stupid! Stupid! Stupid!

An erratic punch of air leaving her, Sin reopened her eyes. 'I'd like to go up now. I just need to rest.'

Gertie watched her brother rush forward and take hold of her arm. Time seemed to freeze. Something electric crackled in the space between them as their eyes locked. Sin's sharp intake of breath had nothing to do with her injuries. Brother Bertie's hand trembled slightly where it rested on her skin, his thumb unconsciously stroking once, twice, as if soothing a frightened bird. The moment shattered when Sin swayed slightly on her feet.

Brother Bertie guided her into the hallway and up the stairs to his room.

Left alone, Gertie filled the kettle, her lips moving in a silent, fervent prayer:

'Almighty Father, unleash your wrath upon the monster who did this. May his flesh rot from his bones while he yet lives. May maggots feast on his putrid soul. And may he suffer the torments of a thousand hells for eternity.' Then she added, 'And if you're too busy, Lord, I reckon my brother might just do the job for you instead.'

She was surprised when Bertram came back minutes later, finding her at the table with a mug of milky Milo warming her cupped hands.

Her fleshy cheeks wobbled with indignation. 'Same ting happened to Mrs Richards' daughter back in Jamaica. She was promised work in Kingston and when she got there the work involved her lying on her back.' Disgust contorted her expression. 'Growing up a woman isn't easy. In the blink of an eye a girl's dream can flip into a nightmare. And there's always some worthless man at the bottom of it.'

'She can't even sleep.' His voice was ragged. 'She's just sitting there, staring into space.'

'She's going to need plenty of time to heal.'

***

Brother Bertie crept back into his room, treading as softly as possible. The last thing he wanted was to disturb Sin if she'd finally found sleep. But she was wide awake, curled into herself on his bed, knees tucked to her chest, arms wrapped around them like a protective shield. When she shifted slightly, her blouse rode up, revealing an angry purple bruise spreading across her stomach.

That fucker had punched her.

Brother Bertie saw red and lost his shit. He strode to the bed, reached underneath, past the hidden bottles of his Lord Have Mercy Rum Punch, and pulled out a wicked cutlass. The blade had travelled with him all the way from Jamaica. Sin shot up, eyes wide with shock. She'd never seen a weapon like it before.

'What are you doing with that?' Her voice quaked, her eyes going wide.

He didn't answer, instead marching to the door like a man possessed. Sin leapt off the bed and threw herself between him and the door. His chest heaved with barely controlled rage. Gone was his usual laid-back cool, replaced by hot-blooded fury.

Sin knew what he was planning. Earlier she'd told him about the horror at the party.

'I won't let you do this.' She planted herself firmly against the door.

He answered in his rawest Jamaican. 'When I hunt that bloodclaat pussy down, I gwan chop his raas into a million pieces.'

'No!'

Bertie shook his head, gripping the handle tighter, shooting her an incredulous glare. 'You think I can let this stand? You're Jimmy's sister.'

'That's why I didn't go to Jimmy. Or Dad. I don't want any more violence. I just want…' Her face crumpled, head falling forward. Fresh sobs tore her apart.

The cutlass clattered to the floor. He gathered her in his arms and guided her back to the bed, laying her down with a gentleness that belied his earlier rage.

'Will you lie next to me?' Her words came out choking and low, barely above a breath. 'I don't feel safe.'

Bertie hesitated, torn. Every instinct screamed to comfort her, but this was Jimmy's little sister. His best mate's flesh and blood. There were lines you didn't cross in their world. But when she looked up at him with those wounded eyes, his resistance crumbled. Slowly, fighting against his better judgment, he lay down and gathered her close. Sin curled into him like she belonged there.

'You're safe,' Brother Bertie whispered, trying to ignore how right she felt against him. 'You'll always be safe with me.'

Chapter Nineteen

Early the following morning, her brother and Sin still asleep, Gertie wheeled the heavy wicker trolley of damp, washed sheets and towels and pushed open the laundrette door with her free hand. The familiar scent of soap and hot metal greeted her, along with the rhythmic rumble of the washing machines. The place was kept shipshape and in order by a woman everyone called Madam Mangler on account of the old-style mangling machines still in use here. You did not want to get in a fight with her. Madam Mangler had left a note stating she'd gone to the shops and would be back in a jiffy.

Gertie was still unsettled by last night's distress with Sin. After her brother had left her in the kitchen, she'd remained sitting at the table, very troubled indeed. Unknown to Bertram, she'd observed him with Jimmy's sister beneath hooded eyes and saw things they probably didn't even know. The ease between them. How they had clung to each other. And more. It was 'the more' that worried her.

A terrible premonition gripped Gertie.

In her heart, she knew that girl was bad news for her Bertram.

Wearily, she made her way to her usual spot in the corner and began unloading some of her washing into the dryer. While she fed shillings and sixpences into the coin slots, the door jingled, and in strutted Ruddy, her signature beehive bobbing.

'Wotcha, Gertie!' Ruddy set her washing basket on a nearby table. 'Busy day ahead at the boarding house?' she enquired.

'You know it,' Gertie replied with a smile. 'The beds don't make themselves, more's the pity.'

Ruddy laughed as she sorted her laundry into piles. 'I don't know how you manage, taking care of all us lodgers. I've got my hands full just with Lady Pru's bits and bobs over in Grosvenor Square.'

Ruddy worked as housekeeper to Lady Prudence, one of London's blue-blooded set who lived in one of the most exclusive parts of town.

'The Good Lord gives us strength for our daily labours,' Gertie said, shaking out a pillowcase. 'And I'm thankful for the work that puts food on the table and keeps the roof over our heads.'

The two women fell into a comfortable natter as they went about their tasks, swapping bits of gossip and commiserating over the rising prices at the grocer's. Ruddy clucked her tongue with a shake of her head when Gertie told her what had happened to Sin. Gertie felt a warmth in her chest that had nothing to do with the heat from the dryer. In the ten years since she'd arrived from Jamaica, these small moments of chit-chat in the laundrette had become precious to her, a balm against the hardship of making a new life in London. Sometimes she got so homesick. Missed Jamaica bad.

The door jingled again, harsher this time, jolting Gertie from her thoughts. She looked up to see a man come stomping inside, a canvas sack slung over his shoulder. Colin Mayhew. Her stomach dropped. The sight of him made her skin crawl. He was a walking embodiment of everything ugly about the East End. His piggy eyes set deep in a face mottled with burst blood vessels, his gut straining against a grubby vest. Even from across the room she could smell the stale beer and cigarettes coming off him. Hatred twisted his doughy features into something truly grotesque.

'Bleedin' cold out there,' he grumbled to no one in particular. His gaze fell on Gertie, and his stare sharpened. He bared his nicotine-stained false teeth. 'You again? Thought I told you not to be washing your filthy rags in the same machines as decent folks.'

You wouldn't know decent if it booted you in your bollocks!

But Gertie didn't voice her scathing put-down, she dropped her gaze instead, focusing on folding a still-warm sheet. She'd learned it was best not to engage with the likes of this smelly, racist old goat. Privately, she cursed him to Hell and back.

But the tosser wasn't finished. He stalked closer, his voice rising. 'Didn't you hear me, you foreign scum? Bad enough we've got to share the neighbourhood with your lot, now you've got to muck up the laundrette, too?'

Gertie's hands stilled on the sheet, anger simmering under her skin. In the corner of her eye, she could see Ruddy rocking with rage.

The mangy dog took another step, close enough that the stench of stale tobacco on his breath hit Gertie in the face. 'Why don't you take your washing back to wherever you came from, eh? Don't they have rivers there?'

Something in Gertie snapped. The righteous fury that she'd tamped down for so long came roaring to the surface, as hot and bright as a Jamaica sun.

She seized a damp sheet from the pile, doubled it over and, quick as a flash, whipped it across Mr Nasty Piece o' Work's face with a resounding snap. He stumbled back, spluttering, his eyes wide with shock.

'Now you listen here, you jackass,' Gertie seethed, the sheet twisted in her fists. 'I work hard for what's mine, same as anyone. I've got as much right to be here as you or anyone else.'

She advanced on him, the sheet raised threateningly. He scrambled backwards, nearly tripping over his own feet.

'You think you're better than me because of the colour of your skin?' Gertie demanded. 'Well, let me tell you, I'd rather be black and proud than a snivelling, stinking, gutter-crawling rat like you.'

She punctuated her words with another swat of the sheet, catching him a good one across the shoulder. He yelped and cowered.

Gertie reared up. 'The Lord says to turn the other cheek, but let me tell you, I'm going to slap your cheeks silly until that dumb head of yours rolls off.'

Ruddy, outraged by what was being done to her friend, had grabbed a wet towel and joined the fray. 'Oi, you manky tosspot!' she hollered, her eyes blazing. 'You want to pick on someone, why don't you try me on for size?'

She snapped the towel, catching him another crack on his arse. He howled, more in surprise than pain, and scurried for cover over to a machine.

'From now on,' Gertie growled, 'you're going to keep a civil tongue in your head, or so help me, I'll hang you out to dry right alongside my washing. Do I make myself clear?'

Blanching, his cracked, thin lips opened and closed like a landed fish, he finally nodded frantically.

Ruddy, not content to let it end there, leaned in close, her voice dropping to a menacing whisper. 'And if I ever catch wind of you giving Gertie anymore bovver, they'll need dental records to identify you after I've finished with you. You know me, so need I remind you that I've got friends in low places, sunshine, and they'd be more than happy to teach you some manners.'

'Good!' Gertie lowered the sheet, breathing hard. 'Now get out of my sight! Don't let me catch you spreading your poison again.'

In two seconds flat he bolted for the door, leaving his laundry sack behind in his haste.

For a long moment, the only sound was the rumble of the machines and the women's ragged breathing. Then, slowly, Ruddy cackled, the sound infectious enough that Gertie found herself joining in.

'Oh, Gertie, that was blinding!' Ruddy exclaimed, wiping tears of mirth from her eyes. 'The look on that wanker's face! I'll treasure it for years.'

Gertie chuckled. She picked up the abandoned sack. 'Reckon he won't be needing this now. Ruddy, want to divvy it up? Finders keepers and all.'

Ruddy's eyes lit up with mischief. 'Why not? Could always use a few extra rags for polishing Lady Pru's silver.' She held up a particularly garish vest, 'I reckon we did that prat a favour. His fashion sense is criminal.'

Gertie snorted, then sobered. 'Thanks for backing me up, Ruddy. It means a lot.'

Ruddy's expression softened. ''Course, babe. Us girls have got to stick together, don't we? Especially with idiots like that running about.'

Gertie nodded, her thoughts turning to her brother and last night. She knew there would be more battles against bigotry to fight, more ignorant fools spouting their racist shit. And if anything were to happen between Bertie and Sin…? She shuddered to think of the storm it might unleash.

'Penny for your thoughts?' Ruddy softly asked, noticing Gertie's troubled expression.

Gertie sighed. 'Just thinking about my brother. And Sin.'

Ruddy's eyes widened in understanding. 'What, Jimmy's sister? Cynthia? Never! They're always going at each other's throats. Like a pair of boxing rabbits.' Her voice slowed with meaning. 'Unless something has happened?'

'Not yet,' Gertie replied, her voice low. 'But I can see the way they look at each other. I don't want my baby brother to get hurt.'

Ruddy asked, surprise evident in her voice, 'I could ask Brother Bertie if him and her are, you know what—?'

'No, no,' Gertie quickly declined her offer. 'Don't worry about it. It's just a feeling I have. But I don't want that for him, Ruddy. I don't want him to have to fight every day of his life just to be with the woman he loves. It's not fair.'

'Life rarely is,' Ruddy responded, softly and sadly. Then she perked up with, 'You're seeing more and more black and white couples these days.'

Gertie gave her a tight nod. Still…her mind rebelled at the thought of Bertram romantically involved with Sin. The thought of her baby brother facing hatred day in and day out, just for loving who he loved, made her stomach churn with dread.

Chapter Twenty

Brother Bertie's fingers drummed against the cheap Formica tabletop, his hat sitting untouched beside him. The memory of last night burned in his gut. Sin curled up against him, trusting him to keep her safe. Him, of all people. Her quiet sobs had torn him up inside, worse than any beating he'd ever taken.

The ancient clock on the wall ticked away the awkward minutes. Gertie had already gone off to do the laundry, leaving him alone with his thoughts. And what a bloody mess those were.

He stiffened at the sound of soft footsteps and hastily stood. Quickly, he jammed his hat on his head, forgetting to tip and tilt it a certain way. Sin appeared in the doorway, her face carefully made up to hide the worst of the bruising on her neck and to bring some much-needed colour to her skin. Their eyes locked, and the air crackled between them. A flush crept up her neck, matching the heat Brother Bertie felt rising in his own cheeks. The memories of them together in his bed last night stood unspoken between them.

He cleared his throat, desperate to break the awkward silence. 'Fancy a cuppa?' He tried for his usual cheeky grin and failed miserably. 'Or maybe a glass of my special rum punch?'

Before Sin could answer, a sharp knock rattled the front door. Her face went white, expression stark and stricken.

'Just Kath,' he reassured her quickly. 'Got word to her last night. No way was I letting you face this alone.'

He opened the door to reveal Sin's best friend and her sister, Dilly. Kath's alarmed gaze widened with concern, while Dilly rapidly blinked. The moment Kath clocked Sin's face, she let out a strangled gasp.

'Oh, pet!' She rushed past Brother Bertie and wrapped Sin in a gentle hug.

Over Sin's shoulder, her eyes met his – grateful but horrified. Dilly followed silently, pressing a soft kiss to Sin's cheek.

Brother Bertie watched the reunion, emotion balling in his chest. He'd done the right thing, hadn't he? Getting Sin's best friend here? But as he observed the tender way Kath fussed over Sin, checking her bruises and murmuring soothing words of comfort, he wished it were him seeing to her needs not someone else.

Sin's eyes caught his across the room. A silent understanding passed between them. What happened last night – her vulnerability, his tenderness – that was theirs alone. Brother Bertie nodded almost imperceptibly, understanding without the need for words.

'We need to get you home, love,' Kath insisted. 'Your mum will be going mental.'

Terror flashed across Sin's face. 'I can't let them see me like this.'

'Stay here then.' Brother Bertie stepped forward. 'Gertie won't mind.'

The gratitude in Sin's eyes made his heart do a stupid little dance. Then another knock boomed through the house.

'Who is it?' Brother Bertie called out once he was in the hallway, tension surging in his gut.

'It's me, you Herbert,' came the smart-mouthed reply.

Jimmy.

The atmosphere in the kitchen changed in an instant. Sin's face drained of colour, her gaze rounding with fear. 'Bertie, please,' she whispered urgently. 'Don't let him know. Promise me! Promise me!'

What could he do but nod and agree, but his conscience was a different story. Lying to Jimmy felt all kinds of wrong. But one look at the humiliation and shame crippling her, and he knew he had no choice.

'Quick,' he told the women. 'Out the back.'

Passing him, Sin hesitated. 'Thank you.'

Their eyes met again and sparked with everything they couldn't say.

Then she was gone, Kath and Dilly in tow, melting into the grey London morning.

Brother Bertie squared his shoulders and went to let his best friend in, the weight of secrets pressing down on him.

***

A nasty case of guilt clung to Brother Bertie inside Jimmy's motor.

'Right then, let's sort this car out,' Jimmy said, gunning the engine. 'Can't have any hiccups when Jan, my Dutch contact comes back to town after my big fight.'

Brother Bertie absently nodded, his mind elsewhere. He could still feel Sin's warmth from last night, the way she'd curled into him seeking safety. It made him sick to think of anyone hurting her.

'Oi, you gone mute and deaf?' Jimmy's voice cut through his teeming thoughts. 'I said, we need to keep the car under wraps until our buyer shows. You listening?'

''Course I am,' Brother Bertie replied, forcing a grin. 'Just thinking about all that lovely dosh we're gonna make.'

Jimmy shot him a sideways glance. 'You're acting queer. What's got into you?'

Brother Bertie was stuck between a rock and a hard place. He'd given his word to Sin, but keeping something this major from his blood brother didn't sit right with him. Should he tell Jimmy? If someone had laid hands on Gertie, he'd want to know straight away. Then again, Sin had trusted him with this. And a man's word was his bond, wasn't it?

'Nothing's got into me,' Brother Bertie finally answered, adopting an exaggerated cockney accent. 'I'm as right as rain, guv'nor. Fancy a knees-up round the old Joanna?'

Jimmy snorted, shaking his head with a roll of his eyes. 'You're a right nutter, y'know that?'

Nearing the garage, Brother Bertie's internal battle raged on. The words danced on the tip of his tongue, begging to be spoken. But every time he opened his mouth, he saw Sin's pleading eyes, felt the weight of her trust in him.

'You sure you're all right?' Jimmy asked, his voice softer now. 'You know you can tell me anything, right? We're brothers, you and me.'

Brother Bertie swallowed hard. 'Yeah, I know. It's just…' He trailed off, unsure how to continue without betraying Sin's confidence.

Jimmy pulled up outside Dabs' garage in Mile End, killing the engine. 'Right, let's have a butcher's at our little goldmine, shall we?'

Approaching the garage, Jimmy fished out the key. Brother Bertie's heart was pounding so hard he was sure Jimmy must hear it. The weight of Sin's gut-wrenching secret pressed down on him, heavier than a docker's load.

'Jimmy, mate…' he began, not quite sure what he was going to say.

'Yeah?' Jimmy paused, key in the lock.

Brother Bertie took a deep breath. 'I just wanted to say… well, you're my best mate, ain't you? And if anything ever happened to you or yours… you'd want me to tell you, right?'

Jimmy's brow furrowed. ''Course I would. What's this about?'

Before he could respond, Jimmy swung open the garage door. The words died in Brother Bertie's throat. They both stared into the empty space before them.

Jimmy stood stock-still, his face a mask of disbelief. 'What the fucking hell?'

The Aston Martin was gone.

Brother Bertie felt the ground shift beneath his feet. This was bad. This was very, very bad.

'Maybe we got the wrong garage?' he feebly offered, knowing full well they hadn't.

Jimmy whirled on him, eyes blazing. 'Don't be a fucking idiot. Someone's nicked our nicked motor!'

Chapter Twenty-One

Mortimer Stiffington, the agent in charge of selling the house on Molasses Quay, hesitated at the entrance of the Voodoo Lounge, his hand hovering over the doorbell. The gaudy neon signs of Soho's notorious sex shops flickered in his peripheral vision, making him squirm with discomfort. This was decidedly not his usual part of town.

At forty-five, he was the very embodiment of his surname – stiff, uptight, and conservative to the core. His stocky frame was always impeccably turned out in a suit that was pressed to within an inch of its life, the creases in his trousers sharp enough to rival a blade. Beneath his bowler hat, his thinning hair was combed over to hide his bald patch and his thin lips seemed permanently set in a disapproving line. He only appeared to warm up when he was with his wife whom he was devoted to.

He'd worked at the same City-based insurance company since leaving school, slowly but steadily climbing the corporate ladder. His crowning achievement was becoming one of the key people managing the business affairs for the estate of the distinguished Blacklock family. In his eyes, this was proof of his upward mobility within the middle class. The task of selling one of their Georgian houses in Sugar Cane Wharf was an honour which he took very seriously.

But under this carefully constructed respectability lay a festering secret. A darkness that, if exposed, would shatter the very foundations of the life he'd so painstakingly built.

He glanced down at the invitation in his hand, then back up at the door. He was here for a charity event. Giving to unfortunates was an important part of Mortimer's life, becoming more so after what had happened all those years ago.

Still, this venue was a strange place to hold such a worthy event.

Taking a deep breath, he pressed the bell.

The door opened, revealing a well-dressed doorman who checked over his invitation. Mortimer's eyes were immediately drawn to a large, ornate display board. In elegant handwritten script it proclaimed:

The Docklands Darlings Foundation. Helping East End Children Find Their Wings.

After giving the doorman his hat, he was escorted to a spacious meeting room. Rows of chairs were neatly arranged facing a small stage with a podium. The room buzzed with activity as elegantly dressed women mingled, sipping champagne and sherry and nibbling on canapés. A striking woman appeared and approached him. She was willowy with a delicately imposing height wearing a pale-pink wool Chanel suit with a triple strand of pearls.

She stretched out her white-gloved hand. 'Mr Stiffington, I presume? I'm Lady Henrietta Featherstonehaugh. We're so delighted you could join us.'

The picture of upper-class grace, her auburn hair was swept up in an elegant chignon, and she exuded an aura of refinement that immediately put him at ease.

Before Mortimer could respond, a shrill voice cut through the chatter. 'Oi, Doreen! Pass us that fancy little sandwich, will ya? Beats the hell outta the crap we usually scoff at the La—' The woman coughed nervously and finished in a squeaky, cut-glass voice, 'I mean, at our regular charitable functions.'

Lady Henrietta's smile never faltered, but Mortimer noticed a slight tightening around her eyes. 'Do excuse me, Mr Stiffington. I must begin the proceedings.'

She glided to the podium, which was the signal for all to take their seats.

'Ladies and gentleman, welcome to The Docklands Darlings Foundation's fundraiser. We're here today to discuss a matter of utmost importance. The plight of East End children.' Her words dripped with emotion and passion. 'I stand before you with a heavy heart and a fervent plea. The children of east London are suffering. Orphaned, abandoned, left to fend for themselves in the unforgiving streets of our great city.'

Mortimer felt his heart swell. This was why he donated to charity. This was what truly mattered. Helping children was everything to him and his wife.

Lady Henrietta marched on, her eyes glittering with unshed tears. 'But we have hope. A beacon of light in the form of a new property on Molasses Quay.'

What? Mortimer was taken by complete surprise. Every eye in the room turned to him. He loosened his tie under their collective hot stare.

Lady Henrietta directly appealed to him. 'Mr Stiffington, with your help, we can transform this house into a sanctuary for these lost children. A place of safety, of nurture, of love.'

Understanding dawned concerning the real reason he'd received an invitation. The charity didn't want his money, it wanted the house he'd been tasked with selling.

Suddenly, a voice rang out from the crowd. ''Scuse me, Your Ladyship, but where's a bird go to powder 'er nose in this joint? I'm burstin' for a slash…I mean, to freshen up.'

Lady Henrietta speared the other woman with a flinty stare. 'Second door on the left, dear.'

After the speech, she made a beeline for Mortimer, steering him towards two plush seats in a quiet alcove.

'I understand you're the man to talk to about the house on Molasses Quay.'

Mortimer nodded, trying to maintain his composure. 'That is correct.'

'We need that house for our new children's home,' she said, continuing the thread of passion she'd shown to the audience. 'These poor darlings, out there and alone. They need a place of safety. We're prepared to make a generous offer. Won't you help us? For the children?'

For a moment, Mortimer wavered. His instructions were to sell the house to someone who was respectable, and the lady before him was the epitome of that. And this was certainly a worthy cause. Nevertheless, he wasn't sure the Blacklock family would appreciate their property being overrun with children from troubled backgrounds. In his mind he saw the house as a place for a loving family to put down roots.

'I'm terribly sorry, Lady Featherstonehaugh,' he stiffly informed her. 'But I'm afraid that's quite out of the question. There are a certain number of protocols and rules I must go through, you understand.'

Just then, the door flew open with a bang. A woman stumbled in, looking like she'd been dragged in by the cat. Yanking down the hem of her way-too-tight skirt, she explained, 'I'm right sorry I'm bloody late! Some knob-nuts tried to nick me charitable donation on the way 'ere!'

Mortimer's jaw dropped. What kind of charity event was this?

Seeing his astonished expression, Lady Henrietta leaned into him. 'We feel that it's important to have some members of the families of the children here. It wouldn't do for us to be seen like we were going in and taking over. The last thing we want is to be called a bunch of do-gooders.'

She moved closer, her knee brushing against his. 'Surely, in a case like this, exceptions can be made?' She pressed her palm on his arm, her touch warm through the fabric of his suit. 'We could make it worth your while…'

Mortimer felt his cheeks redden, a bead of sweat forming on his brow. He jerked back as if burned. 'My dear lady! I don't know what you're implying.' He loved his wife, and adultery was one of the worst sins in his book. 'But I can assure you, rules are rules.'

With that, he stood abruptly, fixing his tie. 'I think it's best I take my leave now. Good afternoon, Lady Featherstonehaugh.'

Hurrying towards the exit, Mortimer couldn't shake the feeling that he'd narrowly escaped something. But what, he couldn't quite say.

***

The moment the house agent was gone, the side door of a neighbouring room was flung open with a bang. Danny Steele emerged. He'd been listening to proceedings. His face was a mask of unbridled fury. Deep creases etched themselves between his brows, and his nostrils flared with each ragged breath. His jaw was clenched so tight it was a wonder his teeth didn't shatter. The very air around him seemed filled with lethal electric.

Confronted with a Danny on the war path, the room ground to a deathly silence.

'All right, you shower!' he roared with barely contained violence. 'Party's over! Everyone out! Fuck off.'

The elegant ladies scattered, revealing themselves to be far less refined than they'd appeared. Stumbling towards the exit, one tripped over her high heels, letting loose a string of curses that would make a sailor blush. Another, in her haste, accidentally dropped her clutch. Its contents spilled across the floor – lipstick, a compact mirror, and unmistakably, a handful of condoms. She scrambled to gather her things, her face red with embarrassment.

Danny's eyes bulged at the sight. 'You brought your working girls to this? You told me that you were going to hire some of those actors from the theatre. God knows there's enough of them needing work. Are you off your rocker?'

Rita, who had been playing her part as 'Lady Henrietta', snatched off her wig. Shrugging, she lit an Embassy and sucked in a much-needed nicotine hit.

'They were all busy so I asked a couple my girls. Beggars can't be choosers, now can they?'

'Fuck's sake!' Danny paced, up and down, his hands balling by his sides. 'You promised me something special that would reel Stiffington in, not this amateur hour bollocks!'

Rita restrained herself from snapping back. Instead, she kept it calm. 'Look! Mortimer Stiffington is as straight as an arrow. So when word reached me he likes to give to the needy, what better way to appeal to his conscience.' She stubbornly folded her arms. 'Anyroads, you thought it was a blinding idea, too, because you gave it the thumbs-up.'

His chest heaved, his breathing noisy in the room.

Rita managed to coax him into a chair, pressing a glass of whisky into his hand. 'Come on, love. It's not the end of the world. We'll think of another way to snag that house.'

Danny took a long swallow, his knuckles white around the glass. 'You don't understand. That house… I need it.'

Gently, Rita perched on the arm of his chair, her brow furrowed. 'Why's it so important?'

Danny's head snapped up, his eyes boring into hers. 'I never said it was important. Times are changing, and I want to diversify my investments. Like you said, it will make a good replacement for the knocking shop on The Sing-Song. Plus, you mark my words, one day property near the river will be worth a mint.'

Rita believed him about property values. The problem was, Danny was using this explanation to mask the truth. Then again, it wasn't her business.

She shared with him something she'd figured out. 'People like Stiffington who give to charity usually do so because they feel guilty about something.'

'What do you mean?'

'Something is burning that man's conscience. A secret.' Smiling, Rita stood to her full height. 'It might take me a while, but I'll find out what it is. And when I do, you bet that house will be yours.'

Chapter Twenty-Two

The man on top of the woman in the bed in the stately bedroom wheezed once, twice, and, with a ripe curse, he reached his completion and collapsed onto her. Viscount Alexander Blacklock, known to most as Lord Xander, having done his duty got off his much younger and very new wife. He didn't need to look at her to know her eyes were squeezed shut, her fingers clawing into the bedsheet. Fucking her was like rutting with a block of ice, making the whole business bloody uncomfortable. But needs must when you required an heir.

Fifteen minutes later, studying himself in the grand mirror, he adjusted his cravat with practiced precision. At sixty-six, he still cut an impressive figure – tall and lean, silver threading through his dark hair adding distinction rather than age. Power and privilege radiated from every pore.

Behind him, barely visible in the mirror's reflection, lay the form of his new bride, twenty-seven-year-old Lady Prudence. Her mousy brown hair fanned out across the pillow, her soft hazel eyes staring blankly at the ceiling, the white satin nightgown clinging to her plump figure. These upper-class families bred their girls to do their duty without any hysterics. Lie back and think of England.

'Off to my club, m'dear.' He didn't bother turning. 'Don't wait up.'

Lady Pru's whisper barely disturbed the air. 'Of course. Have a pleasant evening.'

The girl was proving to be everything he'd hoped for in a wife. Young, submissive, and most importantly, filthy rich. This house had been part of her substantial dowry, along with a country estate and a tidy fortune that would keep him in the style to which he was accustomed for years to come. Also, he needed to beget an heir. He'd been married twice before and only produced girls. Girls were only there to make alliances through marriage to other aristocratic houses, but they could never carry on the family name. That's why he slept with his wife any chance he got, no matter how distasteful he found it.

Smirking, he strode from the opulent bedroom and, descending the sweeping marble staircase, Lord Xander allowed himself a moment to admire his new residence. The entrance hall was a masterpiece of Georgian architecture, with soaring ceilings adorned with intricate plasterwork and chandeliers that glittered and sparkled. Priceless centuries-old artwork lined the walls, and antique furnishings spoke of generations of wealth and taste.

Quite the step up from his crumbling ancestral pile, now mortgaged to the hilt thanks to his gambling weakness. But those days were behind him. Lady Pru's fortune restored his rightful place among London's elite.

As head of the family owning Sugar Cane Wharf, he faced problems. The dock couldn't compete with the new container systems. He'd started the process of offloading everything starting with putting the Molasses Quay house up for sale.

Movement caught his eye at the bottom of the stairs.

'You there!' he barked. 'Fetch my coat and hat.'

The member of staff emerged from the shadows, and Lord Xander's lip curled with disdain seeing Nora Baxter – or 'Ruddy' as she insisted on being called. His wife's housekeeper.

She sneered back at him. 'Do I look like your skivvy, matey?'

Her East End accent grating on his nerves, Ruddy stomped off. Lord Xander gritted his teeth, wishing he could not just sack her on the spot, but boot her and that ridiculous beehive into the gutter where they belonged. But Prudence had made it clear that the hiring and firing of staff was her department, especially Ruddy. When he complained about her insolence, his new wife wouldn't hear a word said against the bloody woman.

How his wife had ended up with an East End boiler for a housekeeper, he'd never know.

He fumed. The butler retrieved his coat and hat and opened the door. Lord Xander stepped out into the balmy evening towards Soho's Voodoo Lounge.

***

Lady Pru remained motionless in the master bedroom, her gaze still fixed on the ceiling.

I will not cry. Will not cry. I won't!

She was a lady, after all, and ladies did not indulge in such vulgar displays of emotion.

A soft knock at the door roused her from her troubled thoughts.

'Come in,' she called, her voice steadier than she felt.

The door creaked open, revealing the concerned face of Ruddy who was holding a silver tea tray. Though only a couple of years separated them in age, with Ruddy being the younger, the gulf between their life experiences was vast. Ruddy's hard-scrabble upbringing in the East End had given her a worldly wisdom that Pru, despite her privileged background, could scarcely fathom. It was as if they'd lived in entirely different centuries, rather than merely different areas of the same city.

'You could use a cuppa and maybe something stronger,' Ruddy said, dropping the formal act once the door closed behind her.

Sitting up, Lady Pru managed a wan smile. 'Ruddy, you are a diamond, always knowing just what to say.'

While Ruddy busied herself with the tea tray, Pru's mind drifted back to the day they'd met, a chance encounter that had changed both their lives forever.

It had been a foggy evening in Whitechapel two years back. Lady Pru had foolishly decided to visit a doctor she knew at The Royal London Hospital in the East End. Instead of allowing her chauffeur to drive her, she had gone on the Underground. At the other end, one wrong turn was all it took for her to get lost in Whitechapel's backstreets. She'd quickly found herself surrounded by a menacing gang of kids. Just as panic had begun to set in, a voice had cut through the fog like a whip.

'Oi! You lot! Clear off before I ride this and turn into the witch from your worst nightmare! You hear me, you raggamuffins!'

The children had scattered, revealing Ruddy, armed with nothing more than a broom that she'd shaken at them and a killer scowl. She'd taken one look at Pru's fine clothes and rolled her eyes. 'What's a posh bint like you doing in a place like this?'

From that moment, an unlikely friendship had blossomed. Ruddy had escorted Pru safely home. When Pru had learned that Ruddy worked as a cleaner, struggling to make ends meet, she'd impulsively offered her a position as housekeeper.

Ruddy had agreed, but on her own terms. 'I ain't living in,' she'd stated firmly. 'And don't think this makes us mistress and servant. No one lords it over me. You need seeing after, and that's what I aim to do.'

Now, as Ruddy handed her a steaming cup of tea, Pru felt a surge of gratitude for her friend's unwavering support.

'So, what's the plan then?' Ruddy asked, perching on the edge of the bed. 'Because if you ask me, that family of yours needs shooting for marrying you off to that randy old cretin. It's clear as day he's only after your money.'

Pru sighed. 'It was my decision. I'm no oil painting, and frankly, I was tired of sitting on the shelf. Xander isn't many people's idea of a dream, but at least he's given me the chance to have children of my own.'

Ruddy smacked her lips, outraged. On the shelf! It was 1967, for fuck's sake. Women shouldn't think they needed a man to get by. Then again, these aristos had some right weird ways. It left Ruddy feeling both frustrated and sad that her friend thought no one would have her because she believed herself to be ugly and too old.

Ruddy snorted. 'What do you need me to do?'

Pru hesitated, then seemed to come to a decision. 'I've decided to go to the country house this week. Xander will probably join me at some point. I've given the staff time off, so I was hoping you could shut up the house for me.'

Ruddy's eyebrows rose slightly, a glint of mischief brightening her gaze. 'Anything else?'

'Just… bless you, Ruddy. For everything.'

Ruddy's face softened. ''Ere, you'll make me blush in a minute. You just rest now. I'll take care of everything.'

Outside, Ruddy allowed her expression of servility to slip. Her features hardened as she thought of Lord Xander and the way he treated her friend. In her years of cleaning for other people, she'd seen her fair share of loveless marriages and cruel husbands, but there was something particularly loathsome about that man.

Wiping thoughts of him from her mind, Ruddy made her way down to the staff's quarters. Suddenly, an idea came to her which had nothing to do with the master and mistress of the house. She thought back to what Gertie had told her had happened to Sin. With the Grosvenor house empty for the week and her ladyship away in the country, there might be an opportunity to…

She needed an urgent sit-down with Brother Bertie.

Ruddy allowed herself a small, grim smile.

Chapter Twenty-Three

Watching the strippers gyrate on the small stage, men with hungry eyes licked their lips in unabashed lust. The Voodoo Lounge pulsed with the raw energy of 1960s Soho after dark. A thick curtain of cigarette smoke hung in the air, mingling with the hum of chat and a steady supply of drink. Xander held court at the roulette table in the club's exclusive casino room, his aristocratic charm on full display. Two stunners were draped over him, giggling at his every word. His smooth, charismatic voice carried across the room, regaling the crowd with an outlandish tale.

'There I was, stark bollock naked, facing down the entire Ascot Ladies' Day Committee,' Xander proclaimed, eyes twinkling with merriment. 'And wouldn't you know it, the duchess herself chose that very instant to make an appearance!'

The assembled group cracked up with raucous laughter. Xander basked in their adoration, carefully concealing the darkness that lurked beneath his polished exterior.

'Go on, Xander!' a portly gentleman urged. 'What happened next?'

Xander cupped the pert bottoms of both his companions. 'I did the only thing a gentleman could do in such a situation. I tipped my hat – the only item of clothing I had left – and said, "Your Grace, I do hope you'll forgive my informal attire. I seem to have misplaced my jodhpurs!"'

The crowd erupted again while slapping Xander on the back, the women attached to him gazing at him adoringly. He was magnetic, drawing people into his orbit with practiced ease.

Yet beneath his jovial exterior, Xander's mood soured. The roulette wheel had not been kind tonight. He was losing. Badly. With each spin, his losses mounted, eating away at the allowance stipulated in his marriage contract with Lady Prudence.

Cunt bitch! he seethed inwardly, careful to maintain his affable facade. Holding the purse strings like some penny-pinching fishwife.

The thought of being financially controlled by a woman four decades younger made him feel like his prick was being slowly chopped down to size. It was galling to a man of his stature. And appetites.

Contemplating risking another substantial bet, a figure suddenly emerged at his elbow. He turned, surprised to see a familiar face he hadn't expected in such an establishment.

The newcomer stood ramrod straight, his greying hair and stoic air commanding instant attention. His impeccably tailored suit spoke of a man who took pride in his appearance. There was an air of quiet authority about him, but there was something else tonight. His guest was wound as tight as someone in a straitjacket. There was an underlying tension Xander had never before witnessed in the man.

Most intriguing!

'We need to talk.' The gentleman's tone, though impeccably polite, left no room for argument.

Xander nodded. 'Of course, old chap. Let's find somewhere a bit more private.'

They retreated to a secluded corner booth, drinks in hand. Up close, Xander could see the strain etched on his companion's face.

'Good God, man,' he remarked. 'You look like you've caught your mistress in bed with the archbishop. What's got you in such a lather?'

The man's jaw worked, another outward sign of his agitation. 'For starters, you know full well that I'd never have a mistress.'

Yes, Xander reminded himself, he was a devoted family man. 'Just me talking. So what's the problem?'

''It's my car,' he ground out. 'My Aston Martin. It's been stolen.'

Xander's eyebrows shot up. It was unlike his acquaintance to be so rattled by mere property loss.

'Surely that's not enough to have you prowling Soho at this hour?'

'You don't understand,' the man hissed, his demeanour shifting, leaning in close. 'It's dear to my heart. It was a gift from my wife.'

Xander's eyes narrowed, suspicion flaring. He studied his guest, noting the tells betraying the man's unease. Sweat pearled on his forehead, unusual for someone legendary for his composure. His left hand twitched against the chair arm. Most revealing was his darting gaze, never meeting Xander's eyes for more than a heartbeat. There was more to this tale. A stolen car, no matter how precious, wouldn't shake someone of his calibre to the core.

'I see,' Xander replied carefully, his tone measured. 'And what exactly do you want me to do about it?'

The man inhaled deeply, squaring his shoulders in an attempt to reclaim his usual authority. 'I know you have… connections. Especially in the East End. Your family are somehow involved there… The Docks…'

'Err, yes indeed.' Xander paled slightly. He never discussed those connections. Even his wife remained ignorant of the full extent of his connections there.

'You know people who might have heard something about my car. I need you to reach out.'

'But surely, in your job, you have colleagues,' Xander said delicately, 'with resources to track it down.'

The man's commanding presence crept back. 'You leave my colleagues to me.' He paused. 'Between us, trusted people are working on it. But I need to maintain… distance from any unsavoury elements. My position demands I remain above reproach.'

Xander's mind raced, scenting an opportunity. He affected casual indifference. 'Consider it done, old boy. I know just the man. Bit rough around the edges, but his nose is well and truly to the ground.'

Relief softened his companion's face. 'Thank you, Xander. I knew I could count on you.'

As the man rose, Xander called after him, 'I'll be in touch. Try not to lose sleep over it.'

His guest's handshake tightened to near pain. 'I trust you can handle this, keeping my name clear of questionable dealings.'

'That goes without saying.'

With a curt nod, the man strode away, once again projecting absolute control.

Xander watched him go, a wolfish grin spreading beneath cold eyes. Whoever was stupid enough to nick that car was in deep shit. They clearly didn't know it belonged to one of London's top cops.

His departed guest.

Commander Reginald Hawthorne.

Chapter Twenty-Four

The crowd's roar shook Walthamstow Dogs while six greyhounds thundered towards the finish line. The iconic racing venue was alive with the electric atmosphere of a Friday night. The Art Deco façade glowed under the floodlights, its famous neon sign a beacon in the East London night.

Inside, up to five thousand punters from all walks of life packed the terraces and grandstand. Bookies bellowed odds while anxious gamblers clutched their betting slips, eyes fixed on the track where sleek greyhounds chased the mechanical hare.

Among the bustling crowd, two figures moved with purpose.

Jimmy Steele and Brother Bertie.

They scanned the faces around them, searching for one in particular.

'There!' Brother Bertie nudged Jimmy, pointing towards a small, portly figure near the fish and chip stand.

Dabs.

The garage owner was in his element, deep in conversation with a couple of locals, like he didn't have a care in the world. He better have an accounting about what had happened to the car they had left in his safe keeping. It had taken them more than a day to hunt him down.

Dabs didn't notice them approaching until it was too late. In one fluid motion, Jimmy and Brother Bertie grabbed one arm each, lifting the diminutive man clean off his feet.

''Ere,' Dabs yelped in protest, his legs kicking uselessly in the air. 'What's the big idea?'

Ignoring his carrying on, they carried him swiftly away from the main crowd, towards the shadows behind the stadium. Once out of sight, they slammed him against the wall, Jimmy's forearm pressed against Dabs' chest.

'Where's the bloody motor?' Jimmy growled, his face inches from the trembling man.

Dabs' mind raced, but he kept his expression neutral. He'd been in tighter spots than this before. 'Now, now, lads. Is this any way to treat an old friend?'

Brother Bertie reared over them both, fucked off as hell. 'Start talking. We ain't in the mood for games.'

Dabs tried to wriggle free, but Jimmy pressed harder, his grip tightening. 'I'm not going to ask again.'

Dabs sighed dramatically. 'All right! All right! I can explain everything. But you might want to ease up a bit. Can't talk if I can't breathe, know what I mean, fellas?'

Reluctantly, Jimmy loosened his hold but kept Dabs pinned to the wall.

Brother Bertie suddenly noticed the bruises on the older man's face. 'What happened to you?'

'I'll tell you what bloody went on…'

***

Yesterday Dabs was on the verge of locking up the garage when the hairs on the back of his neck bristled. In his line of work, instinct was everything. And right now, it screamed that something was off.

'Who's there?' he called out, his voice echoing in the emptiness. 'Show yourself!'

The words barely left his mouth when a weight slammed into him from behind, sending him crashing to the oil-stained concrete. He hit the ground hard, the wind knocked out of him, the taste of dust and grease coating his lips. Dazed, he tried to spin around, but his attacker was too quick. Rough hands grabbed at him, flipping him onto his back, the cold concrete seeping through his thin shirt.

'What the bloody hell?' Dabs gasped, straining against their grip.

There were two of them, that much he could tell, but everything was moving in such a blur he couldn't make out their faces.

One of them barked a laugh. 'Not so cocky now, are ya?'

Dabs opened his mouth, a ripe retort on the tip of his tongue, but a fist to the gut silenced him. He wheezed, doubling over as far as their hold would allow, the pain radiating through his body.

'Get the rope,' the other one ordered, his voice harsh and grating.

Dabs' heart seized.

Within moments, they had his hands and feet bound, the coarse fibres biting into his flesh. By his ankles, they hauled him high, his world going topsy-turvy.

With him swinging gently from the garage's rafters, blood rushed to his head. The smell of rust and metal invaded his nostrils. The swaying made him want to puke up, but it was the reveal of his attackers' identities that knotted his stomach muscles with dread.

Detective Abbot and Detective Long.

Plainclothes coppers he'd had run-ins with before. Dabs inwardly groaned.

Abbot was squat and soft in the middle, with a receding hairline that left him with a large forehead. Long, on the other hand, was a beanpole, all sharp angles and sharper eyes. Eyes that were currently drilling into Dabs with undisguised malice.

'Well, well, well.' Abbot circled Dabs like a shark, his cheap cologne wafting in his wake. 'Fancy meeting you here.'

Despite the throbbing in his skull, Dabs forced a grin, tasting the coppery tang of blood in his mouth. 'Aw, if you wanted to hang out, all you had to do was ask.'

Long's fist lashed out, connecting with Dabs' jaw. Stars exploded behind his eyes. He tasted fresh blood, hot and metallic.

'We're not here to play games,' Long snarled, his breath hot on Dabs' face. 'The Aston Martin. Where is it?'

Dabs' mind whirled. Of course he'd guessed that the car Jimmy and his mate left with him was hot, but never in a million years did he think it involved the boys in blue. No way could he betray himself, so he kept his face neutral, years of practice coming in handy, despite the pain in his jaw and the ache in his limbs.

Abbot's steely gaze bored into him, searching for any flicker that might trap him in his lie. But Dabs was a past master at this game. So he met the copper's stare dead on, keeping his own eyes carefully empty, even as the sweat trickled down his brow.

'Aston Martin?' He hoped his tone was convincingly baffled. 'Mate, I deal with the Ford Cortina crowd, don't I. Wouldn't know what to do with one of them fancy—'

Abbot's hand clamped around his throat, choking off his words, the scent of cigarettes and stale coffee on his breath. 'Don't get smart. We know it came through here.'

Struggling for air, his lungs burning, spots danced in Dabs' vision. When Abbot finally released him, he coughed and spluttered, the cool air burning the back of his throat.

'Look, I don't know what you think you know, but I'm telling you, I ain't seen no Aston Martin.' His voice turned soft and coaxing. 'Don't forget who got your girl that lovely Roller for her wedding, bless her heart. I never took a penny for it, that's because we're mates. Friends. If I knew where this motor was I'd tell you in a heartbeat.'

Long and Abbot exchanged a glance. Then, with a nod, Long stalked over to Dabs' workbench. In one sweeping motion, he sent the contents flying, tools clattering to the floor, the noise deafening in the enclosed space.

'Hey!' Dabs protested, his voice hoarse. 'I just organised that!'

Abbot's smile was razor thin. 'Oh, don't worry. We'll be sure to put everything back. Just as soon as you tell us where the car is.'

Dabs watched helplessly while they trashed his garage, upending drawers and rifling through cabinets, the sound of splintering wood and scattering metal filling his ears. Inside, he was seething, his blood boiling. This was his livelihood they were messing with. But he knew better than to lose his cool with these two.

Long cracked his knuckles menacingly, the sound making Dabs flinch. He swallowed hard, his mouth dry as a bone. He was cornered, and he knew it. The smart play would be to give them what they wanted. But the code of the streets ran deep. You didn't snitch. Not ever.

He closed his eyes, steeling himself, the throbbing in his head intensifying. When he opened them again, his gaze was hard, unwavering, despite the pain that racked his body.

'Do what you want. I can't tell you what I don't know.'

Abbot and Long shared another look, something unspoken passing between them. Then, slowly, they advanced on him, their faces grim, their footsteps echoing on the concrete.

More blows fell, Dabs gritted his teeth against the pain. He'd been in tough spots before, had felt the sting of fists and the crack of bones. But, the garage lights swinging above him, casting strange shadows on the walls, he couldn't shake the feeling that this time, he might be in well over his head.

Jimmy Steele and his friend had dropped him right in it. He'd learned early in the orphanage what trouble smelled like. And this business with the car stank to high heaven.

Maybe he should tell these two crooked cops what they wanted to know.

Chapter Twenty-Five

'The coppers, that's what happened,' Dabs spat out, after relaying his tale to Brother Bertie and Jimmy.

Jimmy lowered him to the ground, stepping back. Dabs furiously straightened his clothes.

'Why would the plod come after the car? You're having a laugh,' Jimmy said, but the tensing of his body betrayed his unease.

Dabs jabbed a finger at his battered face. 'See this? Does that look like I'm having a fucking chuckle?' Moving slightly, he winced. 'Christ, my ribs are still singing from their questions. Lost a day's work cleaning up their mess.'

Brother Bertie shifted nervously. 'Why would the police be interested in the wheels?'

Dabs cupped his hand dramatically near his ear, his gaze going skywards. 'What? You want me to have a chinwag with the Man Upstairs? Maybe get the inside scoop from God Himself?' Pure venom dripped from every word.

Abruptly, his hand dropped flat along with his scathing stare, and he rounded on them both. 'The next time you want to park something hot with me, do us all a favour – give me the full story. I can handle villains, but bent coppers?' He shook his head. 'That's a different kettle altogether.'

Jimmy's features turned to granite. 'Did you tell them anything?'

Dabs stared at him like he'd grown two heads. 'What kind of question is that? 'Course I didn't grass. Whatcha take me for? But I'll tell you something for free – whatever mess you two are mixed up in, it's bigger than just nicking a car. Them two coppers weren't just fishing, they were on a major league safari.'

'So where's the car now?' Jimmy demanded.

'You both want to thank your lucky stars I'd already shifted it to another one of my garages. It's stashed in Hackney.'

Though Jimmy was grateful for the other man's quick thinking, he was still narked about anything happening with the car without his or Brother Bertie's say-so. 'Why didn't you send word to us?'

'Send word?' He seemed on the verge of doing serious damage to Jimmy. 'First off, you two berks do a job without your old man, Danny Steele's, permission. I should've listened to the alarm bells that set off.' His finger tapped the side of his head. 'That's why I used my nut and shifted the motor somewhere else.'

He hissed, 'And now the Old Bill's sniffing up my rear end. I want those luxury wheels gone tonight—'

'Tonight?' Jimmy barked in stunned disbelief. 'That's bare bollocks, because the day's almost bloody over. We're going to need more time than that to find somewhere else to store it.'

'That isn't really my problem, now is it?' But he added, his voice softening, 'But I've never forgotten what you did for my boy, Jimmy, when you were at school with him.'

Jimmy remembered that day crystal clear. Walking across the primary school playground, he'd heard the commotion behind the outdoor toilet block. Three big lads from the top year laying into little Abe. The poor kid's thick glasses crushed under someone's shoe, his nose bleeding, school jumper ripped half off. Something in Jimmy had snapped. Before he knew what was happening, his left hand shot out like it had a mind of its own. One, two, three solid connects. Each bully dropped like a sack of spuds. That was the moment he knew. Knew he had something special in that left hand. The seed of his boxing dream planted right there in that grimy school yard.

'No one dared try it on with my boy after that,' Dab said quietly. 'So I'll give you one more day. You've got till tomorrow night. If you don't put in an appearance, I'll dump it right outside Scotland Yard. Let's see how long it takes our two detective friends to notice an Aston Martin gift-wrapped on their doorstep.'

Brother Bertie and Jimmy exchanged worried glances. What had they got themselves tangled up in?

'Here's a word to the wise, fellas,' Dabs offered before he left. 'The next time you decide to half-inch a car worth more than most people make in a year, find out who it belongs to first. Because, believe you me, if Detective Dickhead and Detective Numbnuts are on the case, someone much bigger than them is at the top of the food chain.'

***

'He's right,' Jimmy told Brother Bertie when they were back inside his car, staring sightlessly through the windscreen. 'What have we got ourselves into?'

'Something's not right about any of this,' Brother Bertie said. 'The way the Old Bill's throwing their weight around, it doesn't add up.'

Jimmy turned to him, the strain of everything written across his face. 'Since when do detectives go around cracking heads over a stolen car?'

'Dear God.' Brother Bertie's skin went a sicky grey-brown. 'Dabs is right. These wheels belong to someone with serious power.'

Jimmy could've given himself a swift kick to the goolies. Hadn't his dad taught him that before you do a job, you put your snout to the ground and find out all the particulars and specifics first?

He felt ice in his gut. 'We've stepped into something deadly this time.'

'Maybe…' Brother Bertie hesitated, choosing his words carefully. 'Maybe you should tell your old man, Jimmy. He might know how to handle this.'

The suggestion hit Jimmy like a physical blow. The image of Stevie's broken body on the dock flooded his mind – Danny's brutal lesson about loyalty and betrayal. If his father could do that to one of his men, what would he do to his own son who'd gone behind his back?

'I can't,' he said, his voice thick. His hands curled tight around the steering wheel, although they were stationary, going nowhere. 'You know how my dad runs things.'

Brother Bertie nodded solemnly. In Danny Steele's world, loyalty was sacred. Breaking it wasn't just betrayal – it was unforgivable. And Danny made sure everyone remembered what happened to traitors.

'And what about your Precious?' Jimmy reminded his friend, meeting his eyes. 'You still need that lawyer, don't you?'

At the mention of his daughter, Brother Bertie's face softened. His mind drifted to a few weeks back when he'd taken her to a family get-together. She'd loved every moment, sparkling and dazzling everyone with her cheeky manners and intelligence.

'She and Gertie are all I've got. The day she was born, I promised her I'd always be there, always take care of her. I can't fail her now.'

Being a father, a family man, wasn't so easy. So many people depended on you.

They sat in suffocating silence, each lost in dark thoughts.

Jimmy finally broke the silence. 'What's our next move?'

His friend's face was grave. 'You're not going to like what I have to say.'

'Tell me.'

'We have to take the car back.'

'What?'

'Something's wrong here.' Brother Bertie pressed his hand over his heart. 'Now we know the filth are involved, my instincts are screaming danger.'

Jimmy was deflated. 'But what about buying the house for Mini? You and Precious?'

'We'll find another way.'

Jimmy thought about telling Mini the news, especially after she'd made the connections for the car. But that meant shattering her dreams of owning her own home? Could he really do that to the woman he loved with all his heart?

Nevertheless, deep down, he knew his friend was right. 'We'll collect the car in the morning—'

Brother Bertie cut him off. 'Can't do morning. I've already arranged to meet Ruddy.' He continued, his voice turning to steel. 'Night will be better. Tomorrow night we get the car and return it exactly where we found it. Then we walk away and never look back.'

Chapter Twenty-Six

Bright and early the following morning, Diego sauntered towards the mansion in Grosvenor Square, his camera equipment bag slung over his shoulder. His heart raced with excitement; he was convinced he'd finally hit the jackpot. This assignment could catapult his career to dizzying heights, erasing the stain of that disastrous incident with Sin Steele.

For a moment his mood turned sour recalling how that East End tart had clobbered one of the fashion industry's biggest names and nearly derailed Diego's career. Didn't she understand the unspoken rules? A quick fumble was often the price of admission in this cutthroat world. Still, her loss was his gain. With Sin out of the picture, if he played his cards right today, Diego was poised to become one of London's most sought-after fashion photographer.

Pausing before the gleaming black door, he smoothed back his goatee and adjusted his crushed velvet jacket. He'd cultivated this continental persona meticulously, burying all traces of Bill from Bethnal Green beneath a veneer of sophistication.

An impeccably dressed butler, who was also a black man, answered his knock. 'Mr Diego, I presume? Her Ladyship is expecting you. This way, please.'

Diego's pulse quickened as he followed him through opulent room after room. A fizz of delight ran through him. This was it! His ticket to the big time!

The butler ushered him into a lavishly appointed drawing room. A woman rose to greet him, resplendent in a Balenciaga gown. Frowning he stared at her ladyship's hair. He never took her as someone who would sport a beehive.

'Mr Diego, how delightful to meet you at last.' She extended a gloved hand. 'I've heard such wonderful things about your work.'

Bowing, he kissed her hand. 'The pleasure is all mine, Your Ladyship. I'm honoured you've considered me for this project.'

'Yes, well, your name came highly recommended. My new husband is quite keen to raise our profile, you see. A feature on the house seemed just the ticket.'

Diego's mind raced with possibilities. 'I have some marvellous suggestions. We could do a series showcasing each room, perhaps with you as a glamorous hostess. And of course, we mustn't neglect the gardens. I'm thinking an al fresco tea party scene.'

Her Ladyship smiled indulgently. 'Why don't we take a tour? You can tell me more about your vision as we go.'

They strolled through sumptuous reception rooms and airy conservatories, Diego's elation growing with each step. This was it, his gateway to the upper echelons of society. No more grubby Soho studios or vacant wannabe models. From now on, it would be only the cream of British society.

'And now,' Her Ladyship's voice brought him back to the present. 'Let me show you something truly special. The pride of the house, really.'

She led him down a narrow staircase. The temperature dropped noticeably the further they descended.

'Our wine cellar,' she announced proudly, pushing open a heavy wooden door. 'Some of these vintages are older than the house itself.'

Diego stepped inside, his eyes adjusting to the dim light. Racks of dusty bottles stretched into the shadows. He turned, a question on his lips... and froze.

The expression on Her Ladyship's face was no longer friendly, in fact it was menacing and cold and behind her loomed the black butler.

Ruddy and Brother Bertie.

Being Lady Pru's housekeeper had its advantages, like knowing exactly when her boss would be away at the country estate, leaving the house perfectly empty for settling old scores.

'What's going on?' Diego stammered, backing away. 'You're not Lady Prudence, are you?'

Ruddy laughed harshly. 'Do you really think a fine person like Lady Blacklock would deal with pond life like you?'

Diego's blood ran cold, becoming suddenly very conscious of his position isolated in the bottom of this house. All alone. 'Who the fuck are you?'

It was Brother Bertie who growled back, 'Who we are doesn't matter.'

'There's been some mistake,' he said, forcing a nervous smile. 'I'm just here to take some photographs...'

'Oh, we know exactly why you're here,' Ruddy spat. 'And we know what you did to Sin Steele.'

Diego's stomach plummeted. 'I don't know what you're talking about. Sin who?'

Brother Bertie advanced on him. 'Don't play the wanker with me, you poxy piece of shit. We know you set her up at that party. Drugged her, trapped her with some fat fuck who tried to rape her.'

'No, no, you've got it all wrong!' Diego protested, his carefully constructed accent slipping into pure Cockney. 'I didn't do nuthin'!'

Ruddy's eyes glittered dangerously. 'See, that's where you're mistaken. Sin didn't put those bruises on herself. You're going to pay.'

Before Diego could react, Brother Bertie seized him, locking his arms in front of him. Ruddy approached, face filled with contempt, holding a bottle of clear liquid in her gloved hand. The perfect weapon, nicked from Diego's own studio.

'Recognise this?' she asked. 'It's the stuff you use to develop your pictures.'

Diego thrashed wildly, but Brother Bertie's grip was like iron. The image of Sin, curled in on herself, lying defeated in his bed, fuelled his strength. Ruddy uncorked the bottle, the acrid chemical smell filling the air.

'No, please!' Diego begged. 'I'll do anything!'

Ruddy's smile widened. 'Too late for that.'

She upended the bottle over Diego's hands. The developer fluid hit his skin like liquid fire. His pristine photographer's hands – his livelihood, his future – bubbled and whitened, the chemical eating into his flesh. The pain was immediate and excruciating. His screams bounced off the cellar walls, his skin blistering and peeling, while the caustic liquid penetrated deeper with each passing second.

'You won't be holding a camera again anytime soon,' Ruddy said coldly. 'Consider this a warning. Try anything like that again, and next time we won't be so gentle.'

Brother Bertie released him, and Diego crumpled to the floor, cradling his ruined hands. The proud fashion photographer was gone, leaving only terrified Bill from Bethnal Green.

'If I ever hear you're doping and setting up women again,' Brother Bertie growled, 'I'm coming after you. And trust me, mate, you don't want that.'

Ruddy knelt beside Diego, her voice low and menacing. 'Now, here's what's going to happen. You're going to walk out of here and never breathe a word of this to anyone. If you do, we'll make sure everyone knows what a sicko, twisted little perv you really are.'

***

'What's really going on with you and Sin?' Ruddy launched straight into, filling two crystal glasses with fancy plonk they'd taken from the cellar.

They were in the large kitchen, sunlight streaming through the high windows, catching the polished surfaces of expensive cooking implements dangling from overhead racks and the gleaming copper pots and white tiles.

Brother Bertie's shoulders stiffened. 'Nothing to tell. Just helping a friend out of a spot of bovver.' He accepted the glass, avoiding her shrewd gaze.

Like hell you were, Ruddy thought, noting how his fingers tightened around the expensive glass.

'Come off it,' she challenged, leaning against the massive cast-iron range. 'All that scrapping between you two, going at each other like cats and dogs. But I ain't blind. I see what's really going on beneath all that fighting.'

'Don't know what you're chatting on about.' Brother Bertie's Jamaican accent thickened, a sure tell he was rattled.

Ruddy pressed on, her voice hardening. 'She's Jimmy's sister. Your best mate's sister. How's he going to feel when he finds out—'

He slammed his wine glass down on the marble countertop with enough force to make Ruddy jump. 'There's nothing to find out,' Brother Bertie bit out, but he wouldn't meet her eyes. 'Leave it, Ruddy.'

Brother Bertie stormed out, his footsteps echoing through the grand house. Ruddy sipped her wine, troubled. Very troubled indeed.

Chapter Twenty-Seven

Sin approached the trendy Soho hairdresser's feeling deflated and down. Up until a few days ago, life had been sweet as sugar. Now? Pure poison. Otis Redding's 'The Dock of the Bay' floated through the salon as she entered, its melancholic tune matching her despairing mood.

The place buzzed with the usual activity, scissors snipping, hairdryers whirring, posh birds getting primped and preened. Some perched at the half-moon-shaped bar, sipping fancy drinks and happily chattering away. Being a hairdresser paid the bills, sure. She loved making women feel like queens, loved the gossip and belly laughs, how clients strutted out feeling like they owned the world.

But was this it for Cynthia Steele? Standing behind a chair listening to pampered dolly birds bang on about their latest shopping sprees while she dreamed of being the cover model on glossy magazines? She was meant for more than following the tired old path of every East End girl, settling for a life mapped out since birth.

And then there was him.

Bertie Watson.

His face materialised in her mind uninvited, sending a hot rush through her veins. Her fingers ghosted over where he'd touched her arm, so gentle it still made goosebumps prickle along her arms. After she'd escaped that nightmare, what in God's name possessed her to run to him of all people?

Brother bloody Bertie.

The cocky git who swaggered about in that daft hat, leading her brother into whatever dodgy business was going. Always running that mouth of his, that cheeky grin stuck to his face like life was one big joke.

But that night…

Sin's breath caught remembering how different he'd been. No swagger, no smart remarks. Just those dark eyes burning with a concern that cut straight through her defences. His touch whisper-soft on her bruised skin.

'You all right, doll?' Kath's concerned voice interrupted her disjointed thoughts. Her friend stood behind the reception desk, worry etched on her face.

Nearby, Dilly slowly swept the floor.

Sin plastered on her brightest camera-ready smile. ''Course I am. Why wouldn't I be?'

Kath hesitated, her gaze darting fretfully away like she was on the verge of announcing someone's death.

Some of Sin's fake cheer faded. 'What is it?'

Kath worriedly glanced at her again and carefully asked, 'Have you heard about Diego?'

Sin instantly stiffened. Fragmented, horrible memories came flooding back. The room spinning, her limbs heavy and unresponsive. The sickening weight of a man's body crushing her, his hot breath on her neck. Bile rose in her throat, panic ripping at her chest. She gasped, struggling to breathe as she snapped back to the present.

Sin had assumed that she'd bounce back from this, brush it off like she did everything else life threw at her. Put it down to one of life's experiences. What a joke that turned out to be. The attack played out live in her head without warning, ambushing her any time of the day or night, leaving her shaken and wanting to curl into a tight ball.

'Forget it.' Kath uttered, seeing her friend's agonising distress. She smoothed her palm nervously down her uniform. 'I shouldn't have… I mean… oh, bloody hell.'

'Tell me.' Sin stepped closer, scowling hard.

Kath sighed, not noticing that her sister had stopped sweeping and was listening, too. 'He's in hospital. Burns all over his hands. Claims it was an accident while he was developing some photos.' She bitterly added, 'Shame it wasn't his face.' One of her brows lifted knowingly. 'If you ask me, it sounds like someone give him his comeuppance.'

The pieces clicked into place in Sin's mind. She knew full well who had doled out the 'comeuppance.' He'd flippin' well promised. That interfering…

Without a word, Sin spun on her heels and stormed out of the salon.

'Where are you going?' Kath's cried out and followed her into the street, but Sin was already gone, a whirlwind of upset and confusion.

***

'I'll get it!' Brother Bertie hollered towards the kitchen where Gertie was cooking, responding to the urgent banging on the front door of the boarding house.

He yanked it open, and a whirlwind of pure fury nearly knocked him backwards.

Sin.

'I know it was you, you interfering so-and-so!' She jabbed an accusing finger into his chest.

Bertie's brow furrowed, though his heart hammered against his ribs. 'What in the heck are you on about?'

His eyes devoured her, raw hunger burning in his gut. Lord above, she was magnificent when she was riled up. Cheeks steamed up with aggro, eyes flashing righteous indignation.

Slipping on his trademark easy-going grin, he drawled, 'Careful, sweetness. Your face might stick that way if you keep scowling like that.'

'Who's that at the door?' Gertie's voice drifted down from the kitchen.

'Just a mate,' Bertie called back.

He grabbed Sin's hand, and the heat of her skin scorched through him. Her delicate fingers seemed to melt into his rougher palm, fitting there like they belonged. He pulled her up the stairs and towards his room.

'Are you all right?' His concern replaced his casualness once they were inside.

Sin could barely contain her anger. 'Did you burn Diego's hands?'

Brother Bertie's jaw worked back and forth, his silence speaking volumes.

'I told you not to do anything!' She exploded. 'Don't you get it? I'm sick to death of all this violence. I grew up in it!'

Her eyes glazed over, lost in a painful memory.

Seven-year-old Sin skipped alongside her dad, Danny, chattering about her day at Kathleen's. The sun was setting, casting long shadows across the East End streets. Suddenly, Danny's eyes locked on to a man across the road. Without a word, he strode over, leaving Sin rooted to the spot.

'Where's my fucking money?' Danny growled, grabbing the man by his collar.

The man stammered, 'I...I'll have it next week, I swear!'

Danny's fist connected with a sickening crunch. Again and again, he pummelled the man, blind to Sin's horrified gaze. Blood sprayed, staining the pavement crimson. The man's pleas turned to gurgles under the domination of Danny's relentless assault.

Sin wanted to run, to scream, but her legs wouldn't move. She watched, paralysed, as her father transformed into a monster before her eyes. The sound of breaking bones echoed in her ears.

When it was finally over, the man lay a motionless mess on the ground. Danny calmly wiped his bloodied knuckles on his handkerchief, then returned to his daughter as if nothing had happened. He took her trembling hand in his. 'Come on, love. Let's get you home for tea.'

Walking away, Sin couldn't help but look back. The man's battered face, barely recognisable, would haunt her dreams for years to come.

Coming back to the present, Sin's voice cracked. 'I'm tired of it all. I want a life free from this shit.'

Although his heart ached for her, nevertheless, he lived by a code. 'I couldn't just stand by after some bastard hurt you,' he said softly. 'You're my spar, Jimmy's sister.'

'That's not your job!' Sin fired back, throwing her head back as if she wanted to scream.

They were toe to toe now, chests heaving, faces inches apart. That old heat, dangerous and familiar flared untamed between them. His pulse roared in his ears, every nerve ending alive to her proximity.

Their lips crashed together. Pure explosion. Everything they'd been fighting – the attraction, the forbidden nature of it all – erupted at once. Bertie's hands tangled in Sin's silken hair, drawing her closer. She matched his passion with her own fierce need, her nails raking fire down his back.

They tumbled onto the bed, a tangle of limbs and unlocked, pent-up desire. His hat tumbled off. Bertie's lips trailed down Sin's neck, eliciting a soft moan that sent shivers down his spine. Her hands roamed under his shirt, exploring the taut muscles of his back. Through the midnight-coloured curls of his hair.

The world outside ceased to exist. All that mattered was the taste of her lips, the feel of her skin against his. Bertie's head swam with the intoxicating scent of her natural perfume. He couldn't get enough of her, every touch, every kiss only feeding his hunger for more.

Sin arched into him, her body responding to his every caress. She'd never felt desire like this before, raw and all-consuming. Her fingers traced the sharp lines of his jaw, memorising every contour of his face.

Their kisses grew more urgent. Feverish. Clothes were hastily pushed aside as they sought to be closer. The heat between them was electric, threatening to consume them both

Suddenly, Brother Bertie jerked back. 'Blood fire! You're Jimmy's sister.'

The words came out strangled. His loyalty to his best friend warred violently with the desperate need to haul Sin back into his arms. Jimmy's face flashed in his mind – his brother in all but blood.

Reality crashed back over Sin, too. She scrambled off the bed like it was burning her, horror at what they'd done written across her face.

Heart still thundering, he pleaded, 'Meet me tomorrow, yeah? The record shop round the corner from where you work.' Even as he said it, he knew he was playing with dynamite.

Sin shook her head violently, her eyes wide with panic, and bolted from the room.

On the stairs, she nearly collided with Gertie, whose knowing gaze flicked between Sin's dishevelled state and her brother standing helplessly in his doorway. Once Sin was outside, he rushed back to his window, watching her disappear down the street, his mind a war zone of desire and guilt.

He pressed his forehead against the cool glass, closing his eyes. What the fuckery had he got himself into? More importantly, what had he done to Jimmy's trust?

Chapter Twenty-Eight

Someone was getting a proper kicking in the bogs inside Holloway Prison. Thirty-eight-year-old Chrissie could hear the brutal grunts and moans the closer she got to the communal bathroom on B Wing. Bathroom? More like a skanky shithole, and she meant that literarily because the stink of crap from them was making her want to puke in the corridor.

You'd think she'd be used to it by now, having been banged up in what she scathingly termed HMP Doss House for the last seven months. The bathroom was just like the rest of the prison – grotty and nasty. Or 'substandard' was how the last official inspection report had more delicately put it when talking about the state of things inside Britain's most infamous women's prison.

HMP Holloway was a right dump, no two ways about it. Located in North London, it was just a stone's throw from Holloway and the Cally Roads. It had a rep for being filthy, strict and violent, including the harsh punishments the screws doled out on a daily basis. Its prime spot in London seemed like it was done on purpose, a warning to women about where they'd end up if they strayed off the straight and narrow. Many a woman buckled under the pressure while banged up here.

Not Chrissie. This place and its ill-fitting bras weren't going to get the better of her.

Not my business! Chrissie determinedly thought. Whoever was getting the bollocks bashed out of them was on their own. Today of all days she couldn't afford to stick her beak in any aggro. She was getting out today. Giving the finger to the prison for good. No way was she messing up her release after putting on the performance of a lifetime for the parole board to get her early release. She'd practically been on her knees in front of that bunch of do-gooders. Bowing and scraping, going on about how she'd learnt her lesson, turned over a new leaf, how she was already on the way to becoming a model citizen who would live happily ever after.

What a pile of horseshite. As if!

Chrissie had written the rule book on living life to the max as a Bad Girl. And one of those rules was when you're backed into a corner, you do what you gotta do to get out of it. This time, it had paid off, very nicely indeed, with her getting her jam roll.

Stepping into the communal bathroom, Chrissie instinctively flinched from the gut-wrenching stench that hit her. The air was thick with the reek of human waste and stale piss. The rank smell of mould and mildew invaded the back of her throat, leaving a disgusting taste in her mouth. The tiled floor had long lost its original colour, replaced by a layer of ingrained grime that had turned the floor a deathly grey. The row of sinks along the wall were chipped and stained, with rusted pipes that constantly dripped, adding to the overall sense of decay. Some of the lavs had doors while others didn't.

By far the worst, the absolute, fucking pits were the showers. It was an open shower set-up with no curtains or walls between them, meaning all the women had to wash in front of each other in their birthday suits. It left many feeling vulnerable and humiliated. No privacy. No dignity.

She and some of the other girls had had a good ole giggle when they heard there were plans to tart up the prison. Grand plans for a swimming pool, education block and gym. It was gonna become a 'place of healing'. They'd pissed themselves silly at that one. The only thing HMP Holloway was good for was being bulldozed to the ground.

The two hatchet-faced cons who had a much smaller prisoner slammed up against the dingy walls had a rep on B Wing. Nan Carter and Jill Ford. Nan was the brains of the outfit while Jill was her gormless gorilla providing the necessary backup. Nan fancied herself as the Queen Bitch of the wing, slinging her bulky weight around like she'd built the fucking place with her own bare hands. She was stocky with broad shoulders and a marked face that had been around the block way too many times. An air of brutal menace hung over her. Jill was tall and lanky with a face full of dead eyes.

Not my business! Chrissie stridently reminded herself.

She was on the verge of walking the other way when she clocked who the two women were fucking over. Bloody hell! Now this became very much her business. It was Maura Reilly, her cellmate. The girl was young with a shy nature that made her easy prey for bullies like Nan.

Maura's features were contorted in pain. The two bruisers pounded and kicked her defenceless body. Nan's fists pummelled Maura's face, leaving angry red bruises in their wake. Jill's heavy prison-issue boots slammed into her ribs, eliciting sharp cries of agony. They showed no mercy, their eyes alight with a sadistic gleam, relishing every second of the young girl's suffering.

Maura's battered face conjured up the memory of another defenceless girl trying desperately to protect herself. A surge of rage coursed through Chrissie's veins.

'Oi! Knock it on the head.' Her demand echoed off the tiled walls. 'Or else I'm going to have to knock both your dumb nuts together.'

The thugs whirled around.

Nan's deadly gaze narrowed giving Chrissie the evil eye. 'Shut your fucking cakehole, dollybird,' she sneered, her Yorkshire accent thick with disdain.

'Yeah,' her muscle backed her up. 'Why don't you cunt off and find your high heels.' Her words ended on a nasty snigger.

Chrissie wasn't surprised at the reception she received. Her striking looks often meant many mistook her for an airhead. Little did they know she'd learnt all the dirty tricks, including kill or be killed growing up in Sugar Cane Wharf.

Chrissie walked over, her fists clenched by her sides. 'Leave her alone, or I'll make your arse and face swap places.'

Eyes glinting with malice, Nan threw her head back with a harsh crack of laughter. 'Think you can take us on, do ya? You're just a pretty face, darlin'. You ain't got the guts.'

Chrissie's lips curled into a smirk. 'You'd be surprised what this pretty face can do.'

Lightning fast, she lunged forward and drove her fist into Nan's jaw. The ferocious blow sent the other woman stumbling back, eyes wide in shock. Jill let out a howl and charged at Chrissie, her talon-like fingers raking for her face. Chrissie seized a fistful of the other woman's hair and yanked back hard. Jill screeched, her nails tearing down Chrissie's arms, leaving angry red welts. Through gritted teeth, Chrissie fought the sting and rammed her knee into Jill's gut. Her opponent crumpled to the floor.

Nan recovered quickly. Fury twisted her face and she launched herself at Chrissie. The two women grappled, trading savage blows. Chrissie grabbed Nan by the back of the neck and hauled her toward the row of toilets. She shoved Nan's protesting face into the bowl, pinned her down one-handed, then reached for the chain. Nan thrashed and sputtered, her screams lost in the water. Chrissie pulled the chain, sending a rush of water cascading over Nan's head.

Finally, she released her grip. Nan slumped to the floor, gasping and choking.

Chrissie hissed, 'You want to thank your lucky stars I wasn't in my heels, because let me tell you for free, I'd have stamped my stiletto straight through that rotten heart of yours.'

She hurried to Maura's side, helping the younger girl to her feet. 'You all right, babes?'

Her cellie had taken a proper battering, no doubt about it. Maura nodded, her eyes brimming with tears of gratitude. 'Thanks, Chrissie. I don't know what I would've done if you hadn't come along.' Her Irish accent softened. 'I'm going to miss you.'

'Any more trouble with those two, you get on the blower to me.'

***

Three hours later, the PO at the exit reception couldn't hide her catty gleam of envy as she handed over the coat Chrissie had been arrested in. A gorgeous Persian lamb fur jacket with tight grey curls and a silky-smooth mauve lining. The scent of another woman was on it. Miss Richards, the screw who ran B Wing. They had reached an arrangement where Miss

Richards had 'looked after' the coat in exchange for ensuring no one took the piss out of Chrissie while she completed her bird at Her Majesty's pleasure. Including the screws.

Chrissie settled the coat around her shoulders with all the swagger of a Hollywood starlet instead of an inmate being released from prison.

'Make sure you keep your fingernails clean, Chrissie.'

With saccharine sweetness, accompanied by a saucy wink, Chrissie answered back, 'Oh, I will, Miss.'

The gate opened and Chrissie waltzed outside. And whispered, 'Oh, I'll keep out of trouble, all right. As surely as my name is Chrissie Steele.'

Chapter Twenty-Nine

'Oi, Danny!' a friendly voice called from Voodoo Lounge's upstairs bar. 'Fancy a bevvy?'

Danny's retort was smart-mouthed and good-natured. 'Still stuffing your face between another man's wife's legs?'

The regulars roared. Everyone knew the guy had recently been caught bang to rights with his pants down with his neighbour's missus.

Pausing inside the main room, Danny soaked up his fill. A sly grin spread across his smug features. This was all his, every last brick. Danny had owned the club for the last five years, a fact not many knew. He preferred to keep his ownership below the radar, along with his other investments. He had his fingers in more pies than a baker's dozen.

But this place? This was different. This was special.

The Voodoo Lounge traded in more than just booze and birds. Secrets were the real currency here, and they flowed as freely as the sex and vice.

Taking the stairs to the basement, Danny felt the familiar shift in atmosphere. Down here was strictly members only, where the high rollers and big shots conducted their dodgy dealings away from prying eyes. Approaching the private casino room, his chest tightened. The person waiting for him always filled him with a weird edge of excitement and dread.

Lord Xander sat in his usual corner, looking for all the world like he owned the place. Danny's gut clenched at the sight of him, a response he'd never quite managed to shake. The older man exuded an aura of effortless superiority that both awed and infuriated Danny.

'Xander,' Danny murmured, lowering his eyes respectfully, hating himself for the automatic deference, but he couldn't seem to help it. 'You wanted to see me?'

The other man's piercing gaze raked over Danny, making him feel like a schoolboy called before the headmaster. 'Ah, Daniel. So good of you to join me. Drink?'

Daniel. No one called him that, not even his old mum had. It was always Danny, or Dan to his mates. But from Lord Xander's lips, it sounded different. Important, somehow. Like he was someone worthy of a proper name.

Danny nodded, accepting the proffered glass of hard liquor. He perched on the edge of his seat, back ramrod straight. Gone was the swagger of the King of the Docks and in its place sat a man desperate for the approval of the other man.

Xander reclined in his seat, radiating aristocratic ease. 'Tell me, Daniel, have you heard whispers about a stolen Aston Martin?'

Danny's brow furrowed because he was genuinely surprised he wanted to meet about some stolen car. 'Can't say I have. Something special about it?'

Xander carefully considered him. 'What I'm about to tell you stays between us.'

'You know better than to say that to me.'

The other man crossed his leg. 'Let's just say that one of our friends in blue has found himself in a bit of a sticky wicket.'

Scowling, Danny threw back, 'Friends in blue? What have the coppers got to do with a stolen motor?'

'This luxury car is his personal vehicle. And he wants it back.'

Danny took a deep swig of his drink. Ran his tongue over the sweet residue left on his lips before asking, 'Which copper are we talking about?'

'Commander Hawthorne?'

That drew a punch of disbelief from Danny. 'Hawthorne? The way I hear it, the man's a straight shooter in a very crooked club.'

Certain members of the Majesty's finest, from high to low, were known for corruption and taking backhanders. Commander Hawthorne wasn't one of them.

Danny's confusion remained. 'Why doesn't he just buy himself a new one?'

Xander's lips curled into a predatory smile that sent a shiver down Danny's spine. 'A gift from his wife apparently. So he needs it back, post-haste. I trust you can handle this little inconvenience?'

Danny felt his chest tighten. Any other geezer asking for a favour like this, he'd be weighing up the profit margin before he even opened his gob. What's in it for me? That was always the first question on his mind. He wasn't in the habit of doing something for nothing. It was bad for business and worse for his reputation.

But this wasn't just any geezer, was it? When it came to His Lordship, all of Danny's usual rules went sailing out the window.

However, this time he hesitated, not happy about doing his usual rollover routine for this man. 'Might be a bit tricky, that,' he heard himself saying, despite his gut screaming at him to shut it and nod. 'Gonna need some resources, like. To pay my boys a bit more…'

Xander's eyebrow arched, a flicker of annoyance behind his eyes. 'Come now, Daniel. Surely the King of the Docks isn't balking at a simple retrieval job?'

''Course not. Just thinking it through, is all. Want to make sure we do this right.'

'Excellent,' Xander purred. 'I knew I could count on you. You've always been resourceful.'

The praise washed over Danny like a warm bath, soothing the edges of his earlier discomfort. He straightened his shoulders, puffing up with pride. 'That's why I'm where I am, isn't it? Know how to get things done, me.'

Suddenly his mind turned to Rita and the house.

'When were you planning to tell me about selling the house on Molasses Quay? Didn't you think I'd find out?' His words were haunted. 'It's on my bloody doorstep. Did you really think I wouldn't find out it was up for sale?'

Lord Xander remained impassive. He took a long drag from his glass, deliberately making Danny wait. 'The insurance company handles all that tedious business,' he drawled, waving his hand dismissively. 'Nothing for you to concern yourself with.'

A muscle in Danny's jaw ticked. 'Funny that. Word on the street says you're particular about who buys it. No criminals need apply.' His voice dropped lower. 'Which leaves me out in the cold, don't it?'

A flash of irritation crossed Xander's face. 'The property needs to transfer to legitimate hands. The right sort of people, you understand.'

'The right sort?' Danny tasted bile. 'And what sort would that be?'

'Oh, come now.' Xander's tone dripped honey-coated poison. 'Let's not pretend we don't both know exactly what I mean.'

He shifted forward, resting his glass on his thigh, studying Danny like a mildly interesting specimen, tone turning hard and unforgiving. 'If I hear you've been near that house and have done something stupid—'

'Like what?' Danny's bottled contempt leaked out. 'Burnt it down? Blown the fucker to kingdom come?'

Xander's expression softened, transformed into a look of practiced sympathy that Danny ached to believe was genuine. 'Still dwelling on the past? Still upset?' Xander clicked his tongue, shaking his head like Danny was some dim-witted child. 'My dear boy, you really must learn to let these things go. It's frightfully common to hold grudges.'

Danny's heart twisted. Even knowing it was all an act, some desperate part of him still craved this man's approval. Always had done, always would. Danny's carefully cultivated mask almost crumbled. He wanted to slam his fist into the brick wall, relishing the sharp sting of pain. Fuck. Why did this poncy git still have such a hold on him? He was Danny Steele, for Christ's sake. The King of the bloody Docks. He didn't bend the knee to any living soul.

Except, apparently, he did.

The silence stretched between them, heavy with history only a few people knew about.

'About that car, get the job done.' Xander brought them back to the point of their meeting. 'Oh, and Daniel? Ensure whoever's responsible is… suitably dealt with.'

Danny didn't need telling twice what that meant.

Whoever had taken Commander Hawthorne's car had to end up dead.

Chapter Thirty

Danny opened his front door, his mind still reeling from the meeting with Lord Xander. Despite the warmth of his home enveloping him, something felt off. Something wasn't right. He froze in his tracks.

Iris appeared in the hallway, her face greyer than a corpse that had washed up on the river's shore, her features stark with worry. She grabbed his arm, pulling him close. The stink of gin on her was stronger than usual. Something had set her off.

Iris whispered urgently, 'She's back.'

His wife didn't need to elaborate. There was only one 'she' that could make Iris look like she'd seen the Devil himself. Danny's heart sank.

'Chrissie's here?' he asked, his voice low and rough.

Iris nodded, her grip on him tightening. 'You know she brings nothing but trouble,' she hissed, her eyes darting towards the living room. 'We should tell her to leave. Sling her hook.'

Danny sighed, running a hand through his hair. Deep down he agreed with Iris. His baby sister was a whirlwind of chaos, leaving destruction in her wake wherever she went. But something inside him, that gnawing guilt that still saw her as the little girl he'd failed to protect all those years ago, couldn't bring himself to turn her away

'Let me talk to her,' he reassured, gently disentangling himself from his wife's grasp. 'I'll sort it out.'

Squaring his shoulders, Danny strode into the living room, prepared for the worst. But nothing could have prepared him for the sight that greeted him.

Chrissie was sprawled across his sofa, one leg thrown over the arm, a joint dangling from her manicured fingers. A decade younger than him she was in fact his half-sister, born from the marriage of their mother to Ezra Steele. A kindly and caring docker who had rescued their unwed mother, Dora, and her two boys, Danny and George, from a desperate situation.

Chrissie was a throwback to the heyday of Diana Dors. Her buxom figure was poured into a figure-hugging wiggle dress that clung to her hourglass curves like a second skin. Platinum-blonde hair fell in soft, sultry waves around her shoulders, framing a heart-shaped face with Cupid's bow lips painted a daring shade of scarlet. She exuded an aura of old

Hollywood glamour mixed with East End brass. Yet beneath the bombshell exterior, there was a vulnerability to Chrissie, a fragility she kept well-hidden behind her scarlet smile and razor-sharp wit. Something unspeakable had happened to Chrissie when she was a girl.

The living room reeked of her wacky-baccy joint, which she leisurely pulled from her mouth when she saw her brother.

'Well, if it isn't the King of the Docks hisself,' she announced with gusto. 'Come to bestow your royal presence upon us commoners, have you?'

Danny felt his resolve wavering. Christ, she looked good. It was easy to forget sometimes that his baby sister wasn't far off knocking on forty's door. She had a way of seeming eternally youthful. Eternally troublesome.

'Christine.' With a curt nod, Danny kept his distance. 'What are you doing here?'

She sat up, taking a long drag on her joint again before stubbing it out in the ashtray on the coffee table. 'What, no "welcome home, darlin' sister, how I've missed ya"?' She ended with a dramatic batting of her false lashes at him.

Danny didn't move. 'Last time I heard, you were living the high life with that flash carpet insurance bloke. What happened to him?'

Chrissie's face darkened for a moment before her smile returned, brittle this time. 'Oh, you know how it is, Danny boy. Turns out his policy didn't cover "acts of wife". The old bat wanted him back, and who was

I to stand in the way of true love?' She paused, then added with a wink, 'Besides, I've always preferred a bit of danger to security. Speaking of which, how's business?'

Danny snorted, choosing to ignore her question. He could well imagine how things had ended with the insurance man. Chrissie had a way of wrapping men around her little finger, then crushing them when she got bored.

'That doesn't explain why you're here. In my house. Uninvited.'

Chrissie stood, smoothing down her dress. 'Can't a girl come visit her favourite brother?' She sauntered towards him. 'Besides, I hear you're still rubbing elbows with the toffs these days. Thought you'd have packed that in by now.'

Danny stiffened. She of all people knew better than to mention Lord Xander.

She carried on. 'Heard anything from George?'

George was their middle brother. He'd run off when he was sixteen, and Danny hadn't heard hide nor hair of him since. And she knew it, which was why he made no comment.

Wrapping her arms around his neck, she cooed, 'I missed you. The world out there's a right nasty place for a girl on her own.'

Danny's arms snaked around her waist, drawing her close despite his better judgment. 'Missed me so much I haven't clapped eyes on you for coming up to two years now. What kind of trouble are you in this time?'

She jerked away, her blue eyes wide and innocent. 'Trouble? Me? Danny, you're breaking my heart. Can't a girl just miss her family?'

Danny looked at her hard, searching for the tell-tale signs of deceit. But Chrissie had always been a good liar, even as a kid. It was part of what made her so dangerous.

'You can stay,' he found himself saying, even while a warning voice in the back of his head screamed at him to reconsider. 'But only for a few days, you hear? And no funny business. I've got enough on my plate without having to clean up your messes.'

Chrissie's face lit up, and for a moment, Danny saw a flash of the little girl she'd once been. 'Oh, Danny, you're a real knight in shining armour, you are!' she exclaimed, planting a kiss on his cheek. 'Don't worry, I'll be as quiet as a mouse. You won't even know I'm here.'

Fat chance of that! He restrained from rolling his eyes.

Chrissie had a way of bringing out the worst in him, of dredging up old guilt and making him do things he'd rather forget. But she was family, and in their world, family stuck together. No matter what.

'I'll take my bags up,' Chrissie chirped, practically skipping towards the door.

'Bags?' Danny called after her.

But she was already gone, leaving Danny alone in the living room with a lingering sense of growing unease.

Iris appeared in the doorway, nervous and upset. 'Tell me you didn't agree to let her stay.'

Danny couldn't meet her eyes. 'Just for a few days.'

'A few days?' Iris hissed. 'Danny, have you lost your mind? You know what she's like. She'll have the place turned upside down before the week's out.'

'She's my sister, Iris,' Danny snapped, his temper rising. 'What am I supposed to do, throw her out on the street?'

'Yes!' Iris shot back. 'That's exactly what you should do. Before she ruins everything.'

Danny opened his mouth to argue, but the sound of Chrissie's heels on the stairs silenced him.

She appeared in the doorway, beaming. 'Now, who's for a drink? A bottle of fancy whisky fell off the back of a lorry straight into my handbag.' With a wink and grin she headed off into the kitchen.

Iris shot her husband an accusatory glare. Sighing heavily, Danny made his way to the kitchen where Chrissie was already pouring generous measures of whisky into two tumblers.

'Just like old times, eh, bruv?' She held out a glass to him. 'You, me, and a bottle of something we probably shouldn't have.'

Danny took it, downing half the contents in one gulp. The booze scalded his throat, the warmth spreading through his chest. Danny welcomed it, that familiar burn that numbed the edges of his world. He had a feeling he was going to need all the liquid courage he could get in the coming days.

His mind turned back to the business he'd agreed to do for Lord Xander. It was time for him to get his firm together to hunt down this car and the idiots who had stolen it.

The dead idiots.

Chapter Thirty-One

'Listen up, you pillock.' Rita's glacial gaze cut Danny down to size. 'I'm not one of your little toerags who comes running when you bark their name. Threaten me, and you better sleep with one eye open in the night because I'll be coming for you in the dark.'

Rita stood with her hands on her hips facing Danny, properly fucked off. They were in his office on the first floor of the River Rat pub. He'd been giving her the third degree about taking her sweet time finding any dirt on Mortimer Stiffington, the agent selling the house. Danny relentlessly paced from one end of the room to the other, each footstep banging through his skull.

Running the docks was child's play compared to all the shit bursting in his brain right now. The top cop's stolen motor, Lord Xander's sneering face, the house on Molasses Quay. And now his troublemaking sister, Chrissie, had crash-landed back at his, spouting off the usual bollocks about changing her ways.

Fuck! Fuck! Fuck! Could life get any worse?

Danny dropped behind his massive teak desk, swiped from a Burma shipment during a customs inspection. The desk was his throne, but today it offered no comfort.

'Just tell me what you've got on that Stiffington wanker. You were the one insisting that he must have a secret.'

His mouth turned sour remembering the fiasco of the so-called charity event Rita had laid on up at the Voodoo Lounge and what a right balls-up that had turned out to be.

Folding her arms across her chest, Rita propped herself against the wall. 'I didn't want to bring you a load of old tripe, now did I. I'm nearly there. I can smell Stiffington's nasty secret in the air.'

'But you're taking too bloody long.' His fist slammed on the desk, the violent sound echoing around the room. 'That house has to be mine.'

'Has to be?' Rita quickly chucked in. Her keen eyes caught his slip. She pulled away from the wall, her crafty and canny glance searching his expression. 'You never did tell me why Molasses Quay means so much.'

Danny stared out the window, at the river below, his backbone rigid. Rita waited and waited, but he remained tight-lipped.

Knowing full well she was getting nowhere, she told him, 'There's this banker in the City who likes to drop by to visit my ladies. He's a man with his nose to the ground. And he's been known to spill interesting facts after a few brandies.'

'It had better work.' He lips twisted menacingly with each word. 'I'm not in the mood for another one of your cockups.'

That put Rita's back up again. She was on the verge of giving him another tongue lashing when voices drifted up from the pub below which signalled that Danny's gang was arriving for their meeting to discuss finding the stolen car.

'Try not to wear a hole in the carpet before I get back.' She headed for the door, then paused. 'Oh, I see Chrissie is back.'

The mention of his sister doubled the pain in Danny's head. 'That didn't take long for that to do the bleedin' rounds.'

Rita paused at the door. 'Couldn't believe it when I clapped eyes on her. She was in full fettle down Sally's caff.'

Danny pinched the bridge of his nose. 'What's she done now?'

'Started a proper tear-up between the Murphy and O'Brien families. Just sat there drinking her tea, laughing while they went at it hammer and tongs. Place is a right mess.'

'Fuck's sake!' Danny exploded. 'She's been back five fucking minutes.'

'Make sure she stays clear of my establishment.' Rita thrust open the door. 'I'm not having her stirring up that sort of grief with my punters.'

She was pulled up short by the sight of Jimmy and Brother Bertie. Her whole face and demeanour lit up when she zeroed in on Jimmy. 'Well, if it ain't my favourite piece of hard rock steel.'

Brother Bertie crowed, tipping his porkpie hat Rita's way. 'Looking ravishing as always, baby-girl.'

Jimmy, however, tensed at her approach. She kept coming and coming, closer and closer, until she pressed herself seductively against him, her curves fitting his frame like a glove.

'All right, Jimmy?' she purred, almost licking her lips. 'Still dreaming about me?'

Smacking his lips, irritated as hell, he quickly disentangled himself. 'Knock it off, Rita. That ship's sailed.'

Before Mini had come into his life, he and Rita had been a casual item, the emphasis on the word casual. Rita threw her head back and laughed, the sound echoing off the walls as she sauntered past more of Danny's men.

Danny waited until his men were settled before his voice cut through the room. 'Right, you lot. Listen up.' Chatter dying down, he carried on. 'We need to hunt down a set of wheels that's been pinched. An Aston Martin, no less. DB4. A real flash and fast bit of kit.'

One of his men asked, 'What's so important about this motor?'

Danny rounded on him with a laser-like glare. 'That's not your business. What is, is you finding it.' He turned in a circle, addressing all present. 'I want every one of you to have your ear to the ground. Check your usual haunts, lean on those in the know. I don't care if you have to turn this city upside fucking down and fucking sideways. Find. That. Car.'

'What about the nonce who nicked it?' Pete, the youngest member of the crew, piped up. 'What do we do with him when we find him?'

The question hung heavy in the air. 'Bring him to me. I'll deal with him. Personally.'

Everyone knew what 'personally' meant in Danny's book. Whoever the five-finger discount fool was, God have mercy on his soul.

'Right then.' Danny clapped his hands together. 'You've got your marching orders. Now get your ugly mugs out of here.'

As the men filed out, Danny beckoned Jimmy over.

Putting his arm around his shoulder, he told him, 'This takes priority over everything else. Even that upcoming fight, son.'

He noticed the way Jimmy's jaw fixed into a hard line, ready to argue the toss. Danny felt that familiar burn in his belly. Didn't his son get it, that boxing was a mug's game? Everyone getting rich except the poor bollocks taking the punches. Promoters, bookies, managers – vultures, the lot of them. His Jimmy was worth more than being some glorified punch bag.

But there was something darker eating away at Danny's guts, something he'd rather cut out his own tongue than admit. Every time Jimmy stepped into that ring, the crowd roaring his name, it twisted Danny up inside with the intensity of barbed wire. His son, the rising star. His son, the one they worshipped and whispered about becoming champion. His son, who didn't need his old man's reputation or connections to make something of himself.

The thought of Jimmy's name in lights, of him breaking free from his shadow was acid in his veins. Success should come through him. Through Danny pulling the strings, keeping his boy exactly where he wanted him. Under his control, like a proper son should be. Some nights, lying awake next to Iris, Danny tortured himself imagining Jimmy's name in the papers:

'Local Boy Makes Good.'

No mention of Danny 'King of the Docks' Steele. Just Jimmy, standing tall on his own two feet. It made Danny's hands itch to smash something.

'But, Dad, this is my shot at—'

'I said it takes priority.' Danny's tone could've stripped paint. 'Now jog on.'

''Course we'll find that motor for you, Mr Steele.' Brother Bertie's smooth voice rolled through the tension.

Danny hadn't even heard him approach.

'Me and Jimmy will ransack this town until we find it.'

That silver-tongued charm that worked on everyone else didn't always wash with Danny. Still, Brother Bertie had a way of defusing situations, and right now Danny's head was banging too hard to argue.

'See that you do.'

Danny watched Brother Bertie's hand land on Jimmy's shoulder, expertly steering his son away before the situation could get sticky. Those two were thick as thieves. Sometimes Danny wondered if that was another thing slipping out of his control.

In fact, he pointedly stared after Jimmy. Truth be told, his boy looked a touch green around the gills, like something had upset him more than getting his priorities sorted out. Danny pondered this awhile before wiping it from his mind. As long as the boy did what he was told, nothing else mattered.

***

'We need to dump it now,' Jimmy exploded, his guts doing backflips while he paced in their usual spot by the river where they sparred and trained. The blood had left his face. 'Now Dad's on the case, we don't have time to take it back where we got it from.'

'In broad daylight?' Brother Bertie shot him a look like he'd gone clean off his nut. 'You gone mental or what?'

'What if my dad's boys suss it's at Dabs' garage in Hackney before we get there?' His panic surged to the pattern of the river's tide before him.

'Char!' Brother Bertie let out a classic sound of Jamaican annoyance, followed by a long and hard kiss of his teeth. He grabbed Jimmy's arm, forcing him to stand still. 'Cool it, bruv. Your old man don't know it was us who half-inched it, yeah? We stick to the plan. Offload it tonight.'

Jimmy dragged in a shaky breath. His dad's face when he'd announced the car theft flashed through his mind. If Danny ever twigged it was him…

'The longer we sit on it—'

'But we aren't sitting on it for long,' Brother Bertie softly reasoned. 'The best crimes are done in the badness of the dark. Trust me on this one.'

Something in his friend's stance changed. His eyes kept darting towards the bridge leading to the main road. Jimmy couldn't help but notice his mate had gone all fidgety, like he had somewhere more pressing to be

'Am I keeping you?' he asked, sarky to the core. 'Got somewhere more important to be?'

For a split second, something flashed across Brother Bertie's face, but then his usual charm switched on, light-bulb bright. 'It's all cool, bruv. We've got this one. Just need to make a quick stop, yeah?'

Before Jimmy could get another word in, Brother Bertie was off, leaving Jimmy standing there like a prize mug.

Watching his best mate's retreating form, he wondered, where was Bertie rushing off to in such a hurry? And more importantly, how were they going to make it through the day without losing their nerve?

If his dad found out it was them who'd nabbed the car, there'd be more than just hell to pay.

Chapter Thirty-Two

Brother Bertie glanced at his watch, his stomach knotting with each passing minute. The record shop in Soho bustled around him, oblivious to his inner turmoil. It was half an hour past the agreed meeting time. His fingers traced over Eric 'Monty' Morris's 'Say What You're Saying' record cover. He'd been an idiot to think she'd actually show.

You proper fool yourself this time, Bertram Watson. One kiss and you think a gal like that will come running to you? You gwan soft in the head, boy.

The truth was, he couldn't get that kiss out of his mind. That kiss had changed everything because it meant he'd had to finally face the truth. He'd lain awake in his bed at three in the bloody morning, his mind circling back to one haunting truth that hit him with bullet precision between the eyes.

Sweet Jesus, he'd been in love with Sin the whole time.

Every cutting remark, every blazing row between them, he couldn't get enough of it. Of her.

Some mornings he'd wake up buzzing, waiting for the moment to get under her skin, watching those eyes flash with temper. Bertram Watson, the man who wouldn't be tied down, the lover of womanhood, had been dancing to Sin Steele's tune without even knowing it.

He loved her. God help him, he loved Cynthia Steele with every breath in his body.

She obviously didn't feel the same because she was a no-show. Letting loose a derisive kiss of his teeth at his own stupidity, he removed his finger from the record with the intention of leaving. Just then, the door chimed.

Sin stepped inside.

Brother Bertie's heart stopped at the sight of her. She wore the simplest of cotton dresses, pale blue and unadorned, yet somehow she made it look like the height of fashion. Her lips were painted that new frosted-pink shade, but it was her natural beauty that lit up the record shop.

Their eyes met across the crowded space. For a moment, neither moved. Sin's heart thundered. What was she doing here? If anyone saw them… But she couldn't stay away, not after that kiss had awakened something inside her she'd never felt before.

Then, as if drawn by an invisible thread, Sin made her way towards him.

'You came,' he uttered with soft wonder, still hardly believing it.

Sin nodded, her eyes darting nervously around. 'I wasn't sure I would.'

Bertie studied her face, searching for any sign of hesitation. 'Are you sure about this? We don't have to—'

Gently, she took his hand in hers. The simple touch set them both on fire. Sin expected him to lead her outside, but instead, he guided her towards the back.

In surprise she asked, 'Where are we going?'

Brother Bertie flashed her a mischievous grin, though Sin noticed a muscle nervously ticking near his mouth. 'Trust me.'

They slipped through a door marked 'Staff Only', then up a narrow staircase. Bertie produced a key, unlocking another door at the top.

'Welcome to Candy's pad.' He ushered Sin inside. 'She's a lady about town who works on...' he gave a delicate cough, 'the stage at night.'

Taking in her surroundings, Sin's gaze widened. Instead of the dingy bedsit she'd imagined, the flat was warm and exotic. Moroccan rugs layered the floor in deep reds and blues, while a gorgeous earth-brown woven blanket draped over the long sofa. A mauve beaded curtain divided the room.

'Your stripper friend has good taste,' Sin remarked, trying to hide how jittery she was behind humour.

Bertie chuckled, but it sounded forced. 'Candy's full of surprises.' Like me being here with my best mate's sister, he thought guiltily.

They stood there for a moment, the air thick with anticipation. Bertie's gaze hungrily roamed over Sin, taking in every detail. The way her pixie cut made her cheekbones stand out. The elegant curve of her neck. How had he never noticed before how perfect she was?

Sin flushed, all the way from the tips of her toes. Brother Bertie's gaze touched her in ways no one else ever had. Like she was precious. Valuable. Not just for her looks or her family name, but for who she was. In his eyes, she wasn't Jimmy Southpaw's sister or Danny Steele's daughter – she was just Sin.

Seeing his chance, he walked boldly over. Cupped his work-roughened palms around her chin. Sin's eyes fluttered closed as he leaned in, his lips meeting hers in a tender kiss. The world fell away. There was no East End, no family expectations, no colour barrier. Just the two of them, lost in each other.

The kiss deepened. Somehow her hands were under his top. On his chest. Against his beating heart. His fingers tangled in her hair, cradling her head.

Their lips broke apart, both of them breathless. Brother Bertie rested his forehead against Sin's, his eyes searching hers.

'I'm a scoundrel,' he warned her.

'My scoundrel.'

My. A thrill rushed through him, followed by a stab of guilt about Jimmy.

'Are you sure?' he asked again, his voice husky.

In response, Sin reached for the buttons of his shirt. Her fingers trembled slightly, undoing them one by one, revealing smooth brown skin beneath. Bertie stood perfectly still, hardly daring to breathe while Sin pushed the shirt from his shoulders. His breath hitched as her fingers trailed lower, tracing the lines of his abdomen.

Unable to hold back any longer, Brother Bertie captured her lips in another searing kiss, his hands finding the zipper of her dress, slowly sliding it down. The fabric pooled at Sin's feet, leaving her in nothing but her undergarments.

Bertie stepped back, drinking in the sight of her. Sin fought the urge to cover herself, unused to being so exposed. But the pure adoration in Bertie's eyes banished her insecurities.

'You're beautiful,' he whispered, glowing with awe.

She let out a startled gasp when he picked her up, carried her through the beaded curtain to the double bed. Their lovemaking was tender, yet passionate. Each touch, each kiss was a revelation.

They moved together, just two young people, expressing their feelings in the most intimate way possible.

Afterwards, they lay tangled together, both dazed, almost speechless at what had just happened. The afternoon sun faded, casting long shadows across the room. He traced lazy patterns on Sin's skin, while she rested her head on his chest. For a while, they simply basked in the afterglow, neither wanting to break the spell. But slowly, reality crept back in.

'What happens now?' the question caught in her throat heavy with fear.

Bertie caught her hand, pressing a kiss to the centre of her palm. 'Now, we take it one day at a time. See where this leads us.'

'It won't be easy,' Sin warned, reality intruding once more.

'Nothing worth having ever is,' Bertie replied with a gentle smile. 'But this feels right, doesn't it?'

Sin nodded, unable to deny it. In this moment, wrapped in his arms, it was easy to imagine a future where they could be together. But the harsh realities of their world loomed large.

Bertie, sensing her inner turmoil, tightened his arms around her as if he alone could protect her from the harshness of life.

'Hey,' he said softly, tilting her chin up to meet his gaze. 'Whatever you're worrying about, let it go. Right now, it's just us. Nothing else matters.'

But she couldn't stop. 'What about Jim—?'

He shifted and moved until she was on her back, him over her. 'Shh! No one else is allowed in our space, just me and you.'

Then he made love to her again, more urgently this time, as if trying to outrun the guilt threatening to consume him. What Brother Bertie didn't want to face up to was the sick feeling in his gut at hearing Jimmy's name. His best mate, the one person who'd always had his back. The man who'd trust him with his life. And now he was sleeping with his sister.

Chapter Thirty-Three

Where the bloody hell is he?

Jimmy was on the verge of hitting the roof when the door finally sprang open and Brother Bertie jumped in as easy as you please into the passenger seat of the car they had stolen.

'Been sitting here, in the dark, freezing my cunty bollocks off, waiting for you. Where have you been?' Jimmy got right into it, not bothering to hide how pissed he was.

He might as well have been talking to the dashboard for all the response he got from his best mate. In fact, Brother Bertie wore one of those soppy grins, looking for all the world like some lovesick poodle.

Brows slashing together, Jimmy scowled disapprovingly. 'It ain't my business who your shagging, but the bird will have to be put on the back burner because we're in some serious shit.'

Abruptly, that strange emotion covered Brother Bertie's features, the same one Jimmy had noticed the other day but couldn't pin down what it was. Now Jimmy would swear it was the spit of guilt. But what would his best friend have to be guilty about?

Lightly touching the brim of his hat, Brother Bertie answered, 'It's all good, man. Let's get this over with, yeah?'

Jimmy said nothing, instead giving his friend the once-over. Something wasn't right, but Jimmy didn't have time to suss it out. They had a job to do. He gunned the engine and peeled away from the kerb, tyres squealing into the night.

The plan was simple. Dump the Aston Martin back outside the townhouse up Mayfair way. Easy in, easy out.

Well, that was the plan, but as they hit the West End, cruising down Piccadilly, that's when their plan went all wrong.

Jimmy checked the rear-view mirror and couldn't believe what he saw.

'Shit!' he hissed. 'Old Bill on our tail.' His eyes narrowed. 'And I'll bet my last sixpence it's those two poncey plods who tried to put the frighteners on Dabs.'

Brother Bertie's head whipped around. His eyes widened when he spotted the police car gaining on them. 'Blood fire! Floor it, Jimmy!'

Jimmy didn't need telling twice. He slammed his foot on the accelerator. The engine roared and they shot forward.

The chase was on.

They weaved through the sparse traffic. Horns blared around them while other drivers swerved to avoid the chaos. Jimmy's heart pounded, adrenaline burning through his veins. Any other time, he would've loved up the thrill of outwitting the coppers at every turn to the absolute max. Not today. All he could think about was getting banged up in Brixton or Pentonville, Mini bringing the kids to visit him. Jimmy visibly flinched; he never wanted his kids to see him behind bars.

'Hold on!' he yelled, determination driving him, cranking the wheel hard, sending them careening around a corner. The tyres screeched, leaving rubber on the tarmac.

Brother Bertie gripped the dashboard, his face a picture of terror. 'Blimey, Jimmy! You trying to put us in an early grave?'

But Jimmy was in the zone, his focus laser-sharp. All of a sudden, a police siren wailed behind them. Sweat beaded on his forehead racking his brain for a way out. Up West wasn't his manor, so he didn't know all the twists and turns of weaving his way out of there, running from the law. He tore down side streets, the buildings a blur on either side. Jimmy's mind raced faster than the car.

'We need to shake them off,' Brother Bertie breathlessly shouted.

'I'm working on it, ain't I? Keep your fucking drawers on!'

Up ahead, a side street rose, wider than an alley but not by much. Jimmy made a split-second decision. Yanking the wheel hard, he sent them hurtling down the narrow passage. For a heart-stopping moment, Jimmy thought they'd made it…they'd driven straight into a dead end.

'Bollocks!' Jimmy slammed his palm against the steering wheel.

The police car screeched to a halt behind them, blocking their escape.

For a second or two there was utter, excruciating silence.

Then two men in suits emerged, guns drawn and pointed squarely at the car they were in. Neither Jimmy nor Brother Bertie needed telling these were definitely the two detectives who had roughed up Dabs.

'You're nicked, you pair of little shits!' the shorter of the two bellowed, his face twisted with malicious glee. 'Come out nice and slow-like, or we'll ventilate that fancy motor of yours!'

The other smoothly added, 'Except, it isn't bloody yours, now is it.'

His partner chimed in, his voice dripping with menace. 'And don't think about pulling a fast one. I'm just itching for an excuse to pull this trigger.'

Brother Bertie was already moving. 'Switch places,' he hissed urgently. 'Now! If they get too close they'll clock our faces!'

No questions asked, Jimmy scrambled over the gearstick while Brother Bertie urgently slid under into the driver's seat. The detectives were advancing cautiously, step by step, their eyes gleaming with the anticipation of a job well done.

Brother Bertie gripped the wheel. Jimmy could see the sweat falling down his friend's face, could practically hear the rapid boom-boom of his heart. For a moment, he wondered if Bertie had lost his nerve.

But then a steely determination settled over his mate's features. In one fluid motion, he stomped on the accelerator and cranked the wheel hard. He shot the car into reverse, engine roaring with the desperate power of a caged beast finally set free. The cops' eyes widened in shock, their triumphant expressions morphing into panic when they realised what was happening. That if they didn't get out of the way…

They dove for cover. One going left, the other right.

With a sickening crunch of metal on metal, the Aston Martin ploughed into the police car. The impact rattled Jimmy's teeth, but Brother Bertie didn't hesitate. In fact, he was grinning for all he was worth. There had always been a kill-thrill side to his personality, a love of danger. He drove forward and back into the other motor, shunting it to the side. This time he didn't stop; the sides of the Aston Martin scraped against the brick walls, showering sparks pushing past the police vehicle.

Tyres squealing, the stolen car shot backwards out of the street. With an expert twist of his hands at the wheel, Brother Bertie swung the car forward and then tore through the ink-black streets of London, his driving even more reckless than Jimmy's had been. It was a brown-knuckle ride that seemed to last forever, but finally, they hit the open road heading towards Essex. Jimmy's madly beating pulse slowed.

The best friends looked at each other, dead serious. Abruptly, Jimmy let out a whoop of triumph, pounding the dashboard with both hands. Brother Bertie threw his head back and let out a wild laugh, his hat jigging on his head.

'Bloody hell, mate! We did it!' Jimmy hollered, his silver-grey eyes wild with delighted excitement.

His friend's grin was a mile wide. 'Did you see those coppers' faces when I reversed into them? Thought their eyeballs were gonna pop right outta out their dumb skulls!'

Jimmy reached over and clapped Brother Bertie on the shoulder. 'You're a fucking genius, bruv. That move was mental!'

More raucous laughter and high-fiving tore up the inside of the motor, which swerved, Brother Bertie struggled to control it through his elation.

'I thought we was goners for sure,' Jimmy gasped, wiping tears of mirth from his eyes.

Bertie's chest swelled with pride. 'Not a chance, Jimmy boy. Not with Bertram Watson from St Ann's Parish in Jamaica at the helm.'

Getting closer to Essex their verbal high-fiving dribbled away, the enormity of their situation kicking back in. More importantly, they still had the car on their hands, which they parked in a secluded spot.

It was Brother Bertie who said, 'Dabs was right, this car is hotter than the Devil's own kitchen. Someone wants it back for a reason.' He fidgeted uncomfortably in his seat. 'There's something about this motor I don't like. These wheels have got secrets.'

Brows slashing together, Jimmy asked, 'Did you find anything dodgy when you searched it, like in the boot?'

His friend stabbed him with an expression of stunned confusion. 'Search the car? I never did that. The boot? I thought you'd sorted that out. Gone through it with a fine-tooth comb.'

'Me?' Jimmy's voice rose. 'When the fuck would I have had time to do that?'

'Well, I didn't fuckery-bloody do it either!' Brother Bertie shot back.

They glared at each other, the silence thick with tension and unspoken accusations.

'Fuck's sake!' Jimmy muttered, running a hand through his hair. 'We need to check it now. Could be anything in there.'

Finally, Brother Bertie clicked open his door. The sound cut through the silence like a gunshot. On the other side, Jimmy's door creaked open, then slammed shut, the noise swallowed by the vastness of the darkness around them.

Making their way to the rear of the car, their shoes crunched on loose gravel. A fox screamed somewhere in the darkness. Jimmy flinched. Brother Bertie pretended not to notice.

A sour, metallic smell hit their nostrils the instant Jimmy cracked open the boot. A strange odour crawled over his face.

'Get the torch we found in the glove box, yeah?' Jimmy's voice betrayed his unease.

Brother Bertie jogged round to the passenger side, returning moments later with the heavy-duty torch. His porkpie hat cast odd shadows across his face. Jimmy snatched the torch, the beam cutting through the darkness, illuminating something large and white. A box.

'What's that?' Brother Bertie swung the beam of the torch over it.

'Looks like one of them posh ice boxes.' Jimmy leaned in closer. 'Motor car refrigerator thing.'

'Why would a fridge be in a car? Maybe the guy who owns the car liked to take the kids and the missus on family picnics.'

But something felt wrong. The air around the ice box felt different. Heavy with menace.

'Open it,' Jimmy muttered.

Brother Bertie hesitated, then reached for the catch. The lid resisted slightly before it opened. It sent a blast of frigid air into their faces, carrying with it a metallic stench that made Jimmy's stomach roll.

The light revealed red and pink shapes scattered through half-melted ice like some mad butcher's window display. But this wasn't meat for Sunday dinner.

'That's a hand,' Brother Bertie said, voice tight. The torch shook violently in his hand. 'And a foot… Another foot.'

Jimmy's breath came in short gasps. 'There's more. Christ, there's more.'

The torch swept across the horror, limbs and chunks of flesh dismembered like some grotesque jigsaw puzzle. Red ice. Pink ice. Marbled ice.

Brother Bertie's composure cracked. 'There's no head.'

Then Jimmy lost it, staggering backwards, gagging. He doubled over, heaving his guts onto the grass.

Chapter Thirty-Four

Brother Bertie remained frozen, staring into the box. His face had gone the colour of a deathly brown, but his voice stayed steady. 'We need to think this through, Jimmy. Nice and calm like.'

'Calm? Calm?' Jimmy was practically shrieking. 'There's bits of some poor bollocks chopped up in there!'

'Keep your voice down.' Brother Bertie gently closed the lid, though his hands weren't quite as steady as his voice. 'Last thing we need is some nosey parker stumbling across this.'

Jimmy straightened up, wiping his mouth with the back of his hand. He was shaking like a leaf in a storm. 'Who'd do something like that? Cut someone up into… into pieces?'

'Someone who didn't want the body found in one piece, that's who.' Brother Bertie pulled out a small flask of Lord Have Mercy Rum Punch and knocked it back. It took the edge of his shock. 'Question is, what's it doing in this car?'

'I can't…' Jimmy's voice cracked. 'I can't stop seeing that foot.'

Brother Bertie passed the flask to him, and Jimmy couldn't get enough of the potent drink.

Getting his breath back, Jimmy said, 'At least we now know why someone is after this car.'

'Who do you reckon that someone is?'

Passing the flask back to his friend, Jimmy paused, thinking on the question. 'If a couple of crooked cops are on this then it's most likely to be some big-time criminal. A major league Face who has them in his pocket.'

'Unless it's the two coppers behind this themselves,' Brother Bertie added a new perspective. 'From what Dabs said they're as bent as a butcher's hook. What if someone they were in business with double-crossed them. And now won't be double-crossing anyone ever again.'

By rights, Brother Bertie should've been stunned that two police officers were involved in this. But this was 1967. Nothing surprised him anymore when it came to the filth. Half of them were worse than the villains they pretended to chase, pocketing bungs left, right and centre, doing dodgy jobs for whoever paid the highest price. The only difference between a cop and a crook these days was the uniform.

The horror of their situation sank in. Jimmy slumped against the car, legs barely holding him up.

The stench of death smothered him. Sweet, rotten, and sickening. He'd seen brutal things working the docks, but this was on a whole other vicious level. Arms, legs, torso. Brother Bertie stood rigid, brain ticking away. both men knowing their night had just turned into a nightmare. And it was far from over.

'We need to figure out our next move. Carefully.' Brother Bertie broke through the dreadful quiet. 'One step at a time. First step, we need supplies. Shovels.'

'You saying we should bury him?' Jimmy was incredulous.

'Well, we ain't gonna try to raise him up from the dead.'

Jimmy nodded numbly. 'But where are we going to get shovels from?'

Scowling, Brother Bertie thought hard before an idea came to him. 'We passed a cricket ground five minutes or so back. There's bound to be a groundkeeper's shed or something with tools inside.'

While his shellshocked mate made the trek, Brother Bertie slumped against the side of the car, his mind reeling. How had it come to this? He was supposed to be making something of himself, not getting mixed up in whatever this was. Only hours ago, he'd been lying in the arms of delicious Sin.

His thoughts drifted to his sister who'd sacrificed so much for him to have a flying start to a good life in England. The memory of their last day together in Jamaica back in '57 washed over him.

Gertie sat down her fifteen-year-old brother on the step outside their house. On her lap was a box.

'Don't go, Gertie,' he pleaded, his voice choked with sobs. 'Please don't leave me.'

Gertie's eyes glistened with unshed tears. She cupped his face, her touch gentle but firm.

'Listen to me, little man.' She was battling harsh emotions, but her voice never wavered. 'I have to go. It's the only way I can make a better life for us both.'

Bertram sniffled, his bottom lip trembling. 'But what about me?'

Gertie smiled softly. 'I'll send for you, you hear? Just as soon as I get settled.' She opened the box, revealing a well-worn porkpie hat. 'This was Daddy's. Grandfather thought you should have it now.'

His eyes lit up when Gertie placed it on his head. It was too big, slipping down over his eyes, making his sister chuckle.

'You'll grow into it,' she reassured him, adjusting it. 'And when you do, remember Daddy's words: "A man's hat is his crown. Wear it with pride and honour."'

Bertram nodded solemnly, his small hands gripping the brim. 'I'll make Daddy proud. I'll be a good man, just like him.'

Gertie hugged him tightly, her voice thick with emotion. 'You already are, little brother. Just keep that good heart of yours and stay on the right path. And one day, when you're older, you'll join me in England. We'll be together again.' She stood, wiping her eyes. 'I have to go now. Be good for Grandfather, yeah? Make me proud.'

The memory fading, Brother Bertie touched the brim of the same porkpie hat with a bitter taste in his mouth. 'Make her proud' echoed in his head, mocking him. If Gertie could see him now, getting ready to bury a dismembered body... He felt revolted with himself.

Jimmy appeared with all they needed, including, to Brother Bertie's surprise, a can of petrol.

'Thought we might need to torch the car,' Jimmy explained, noticing Brother Bertie's questioning look.

Brother Bertie shook his head. 'Nah, bruv! If these wheels do belong to some top dog, they'll be shitting themselves wondering if the thieves have found the body. And we'll be the only ones who know where the body is. If tings get rough then that faceless body becomes our bargaining tool. Our leverage.'

They set to work, the shovels biting into the soft earth of the lay-by. The night air grew thick with the smell of freshly turned soil and something far less pleasant.

Brother Bertie paused, leaning on his shovel. 'Jimmy, we just gotta keep our heads down, yeah? Act normal. Prepare for your big fight.' He didn't feel nearly as confident as he sounded.

'This is fucked up.' Jimmy grunted.

It was gruelling work, taking them four to five hours. Finally they stood back, both staring at the freshly covered grave.

An exhausted Brother Bertie laid out their plan. 'At the moment, only me and you and a few bad people know about the body. The bad people aren't going to be broadcasting it from the rooftops about some dead guy.' He continued. 'The cops never saw our faces. No one knows we have the car. So I say we hang on to it. Keep it hidden, then when the fuss has died down, after your fight we give your contact in Amsterdam a little bell—'

Jimmy finished, 'And the deal is still on.'

'Where are we going to hide the car?'

A knowing look darkened Jimmy's face. 'I know just the place.'

Chapter Thirty-Five

Sugar Cane Wharf rose up ahead, a mass of cranes and containers against the inky sky. Jimmy turned the car down a narrow cobbled alley, barely wide enough for the motor. The ancient stones were slick with decades of Thames mist, forcing him to crawl along at a snail's pace.

'I hate this place at night, much less the early hours of the morning,' Brother Bertie mumbled, a shiver passing through him, his usual easy-going vibes nowhere in sight. 'Puts me in mind of what Hell would be like without the fire.'

The cobbles rattled the car, each bump and dip making him flinch. Something about the docks after dark set his teeth on edge. The air felt different here, heavy, restless, like the souls of dead dockers still wandered these alleys, watching with hollow eyes. Even the shadows seemed alive.

Jimmy killed the engine in front of a hulking warehouse. It looked about ready to keel over, its brick walls stained black with a century of grime and pollution. Most thought it abandoned, just another corpse of London's dying docklands.

'Let's get this over with,' Brother Bertie said, fidgeting with his porkpie hat before stepping outside.

Jimmy followed with the torch they'd used to help bury the body. The distant swish of the Thames was the only sound apart from their erratic breathing.

Reaching the warehouse's side door, its rusted hinges screaming neglect, Jimmy fumbled with his keys.

'Raas! Hurry up, bruv.' Brother Bertie glanced fretfully around the darkness. 'This place… it's like someone – something – is watching.'

Brother Bertie could handle most things the criminal life threw at him, including, as he'd just demonstrated, dead bodies. But there was something spooky about this stretch of Sugar Cane Wharf in the dark that made him want to hightail it the other way.

The lock gave with a grinding screech, and they slipped inside, plunging into darkness thick as treacle. Jimmy flicked on his torch, its weak beam barely cutting through the gloom. The place was a huge cavernous space filled with old crates and rusty machinery. They made their way to the back where they found a hidden switch, a small knot in the wall that yielded under his fingers. With a sound resembling grinding bones, a section of wall swung inwards, revealing a ramp.

'Fuck me sideways.' Bertie gaped at the yawning darkness beyond.

Few knew about these hidden tunnels and forgotten spaces beneath the docks. Over centuries, smugglers and thieves had carved out their own secret, criminal world down there.

The stench that wafted up nearly knocked them off their feet. Stagnant water, rot, and secrets best left buried.

'We gotta get the motor down there,' Jimmy said, already dreading the task ahead. The ramp plunged at a brutal angle into the bowels of Sugar Cane Wharf, worn concrete crumbling at the edges.

'Jesus,' Brother Bertie hissed through clenched teeth. 'One wrong move and we'll wreck the Aston. She's worth nothing if we damage her more than she already is after that chase with the coppers.'

The next twenty minutes were pure hell. Jimmy crawled the stolen car forward while his best friend guided him, both of them sweating despite the bitter cold that crept up from below. The air down here was different, raw and vicious. The Thames crashed against the wharf's foundations, the roaring echo bouncing off stone walls.

Suddenly, metal shrieked against concrete as the car's undercarriage caught the ramp. They froze, hearts hammering. With a delicate move, Jimmy managed to get the car moving again.

Another gut-wrenching scrape had Jimmy gripping the wheel until his knuckles went white. But inch by agonising inch, they guided the Aston Martin down. The darkness swallowed it whole, leaving only the red glow of brake lights reflecting off grimy walls.

The river's fury was deafening now, the sound mixing with the drip-drip-drip of water from ancient pipes. This deep under the wharf, the cold went straight to your bones. The type of cold that reminded you of all the bodies the Thames had claimed over the centuries.

Finally, the car reached the bottom of the ramp. They got out, and, chests heaving, both wiped down inside to get rid of their fingerprints.

'We should check it out,' Jimmy said, his voice hollow. 'Make sure there's no nasty surprises.'

Brother Bertie's jaw dropped in surprise. 'Fuckery, Jimmy! You for real!' Seeing his mate wasn't about to budge, he shook his head and said, with a wave of his hand, 'After you, bruv.'

The tunnel opened into a vast chamber that swallowed their torch beam whole. Massive wooden beams loomed while the walls weeping moisture. Here and there, crumbling brickwork revealed patches of bare earth, like the very ground was trying to reclaim this secret space.

'How deep this ting go?' Brother Bertie couldn't believe his eyes.

Jimmy shook his head. 'Dad said even he doesn't know how long these tunnels run for. Thinks it's under the whole bloody East End. Old smugglers' routes, he reckoned.'

They pushed on, the darkness pressing in. The air grew thick, each breath a struggle against the damp and decay. Their torch beam danced across the walls, revealing grotesque shadows that seemed to move of their own accord.

The tunnel forked, one path sloping deeper into the earth, the other curving away into impenetrable blackness. Jimmy hesitated, then chose the path that curved. The floor beneath their feet changed from stone to packed earth, squelching with each step.

Rusted chains hung from the ceiling, swaying slightly in a breeze they couldn't feel. The clink of metal on metal sent shivers down their spines. In places, the tunnel widened into small chambers, filled with rotting wooden crates and the remnants of long-forgotten contraband.

Abruptly Jimmy frowned. 'If I'm not mistaken, I think that path may lead to the house Mini's got her heart set on in Molasses Quay.' His words dribbled away because he'd never thought the house might have access to a tunnel. Now that could come in really useful.

'This place is like a bloody maze. We could get lost down here forever.'

Jimmy nodded grimly. 'That's the idea, innit? Perfect place to hide things you don't want found.'

The torchlight caught flashes of movement. Rats with eyes like hellfire, scurrying away from the light. But there were other things, too, shapes just at the edge of their vision that vanished when they tried to focus on them.

The stench was overwhelming now. It clung to their clothes, their skin, seeping into their very pores. Jimmy's mind flashed to the body parts in the boot, that retching sensation coming over him again.

Bertie crossed himself, muttering something that sounded like a prayer. 'We shouldn't be here. The place is full of spirits and duppies.'

Jimmy had learned from his friend that duppies were evil spirits from Jamaican folklore, shadow creatures that haunted dark places like this. According to Brother Bertie, they had a nasty habit of leading people to their doom. For once, Jimmy heeded his friend's superstitions and got them out of there.

Chapter Thirty-Six

A few days later, Iris sat at the kitchen table, the slight steam from the steak and kidney pudding she was cooking on the stove drifting in the air. Her bony fingers traced the rim of the empty glass beside her. The burning, intoxicating taste of gin lingered on her tongue and the back of her throat. Her gaze fell upon the package before her, beautifully wrapped in crisp brown paper and tied with a delicate bow of string. Mini had done the wrapping for her because, being a seamstress, she had such a delicate hand and an eye for turning something out right.

The sound of the front door opening and closing jolted Iris from her thoughts.

'Jimmy?' she called out. Her body swelled with anticipation.

Heavy footsteps echoed down the passage, and a moment later, he appeared in the doorway. Instantly she was struck by how tired he seemed. Exhaustion seeped from his very pores, carving deep lines of weariness into his handsome face.

Unbidden, a memory from long ago rose to the surface of her mind. 1941, in the midst of a relentless Blitz raid, she had brought Jimmy into this world with the help of a few stalwart neighbouring women. He had been a big baby, his birth a brutal, drawn-out ordeal that had nearly claimed Iris' life. Yet, as she had cradled his wriggling form against her chest for the first time, every ounce of pain had melted away, replaced by a surge of love so fierce it had stolen her breath. The sheer pride and joy on Danny's face when he'd first laid eyes on his son was a sight she would treasure until her dying day. It was that image she conjured and held on to when another tale of her husband's cheating ways reached her.

Blinking away the poignant memory, Iris gestured to the chair opposite her. 'Sit yourself down, lad. I've got something for you.'

Jimmy eyed the package curiously lowering himself into the seat. 'What's all this then?'

'Open it and see,' Iris urged, a tentative smile playing at the corners of her mouth.

With careful fingers, Jimmy untied the bow and peeled back the paper. He lifted the lid of the box, revealing a pair of immaculate boxing gloves nestled within. His eyes widened in wonder.

'Mum!' he breathed, thick with emotion. 'Where did you get these?'

Eyes sparkling, Iris lengthened her neck with pride. 'I had a word with a captain on a ship I've got to know very well over the years, called in a favour. He brought them back special from his last trip to Mexico. I've heard they make the finest gloves in the world there.'

The gloves were a work of art, crafted with meticulous attention to detail. The supple leather, dyed a rich shade of chestnut, almost glowed in the soft kitchen light. It was sewn with intricate handmade stitching. The laces, woven from the finest cotton, were a pristine white, begging to be tied. Lifting one of the gloves from the box, Jimmy marvelled at the perfect balance of weight and suppleness in his hand. These were gloves made for a champion.

He met his mother's gentle gaze, tears pricking at the corners of his eyes.

'I don't know what to say. They're perfect.'

Iris reached across the table, clasping her son's free hand in her own. 'When you knock out the current champ and take that local heavyweight title, I want it to be with these gloves. I want the world to see my boy for the champion he is.'

Jimmy brought her hand to his lips, pressing a tender kiss to her weathered knuckles. 'I won't let you down, Mum. I swear it.'

Suddenly, her tone grew heavy with emotion. 'I want better for you, Jimmy. I never wanted this life for you, following in your father's footsteps. You're meant for greater things. Straighter things.'

A shadow passed over Jimmy's face, the tendons in his neck straining with the weight of unspoken words. 'I love you, Mum.'

Iris' heart clenched with hope, because in the warmth of the kitchen, with the promise of glory wrapped in leather and love, anything seemed possible. Jimmy departed, the gloves clutched protectively to his chest. Slowly standing, Iris went over to the kitchen cupboard and took out the gin she always kept handy. She knocked it back straight from the bottle. One more slug of Mother's Ruin, to steady her nerves and fortify her spirit. For in this world of violence and vice, a mother's love was the strongest tonic of all.

Chapter Thirty-Seven

'You look like you've seen Christopher Lee in one of them Dracula films!'

Sin jerked her head up at her friend's frank statement. She forced a wan smile for Kath. The waters of the river lapped against the shoreline. Sin was perched on a crumbling stone wall, her legs swinging idly. Beside her, Kath unwrapped newspaper parcels, revealing steaming portions of fish and chips.

'Careful, love,' Kath cautioned, handing a paper cone to her sister, Dilly.

The young woman's eyes stared unseeing at the river, but her fingers curled instinctively around the warm package.

Sin gazed out at the hulking silhouettes of cargo ships and cranes looming against the grey sky. Sugar Cane Wharf bustled with activity even with dusk settling in over the docks. The clanging of metal and shouts of workers carried across the water, a cacophony Sin had known all her life.

'Ta,' Sin mumbled, accepting her own portion from Kathleen. The salt and vinegar made her mouth water, but she found herself picking at the food listlessly.

Kath settled beside them, trying to perk up proceedings with her sunny smile. 'This is a right treat, eh? We don't get to splash out like this often.'

Sin nodded absently, her mind elsewhere. She was consumed with thoughts of her and Bertie. They'd managed to meet a few more times, and each time was the same. Seventh heaven. They couldn't wait to get their clothes off quickly enough. Her skin tingled at the memory of his gentle caresses, his touch exploring her body that left her aching and breathless. But reality always came crashing back, leaving her down and depressed. Their love, burning bright behind closed doors, might never see the light of day. The joy of their stolen moments was always tinged with a deep, gnawing despair.

Kath's cheerful voice broke through her agony. 'You'll never guess what happened the other day. That Anglo-Merchant bank up in the City sent another letter, all official-like. Said they're increasing the monthly payments!'

Sin blinked, focusing on her friend. 'What? What monthly payments?'

'You know the ones. Been sending money ever since Dilly's accident.' Kath stroked her sister's arm gently. 'I remember the first time the money arrived.

Da's ticker nearly went on the blink. Thought it was a mistake.'

Bless his soul! Seven years ago Kath's father had died on the docks when a crane's cable had snapped, sending a half-tonne of bacon crashing down on him, killing him instantly.

Sin added slowly, 'But you never found out who sent the money or set up the account?'

Kath shook her head. 'Not a clue. Da didn't have two pennies to rub together most days, let alone a fancy bank account. Just a working man down Sugar Cane Wharf, same as all the other dockers.' She popped a chip in her mouth, chewing thoughtfully. 'It was dead strange, but we were so hard up after the accident. Da hardly touched it at first, but then Dilly needed all that special care…' She glanced at her sister with love and sadness.

Sin felt a pang of guilt. Here was Kath, supporting her sister, while she was tied up in knots over a secret love affair. The weight of it pressed down on her chest until she thought she might suffocate if she didn't speak the words aloud.

'I'm seeing someone,' she blurted out.

Kath's eyes lit up. 'Ooooo! Who's the lucky fella? Anyone I know?'

Sin's stomach churned. She forced herself to meet Kath's eager gaze. 'Brother Bertie.'

Kath's jaw went south. For a long moment, the only sounds were the lap of water against stone and Dilly's quiet munching.

'Bertie?' Kath whispered finally. 'Jimmy's best mate, Brother Bertie? Jamaican Bertie?'

Sin nodded mutely, her cheeks burning.

'Blimey,' Kath breathed. Then, to Sin's surprise, a huge, radiant grin lit up her face. 'Well, he is a bit of all right, ain't he? Always laughing, that one.'

Sin let out a shaky breath. 'You're not shocked?'

The skin on Kath's forehead wrinkled slightly. 'Well, it's not exactly common round here, is it? But…' She paused, choosing her words carefully. 'Jimmy's not prejudiced or nothing. And Bertie's like family to him. Maybe it'll be all right?'

Sin's heart clenched. Sweet, naive Kathleen. If only it were that simple.

'My dad would go spare,' Sin said quietly. 'You know what he's like. And what if Jimmy…?' She was unable to voice her deepest fear. That this might shatter the bond between her brother and his best friend. Mind you, her brother had fallen head over heels for someone who was meant to be forbidden to him.

Kath was silent for a long moment, absently brushing chip crumbs from Dilly's lap. When she spoke again, her voice was uncharacteristically serious.

'You know what I reckon? One day – maybe not soon, but someday – we'll live in a world where people can just love each other. No hatred, no fuss about who's with who. Wouldn't that be lovely?'

Sin stared at her friend, struck by the simple wisdom of her words. 'Yeah,' she agreed softly. 'That would be something.'

A mischievous glint appeared in Kath's eye. 'So, what's IT like? Y'know, the in and out IT?'

'Kathleen!' Sin gasped, her face flaming.

'Oh, come off it! I've only ever kissed a bloke a couple of times. You've got to give me something!'

Despite herself, Sin felt a giggle bubble up in her throat. Soon both girls were giggling, the sound echoing across the water. Even Dilly wore a faint smile ghosting across her lips.

Sin found herself opening up. 'Before Bertie, I did it a couple of times before with this guy—'

'Cynthia Steele! You never!' Kath squealed.

'Between me and you, he wouldn't know pleasure if it smacked him in the kisser.' Kath roared with laughter. 'Now with Bertie it's like nothing I've ever felt before. When he looks at me, it's like I'm the only person in the world. And when he touches me…'

Kath leaned in, eyes wide. 'Yeah?'

Sin bit her lip, remembering the electric feel of Bertie's hands on her skin, the way her body came alive under his touch. 'It's like I'm on fire,' she whispered. 'Like I'll die if he stops.'

Kath sighed dreamily. 'Sounds proper romantic.'

Sin's smile faded, reality reasserting itself. 'But it's dangerous, too. If anyone found out…'

'You really love him, don't you?'

Sin nodded, tears pricking at her eyes. 'Christ almighty, I do. All that time we spent at each other's throats, trading insults like punches, truth was, every bloody word between us was just masking what was really happening in our hearts.'

Kath reached out and squeezed her hand. 'Then that's all that matters, ain't it? The rest, well, we'll cross that bridge when we come to it.'

Sin wished she could share her friend's optimism. Her stomach knotted with worry. How long could she and Bertie keep sneaking around? God, she loved him so much it hurt. But was love enough to overcome the prejudice and hatred they might face? Sin's chest tightened. She couldn't bear the thought of losing him, but she couldn't see a way forward either.

Sin stared out at the darkening river, wondering how something that felt so right other people could think was so wrong.

Chapter Thirty-Eight

Lying on the gaudy bed in her black silk baby doll with red trim made Rita's skin crawl. You'd think she'd be used to it by now. The pawing hands, the sour breath, the sticky press of sweaty flesh against her own. But some things you never got used to, no matter how many times you went through the motions. The Sing-Song Lady creaked and groaned, rocking gently on the Thames.

The door opened with an abrupt click. Her special visitor had arrived. In waddled Horace Dunbar, a roly-poly banker with thinning grey hair and piggy eyes that greedily roved over Rita's body. She fought back a shudder, plastering on a coquettish smile instead.

'Well, well! Horace. Been expecting you.'

He grunted, already fumbling with his belt. 'Let's skip the pleasantries. Spread those naughty thighs for Uncle Horace.'

What a charmer!

Getting up, nice and slow, so he got an eyeful, Rita glided over to him, putting her sexiest swing into her hips. 'Now, now! What's the rush? Why don't we have a little natter first?'

He squinted, baffled. 'Natter? Since when do I come here to talk?'

She ran a finger down his chest, fighting the urge to recoil. 'I've got a teeny-weeny favour to ask…Big Boy.'

That was his kink, being called 'Big Boy'. He got a hefty hard-on from it. Probably because his 'big boy' was in truth a very 'small boy.' Squirming with renewed excitement, he licked his lips.

Rita pressed her advantage. 'This favour is nothing major. Just some info about a certain person.'

The banker's face went slack with surprise. 'What person?'

'Someone who works up the City way. He's called Mortimer Stiffington.'

Rita had carefully scrolled through the brothel's client base to pinpoint which one would most likely have potential information on the agent selling the house on Molasses Quay. Stiffington was hiding a secret, she just knew. All she had to do was find out what it was.

I knew it! Rita crowed when she saw recognition of the name cross the banker's face.

He slowly asked, 'What are you interested in that dry stick for?'

'Let's just say I've got a vested interest,' she purred back, rubbing her body against his. 'Come on, Big Boy. I bet there's something juicy. Everyone's hiding something under their mattress.'

Horace hesitated, clearly torn between his lust and his professional discretion. To ensure he made the right choice, Rita trailed her tongue along the flabby skin of his neck.

'Tell you what,' she tantalisingly continued in a low, husky tone. 'You scratch my back, and I'll do that thing my girls say you like so much. The one with the feather.'

That did it. A shiver of intense pleasure coursed through him, his resolve crumbling as his cock stood to attention in his trousers.

'Stiffington's been making monthly payments to an account for the past decade. Same amount, like clockwork.'

Rita's heart raced. This was it. 'Who does the account belong to?'

'That I don't know because it's all hush-hush, but it's enough to put a smile on someone's face every month, if you catch my drift.'

Rita's mind rushed with the possibilities of what this could mean. Was Stiffington being blackmailed? Supporting a secret family? A boyfriend tucked away in a secret love nest?

'Thanks, sugar,' she cooed and led him to the bed where she lay down. 'Now, how about that feather?'

But Horace had other ideas. Before Rita could react, he'd produced a gag from his pocket and shoved it in her mouth. Terror gripped her like an icy fist around her heart. The room shrank, walls closing in while his bulk loomed over her. His gaze gleamed with cruel excitement, his breath hot and rancid on her face.

'Not so chatty now, are we?'

Rita thrashed wildly, her muffled screams choking inside her mouth. Her nails raked across his face, drawing blood, but he only laughed, pinning her arms above her head with one meaty hand.

The world narrowed to a pinpoint of fear and desperation. Rita bucked and writhed, but the banker's weight crushed her, suffocating. Panic clawed at her throat while memories flooded back…

She was sixteen again, walking the streets for the first time, trapped beneath a john who'd paid for submission she hadn't agreed to give. After he'd finished, he'd beaten her black and blue.

Horace's free hand roamed her body, rough and possessive. Rita squeezed her eyes shut, willing it to be over, praying for salvation that wouldn't come. The rank stench of sweat chocked her. The head of his cock stabbed the inside of her thigh.

No fucking way was he getting inside her!

Her fingers scrabbled desperately at the nightstand, managing to throw the top drawer open. Just when his weight shifted, him preparing to violate her, Rita's hand closed around the cold metal of the gun. Without hesitation, she brought it down and fired.

The shot rang out, impossibly loud in the confined cabin. Horace howled, clutching his bleeding leg while he toppled to the floor. Rita scrambled away, her back hitting the cabin wall, keeping the gun trained on him with shaking hands.

She spat out the gag, gulping air and more air. Her entire body trembled, wave after wave of chills rushing across her skin. Horace writhed on the floor, screaming while he tried to stem the bleeding.

'Tiny!' Rita's voice was hoarse, barely recognisable. 'Get in here!'

The door burst open, and Tiny filled the frame. His eyes widened at the scene before him. With murderous intent, he advanced on Horace with raging bull intent, growling, 'I'll have his knackers.' He laid into Rita's attacker with savage punch after savage punch.

'That's enough!' Rita snarled. 'Get this piece of offal outta here and dump him outside The London. And make sure he knows what'll happen if he breathes a word of this to a soul, including them doctors.'

Tiny nodded, understanding his boss lady wanted her attacker to be left outside the Royal London Hospital in Whitechapel. Hauling the moaning almost unconscious Horace to his feet, he answered, 'You got it.'

When the door closed behind them, Rita sagged onto the bed, her legs suddenly unable to support her. The gun slipped from her numb fingers, clattering to the floor. She was shaking all over, her breath coming in short, sharp gasps. That was one of the big problems with the oldest profession in the world, some punters took it into their violent minds that ponying up money gave them the right to batter a woman every which way. This tosser was worse because he'd got it into his thick skull that Rita owed him something special. Like passing on a bit of tasty info gave him bleedin' ownership rights over her body.

'Fucking hell.' She ran a shaky hand through her hair.

She was sick of this life. Sick of the leering men, the constant danger, the stench of river damp that never quite left her clothes. Once she'd helped Danny secure that bloody house on Molasses Quay, she was done. Done with him, done with the East End, done with it all.

It was time to set her sights higher. The West End was calling, with its posh shops and even posher gents. Rita could see it now: a rich husband, a gaff in Mayfair, respectability at last. No more groping hands and sweaty bodies.

No more fear.

But first, she had to finish what she'd started. Find out who Stiffington was paying, and why. Then she could leverage that information, help Danny get his precious house, and finally break free.

She inhaled a deep breath, steadying herself. She couldn't fall apart now. Not when she was so close.

Rita made her way to the small mirror above the dresser. Her mascara had run, leaving dark trails down her cheeks. She wiped them away, reapplying her slap with a steady hand.

'Pull yourself together, girl.' She glared at her reflection. 'You've come too far to crack now.'

Rita smoothed down her baby doll and checked her reflection one last time. The scared sixteen-year-old was gone, replaced by the hard-eyed woman who'd clawed her way up from nothing.

After putting on a dressing gown, she went to the upper deck and lit up an Embassy. The night air was cool on her flushed skin, carrying the rank smell of the Thames and the distant rumble of the city.

Rita took a final drag of her cigarette, her mind racing with plans and possibilities. A grim smile played on her lips while she flicked the butt into the murky waters below.

Why would Mortimer Stiffington be paying money to someone every month?

Chapter Thirty-Nine

The money was gone. In his bedroom, Danny rifled through his wallet for the third time. The crisp notes he'd counted out last night weren't there, vanished like cargo off a docker's hook. He knew exactly how much should've been there, but all his hand found now was thin air.

His teeth ground together. There was going to be all-out murder in this house by the time he was finished!

Grim-faced, shoving the wallet into his back pocket, Danny thundered down the stairs, each step vibrating with his growing anger. In the kitchen, Iris was busy at the stove, the smell of bacon filling the air. Chrissie was at the table.

'Morning, Danny-boy,' his sister drawled, lounging back in all her glory like she was Elizabeth Taylor in Cleo-fucking-patra.

Well, that's what it seemed like to Danny. She took out a new Du Maurier from her fancy gold cigarette case with an exaggerated flourish, tapping it twice like she'd seen them do in the pictures before slipping it into her long black holder with practiced elegance.

'Your face is all wonky, like your Y-fronts are a bit far up the ole bum-aroo, bruv.' She suddenly peered at him intently through a cloud of smoke, her expression changing to one of real concern. 'You all right?'

Ignoring her, Danny settled his full attention on his wife. 'Has anyone been in our room?'

Iris glanced over her shoulder, brow furrowed. 'No one but me. Why?'

'Because there's money missing from my wallet,' he seethed, low and dangerous. 'A fair bit of it, too.'

An ominous silence fell over the kitchen, save for the crack and sizzle of bacon in the pan. Chrissie pulled the Du Maurier from its holder, stubbing it out deliberately slow and theatrical, a shadow masking her features. 'You probably spent it down the River Rat. You've been having a lot of meetings with your men down there lately.'

Danny's temper went on the rise, and he rounded on his sister. 'I ain't some divvy who can't keep track of his own dough. There was no thieving in this house before you showed up.'

'Tea-leafing?' Chrissie shot daggers at him. 'You better not be pointing your fucking finger at me.'

'I think you know bloody well what I'm implying,' Danny growled.

Iris stepped between them, spatula in hand like a peace offering. 'Now, now! Let's not jump to conclusions. I'm sure there's a perfectly reasonable explanation.'

But Danny appeared to be beyond reason. Days of pent-up frustration at the uninvited appearance of his sister came pouring out. 'Reasonable? There's nothing reasonable about this one.' He jabbed his thumb at Chrissie. 'She blows in here, eats our food, sleeps under our roof, and this is how she repays us?'

Chrissie rose with a deliberate slowness, her full figure clinging to the seams of the tight dress she wore. 'Big words from the big man,' she sneered. 'King of the Docks, are ya? More like king of jumping to the wrong conclusion.'

Danny raved back. 'Going around with your nose in the air like being banged up at Holloway was a stint up at Butlins.'

The words hung in the air, heavy and poisonous.

For the first time, Chrissie looked uncertain. 'Holloway? Who said I've been in Holloway?'

Danny laughed with not an ounce of humour. 'Do you really think I swallowed that cock-and-bull about you being on the continent? Word reached me months back about my baby sis being banged up.'

Chrissie's face contorted with rage. 'You bastard!' she hissed. 'After everything I've been through, you dare accuse me?'

She lunged at him, talon-like nails ready to rake across his face. But Danny managed to stumble back.

Spatula still in hand, a shocked Iris tried to get between them again, crying out, 'Stop it! Both of you!'

They took not a blind bit of notice of her, and no wonder, because when the Steele siblings were going at each other's throats, even the Second Coming wouldn't stop them. Storming forward, Danny grabbed his sister's wrists, holding her at arm's length.

'You want to have a go, do you?' He spat out between clenched teeth. 'Fine by me! Let's take this outside and give the neighbours something to gawk at, eh?' He dragged a kicking and swearing Chrissie towards the door.

Wringing her hands, Iris again tried to calm the situation. 'Danny, please! Think about the neighbours.'

'I don't give two fucks about the neighbours. In fact, let's give them a proper show like they're in the front row down The Palladium.'

With one hand he threw open the front door.

Iris pleaded one more time. 'Danny, think about what you're doing.'

But her husband was beyond thinking. All he knew was the red mist of anger clouding his vision and the feel of his tea-leafing sister struggling against him.

They burst out onto the street, the morning sun casting long shadows across the weathered brick of the terraced houses. A few early risers stopped to watch, and Danny could almost hear the curtains twitching up and down the street.

He released Chrissie, who staggered back, her blonde hair a dead ringer for a bird's nest around her face.

'Go on then,' she taunted. 'Show everyone what a top man you are, beating on your little sister.'

'I ain't going to lay a finger on ya,' Danny spat. 'But I want you gone. Now. You're not welcome here no more.'

A small crowd had gathered, keeping a respectful distance. Danny was aware of the whispers, the sideways glances. He was the King of the Docks, respected and feared in equal measure, but even kings had their dirty laundry, and his was currently on full, filthy display for all to see.

Chrissie laughed, a harsh, bitter sound. 'Gone? Where am I supposed to go? Back into the arms of Her Majesty's pleasure?'

'I don't give a monkey's arse where you go,' Danny roared. 'You've outstayed your welcome, you light-fingered cow!'

The accusation hung in the air, and Danny saw something flicker in Chrissie's eyes. Hurt maybe, or guilt. But it was gone in an instant, replaced by that familiar defiance.

'You want me gone?' Chrissie sneered. 'Fine. But don't think this is over, Danny Steele. You'll regret this, mark my words.'

Danny turned on his heel, storming back into the house, past his wife who stood with her back against the hallway wall. He bounded up the stairs two at a time to Chrissie's room where he snatched her battered suitcase, hurled it onto the bed and ripped it open. Then he proceeded to yank open drawers and the wardrobe, wrenching out clothes. Dresses, undergarments, stockings, blouses, he threw them in the suitcase in one big jumbled mess of fabric and fury.

Iris appeared in the doorway, pale, expression riddle with consternation. 'Love, please. This isn't the way.'

He slammed the suitcase shut, the clasps barely containing its overstuffed contents. With a grunt, he hefted it to the window, throwing it open with his free hand.

Outside, Chrissie stood in the middle of the street, arms crossed, cheeks scalded red with rage. The small crowd of onlookers had grown, faces both familiar and strange turning up to watch the drama unfold.

'Oi, Chrissie!' Danny bellowed. 'Here's your bleedin' luggage!'

With a heave, he sent the suitcase sailing out of the window. It arced through the air before crashing to the pavement at Chrissie's feet. The impact sent the clasps flying open, spilling her belongings across the street. A gasp went up from the crowd. Chrissie stood stock-still, staring at the sad pile of her possessions.

Face hot with exertion and anger, Danny leaned out of the window. 'And don't think of coming back, you hear? You're done in this house!'

For a moment, Chrissie didn't move. Then, with a dramatic twist of her mouth and taking her sweet time, she scooped up her scattered belongings and carefully placed them in her suitcase. Straightening up, she pulled out her compact and a deep-red lipstick, raising her head. Her eyes locked with her brother's. Then she carefully applied her lippy. He felt a chill run down his spine. There was something in her movements, not just anger or hurt, but something colder, more calculating.

'You'll be sorry, Danny,' she called, her voice carrying clearly in the hushed street. 'Payback's coming, bruv.'

Then his sister and her suitcase were gone.

Danny slumped against the window frame, the adrenaline draining out of him. He became aware of Iris' presence behind him, could feel the weight of her disappointment without turning to look at her.

'Was that really necessary?' she quietly enquired behind him, a heavy note of exasperation in her tone.

Danny didn't answer. His eyes were fixed on the spot where Chrissie had vanished, a gnawing feeling in his gut telling him this was far from over.

Outside, the gawkers began to disperse, no doubt eager to start whispering with relish on the East End gossip vine. The shenanigans at his gaff would no doubt be the talk of the docks by lunchtime. Danny didn't give an effing monkey's.

Still, his sister's words echoed in his mind, a promise and a threat rolled into one.

'You'll be sorry, Danny. Payback's coming. bruv.'

Chapter Forty

'We don't want to kill a copper. Not yet anyway.'

The command rumbled from Batters as he towered over the terrified man kneeling before him. He was gathered with a few of his men and Lucas inside one of the salt warehouses in Sugar Cane Wharf. The unfortunate man was a detective sergeant, one of several bent coppers in his pocket. Greedy bastards, the lot of them, in his opinion. Always happy to look the other way for a brown envelope stuffed with enough for a little drink. But this one had been holding out on him, and that wouldn't do.

So Batters had him kneeling on jagged rock salt crystals digging deeper into his shredded knees. The cop's face twisted in raw agony with every tiny movement, grinding the salt further into his wounds, sending white-hot flashes of pain shooting up his legs.

Salt warehouses stank of the sea, even this far up the Thames. Perfect place for teaching lessons to those who thought they could play him for a fool.

'One more time.' Leisurely puffing on his Montecristo Cuban cigar, Batters circled his prey, boots crunching on the crystalline floor. 'What are these whispers I'm hearing about top brass Hawthorne's motor going walkies?'

The cop's split lips trembled. 'I swear on my life—'

Lucas, Batters' ever-present shadow, obliged with a solid kick that sent the man face-first into the salt. Rough crystals found every cut, every scrape on his face, causing him to shriek which echoed off the warehouse walls. The salt seared into his wounds like liquid fire, drawing another blood-curdling scream from deep in his gut.

Music to Batters' ears.

'Wrong answer,' he grunted around his cigar.

His son grabbed a fistful of hair, yanking their victim's head back. Salt clung to the blood on the copper's face. Tears streamed down his cheeks, cutting trails through the bloody salt.

After a couple of leisurely puffs, Batters carried on. 'See, you've been on my payroll long enough to know better. When I hear about some high-ranking copper's motor getting nicked, and him wanting it back, lively-like, and you suddenly go quiet on me?' He clicked his tongue. 'That's not how our arrangement works.'

Blood and spittle dribbled down the man's chin. 'Please… Mr Rogers…'

'Calling me Mr Rogers won't save your worthless hide.'

Lucas pulled his knuckleduster from his pocket, sliding it on with practiced ease. The brass gleamed dully in the weak light filtering through grimy windows.

'Now, how about we try this again?'

The man's eyes bulged at the sight. The punch that followed caught him in the ribs. The force sent him sprawling sideways into the salt. His howl of agony filled the warehouse as salt crystals went into his fresh cuts and gouges, setting every nerve ending on fire. He thrashed helplessly, which only worked the salt deeper into his wounds.

'The way I hear it,' Batters casually informed his captive, 'is someone's been given the job of finding that motor. And you know who it is.'

'I was keeping my head down!' The guy wheezed through broken teeth, choking on his own screams. 'Trying to stay alive!'

Batters grabbed him by the throat, forcing his face closer to the salt-covered floor. 'Keep your head down any longer and you'll be eating this lot.'

'Danny Steele!' the cop finally choked out. 'It's Danny fucking Steele! Commander Hawthorne's got a friend who's connected to Danny. This friend has got Steele hunting for the car and those that took it.'

Batters' hand went slack. He straightened slowly, exchanging a surprised glance with his son.

Danny Steele. Now that was interesting.

'Gov! Gov'nor!' a voice yelled.

Batters turned to find one of his younger lads, a scrawny kid named Ray, jogging towards him, out of breath.

Batters was annoyed. 'This had better be important.'

Ray doubled over, hands on his knees, gasping for air. 'There's a certain someone at the Dockside Devil, Boss. You're gonna want to see this.'

The River Rat was Danny Steele's HQ, and the Dockside Devil, on the other side of the wharf, was Batters'.

Batters squinted. 'That's what a boozer is. It has folk drinking in it.'

'Nah.' The lad shook his head. 'The Dockside Devil has never had this person in it before.'

Batters was getting tired of this runaround. The boy was that close to earning himself a clip around that stupid noodle of his. 'Spit it the bollocks out.'

Hesitating, the young man leaned in close his boss, clearly nervous about delivering the news, and finally told him in a hushed tone.

Batters went stock-still. All manner of thoughts stormed through his head. He yanked the boy by the front of his work shirt. 'You sure?'

The boy did a quick cross over his heart. 'Swear on my life. With my own eyes, I seen it.'

Gently, letting him go, Batters smiled so wide his gold molars were on display. A golden goose might've just fallen into his lap.

***

When Batters entered the Dockside Devil the place went deathly quiet. There was always a silence that accompanied his entrance, but the quiet today was different. Those present must've picked up on his mood, that something was different, because their attention today was sharp and expectant. Like they sensed something bad was going to go down. And, no wonder; they all knew who the unexpected person currently hunched at the bar was.

Batters' self-satisfied gaze fixed on the figure, the only one who wasn't giving him the eye. Even from behind, he'd recognise that bottle-blonde hair and curvaceous figure anywhere.

Chrissie Steele.

Squaring his shoulders, he strutted over, a signal for the customers to start chatting again and, more importantly, to mind their own business.

He sidled up right next to her. 'Well, well, well. If it ain't little Chrissie Steele. To what does the Dockside Devil owe this pleasure?'

Chrissie turned to face him, and Batters felt a jolt of surprise. The years hadn't been kind to her. Oh, she was still a stunner, no doubt about that, but there was a hardness to her features now, a weariness in her eyes that spoke of a life lived way too fast.

'Batters.' She let out a sad smile, the lines fanning at the corners of her eyes. 'Long time no see.'

'Aye, that it is.' He motioned to the barman for a drink. 'Heard you were back in our neck of the woods.

I must admit I never thought to see you in this part of the Wharf.'

Eyes suddenly flashing, she took a deep swig from her glass, the muscles in her throat working. 'Just fancied a change of scenery. That a crime now?'

Batters chuckled, laying on the charm. ''Course not, love. My house is your house and all that bollocks. But I can't help but wonder why you'd choose my boozer, of all places. Your brother and I ain't exactly on the best of terms, if you catch my drift.'

She slammed down her glass, her features screwed up into a snarl. 'That bastard can rot in Hell for all I care.'

Interesting!

Batters shifted his elbow closer. 'Trouble in paradise, eh? What's ole Danny gone and done now?'

For a moment, Chrissie seemed to war with herself, clearly unsure whether to confide in him. Then, like a dam bursting, it all came pouring out.

'The effing prick threw me out!' she spat, ugly and hurt. 'After everything I've done for him, after all the shit I've put up with over the years. Says I'm nothing but trouble.' Her gaze was wild with fury. 'He accused me of stealing from him. I'm a lot of things, but I ain't no tea leaf.'

Batters listened, nodding sympathetically while she ranted and raved. He could see the pain beneath her anger, the vulnerability she was trying so hard to hide. In normal circumstances he might feel sorry for her but she was a Steele. That name was poison in his mouth, bitter with years of festering bad blood between them. The Steeles had taken everything that mattered, piece by bloody piece. His precious Mini, choosing Jimmy over her own flesh and blood. And that wasn't the only wound. There was one that went years farther back than that. Too old and deep to think about.

If there was a rift between brother and sister, this could be the leverage he needed to finally get one over on Danny. Maybe Chrissie knew about her brother looking for Commander Hawthorne's car?

But Batters had to play this smart.

He tutted with mock sympathy. 'That's rough.' He placed one of his huge, meaty hands on her arm, a gesture of comfort. 'Your own flesh and blood turning on you like that. What's the world coming to? Where are you staying now?'

Chrissie's shoulders slumped. 'Nowhere. I've got hardly any money. No place to go.' She trailed off, biting her lip, looking lost and alone.

Batters saw his chance and seized it. 'Now, we can't have that, can we? A classy bird like you sleeping rough? No, that won't do at all.'

He paused, making a show of considering his options. 'Tell you what, why don't you come and rest your weary head at my drum for a bit? I've got plenty of room, and it's the least I can do for an old friend.'

Her eyes widened in surprise. 'You'd do that for me?' Abruptly, her expression stiffened. Lengthening her neck, she told him flat out, 'If you're thinking about me becoming a football between you and Danny, you'd better think again.'

He played it like he was genuinely upset, his hand leaving her arm and covering his heart. 'Me? Mug you off? Never.' A twinkle entered his gaze. 'Don't forget I remember when you used to run around as a young 'un with no knickers on.'

Chrissie let out a gasp of pretend outrage and elbowed him good-naturedly in the side. 'I most certainly did not.'

Batters gave her his most charming smile, softening the harsh angles of his face. 'I've always had a soft spot for you. What d'you say?'

For a long moment, Chrissie assessed him, searching for any sign of deception. Then, slowly, she nodded. 'All right. You're on. Thank you, Batters. I mean it.'

As they finished their drinks and prepared to leave, Batters felt a surge of triumph. He'd done it. He'd got Danny Steele's sister under his roof, and with her, a wealth of potential information. This could be the key to finally bringing Danny down and cementing his control over the docks.

Guiding Chrissie out of the pub with a gentle hand on her lower back, Batters couldn't keep the satisfied grin off his face. Oh yes, things were looking up indeed. Danny Steele wouldn't know what hit him.

Chapter Forty-One

Sin screamed her head off. She and Brother Bertie hurtled down the Helter Skelter. The world spun in a blur of red and white stripes, punctuated by flashes of Brighton's bustling pier below. She nestled between Bertie's legs, his strong hands gripping her shoulders, their bodies pressed close on the rough hemp mat.

'Hold tight!' he shouted, his deep laugh rumbling against her back.

The wooden slide rattled beneath them as they whizzed round and round. Sin's heart raced, a giddy mixture of fear and exhilaration. Nearing the bottom, she leaned back into Bertie's chest, savouring his warmth, his scent. His grip tightened, protective and thrilling all at once. They hit the final turn with a jolt that sent them airborne for a split second before crashing onto the landing mat in a tangle of limbs and laughter.

Breathless and dizzy, Sin turned to Bertie, his face split by that gorgeous grin she adored. In his eyes, she saw the same wild joy she felt. Sod the rest of the world. Right now, this was all that mattered.

Sin stumbled off the slide on wobbly legs, giggling uncontrollably. Bertie caught her, pulling her close.

'All right there, baby?' he murmured, dark eyes twinkling with mischief.

Sin grinned up at him, still breathless. 'Never better.'

Hand in hand, they strolled along Brighton Pier, the setting sun painting the sky in brilliant shades of orange and pink. Sin marvelled at how natural it felt, being here with Bertie. No furtive glances over their shoulders because they feared being spotted by someone who knew them. Just two young lovers enjoying a day out at the seaside.

For the past few weeks, they'd been meeting almost every day, in his friend's place in Soho. They couldn't get enough of each other. Each time they made love it seemed to be with more aching desperation. This trip to Brighton felt like coming up for air after being underwater for too long.

'Fancy a bite?' Brother Bertie asked, nodding towards a chippy.

Sin's stomach growled in response. 'Starving.'

They joined the queue, Sin nestling comfortably against Bertie's chest.

An elderly couple in front of them smiled indulgently.

'Young love,' the woman said to her husband. 'Reminds me of us, back in the day.'

Sin felt a warm glow of pride. This was how it should be, she thought. Just two people in love, no different from anyone else. She remembered Kath's words from a few weeks ago, about a future where people could love freely, without judgment. It had seemed like a beautiful dream then, and now, in this moment, it felt tantalisingly close to reality. Plus, it also reminded Sin that not everyone was against their type of love. These small moments of acceptance were precious, little lights in the darkness.

As they sat on a bench overlooking the beach, tucking into their steaming parcels of fish and chips, a group of lads swaggered past. One of them did a double-take, his face twisting into an ugly sneer.

'You! Yeah, you!' he called out to Brother Bertie. 'You lost or something? Jungle's that way!'

His mates sniggered, emboldened by his cruelty.

Another chimed in, 'What you doing with one of our women, eh?'

Sin felt her lover stiffen beside her. She gripped his arm, heart pounding, and urgently whispered, 'Ignore them.'

But the men weren't done. They formed a loose circle around the bench, leering and jeering.

'What's the matter, sweetheart?' one taunted Sin. 'Couldn't find a proper English bloke?'

'Piss off!' Sin spat, fury rising in her chest.

The ringleader's eyes narrowed dangerously. 'What did you say, you little—'

In a flash, Brother Bertie was on his feet, his fist connecting solidly with the bastard's jaw. The crack of bone meeting bone echoed in Sin's ears.

The others lunged forward, but Brother Bertie was ready. He might not have Jimmy's raw power, but years of sparring in the ring had honed his reflexes to a razor's edge. He ducked under a wild swing, coming up with a vicious uppercut that sent another attacker reeling.

Sin watched in horror and awe as Bertie weaved and bobbed, his movements fluid and precise. He landed a flurry of quick jabs to one lad's ribs, driving the wind from him. Another rushed in, only to be met with a devastating hook that dropped him out cold.

But there were too many of them. While Brother Bertie grappled with one, another caught him with a glancing blow to the temple. Sin saw a flash of red as blood trickled down his face. He stumbled backwards, momentarily dazed.

'Bertie!' Sin cried out.

She grabbed an empty bottle from a nearby bin, brandishing it like a club.

The sight of her armed seemed to give Bertie a second wind. He shook his head, clearing the fog, and reached into his jacket. The small revolver appeared in his hand as if by magic.

The sight of it stopped the thugs in their tracks. Even the ringleader, nursing his bruised jaw, took a step back.

'Back. The. Fuck. Off.' Brother Bertie's voice was low and dangerous.

For a tense moment, no one moved. Sin could hear her own heartbeat pounding in her ears. Then, muttering curses, the group began to retreat.

'Fucking animals,' one spat as they slunk away.

Sin sagged with relief, her legs trembling. Brother Bertie tucked the gun away and turned to her, his eyes full of concern.

'You all right, baby?'

She nodded shakily, unable to speak. He pulled her close, and she buried her face in his chest. However, she didn't stay there long, snapping her face up.

'We've got to get out of here before someone calls the coppers.'

On the train, Brother Bertie tried to guide Sin to a pair of seats, but she hesitated.

'Maybe we should sit separately,' she said quietly, hating herself for the words even as they left her mouth.

Hurt flashed across Bertie's face, quickly replaced by understanding. 'If that's what you want.'

Sin watched him make his way down the carriage, throat tight with unshed tears. In misery, she sank into her own seat

Her stomach churned with self-loathing. She was caving, bowing to the pressure of narrow-minded tossers instead of standing tall. What kind of coward was she? It wasn't her way to run scared instead of facing the world head-on. She'd always prided herself on being a fighter, on sticking two fingers up at anyone who tried to push her around. Now here she was, ready to shove their precious love away just because some pricks couldn't handle seeing them together. It made her skin crawl with shame.

Sin felt like she was betraying not just Bertie, but everything she believed in. She was crucifying the memory of every brave soul who'd fought for change, every couple who'd weathered the storm of prejudice before them. The taste of her own weakness was bitter, threatening to choke her.

Chrissakes! This was 1967!

The world had colour tellies and was showcasing the future of supersonic planes, but a black man and a white woman couldn't walk down the street together without fear.

It was madness. She glanced down the carriage to where Bertie sat, his handsome profile silhouetted against the window. Sin ached to go to him, to curl up in the safety of his arms. But the memory of those hateful men held her back.

Chapter Forty-Two

Gertie stood before the mirror, her nimble fingers adjusting her trademark vibrant red, gold, and green wrap that adorned her head. She paused, examining her reflection with a critical eye. The gravity of her mission today was evident in the determined compression of her lips and the steely glint in her deep-brown eyes. Satisfied with her appearance, she picked up her well-worn leather frame handbag and stepped out into the bustling streets of Whitechapel.

Striding purposefully towards the Underground station, Gertie passed the familiar group of winos who often congregated outside. One of them, a wiry man with an alcohol-seasoned complexion, raised a bottle of VP wine in salute.

'Mornin', Gertie!' his slurred words rang out, his bloodshot eyes squinting. 'Lookin' mighty serious today. Everything all right?'

Everyone knew Gertie in this part of the East End, including the drunks outside the station. Unlike others, she didn't sniff or raise her nose in the air at them. In her eyes they were God's children, too. When they wanted something to eat they knew a bellyful of homemade food would always be waiting for them at her back door.

Managing a tight smile, Gertie briskly nodded. 'Charlie, sometimes life is in God's hands. While at other times you can't wait for the Lord to come along and so have to get things done yourself.'

She didn't slow her pace, leaving the men to their cheap booze and idle chat. Gertie rarely ventured Up West, and for good reason. The city's posh districts, with their glitzy shops and trendy cafés, felt like a world apart from east London's close-knit community. Plus, as a God-fearing woman, she couldn't shake the feeling that beneath all that sparkle, Satan himself was at work, especially in the seedy streets of Soho come nightfall. But today, she had no choice.

Less than an hour later, Gertie eyed Leicester Square Tube's escalators warily. She never did trust those moving stairs, with their endless wooden teeth and relentless motion. Each time she stepped onto them, she whispered a fervent prayer of deliverance to the Almighty, asking for safe passage through this unnatural contraption.

Outside, Gertie took a moment to get her bearings in Soho. The streets here were a riot of colour and sound, with people parading about in the latest styles and fashion. She consulted the scrap of paper where she'd jotted down the address of Sin's workplace, a trendy hair salon catering to the young and hip.

Approaching the sleek storefront, Gertie could hear the sweet, soulful sound of Lulu singing, 'To Sir With Love' coming from inside. Stepping in, she entered a world that was completely different to the one she knew with furniture that, in her opinion, looked plain bad for your back. The salon was packed, doing a very brisk trade.

Amidst the bustle of stylists and clients, it was Dilly, Kath's sister, who first noticed Gertie's arrival. She tugged Kath's top to get her attention and nodded towards the entrance. Kath's eyes widened at the incongruous sight of Gertie, resplendent in her eye-grabbing hair wrap, standing amidst the sea of fashionable Londoners.

Hurrying over, she greeted Gertie with an uneasy smile. 'Gertie! What a surprise. Is everything all right?'

Gertie fixed Kath with a steady gaze. 'I need to speak with Cynthia. It's important.'

Kath lost her smile, sensing the gravity in Gertie's tone. 'Let me fetch her for you,' she offered, her concern clear in her tone.

After the younger woman's departure, Gertie felt the curious stares of the other clients and stylists boring into her. Lengthening her neck, compressing her lips, she refused to be cowed by their scrutiny. She was here for Bertram, and no amount of curious glances could deter her from her purpose.

'Love the headscarf!' a young, smiling stylist exclaimed, pausing with scissors poised. 'That red-and-gold pattern with the green is absolutely fab. Did you get it from Portobello?'

Before Gertie could answer, another girl chimed in, 'The colours are groovy! Really out there.'

'It's bang on trend,' the first stylist declared. 'Everyone's going mad for prints this season.'

Momentarily wrong-footed by their genuine enthusiasm, Gertie was speechless. She'd expected sideways looks, not compliments. Nevertheless, she was glad when Sin emerged, her form-fitting capri trousers showing off her tiny waist and shapely legs. Surprise flickered across her face, quickly replaced by a guarded expression.

'What brings you here?' Sin warily questioned, alarm lighting her eyes, too.

Gertie inclined her head towards the back of the salon. 'We need to talk. Privately.'

Sin hesitated, glancing around at the watchful eyes of her colleagues. 'Let's go to the kitchen.'

The two women wound their way through the salon, past the rows of vinyl and leather styling chairs and the hum of hair dryers. Once in the small kitchen, Sin turned to face Gertie, arms crossed defensively over her chest.

'What's this about, Gertie?' Sin's words carried a hint of rebellion.

Gertie met Sin's gaze unflinchingly. 'It's about you and Bertram. I know what's been going on between you two,' she stated bluntly.

Sin's eyes widened, a flash of panic crossing her features before she schooled them into a mask of indifference. 'I don't know what you're talking about,' she managed, strain evident in every word.

'Don't play games with me, girl,' Gertie warned, the words low and serious. 'I don't know where you and him went the other day, but he's not been himself since.'

Sin's face crumbled, her shoulders sagging. She averted her gaze. 'Brighton,' she whispered, so softly Gertie could barely hear it. 'We went to Brighton.'

Gertie's gut clenched, remembering the haunted look in her brother's eyes when he'd returned home. She didn't know the details, but she could guess at the ugliness they must have encountered. She'd known something terrible had gone on because when she'd tried to tempt him with her salt fish fritters, one of her homemade treats he couldn't get enough of, he hadn't wanted to know, locking himself away in his room.

'Look, child,' Gertie softened slightly. 'You know how tings run. A black man and a white woman together... it's pure madness and trouble.'

Sin's head snapped up, her eyes blazing with bold insolence. 'I don't care what people think!' The words burst from her. 'I love him, Gertie. And he loves me.'

Gertie's anger surged, hot and intense.

Did this girl have rice and peas for brains!

Her next words lashed into Sin with the sting of a whip. 'You listen to me, young lady. You have no idea what it's like, walking down these streets with skin like mine.' Rage trembled through each syllable. 'The stares, the whispers, the hatred in some eyes. It's like I'm invisible and a threat all at once.'

Her hands clenched into fists, straining at her sides. 'I've been spat on, called names that would make your ears bleed. I've had doors slammed in my face and been turned away from shops just for being who I am.' She jabbed a finger at Sin, dropping to a low, intense whisper that vibrated with emotion. 'But I keep my head high because I know my worth. I won't let ignorance and hate break me.'

Gertie sighed heavily, the weight of her next words settling on her shoulders like a physical burden. 'If you don't give him up,' she pressed each word slowly, deliberately, 'then you will be the ruin of my brother.'

Sin recoiled, the blood suddenly deserting her face. 'You can't mean that,' she choked out, barely able to form the words.

'I do,' Gertie affirmed, though her heart ached at the anguish in Sin's eyes. 'Bertram's got a good heart, but he's not built for the kind of trouble this will bring. I know he'll have told you about what's happening with his little girl. He doesn't need more problems in his life.'

Sin's lower lip trembled, her eyes glistening with unshed tears. 'I can't just stop loving him, Gertie. I can't.' The words broke from her, cracked and raw.

The song playing in the salon changed to 'Standing in the Shadows of Love' by The Four Tops.

Gertie reached out, clasping Sin's hands in her own work-roughened ones. 'Sometimes, loving someone means doing what's best for them, even if it breaks your own heart.'

Sin yanked her hands back, her eyes flashing with a turbulent mix of anger and despair. 'You don't understand. Bertie, he's the only one who sees me for who I really am,' she burst out. 'Not just Danny Steele's daughter or some East End dolly bird with a pretty face. He sees my heart, my soul.'

Gertie's heart twisted painfully at the despair laid bare before her. She understood all too well the yearning for a love that saw beyond the surface, that accepted and cherished the true self hidden beneath. But she also knew the cruel realities of the world they lived in.

'I know it feels like your whole world is wrapped up in him right now,' Gertie murmured with painful compassion. 'But you've got to think of his future, too. What kind of life can you two have together? Always looking over your shoulders? Always waiting for the next ugly word or fist to come flying?'

Sin flinched, her body vibrating with intensity. 'I can't give him up. It would be like cutting out my own heart,' she rasped. 'I love him more than anything in this world. And I won't let anyone take that away from me. Not even you.'

Gertie straightened her shoulders, her expression hardening with resolve. And stepped back. 'Then you mark my words,' the warning rang with dire certainty. 'This love you say you have for him and he has for you -- it will destroy you both.'

Her final words were ones Sin would never forget.

'You will watch as love turns to hate.'

Chapter Forty-Three

'Come in,' Danny barked after the sharp rap on the door of his office at the back of the River Rat. He was sitting behind his massive desk, the polished surface gleaming under the glow of the yellow light. Less than a minute ago, his meaty fist had slammed down, rattling the contents of the desk.

'Bloody useless!' he'd snarled, his scarred cheek contorting with rage.

Two weeks had passed, and the trail on the car thief hadn't just gone cold, it was Baltic. His reputation was on the line, and with Lord Xander of all people. He was the last person he wanted to appear useless in front of.

Something was doing his head in, big time. Eating away at him, turning his thoughts dark and restless. His gut had never been wrong in the decades of running criminal rackets through the East End, and right now it was screaming that he was missing something critical. Something staring him right in the bloody face.

His visitor was Pete, his teenage runner. The lad's eyes were large with excitement, with a touch of awe staring at who he considered to be the most powerful man in the East End. He swallowed hard, Adam's apple bobbing.

'Spit it out!' Danny wasn't in the mood.

Pete's reply tumbled out. 'I got word on them car thieves, boss.'

Danny stiffened. 'Who is it?'

'It's not one. There are two of them.'

Danny mulled that surprising drop of information. He and everyone else had assumed it was one toerag they were after.

'What else?' he added, suspecting that Pete hadn't finished his tale.

'These two bokes are young.' Confidence pushed Pete closer to his boss. 'One's white, the other, coloured.'

The words hit Danny like a sledgehammer to the gut. His mind raced. A white lad and a black lad working together? His brain kicked into gear because that was a very unusual combination in 1960s London. Then the realisation hit of what he'd been told. It was like his head was being held underwater, stealing his breath.

Nah! No way! It couldn't be.

Not his Jimmy and that Watson lad?

If he hadn't been sitting down Danny would've staggered back. He gripped the edge of his desk until his knuckles were a ghostly white.

Have I been hunting my own son all this time?

'You sure about this?' The words came out weak, sounding unreal to his ears.

Pete nodded but clearly confused by the way all the colour had drained from his gaffer's face. He didn't understand what he'd said wrong. He'd only been doing his job, keeping his eyes and ears open like the bossman had told him. Truth be told, at eighteen, despite growing up in Sugar Cane Wharf, he was still green to the darker sides of gangland politics. His mum still made him jam sarnies for his lunch. He hadn't yet learned how to spot when information could be a loaded gun.

Instead, his chest puffed out, swelling with pride that he was the one giving the King of the Docks this news.

'Dead sure. This old soak I know tells me that he saw a flash motor with a black and white guy inside being chased by the Old Bill down Piccadilly way a few weeks back.'

Danny's jaw clenched. He'd held a meeting almost the same time and cast his mind back to it. Yeah, Jimmy and Brother Bertie had been there, acting strange. Quiet. Shifty.

'Pete,' Danny's voice was dangerously calm. 'Does anyone else know about this info? About you coming to see me?'

The younger man shook his head. 'Apart from the drunk, whose sozzled most days, I came straight here to tell you. Thought you'd want to know right away.'

Pete stood a little taller, chin lifting, basking, in his eyes, in a giant's approval. He'd done good, and he knew it. The lad's hands, which had been fidgeting nervously at his sides, now rested easily in his pockets.

Danny's hard expression softened. 'Good lad. You did the right thing.'

A nervous smile broke across Pete's face, his cheeks growing rosy. 'Oh, and boss, I don't know if you heard, but me and Lizzie, we had our baby girl last week.'

Danny's face lit up. 'That right? Congratulations, son.'

He got up and clapped the younger man on the back. 'This calls for a celebration. Come on, I've got a special bottle in the back.' He placed his arm around his shoulder. 'Ever heard of Bowmore '64? Smooth as silk and rarer than hen's teeth. Just got a case off a ship from Scotland last week. Not even on the market yet, this stuff.'

Danny led Pete to the rear of the pub, where worn stone stairs descended to the murky Thames.

The Executioner's Steps.

As they reached the top of the stairs, Danny paused.

'You know, Pete,' he said casually. 'Loyalty's a funny thing. It's valuable. But it can also be dangerous.'

Before his runner could figure out what he meant, Danny shoved him hard.

Pete's arms windmilled uselessly in the air, a strangled cry escaping his lips. His body tumbled backwards and bounced off each stone step like a ragdoll. The final impact drove the air from his lungs in a harsh gasp. His neck snapped with a sickening crunch as he hit the bottom, head twisted at an impossible angle.

He lay misshapen and crooked on the shoreline of the river, limbs splayed and broken. One of his arms twitched, a last message from his shattered body, then went still.

Danny descended quickly, his alert gaze scanning the darkness, checking for witnesses. Satisfied it was just him, the rats, and river for company, he pulled a flask from his jacket and pried open Pete's lifeless mouth and poured whisky into it and splashed some over his clothes.

'Sorry, mate,' Danny muttered. 'Can't have loose ends.'

No one – no one – could know this business might involve Jimmy.

Might?

Who was he kidding.

He knew that his son was up to his neck in this as sure as he was standing over a dead body.

He arranged the body to look like a drunken fall. Mud squelching beneath his boots, Danny crouched at the river's edge and dipped his hands into the murky water to get rid of any blood and alcohol. Its coldness stung against his flesh, turning a dirty brown as he scrubbed Pete's blood from his skin.

He watched the crimson swirls disappear into the sluggish current, his face a mask of grim determination. The river had swallowed worse secrets than this. It would keep his, too.

The incoming tide slapped against Pete's body, already beginning to drag him towards the river's dark embrace.

Alone again in his office, Danny let his mind drift back. Fifteen years ago, on a dank evening down at these very docks.

Young Jimmy stood wide-eyed beside him. The Thames gushed at the wooden pilings, the water black and oily in the dim light. At their feet knelt a man, face bloodied and swollen.

'You see this sorry bastard, Jimmy?' Danny's voice was ice. 'Thought he could nick from us. From our family.'

The boy nodded, not fully grasping the gravity of the situation.

'In our world, family is all you've got,' Danny continued. 'We protect our own. And we punish those who betray us.' His gaze bored into his son. 'Even if it's family who does the betraying. You understand?'

Another nod, distress and confusion mingling in Jimmy's expression.

Danny grabbed the kneeling man by the hair, yanking his head back. 'Tell my boy what you did.'

'Please,' the man whimpered. 'I didn't.'

A vicious backhand silenced him. 'Tell him!'

'I… I stole from you,' the man choked out. 'From the family.'

Danny's grip tightened. 'And what happens to thieves in our world, Jimmy?'

Young Jimmy's voice trembled. 'They get punished.'

'That's right, son.' Danny's smile was cold. 'And you're going to help me. Show me you understand what family means.'

He thrust a length of heavy chain into Jimmy's small hands. The boy's eyes widened in horror.

'Dad, I… I can't.'

'You can and you will,' Danny snarled. 'Family first, Jimmy. Always.'

Stiffening, Jimmy stared at the chain. Then he looked nervously up to his father, his face stark white.

'Do it!' Danny deliberately commanded with force, because his son had to understand that in life sometimes you had to get your hands dirty.

Inhaling deeply, Jimmy turned to the kneeling man. Raised the chain high and whacked him in his head. Crying out, their captive wobbled but didn't fall.

'Harder!' Danny ordered.

This time when he raised the chain, Jimmy kept hitting. And hitting. What followed was a brutal lesson in loyalty and consequences. The sound of the chain striking flesh echoed across the empty docks, punctuated by the man's agonised screams and the gentle sloshing of the river.

When it was over, Danny took the bloodied chain from his son's shaking hands. He wrapped it around the barely conscious man's legs.

'Finish it, Jimmy,' he said softly. 'Push him in.'

Tears streamed down the boy's face, but he did as he was told. The splash was lost in the sound of a passing barge.

Danny put his hand on Jimmy's shoulder. 'That's my boy. Family first. Never forget.'

The memory faded, leaving Danny alone with his fury. A guttural roar tore from his throat. His arm swept across the desk, sending everything crashing to the floor. The framed photo of young Jimmy smashed against the wall.

He grabbed a fresh rum bottle, not bothering with a glass. The rich, brown liquid burned his throat, doing nothing to quell the inferno raging inside him.

His own flesh and blood, going behind his back? After everything he'd done for the boy? Taught him the rules of their world? Shown him what it meant to be a Steele?

Danny's grip tightened on the bottle. The neck shattered, shards of glass slicing into his palm. He barely noticed the blood dripping onto the old wooden floorboards.

'Ungrateful little prick,' he snarled, hurling the broken bottle against the wall where it exploded in a shower of glass and liquor. 'I'll fucking kill him,' he muttered, his voice rich with rage and betrayal. 'I'll wring his scrawny neck myself.'

Suddenly, Danny went still. Cleared his mind. Gulped in three shots of deep air. He'd learned this technique from an old sailor hailing from Thailand. You met all sorts through the docks. He had to think this through. Carefully and slowly. He began to prioritise.

Lord Xander was up first. He'd been needling Danny for the last week wanting to know his progress, wanting results. Danny had a big decision to make.

Would he tell Lord Xander that one of the thieves was his son?

And as for Jimmy and that smart-mouthed, headgear-wearing ponce sidekick of his.

Danny would choose his moment perfectly.

They wouldn't see him coming.

Chapter Forty-Four

Danny banged the heavy knocker against the glossy black door of the Grosvenor Square mansion. The posh neighbourhood stood in stark contrast to his East End roots, a reminder of the vast gulf between his two worlds.

The door opened, revealing a snooty-nosed butler who eyed Danny with thinly veiled contempt. 'The tradesmen's entrance is round the back.' He sniffed.

You fucking what?

Danny drew himself up to his full height. He'd have given this stuffed penguin a right-hander if they'd been anywhere else. 'I'm here to see the lord of the house. And I ain't no bollocks tradesman.'

The butler's eyes widened; he was clearly caught off-guard by Danny's threatening manner. He hesitated, mouth opening and closing like a fish out of water.

'Well?' Danny barked. 'You gonna let me in or leave me standing here doing an impression of a tom waiting for her next punter?'

Reluctantly, the butler stepped aside, allowing Danny to enter the opulent foyer. While the butler led him towards a small side room, a familiar voice called out from the grand staircase. 'Well, well. If it ain't the King of the Docks hisself.'

His head snapped up, Danny's alert gaze found Ruddy and her knowing expression. 'What you doing here?'

Ruddy descended the stairs, her features changing to one of curiosity. 'I could ask you the same thing?' Her shrewd expression swept him. 'All them rumours years back, seems they was true, after all'

'Mind your own business,' Danny grunted, but blood flushed his skin.

Unfazed by his outburst, Ruddy raised a calculating brow. 'Touch a nerve, did I?' She turned to the butler and told him, 'I'll take it from here.'

Looking more than relieved, after sending Ruddy a grateful nod, the butler left her to it.

Ruddy jerked her head towards a door off to the side. 'In there.' Then she became very serious. 'He's not going to be best pleased you've shown your face here.'

Danny shouldered past her, muttering a string of curses. The room he entered was small, clearly meant for less important visitors. The insult made him bristle.

Lord Xander burst through the door moments later, his normally perfectly coiffed hair slightly dishevelled, face flushed with seething annoyance.

'What the bloody hell do you think you're playing at, coming here? You know our business is always done at the club.'

Danny met his gaze unflinchingly. 'What's the matter? Ashamed everyone's gonna find out who I am?' He stared the other man square in the eye, struggling to keep a rein on the emotions kicking off inside him.

'Don't want anyone to hear about me being your wrong-side-of-the-blanket son?'

Panic drew the blood from the older man's face. He closed the door, hissing, 'Keep your voice down!'

'Why should I?' Danny challenged, years of pent-up resentment bubbling to the surface. 'Scared your toff mates will find out you knocked up one of your family's housemaids? Not once, but twice.'

Xander's face paled even further. 'That was a long time ago. I was young, frightened—'

'Frightened?' Danny scoffed. 'What about my mum? What about me and George? You think we weren't scared?'

The words hung heavy in the air between them. Danny's chest heaved, emotions he'd long suppressed threatening to crush him. He could feel his heart galloping, a lump forming in his throat. For a moment, he was that little boy again, desperate for his father's love and acknowledgement.

Suddenly, Danny caught a glimpse of himself in one of the room's ornate mirrors. The resemblance to Viscount Alexander Blacklock was startling. The same height, the same sharp jawline, the same brown eyes. But it was inside where the real likeness lay. In their cunning nature, the way they'd throw their loved ones under the bus to get what they were after. It hit him like a punch to the gut. He was more like this man than he cared to admit.

Danny continued, his biting tone becoming more savage. 'I had to hear it from the mouth of strangers at the club that my own father had got himself married.' He deliberately exaggerated his Cockney accent. 'Tied the knot with some pretty little piece from a family with loads of bread.'

His gaze snapped harshly around the room, taking in the expensive furnishings, the oil paintings on the walls. All the trappings of a life he'd been denied. His mother's face flashed in his mind. Her soft eyes, her gentle smile. She'd been so different from Xander, so innocent and caring.

Xander moved over to the small drinks cabinet and poured a stiff whisky without bothering to offer his son one. After taking two sips, he told Danny, 'I didn't have a choice. I had to get married because I need an heir.'

The familiar rage bubbled up in Danny's gut. 'What about the heir you already got?' His voice came out rough. 'Or don't I count for anything?'

Xander's smile never reached his eyes. 'Oh, come now. You can't seriously expect a housemaid's bastard to inherit the Blacklock title?' He studied his drink thoughtfully. 'The very notion. What would people say?'

Danny's hands curled into fists, nails digging deep into his palms. All those years he'd spent building his empire on the docks, becoming someone of consequence. For what? So his own father could look right through him?

'I built something,' Danny ground out. 'Made myself more than what you thought I'd be. While you've been pissing away your family's fortune.'

'Indeed you have.' Xander's tone dripped with venomous sarcasm. 'Strong-arming dockers, running protection rackets. Such entrepreneurial spirit.' His lips curved. 'My heir has got to be legitimate and come with blue blood in his veins.'

Each word was a knife in Danny's heart. He thought of his own boy, Jimmy. How many times had he cut Jimmy down, made him feel small? Christ, he was no better than this preening ponce in front of him.

'Your mother understood her position,' Xander mused, momentarily glancing into his drink. 'Sweet girl but practical. She never harboured silly notions about going above her station and marrying a member of one of Britain's finest families.'

Danny's vision blurred red. He could still remember her crying herself to sleep, thinking he couldn't hear. The scar on his cheek throbbed with every heartbeat.

'She was worth a hundred of your fancy birds.'

'Was she?' Xander's eyes glittered with calculated malice. 'Tell me, what exactly made her so special? Besides spreading her legs for the young master?'

Enraged, Danny went for him, but the door opening stopped him dead. A young woman with skin tanned from the outdoors and wide, innocent eyes. Danny instantly sussed who she was. Lady Prudence, his father's new and much younger bride.

To Danny's critical eyes she was nothing to write home about. Her mousy brown hair was pulled back in a style that did her no favours, emphasising her round, unremarkable face. She wore a dress that probably cost more than most families in Sugar Cane Wharf made in a lifetime, but it couldn't hide the fact she had the build of a bleedin' barrel.

Danny felt a surge of bitterness. This plain little number got to be on his father's arm, while he, flesh and blood, was treated like dirt on the old bastard's shoe. Money really could buy anything in this world. He refused to admit to himself that he was jealous of her.

'Oh!' she exclaimed, clearly startled to find the room occupied. 'I'm so sorry, I didn't realise you had company, darling.'

Xander's demeanour changed in an instant, his charm slipping back into place as smooth as his silk cravat. 'Not to worry, m'dear. This is an associate of mine. Daniel Steele.'

Lady Prudence's eyes lit up with friendliness. 'How lovely to meet you, Mr Steele. I don't believe

Xander's ever mentioned you before. How do you two know each other?'

Something inside Danny knotted at her words. Of course Xander had never mentioned him. Why would he mention his bastard boy?

'Business,' Danny replied gruffly. 'Just business.'

'I see,' Lady Prudence said, though her tone suggested she didn't see at all. 'Well, I won't keep you. It was lovely to meet you.' She nodded Danny's way.

When the door clicked shut behind her, Danny turned back to Xander. 'I see your young bride's brought you some newfound wealth,' he remarked, gesturing to the swanky surroundings.

Xander's jaw tightened. 'We're not here to discuss my personal affairs.'

'No,' Danny agreed. He cut off the pain. Froze out the past. 'We're here about the car.'

'Have you found it?'

Danny hesitated. The information he'd received burned in his gut. His own son, his Jimmy, involved in this mess. Could he really trade his flesh and blood for a scrap of approval from this man who'd never been a true father to him?

'I may be getting closer to the geezer who pulled this stunt.' No way on this earth was he handing his son over this man, of all people, on a plate. He'd get the car back and deal with Jimmy in his way. He expertly shifted the conversation. 'Why is this motor so important? It's all a touch fishy to me.'

Xander's expression became distant. 'What do you mean, fishy?'

'Just a feeling,' Danny replied. 'Seems like a lot of fuss over one car.'

'It's not just any car,' Xander snapped. He thought for a moment and then blurted out, 'Like I told you before, it belongs to Commander Hawthorne and he wants it back for sentimental reasons.' His lips pursed in displeasure. 'This matter has been dragging on for too long. It needs to be resolved. I assured Hawthorne that I had the right man for the job. Now if you're not up for it, I can always find someone else.'

'Yeah, yeah,' Danny muttered, already turning to leave. 'I know how to do my job. The car will be back with you soon, and the dickhead who took it won't be troubling anyone ever again.'

While he reached for the door handle, Xander's voice stopped him. 'Daniel?'

He paused, not turning back.

'I am proud of you, you know. In my own way.'

Danny's hand tightened on the doorknob, his throat constricting. For a fleeting moment, he was that little boy again.

He yanked the door open and strode out, ignoring the stares of two maids while he made his way to the front door. The cool air hit his face when he stepped outside, and he took a deep, shuddering breath.

Deliberately, he turned down a deserted side street, and his carefully cultivated mask crumbled. He slammed his fist into the brick wall, relishing the sharp sting of pain. Fuck. Why did the father who refused to acknowledge him still have such a hold on him? He was Danny Steele, for crying out loud. The

King of the bloody Docks. Bow and scrape to another human being? Fuck off!

Except, apparently, he did.

Then he banished his blood father from his mind and focused on his son. He'd protected Jimmy. For now. But at what cost? He had to get this mess sorted out before it blew up in his face.

Chapter Forty-Five

Iris heard the front door slam shut, the sound reverberating through the house. She tensed, her hands stilling over the pot of stew she'd been stirring. There was only one thing that made Danny come home in such a state.

She wiped her hands on her apron and stepped into the narrow hallway. He stood there, his broad shoulders hunched, his face a picture of hurt and fury. His eyes were bloodshot, sunken into dark hollows, and his jawline so tight she could almost hear his teeth grinding. The grooves around his mouth seemed deeper. It was an expression that spoke of a soul in torment, of a man grappling with demons he couldn't quite vanquish.

Iris' heart clenched. She'd seen that look too many times over the years.

'You've seen him, haven't you?' she asked softly.

They both knew who 'him' was. His bloody father.

His eyes meeting hers, the anguish in their depths made her want to weep. He didn't need to speak; his tortured expression said it all.

'Oh, hun.' Iris sighed, stepping closer. 'I can always tell. You're always the same way after seeing That Man.'

A bitter laugh escaped Danny's lips. 'That obvious, am I?'

Iris reached out, her fingers brushing against his cheek. 'Only to me.'

For a moment, Danny leaned into her touch, his eyes closing. Iris felt a flicker of the old warmth between them, a ghost of what they'd once shared. But then Danny stiffened, pulling away.

'I'm fine,' he muttered and shrugged off his coat. 'It's nothing.'

He trudged into the kitchen, slumping down heavily at the table. Iris followed, her heart aching at the sight of her once-proud husband appearing so defeated. She moved to the kettle, filling it and setting it to boil. A cuppa wouldn't solve anything, but it was all she knew to do in moments like these.

'Danny,' she said gently, preparing the cups. 'Talk to me. Please.'

He turned away, his fists clenching at his sides. 'What's there to say? I'm still not good enough, am I? Never have been, never will be.'

The bitterness in his voice made Iris flinch. 'That's not true—'

'Ain't it?' Danny's eyes blazed, even though his body remained slumped in the chair. 'I'm his firstborn, Iris. His fuckin' firstborn!'

Deep down, she'd always suspected that Danny's ruthless ambition, his drive to conquer the docks, came from a desperate need to prove himself. To show the world, to show That Man, that he was worth something. But seeing him like this, so exposed and vulnerable, brought home just how deeply that need ran.

Placing the steaming mug in front of him, Iris found herself lost in thought. How many times had she watched Danny tear himself apart, trying to live up to an impossible standard? How many nights had she lain awake, listening to him toss and turn, haunted by dreams of a life he could never have?

This obsession with being his father's heir was eating Danny alive. It had twisted him, turned him hard and cruel in ways that sometimes frightened her. The young man she'd fallen in love with was still in there, somewhere, but he was buried beneath layers of bitterness and hostility.

'He's got himself a posh new bride now,' Danny told her. 'Probably trying to breed her every night to get an heir on her. As if I don't even exist!'

She wanted to hold him, to soothe away the pain like she used to. But those days were long gone.

Her husband ran a hand through his hair, his shoulders sagging. 'I've built all this, haven't I?' He gestured vaguely, indicating their home, his empire beyond on the docks. 'I'm the King of the fuckin'

Docks. But to him… to him, I'll always be that dirty little secret. Me and George. The bastard brothers he wishes he could forget.'

Iris got pissed off on his behalf. 'You're worth a hundred of him. You always have been.'

For an instant, something softened in Danny's face. He looked at her, really looked at her, in a way he hadn't in years. 'Iris…'

He started to reach for her, and for a heartbeat, Iris thought he might pull her close, might kiss her with searing passion like he once had. A flicker of longing sparked within her, yearning for that connection they'd lost years back, when Sin was fifteen. But deep in her core, where all the hurt and betrayals festered, she froze.

Danny must have sensed it because his hand stopped, a flicker of regret passing over his features. The moment stretched between them, heavy with all the things left unsaid.

The sudden knock at the door startled them both. Danny's expression hardened, that moment of rare open emotion vanishing behind his usual expression of control.

'I'll get it.' He pushed up from the table.

Iris stayed in the kitchen, straining to hear. She caught snatches of Danny's voice, growing increasingly agitated. That was definitely their neighbour, Norma, he was talking to.

'You what?' she heard him exclaim.

Then, a while later, 'I don't bloody believe you!'

The conversation continued, too low for Iris to make out more words, but when Danny finally returned to the kitchen, Iris gasped. He was colourless, ashen and shaken. Whatever he'd heard at the door had rocked him to the core.

'Danny?' She wrung her hands, suddenly afraid. 'What's happened? Who did Norma want?'

For a long second, Danny said nothing. Then, very quietly, he spoke, his voice flat and devoid of feeling.

'Get Jimmy here. Now.'

Chapter Forty-Six

Sin floated through her front door, humming Gladys Knight & the Pip's 'I Heard It Through The Grapevine', heart still dancing from being with Bertie. She'd skipped most of the way home, giddy with happiness, feeling like the luckiest girl in all of London. But that feeling drained away the instant her gaze landed on the spot where her dad's boots should've been. Danny Steele was obsessive about his work boots, never walked through the house with them on, very particular about keeping the floors clean. Sin reckoned it was something to do with his upbringing, not that he ever talked about that.

Every last trace of her happiness evaporated. Her dad had his rituals, and fucking over his family was his biggest one – least in her eyes. With a long-suffering groan, she leaned heavily against the door, briefly closing her eyes. Whatever fresh aggro was brewing, she wanted no part of it. Probably something to do with the docks, she concluded.

She decided to slip quietly up the stairs to her room…

'Cynthia?' At the sound of her mum's questioning call coming from the sitting room, she froze on the second step. 'Be a love and come in here for a second.'

Why did her mum sound so upset? Tone so strained? All of a sudden she was breathless, a mix of fear and anxiety twisting in her lurching gut. If that bastard dad of hers had done something to upset her mum…

Sin saw red.

Her father appeared like the Devil in the sitting room doorway. His face was mottled, almost purpled with building rage. The cords in his neck strained against his skin, and his fists pumped by his sides.

'You've been seen, girl,' her father spat the accusation at her.

The ugly words changed the shape of his lips, leaving them crooked and gnarled, unrecognisable as his mouth.

Usually Sin would stand her ground, but this time there was something unnerving about the way he held his body that left her breathless. That cold expression in his gaze made her come over with icy dread.

Recovering, she tried to brush off the growing bad feeling with a dismissive slight roll of her eyes and a tut. 'You'll have to be a bit more specific than that.' Even though she knew it would royally wind him up, she was bolshy to the core, using her best posh-nosh voice. 'In my line of professional work, I'm seen with lots of people. Classy people.'

From the murderous expression on her dad's face, Sin quickly twigged she should've kept her trap shut. Poking the bear when he was this fucked off – she must have a death wish.

She let out a startled shriek when her dad sprang towards her, a charge that was so unexpected Sin had no chance to react. His fingers clawed in her hair, his talon-like nails digging into her scalp.

'Let me go! Let me go!'

She might as well have been pleading with the moon because he took sod all notice, his grip savage like he was trying to rip her bloody head clean off her shoulders. Using all his might, he dragged her by the hair into the sitting room. Sin went kicking and screaming all the way, the unnatural angle of her neck resulting in pain so fierce she thought her neck was about to break. Deep inside the room he finally let go, chucking her to the floor like she was a sack of shit.

In a tangle, Sin landed on one side of her face, her hair matted about her, obscuring her vision. She tried desperately to capture her breath; the motion of her chest pumped up and down wildly. Her dad was really angry, which meant she had to tread very carefully. Tread on Danny's tail when he was raving, you never knew how he was going to react.

So she sat up and, after pushing the hair off her face, her stricken gaze darted around the room. And there was her mum, as expected, sitting in her usual chair, her distress clear in the bright fright of her gaze and her clenched hands in her lap. Sin knew her mother wouldn't utter a word. In her eyes, Danny was the head of the household and what he said went.

What stunned Sin was the presence of her brother, Jimmy. It wasn't like him to stand there and allow their dad to brutalise her any which way. Which made her suss something bad was going on here. She sent her brother a questioning gaze, but he deliberately turned away.

Now Sin got scared.

What the fuck was going on?

Her dad soon answered, rearing over her with disgust, his fury evident in the audible sound of his erratic breathing. 'You were seen. With one of those West Indian chaps.'

Sin's heart fell; the blood in her veins froze over.

Shit! Bertie!

Instinctively, her eyes fluttered to disguise her initial shock. Who the hell had seen them? They'd been so careful… except for that time. They say that love is blind, what they don't tell you, though, is that love can be stupid. Real stupid. Brighton. That one time they had allowed their feelings to forget what the real world was like.

Deciding to tough it out, Sin stared boldly right back. 'I don't know who's been telling tales, but I can guess.' Thinking quick on her feet, she added, 'the man I was seen with is a client from America. The photographers have contacts all over the world—'

'Go around kissing all your fucking clients, do ya?' If you asked Danny, all that kissing that went on in that modelling business wasn't natural. 'His black mouth on yours.'

In disbelief, Sin responded, 'I never took you to be prejudiced. You fought tooth and nail for Mr and Mrs Pascal when they came over from Grenada and the council wouldn't house them. You got them their flat.'

'That's business. That's what I do, look out for everyone, everyone in this here community.' The fierce rush of his breath pushed his chest out. 'Family is different. They have their women and we have ours. Touching my daughter…' Revulsion rippled across his features, along with a wrinkle of his nose. 'Letting him touch you. Opening your legs for him—'

'That's enough, Dad.' From the clenched tone of his voice, it was obvious that Jimmy couldn't hold back from intervening anymore.

Danny turned on his son. 'Enough? You should be ashamed of her—'

'Nah, Dad.' Jimmy emphatically shook his head. 'You know I don't hold with none of that racist claptrap. We all bleed red blood. You've never had a problem with Bertie—'

'That's friends, isn't it? They can be mates. Besides, Bertie's different after what he did for you that night in '63. Anyway, we're not talking about your friend here.'

They don't know it was Bertie. Thank God. Sin breathed slightly easier.

She watched her father turn back to her. The set of his features chilled her to the bone. He appeared so calm now. Too calm. A calm Danny Steele could be a nightmare. Face wiped clean of emotion, he began to take off his belt. It was black and leather, worn now after years of use with a square brass buckle. He'd had it specially made by a skilled leather worker down Petticoat Lane Market.

Sin couldn't believe what she was seeing. Her dad had never hit her with an object in her life. His hand yeah, a swift clip around the ear or her head when she was a young one when he deemed she'd stepped out of line. But a belt? Never.

Then he did something that shook her whole world.

He held the belt out towards Jimmy. And told him, 'You've got to do this, son. You'll be the head of the house when I'm gone so you need to stamp your authority from the off.'

Dazed, head shaking from side to side in disbelief, Jimmy backed away, expression gripped with horror. 'No way! I ain't doing it, Dad.'

Danny shook the belt at him like a deadly snake. 'What do you think folk are going to say when they find out? Eh? She's brought down shame on our family. Shame on the Steele name.' That seductive, charming tone he was known for took over. 'Don't forget, son, FAMILY is everything. Everything.'

Sin welled up, a storm of bitter tears rising inside her. 'You've always hated me. And we know why. You've been biding your time for nine years. This is payback.'

Self-consciously, Danny's finger ran the length of the scar on his cheek. The story he'd put about how he'd earned it, in a fight down the docks, was legendary. The only problem was, it was a lie.

Chapter Forty-Seven

1958

'He likes my tits better than yours.'

The woman yelled the shocking words outside the Steele family house, her voice slurred with booze and loud enough to wake the dead. It was Sunday, and the Steeles were sitting down to a good ole roast on their best china plates. You could say a lot about Iris Steele – preferably behind her back so her old man never heard – but you couldn't fault her Sunday spreads. You didn't even need to see the food; the delicious aroma permeating the house was enough to make your mouth water.

Everyone at the table froze at the crude shouts from outside. Seventeen-year-old Jimmy and fifteen-year-old Sin flicked quick, nervous glances at each other before staring down at their plates. Iris' lips tightened while her fingers fluttered in her lap.

The only person who carried on like everything was normal was Danny. He got to his feet, presiding at the top of the table with a pair of knives in his hands. They were a fancy pair of blades he'd had specially brought in at the docks via Turkey. Silver handles, beautifully decorated, that felt heavy and good in his hands. He honed the blades together with that distinctive scraping sound before carving into the succulent pork.

In reality, Danny was seething. The bitch would dare come to his house. His fucking home. Right on his doorstep. A married man having a Doris on the side was to be expected; what wasn't was for it to be broadcast to the whole fucking world by the tart who'd dropped her knickers. There were rules and you abided by them.

He rued the day he'd clapped eyes on Carol Wilson. He'd met her in a boozer in Whitechapel. Recently widowed, down on her luck and lonely, she was on the prowl for a man to warm her bed. Considering she wasn't a bad-looking sort, Danny had taken her up on her invitation. It didn't take him long to figure out he'd made a big-time mistake. At first, things were nice and cosy – he'd drop by her place off New Road, she'd provide him with a satisfying pair of thighs to ease the troubles of life away. Shy of two months into their relationship, that's when the brass started to spoil things. Popping up like a flipping Janet-in-the-box down the Docks and the

River Rat like she had a claim on him. Nah! He couldn't have that. So he'd dumped her, not rough, mind – Danny was never rough about it. Women appreciated sweet words, making them still feel great about themselves, and then he waltzed out the door.

Obviously, it hadn't worked in Carol's case. Continuing to carve, he ignored her presence outside, hoping she'd do the decent thing and piss off. He was proved wrong when her voice came louder and coarser.

'Iris Steele, you hear me? He's tired of having to stare at your saggy pair. No wonder they call you One O'clock Iris, knocking it back so much that you don't get out of bed until come one in the afternoon.'

Iris raised her head and stared into the distance, a blank expression settling in her eyes. Her lips started moving. Beneath her breath, she slowly recited, 'The Lord is my Shepherd, I shall not want…'

Jimmy sprang out of his chair so quickly that it tipped backwards, tottered on its legs before managing to right itself. His hands clenched so tight into fists, his knuckles were visible. He told his dad, 'I ain't standing for this. Someone needs to—'

Danny cut his son off. 'Sit back down and enjoy the beautiful spread your mum has put on.'

Jimmy wavered, the anger vibrating off him leaving his face a furious red.

Danny wasn't bothered because he would fucking sort the bitch out. In good time. Always do everything in good time. When they least expected it. Plus, he knew what would happen next, which it did a few minutes later.

'Oi! Slaggie Maggie! Sling your skanky hook.' That was Norma, their neighbour two doors down. 'No one wants your poxy yo-yoing panty sort around here.'

'Who you calling yo-yoing panty?'

Carol must have had a death wish because no one mixed it with Norma. She was built like a navvy and had been a noted boxer in her day, part of the underground women's boxing scene. After retiring, she'd become Danny's eyes and ears on the street. That's why Danny had told Jimmy to retake his seat – because Norma would see to things.

'Go on! Get out of here.' That was the chorus from some of the other women who lived on the street.

There was also a lot of loyalty towards Iris around here. She might have had a fast and loose relationship with the bottle, but she would give the blouse off her back to a stranger in need.

'Your sort isn't welcome here.' Danny imagined Norma with her meaty arms folded across her middle. 'Find your own man and stop stealing others.'

Of course, this wasn't Danny's fault, most women on his street thought. The woman must've tempted him away from his wedding vows. In these situations, the scarlet woman was always to blame. Right?

Sensing the danger, Carol was off on her toes as quick as she'd come.

Inwardly promising to thank Norma later, Danny got on with his family Sunday meal like nothing had happened. The problem was, Iris wouldn't stop reciting from the Bible:

'I say to you that everyone who looks at a woman with lustful intent has already committed adultery...'

He tried his best to cut her voice out, but it wouldn't work.

'Many men will say, "I am just looking; that doesn't hurt anyone..."'

He slammed one of the carving knives down. 'Will you effing well knock it on the head.' He'd had a bellyful of her religious gibberish.

Suddenly, Sin flew up and leaned over the table, shouting at her father, 'I hate you.'

Danny stared at her as if she'd lost her mind. What the fuck were they teaching kids these days in these new comprehensive schools? Certainly not how to honour and obey their father. The girl wanted to thank her lucky stars he hadn't pulled her out of school like plenty of his mates were doing to their eldest girls to help their mums with the other kids and take care of their homes. Truth be told, his daughter had been grating on his nerves lately. Something about the way she carried herself, with that nose of hers stuck in the air.

Danny snarled, 'You better sit down—'

'I'm sick to death of you treating Mum like this,' Sin wailed over him. 'Shoving your fancy women in her face.'

Danny moved around the table. The girl had gone too far. And that's when it happened. In a flash of a blur that no one would ever be able to recount exactly what occurred next. Somehow one of the Turkish knives was in Sin's hand and she sliced it across her father's cheek.

A terrible silence shrouded the room, along with stunned shock. No one could believe what had just occurred. The blood bloomed on Danny's right cheek. The scent of blood was in the air.

It was Iris, of all people, who went into action.

Hurriedly, she turned to Jimmy. 'Get your sister to Sister Bernadette down the convent. Now.' He didn't move. Her order hardened. 'I said now, boy.'

Jimmy reacted the exact time Danny slowly covered his fingers down the side of his face in a daze. His daughter had just… the fury broke inside him and boiled over. He lunged for Sin, but his wife niftily stepped in his way. Iris proved to be a lot stronger than her fragile appearance suggested. Grabbing her husband's arms, she fought with him, regardless of knowing it was useless – there was only ever going to be one winner.

She shouted at Jimmy, 'Out the back so no one sees you.'

Finally, Jimmy did what his mother ordered and dragged his sister out of the house.

Enraged and with a roar, Danny knocked his wife to the floor and ran towards the back door in the kitchen.

On her knees, Iris pleaded after him, 'Don't, Danny. I beg you. Please.'

Abruptly, Danny froze. He stared back at his wife, the blood dripping down his neck into the top of his vest. 'But she cut me.'

''I know, sweetheart.' Iris scrambled to her knees, her shaking hands holding on to a chair to get to her feet. She clucked her tongue like she was talking to a child. 'You've only gone and hurt yourself, haven't you.'

She got him sat down, and as she ministered to the damage done to his face, she whispered, 'You rush out that door and folk will know that it was Sin who did this. What are they going to think, eh, Danny, if they hear your girl got the better of you?'

'What?' He was coming out of his daze.

Iris clucked her tongue gently again. 'It might ruin your reputation. Now if they thought you got that mark in a fight down the docks, that's going to raise you up. Boost your standing.'

Her words penetrated his fog. And made sense.

Like a lullaby in his ear, she told him, 'You leave Cynthia to me. You'll see, it will all work itself out.'

For a week, Sin remained at St Philomena Convent until her mum arrived with all her belongings packed in a grip-style suitcase. Sister Bernadette had secured her a place in a convent school in Kent. Sin cried buckets when she found out it was a boarding school, but she knew better than to plead to stay at home. If that happened there was only one outcome. Her dad would kill her.

As for Carol Wilson, a few days later she was brought into The London Hospital as an emergency on account of her face being slashed to bloody ribbons. Despite swearing he hadn't ordered it, no one believed Danny.

Chapter Forty-Eight

Now

Like a man hypnotised, Jimmy couldn't tear his stare away from the thick belt dangling from his dad's large hand. What the fuck was he supposed to do? Go against his father, the mighty Danny Steele, King of the Docks? Or beat the living daylights out of his sister? The same sister he'd sworn to protect since she was a baby?

That was the terrible choice facing Jimmy. And he needed to make it soon because there was going to be trouble otherwise. Then again, whichever way he went, trouble would be waiting at the end of it.

Swallowing convulsively, he stared hard at his sister on the floor. Most in her position would be clutching the bottom of his trousers pleading, bawling their head off, begging for mercy. Not Sin. Her stare was defiant, her chin proudly tilted.

His dad's silky persuasive instruction intruded. 'You've got to do it, son. How are you going to maintain order when you start out with your own firm if you can't do it within the four walls of your home? Eh?'

It was like Jimmy could feel his father's hot breath on the back of his neck.

His father wouldn't stop. 'There are rules. What are you going to do if someone goes against you? Gets out of order? Have a pint with them? Let them off? Nah! You're going to have to teach them some manners they will never forget…'

On and on his father went, viciously, turning the knife in a wound that was festering and exposed. However, Jimmy couldn't fault his dad about one thing he was on the money about. Outside this door he had to maintain order or people were going to take the piss. Jimmy Southpaw seen as a soft touch. A pussy. He'd become the bloody laughingstock of the East End underworld.

His eyes lifted to his dad's; his decision was there, clear for his father to see.

The corner of his mouth twitching like he was suppressing a triumphant grin, Danny handed the belt to his Jimmy who flinched at the surprising weight of it. Much heavier than he was expecting. Flipping hell, if he really laid into her, he was going to do some severe damage. Something else struck him. The buckle dangled at the end. If he hit Sin with that she might be scarred for life, her dreams of being a model over for good.

Was that their dad's intention all along? To fuck over her future? No way was Jimmy going to be a party to that. Heart thumping with fury, nerves itching beneath his skin, he strode over to his sister. Their gazes met and clashed. She didn't flinch like he did. Her fierce expression was loaded with fire and bravery.

Do your worst. You won't break my spirit.

Jimmy despised himself, nevertheless, the old man was right, there were rules. In the East End, you broke one, you paid the price.

Turning the belt so that the buckle end was in his palm, he wrapped some of the belt around his hand. Knowing what was coming, Sin turned her face but never cowered. He raised the belt and was careful to bring it down with minimal force across her back. Even though he used the lightest of movements, the impact of leather against flesh vibrated right through him, the sound ripping through the air.

Barely able to breathe, Jimmy watched his sister's body jerk. Her teeth sank into her bottom lip; she was clearly trying to hold the sound of pain back, but she couldn't stop the tiny moan that entered the room. Sweat covered Jimmy's forehead as he raised the belt, but it never fell because his father moved close to him.

And whispered in his ear, 'No, no, no. That won't do, son.' He proceeded to instruct him like he was teaching Jimmy the proper etiquette of how to ride a bike. 'She needs to learn her lesson. Needs to feel her mistake. So hard, son. HARDER.'

I can't do this. Can't.

But the voice of the lad Danny had brought up to be tough fought back: You have to. You don't have a choice.

Shoving back all his emotions, Jimmy held the belt high again and this time brought it down with force. Sin screamed, her body visibly vibrating with pain. She curled into a protective ball. He did it again and again, blocking out the sounds of her bloodcurdling agony. Three more times he tore into Sin. Then he threw the belt to the floor with self-loathing, fighting the waves of nausea that threatened to spew out of him. His sister was a weeping mess, her body twisting with the violence he had inflicted upon her.

He scooped Sin into his arms, held her close to his chest and swept past their father, but not without noticing the conceited curve of his mouth and the gleam that turned the skin of his face into the oily self-satisfied sheen of a man who had iron-clad control over his family.

Taking the stairs two at a time, Jimmy carried Sin with the gentleness of a newborn to her room. He caught his reflection in the mirror of her dressing table. His expression was harrowing, his skin a ghostly pale. But the biggest thing staring ominously back at him was revulsion. Sickened that he could've done this to the sister he loved so much.

Gently, he placed her on her bed. Watching the tears roll down her unhappy face, Jimmy felt his heart breaking.

He told her, 'I had to do it.'

Her trembling hand touched his arm. 'No one goes against Danny Steele.'

His brows slashed together. 'But why did you do it? You know word would reach Dad if you were seen with a coloured man.'

Her cheeks tinted with annoyance. 'Not you, too, Jimmy? For heaven's sake. I'd expect better from the man who went against everyone and married the daughter of his father's worst enemy.'

Jimmy had the heart to look ashamed. Eventually he explained, 'But that's different—'

'Why? Because your wife is the same colour as you? What would you do if it was your mate, Brother Bertie, I was seen with?'

Jimmy's anxious gaze shifted away, desperately trying to deal with his churning conflict. Bertie was no mere friend, he was a brother. No doubt about it. But would he want him marrying his sister? He dismissed the idea as quickly as it had come on account of those two not being able to stand the sight of each other.

He answered adamantly, 'But it wasn't Bertie.'

Sin shook her head, a long, weary sigh escaping her. 'Anyway, whoever whispered tales in Dad's ear got it wrong. You know what it's like at the hair salon, everyone's all kissy-kissy. That's all they saw.'

Jimmy bowed his head. 'I hate myself, Sin.'

The pressure of her fingers increased. 'I'll love you till the day I die.'

Despite his sister's attempts at smoothing things over after the wickedness he'd perpetrated against her, Jimmy knew the truth. Their relationship would never be the same again. Some wounds, Jimmy realised, went deeper than any belt could strike.

Chapter Forty-Nine

'Jimmy? Are you all right?'

Gertie's concerned cry cut through the fog in Jimmy's mind. He stood at her boarding house door, the taste of bile burning his throat. The memory of what he'd just committed against Sin made him want to throw up in the gutter. How could he face Gertie? Her warm, kind heart would turn to stone if she knew what these hands had done.

Gertie's eyes narrowed, her lips pressed into a thin line of worry beneath her headwrap. 'You don't seem yourself, at all. What's wrong?'

Jimmy swallowed hard against the acid in his mouth. 'Is Bertie in? It's important.'

'He's upstairs in his room.' Scowling hard, Gertie stepped aside to let him through, her eyes boring into him. 'But, Jimmy...'

He brushed past her, taking the stairs two at a time. The pounding of his feet matched the thundering in his chest, each step an echo of the belt striking flesh.

Music drifted from behind Brother Bertie's closed door, Jimmy Cliff's, 'Hard Road To Travel' blasting from the gram. Jimmy pushed the door open and found his friend lounging on his bed, his hat tipped back, a glass of his infamous Lord Have Mercy Rum Punch dangling from his fingers. His easy expression vanished, replaced by concern when he took in Jimmy's wild eyes and dishevelled appearance.

Urgently setting his drink aside, Brother Bertie sat up, his searching gaze all over his best friend. 'What's going on, spar?' An alarming thought came to him. 'Was it the coppers? Did they find you?'

Jimmy slumped against the doorframe. 'I can't…' His voice cracked. He shook his head, unable to form the words. He pulled in a huge punch of air, and his chest trembled.

Brother Bertie was up and across crossed the room in two strides flat. He gripped Jimmy's forearms, forcing him to directly stare him in the eye. 'Talk to me.'

When he released Jimmy's arms, his friend staggered and sat heavily on the bed. Jimmy stared at his hands, turning them over slowly.

Strong hands. Scarred hands. Knuckles thick and gnarled from untold punches thrown in the ring. The calluses told stories of working the speed bag until his skin split and bled. Boxing hands that had earned respect in boxing gyms across the East End.

These were the hands that had gently caressed Mini with so much wonder on their wedding night. The hands that cradled Violet and Robbie when they came into this world. His dad had always said you could tell a man's worth by studying his hands. Jimmy's were working hands, fighting hands. Champion's hands.

And now they were coward's hands. The same hands that were meant to protect his beloved sister had become the worst weapon against her. He flexed his fingers, seeing Sin's terrified face flash before his eyes.

Barely above a hush, he said, 'See these?' He felt his friend's eyes shift to his hands. 'These are meant for glory in the ring. I always said I'd never use these against anyone in my family. Never against anyone I loved.'

'Jimmy.' Brother Bertie's voice was filled with shock. 'Was it your dad? Did he find out it was us who took the car?'

'No,' Jimmy quickly reassured him. 'I wish I had stood up to him. For once in my miserable life, I wish I had just fucking well told him "no". That I'm my own man, standing on my own two feet.'

'What did he make you do?' Brother Bertie didn't understand why, but his heart started kicking up a fuss inside him. Banging and beating as if the worst thing in the world had happened. Like he had a premonition of something that was badly wrong.

'All these years.' Brother Bertie heard the bitter, self-hatred in Jimmy's words. 'Everything I do, it's never enough for him. Champion boxer? Nah, waste of time, he says. Should be focusing on the firm. Give me money to help me and Mini get our feet up on the property ladder? Nah, stay under his roof for the rest of eternity.'

Brother Bertie felt easier because for a moment there he'd thought something had happened with Sin. He nodded sympathetically. 'Fathers and sons, yeah? It's like they're scared of us becoming more than they were.'

He'd spotted it years back. The way Danny Steele kept his son under his thumb, how he'd chip away at Jimmy's dreams of being champ. 'Under manners' was how they would put it in Jamaica, meaning under control. Danny kept his son under manners.

But Brother Bertie had kept well out of it because family business was sacred ground. No matter how close you were to someone, you never stuck your nose in their blood business. Even when you saw the truth plain as day, you kept your mouth shut and waited for them to figure it out themselves. At least Jimmy was finally seeing his father for what he was.

Jimmy's hands rolled into fists. 'He's got this power. One word from him and I'm that little kid again, desperate to make him proud. Desperate enough to…'

He swallowed hard. He told his blood brother everything. Everything. But beating Sin – never! He couldn't tell Bertie what he'd done and be able to look him in the eye ever again.

'Sometimes I think the day we nicked that motor,' Jimmy carried on, 'everything started going to shit. Like we opened up something evil.'

'True talk. Finding that body in the boot.' Brother Bertie shuddered. 'Never thought I'd be digging a grave in the dead of night.'

'We've got to end it.' Jimmy's hands balled into fists.

His mate frowned. 'End what?'

'Get shot of that car before it destroys everything.'

'The last time we tried that, the filth ambushed us. What about your Dutch guy?'

Jimmy shook his head. 'For some reason I can't get him. Bollocks.' Jimmy drew the words out, slow with hesitation. 'There's someone who might take the car off our hands.'

Brother Bertie studied his friend's face. The change that came over Jimmy's features made him step back. Gone was the tortured guilt, replaced by something cold and deadly. Brother Bertie had seen that exact same expression the night they'd buried the body. But this was worse. This was the face of a man ready to make a deal with the Devil himself.

'No fuckery way!' Brother Bertie's stomach twisted. 'You can't mean who I think you mean. That's suicide, bruv. A whole other level of madness.'

'What choice do we have?' Jimmy stood, his hands now steady. 'We need that car gone. Whatever it takes.'

Chapter Fifty

Jimmy's fist thundered against the Dockside Devil Pub's back door. For a moment he closed his eyes, still trying to take in the enormity of what he was doing. There was no coming back from this.

How the fuck had his life come to this?

Brother Bertie pressed close to him in the grimy alley. 'We don't have to do this. There has to be another way. I know some brothers from West London way who could—'

'If that was true, you'd have already put the feelers out.' Jimmy sucked in a lungful of river air. 'Ain't no other choice. We need this sorted, and fast.'

He pounded at the door again. If someone didn't open up soon he was going to boot the thing in. For a long moment, there was nothing but the churring and slapping of the nearby river against the rotting wooden pilings of the docks. Finally, there was the scrape of a bolt being drawn back.

The door creaked open, revealing Lucas, Jimmy's brother-in-law. Not that the mountain of a man had ever publicly acknowledged him as such.

The other man squinted, features setting into shock. 'What's happened? Is it Mini? The kids?'

'She's fine,' Jimmy assured him quickly. 'We need to see your dad. It's important.'

His wife's brother's expression switched in an instant, his body stiffening with hostility. 'Fuck. Off.' His chin pointed dangerously towards the river. 'That's where the offal and crap belong.'

He started to slam the door, but Jimmy's foot got there first.

'Like I said, we need to see Batters.'

Lucas' narrowed gaze sized them up. After what felt like a lifetime, he stepped aside. 'Your fucking funeral.' He grunted in disgust. 'Rats like you end up floating in the Thames every day round here.'

Jimmy thought Mini's brother was going to play true to form and parade him and Bertie in the main taproom to be verbally gobbed on and ridiculed by Batters' assembled gang. However, the big guy surprised him by bypassing the main room and instead herding them towards a door at the back of the pub. A narrow, winding staircase led down into the dark depths of the building. With each step, the air cooled, the stairs squeaking louder.

At the bottom, they found themselves in a cavernous room and froze at the terrible sight before them. Jimmy's breath caught in his throat. If he was a praying man, he'd have made the sign of the cross. In the middle of the room was an old wooden gallows with a noose hanging from it. The lighting amplified the shadow of the noose against the wall, making it big and scary. It was like the ghosts of those who had danced and died at the end of the rope were still there.

And there, seated beneath the gallows like the chief executioner, was Batters. Thick smoke from a Willem II cigar wafted above his face, which jolted with disbelief for a split second before he masked his emotions again.

'Well, this is unexpected.' His voice dripped with false warmth. 'What brings Danny Steele's golden boy, my son-in-law, to my door?'

Jimmy felt rough hands seize him from behind, forcing him to his knees. Brother Bertie had other ideas. Twisting free, he quickly backed up against the damp wall. A gun appeared in his hand. Jimmy's mouth nearly dropped open because he hadn't seen this coming. The air crackled with shocked silence. No one moved. No one breathed.

'Back the fuckery up!' Brother Bertie blasted. Gone was the laughing, carefree man everyone loved to call 'brother'. In his place stood a man who was fearless. The gun didn't waver in his grip.

'You stupid bastard!' Batters launched to his feet, face knotted with apoplectic rage. 'You dare pull a shooter in my manor?'

The underground room hummed with lethal tension. Batters' men had their hands hovering over their own weapons, muscles coiled tight as springs, waiting for the signal to blow Bertie away.

'Bertie, put it down,' Jimmy urged, still on his knees. 'Nothing's gonna happen to us here.'

'That right?' Brother Bertie's lips curled. His steadfast gaze never left Batters. 'Your father-in-law here gonna play nice all of a sudden?'

'I ought to have you cut into pieces,' Batters snarled, his spit flying through the air. 'Coming into my gaff, pointing that shooter at me, shouting the odds. Who the fuck do you think you are?'

'The man holding the gun.' His Jamaican accent grew stronger, a sign Jimmy knew meant his friend was running on pure adrenaline.

'Listen to me.' Jimmy kept his voice level, reasonable. 'We need his help. This ain't the way.'

For several heart-stopping seconds, no one moved. The shadow of the gallows noose danced on the wall behind them, a grim reminder of the consequences. Sweat trickled down Bertie's temple.

Finally, he relaxed, lowering the gun.

Batters' men pounced, forcing him roughly to his knees beside Jimmy. The shooter clattered across the floor, coming to rest beneath the gallows.

'Your West Indian friend's got some bollocks on him,' Batters spat, his face still flushed with fury. 'I'll give him that.'

He retook his seat and went back to his cigar, puffing away. Then he gave his daughter's husband all his attention again, assessing gaze glinting with malicious glee. 'You must be desperate. For your mate there to come tooled up you must be in some kinda fix. What could drive a poxy Steele to risk coming here?'

Jimmy swallowed hard, fighting to keep his voice steady. 'Mr Rogers, we need your help.'

Batters sucked down more smoke, taking his sweet time. 'Help? From me? I'm lovin' this, every last second of it.'

He ground out his cigar. Then slowly stood, broad and large, deepening the intimidating presence in the underground room. He prowled closer to the younger men, moving with the calculated intent of a man who'd broken more bones than he could count. The room suddenly felt smaller, more confined. Batters took his time circling them, a shark scenting blood in the water. His boots crunched over the old floor.

'And why should I lift a finger to help Danny Steele's git?'

'It ain't about my old man.' Jimmy hoped his desperation wasn't showing. 'It's personal.'

Batters grinned, his gold back teeth shining. 'It's always personal.'

After drawing in a deep breath, Jimmy confessed, 'I've got a motor that's running a bit hot. I need it taking off my hands.'

Batters froze, every muscle in his bull-like frame turning to granite. His face twisted through a dozen expressions before settling into something that would make most men run the other way – pure fucking delight.

'You nicked those wheels, didn't you?' The ugliest laughter imaginable erupted from deep within his belly.

The savage joy dancing in his eyes made him look ten years younger. Christmas had come early for Eric 'Batters' Rogers.

'Half the Old Bill in London are turning the City upside down looking for that particular bucket of trouble.' He rocked back on his heels, practically glowing with satisfaction. 'And here it is, gift-wrapped and delivered by Danny Steel's own flesh and blood.'

Jimmy dared to ask, 'Why are the coppers after it?'

Batters' gleeful expression drained away, his stare turned to chips of ice. He crouched, getting right into Jimmy's face, his hot breath beating against his skin.

'This is exactly why my Mini should've run screaming in the opposite direction when you came sniffing round. What kind of mug half-inches a motor without knowing who he's stealing from?' He shook his head, disgust twisting his features. 'My daughter married a bloody liability.'

Jimmy's heart thundered against his ribs. 'Who owns it?'

He thought back to the gruesome chopped-up body in the boot.

Without answering, Batters stood tall again and stared over at the old gallows. 'Back in the day, they used to string up river pirates from these very beams. Then hang there outside for days, rotting in the sun and the rain, a warning to any other poor bollocks who thought about crossing the wrong people. Nasty business.'

Jimmy's mouth went dry. This was it. His best friend was right, they were done for.

Batters faced him again, a calculating expression in his eye. 'I could turn you in to the coppers who I'm sure would show their appreciation with a little drink for me. It'd be the smart play.'

'Please, Mr Rogers.' Jimmy hated that he was on his knees before this particular man, pleading and grovelling. He fucking hated very last minute of it. But he had no choice. 'I know I ain't got no right to ask, but—'

'You're damn straight, you've got no right!' Batters exploded, face contorting with rage. 'You took my little girl from right under my nose, you piece of filth!'

For a moment, raw emotion flashed across his face. But, quick as a gallows rope snaps a neck, it was gone.

'Lucky for you, I'm in a generous mood,' Batters crowed. 'I'll lend you a helping hand with your problem.'

Relief washed over Jimmy, quickly followed by suspicion. 'Just like that? What's the catch?'

Batters grinned, broad and wide. 'Oh, there's always a catch, boy. You of all people should know that. You took Mini from me, Steele. That's a debt that can never be repaid.'

He retreated to his desk and pulled another cigar from his tin and lit up. After a few puffs he told Jimmy, 'Consider this a favour. One that I'll collect on when the time is right.'

Jimmy nodded, knowing he was making a deal with the devil.

God, if word got back to his father that he was making deals with his enemy, it was game over. But at least that motor would be gone. The trouble that car brought couldn't hurt him and those he loved anymore.

Chapter Fifty-One

Stubbing out his Saint Luos Rey cigar, Batters lounged in his tatty armchair, feet propped on a scuffed ottoman. His terraced house near Sugar Cane Wharf wasn't much, but it was home. He was feeling as smug as a gangster with an alibi because that flash motor had been delivered into his possession. All fucking his.

Chrissie was perched on the sofa opposite, a joint dangling between her slender fingers. The pungent smoke curled lazily in the air. She'd gone all out to look the epitome of sixties chic. She wore slim-fitting black cigarette pants that hugged her curves, paired with a crisp white shirt rolled up at the sleeves and half buttoned to showcase her breasts. A scarlet silk scarf was knotted loosely around her neck, adding a pop of vibrant colour. The overall effect was both elegant and edgy, like Audrey Hepburn with a dangerous vibe.

'Eric, honey-bun,' Chrissie purred, her voice husky from the smoke. 'You've been ever so good to me.'

In a slo-mo movement, she uncrossed her legs in a very sexy movement. Batters' mouth went dry. Chrissie was a right sort, no doubt about it. But…

'Now, now, Chris,' he murmured, clearing his throat. 'Let's not get carried away.'

Her eyes widened, genuine surprise flickering across her face. 'What's the matter, darlin'? Don't you fancy me?'

She'd been living under his roof, settled in the spare room and a lonely bed. Chrissie had decided that today was the day to make her move.

Batters shifted in his seat, uncomfortable. 'Any man with eyes would. But…'

'But soddin' what?' Chrissie snapped, highly offended.

She leaned forward, her shirt gaping open, giving him an eyeful. Yeah, see if you can resist these puppies, matey.

Batters scrubbed a hand over his face. 'Look, Chris, you're Danny's little sister. I've known you since you was knee-high to a nipper. Can't shake that image, y'know?'

Chrissie's seductive smile faltered. 'I remember you and Danny being thick as thieves back then. Best mates, weren't you?'

Batters nodded, a hint of surprise in his eyes. 'Didn't think you'd remember that.'

'I might've been young, but I did possess a pair of eyes,' Chrissie remarked. 'You two were inseparable. I always wondered what happened?'

Not many round these parts remembered how it used to be. Time had a way of burying the truth under layers of hatred and violence. Back in their teenage years, Batters and Danny had been tight, more brothers than friends. These days, the sight of them trying to kill each other made folks forget they'd once shared everything. The real reason for their fall-out remained locked away, a secret neither man discussed.

A shadow clouded Batters' features. 'Life happened. People change. Loyalties shift. Betrayal comes a-callin'.'

Of course Chrissie knew there was more to the story, but she didn't push. Instead, she asked, 'So what's all this about Jimmy? Earlier you said he paid you a visit, but you didn't elaborate. Knowing the bad blood between you, why would my nephew turn up on your doorstep?'

Batters' expression darkened. 'Yeah, yesterday. Him and that black lad he knocks about with. Seems they've got themselves in a bit of major league bovver.'

'Oh?' Chrissie's ears pricked up, her expression deadly serious.

'Took something that didn't belong to them.' Batters chuckled without humour. 'Now they're fucking running scared.'

Jimmy's in trouble, Chrissie's horrified mind screamed. Inside, her guts twisted horribly with anxiety. She took another drag on her weed, hard and long this time, to steady her nerves.

'Too right.' Batters was too busy lapping up his own victory to notice the change in her manner. 'Your nephew came crawling to me. You should've seen him, practically kissing my ring on his knees.'

'What'd you tell him?'

Batters' eyes glittered dangerously. 'He's already delivered the car—'

'What car?'

It hadn't taken Batters long to figure out that Danny's sister was no use to him, except that little nugget of information she'd passed on about another of Danny's warehouses. No matter how much he'd tried to nudge her in the right direction, the reality was she knew sod all about her brother being tasked to find Commander Hawthorne's Aston Martin. By rights, he should've shown her the pavement. But something about Chrissie got under his skin. She was funny, had the brass to speak her mind to him. Still, he suspected that beneath all that banter she was two steps away from being unhinged.

Then again, Batters had always liked playing with fire.

Rearranging his body so he was sitting straight, he told her, 'It's too long a story to tell for that pretty brain of yours. I don't give a monkey's about that motor because all I'm thinking is how sweet revenge is gonna taste.'

'Revenge?' Chrissie echoed. She crossed her legs again, fingers tightening around her spliff. 'So you're out to get retribution to even the score about the past?'

He began shouting the odds, his temper rising. 'Too right! Danny stealing what he knew wasn't his, Jimmy taking my little girl. The Steeles have taken everything from me!'

Chrissie was baffled, her brows shooting up. 'Whatcha mean Danny stole what wasn't his?'

He clammed up, his eyes distant, like he wasn't even in the room. 'Revenge has kept me going, and believe you me, it's time for me to strike.'

No one ever dared challenge Batters, his reputation for violence preceding him. But Chrissie wasn't just anyone.

'Now hang on a bloody mo.' Her voice was filled with righteous indignation. 'What about what Mini wanted? Did you ever think about your daughter's needs?'

Batters stared at her, gobsmacked, like she'd truly lost her marbles. 'You what?'

'I remember your Fleur, God rest her soul,' Chrissie continued softly. 'She was a kindly woman. A proper lady. Class. Gentle to everyone, even us kids running wild causing trouble. Don't you think she'd want her daughter to be happy, even if it meant letting her go?'

His fury drained away, leaving behind a pain so deep Chrissie hardly recognised the bruiser before her. If she wasn't who she was, she'd probably have gone and comforted him.

'Fleur.' He emitted the name of his wife with such trembling emotion. 'She was everything to me.'

For a moment, the feared gangland boss disappeared, replaced by a man still grieving for his lost love.

'We were so young when we had Lucas, and then my beautiful Mini comes along.'

Chrissie heard his blatant love for his daughter.

'Mini was the spit of her mum. Small and delicate. My little princess. Fleur, she doted on that girl. Said she was gonna make sure Mini had all the chances she never did. When Fleur got sick…' He swallowed hard, the words broken glass in the back of his throat. 'She made me promise. Cross my heart that I'd watch over our little girl with my life.' His voice cracked. 'How am I supposed to do that when Mini spat in my eye and betrayed me?'

'Fucking grow up.'

Batters was outraged. 'What did you say?'

Chrissie's heart ached for him, but, at the same time, it was time to tell him some home truths.

She took another deep drag on her joint, its fruity earthiness flavour coating her mouth while she considered her words carefully.

'You heard! We're three years off 1970. Times are changing. Women, we're not just sitting at home waiting for our dads to tell us who to marry anymore. Waiting for our old fellas to come home to present them with their dinner and slippers by the fucking fire. We want more out of life.'

Batters scoffed. 'What's that got to do with anything?'

'Everything!' Chrissie pressed on, emboldened. 'Mini's a grown woman. She's made her choice. Maybe instead of fighting it, you could try to understand it?'

'Understand?' Batters' voice rose, his old fire returning. 'Understand what? That she chose them over me? That she'd rather be with that Steele boy than her own flesh and blood?'

Chrissie held her ground. 'She chose love, you dumbo. Ain't that what your Fleur would've wanted?'

The mention of his dead wife's name seemed to deflate Batters again. He slumped in his chair, suddenly appearing every one of his years. His flesh sagged, his gaze haunted by the ghosts of his past.

'It's not too late,' Chrissie suggested gently. 'Mini's got kids of her own now. Your grandkids. Your kith 'n' kin. Maybe it's time to build some bridges?'

For a long moment, Batters was silent, lost in thought. Chrissie watched him, wondering if she'd pushed too far. Finally, he spoke, his voice barely above a whisper.

'I see her sometimes, y'know. In the street. She seems… happy.'

Chrissie nodded encouragingly. 'That's good, ain't it? That's what you and Fleur wanted for her.'

For a moment, it looked like he might listen to her. Then, like a switch being flipped, his bristling anger returned.

'Nah!' He sneered, voice cold. 'That ship's sailed. But I'll tell you what I am gonna do. I'm gonna make the Steeles pay. All of 'em.' He paused, winking at Chrissie. 'Except you, of course, sweetheart. You're all right in my book.'

'Of course I am, love.' Chrissie laughed, and then her expression suddenly darkened. 'I don't approve of you attacking my nephew… But as for his father.' A pulse in her cheek ticked beneath her face powder. 'After the way he treated me. Made a total show of me in front of the neighbours—'

Batters cut in. 'Don't you worry, girl. The King of the Docks is going to get what's coming to him.'

Her eyes lit up. 'What's this plan of revenge of yours?'

Batters shuffled to the edge of his armchair, his voice dropping to a conspiratorial whisper. 'Right, here's what we're gonna do…'

Chapter Fifty-Two

The day of reckoning had finally arrived. Jimmy 'Southpaw' Steele's shot at the local heavyweight boxing championship was a mere four hours away. Inside the Steele family home, anticipation hung thick in the air. Jimmy sat at the dining table, his broad shoulders hunched forward, eyes fixed on the mammoth steak Mini had just placed in front of him.

'Get that down you, son,' Danny Steele barked, his voice gruff with pride. 'That's what a red-blooded boxer needs to win. Proper fuel, that is.'

Jimmy nodded, sawing into the meat with gusto. The rich aroma of the steak filled his nostrils, but his mind was elsewhere. His fingers twitched slightly as he gripped the knife and fork, almost feeling the weight of the gloves on his hands.

'You all right there, son?' His father's voice cut through his musings. 'You've gone all quiet on us.'

Jimmy glanced up, forcing a smile. 'Yeah, Dad. Just… thinking, y'know?'

Danny nodded, understanding in his eyes. 'It's the Big One tonight. But remember, you're a Steele. We don't lose.'

The words hung heavy with expectation. Jimmy felt the burden of them on his shoulders, adding to the pressure already building inside him. His heart raced with a mixture of excitement and nerves. This was it. The moment he'd been dreaming of since he'd first laced up a pair of gloves. He could almost taste the victory, sweet and tangy on his tongue.

Iris beamed at her boy, her silver-grey eyes – so like Jimmy's own – brimming with pride. 'You're gonna do us proud tonight, our Jimmy,' she said, reaching across to squeeze his hand. 'Show 'em what a Steele is made of.'

'Too right,' Sin piped up, but Jimmy couldn't help noticing the strain in his sister's voice.

She'd been off lately, quieter than usual. Guilt and shame twisted in his gut remembering what he'd done to her. No wonder she was the picture of unhappiness.

Jimmy made himself a promise. After he'd won the championship he was going to take her out for a slap-up meal at Blooms in Whitechapel.

Even as warmth surged in his chest at his family's support, Jimmy couldn't quite quell the nagging worry in his gut. He glanced at Mini, his beloved wife, her belly gently rounding with their third child. She smiled at him, her eyes shining with unconditional love. Jimmy felt sick. He still hadn't told her about the house, that her dream of moving out of his parents' place had pissed itself down the drain. He'd let his beloved wife down, plain and simple. The house had meant so much to her.

At least that cursed car was gone. When he and Brother Bertie had handed it over to Batters, they couldn't get away quickly enough.

Although, an unsettled feeling nagged away at him; why did Batters really want the car? Maybe he was involved with the body that had been found in it?

I'll tell her after the fight, he vowed silently. Win or lose, she deserves to know.

'Earth to Jimmy!' Sin's voice broke through his thoughts. 'You gonna eat that steak or just stare at it all night?'

Jimmy blinked, realising he'd been lost in thought. 'Sorry, just—'

Sin's eyes softened. 'You've got this, big brother. We believe in you.'

As Jimmy polished off the last of his meal, his father beckoned him over to a quiet corner of the room where he poured them both two glasses of rum.

'Here, son. A little Dutch courage, eh?'

Jimmy's eyes widened. 'No way, Dad. I can't drink before the fight.'

Danny chuckled, a sound like gravel in a tin can. 'Don't be soft. All the greats knocked back a bit of the hard stuff before a big bout in my day. Steadies the nerves.'

'Thanks, but I'll pass,' Jimmy said firmly. 'I need a clear head tonight.'

A flicker of something – disappointment? anger? – crossed Danny's face, but it was gone in an instant. Jimmy watched his father knock back both shots, a familiar unease settling in his gut. Danny Steele was a hard man to please, always expecting more, always pushing harder. Sometimes Jimmy wondered if anything he did would ever be enough.

But tonight wasn't about his father. It was about proving something to himself. About taking that first step towards the life he wanted for Mini and the kids. Towards being his own man. The prize money wasn't going to be much, but he'd put it away to contribute to buying a house.

A sharp knock at the door announced his best friend's arrival.

'All right there, Jimmy boy?' Brother Bertie grinned. 'Your chariot awaits, primed and ready to deliver London's next heavyweight champ.'

Jimmy couldn't help but smile back. Good ole Bertie, loyal as they come. They were going to the venue early to get a feel for the place and then get ready for the fight. The last thing they wanted was to be in a rush.

'Give us a minute, yeah?' he told his best friend before turning to Mini and pulling her close. She felt so small in his arms, so precious.

'I love you,' he murmured into her hair. 'You and the kids, you're everything to me. You know that, right?'

Mini gazed up at him, her eyes misty. ''Course I do, you big softie. Now go on, get out there and show 'em what you're made of.'

Jimmy kissed her deeply, trying to pour all his love and silent apology into that one gesture. Mini had decided against attending the fight stating that her nerves would be shot watching which wouldn't be good for the baby.

When they broke apart, he saw his father grabbing his coat.

Danny explained, 'Just got a bit of business to take care of first. Then I'll come and pick your mum and Sin up. We'll be there cheering you on, don't you worry.'

A sudden surge of emotion fired through Jimmy. Despite everything, despite the pressure and the expectations, his parents were here for him. Supporting him in their own way.

'Mum, Dad,' he called out, his voice thick. 'Thanks. For everything.'

Iris hurried over, enveloping him in a fierce hug. 'Oh, my boy,' she whispered. That was it, nothing more, an embrace filled with a mother's love.

Even Danny appeared touched, clapping a hand on Jimmy's shoulder. 'Make us proud, son.'

Brother Bertie's searching eyes scanned the room. 'Where's Sin gone?'

'She was here a minute ago.' Iris frowned. 'Must've slipped out.'

'Right then,' Jimmy said, squaring his shoulders, missing the distress on his friend's face that his sister wasn't there. 'Let's do this.'

***

Jimmy stepped out of his parents' house and stopped dead in his tracks. His jaw dropped in astonishment at the sight before him.

The whole bloody street had turned out.

Some were on their doorsteps, others in the street.

Old Tom Jenkins was one of those on his doorstep, his old sailor's pipe clenched between his teeth, nodding solemnly. The Baxter twins whooped and hollered from their perch on the garden wall. Even old Mrs Gates tottered at the edge of her front garden, gripping her fancy walking frame for dear life.

'Blimey, mate,' Brother Bertie whispered, dark eyes wide. 'The whole East End's come to see you off.'

A thunderous stamping of feet began, the rhythm matching Jimmy's racing pulse. The very ground seemed to vibrate with the force of it.

'Knock 'em dead, Southpaw!' bellowed Norma from two doors down.

'Show 'em what a real East End boy can do!' shrieked Mrs Collins, her hair in curlers.

Jimmy's gaze landed on Rita Lawless, dolled up to the nines. She winked, blowing him a kiss. 'Give 'em hell, handsome!'

Jimmy was blown away, his heart swelling, threatening to burst right out of his chest. This wasn't just a send-off; it was a bloody coronation. His eyes stung, and he blinked rapidly, refusing to let the tears fall. Pride coursed through his veins. These were his people. His streets. His manor.

For a moment, panic gripped him. What if he let them down? What if he couldn't bring that title home? The doubt flickered, a shadow across his heart. But then he caught sight of old Mr Thompson, the retired docker who'd lost three fingers to the job. The old man's eyes shone with a fierce pride that seemed to say, 'You're one of us, boy. You can't fail.'

Jimmy's resolve hardened. He'd fight for more than just himself tonight. He'd fight for every callused hand that had ever grafted on these streets, for every dream that had been born in these cramped houses and narrow alleys.

This wasn't just support, it was love.

Raw, unfiltered East End love.

It filled him up, made him feel ten feet tall and bulletproof.

The crowd parted as Jimmy and Brother Bertie made their way down the street, every step feeling like they were walking on air. Hands reached out to pat Jimmy's back, ruffle his hair, squeeze his shoulder.

When they reached the end of the street, a chant started. Low at first, then swelling until it echoed off the brick buildings all the way down to the docks on Sugar Cane Wharf.

'Southpaw! Southpaw! Southpaw!'

A grinning Brother Bertie slapped Jimmy on the back. 'Better than any entrance music. Now let's go make these streets proud.'

Chapter Fifty-Three

'What the fuckery is that van doing?' Brother Bertie relayed, bemused, his knuckles aching from gripping the steering wheel so tightly.

Jimmy twisted in his seat, peering through the rear window of the Morris Minor. A battered white van prowled menacingly close, its headlights blazing.

'Dunno. I don't like the look of this, though.'

Suddenly, the van surged forward, its bumper kissing the Minor's tail. Brother Bertie swore, swerving trying to avoid the impact. It's tyres screeched against the road, and the acrid smell of burning rubber filled the car.

This can't be happening, Jimmy thought, not now, of all times. I've got to get to the fight.

The van struck again. Harder. Stronger. The car fishtailed wildly. Brother Bertie fought for control, his features set with disbelief. But it was no use. They spun off the road, the world outside the windows becoming a dizzying blur of shadows and streetlights.

The crash came with a sickening crunch of metal. Jimmy's head snapped forward, then back, stars exploding behind his eyes. For a moment, everything went black.

When he came to, rough hands were dragging him from the wreckage. Jimmy lashed out blindly, his boxer's instincts kicking in. His fist connected with something solid, eliciting a grunt of pain.

'Hold the cunt down!' a gruff voice barked.

More hands grabbed him, pinning his arms.

Jimmy thrashed wildly, roaring his defiance. 'Get off me, you bastards!'

Out of the corner of his eye, he saw Brother Bertie putting up his own fight, landing a solid right hook on one of their attackers.

'Jimmy!' he yelled. 'Don't let them—'

Something hard cracked against the back of Jimmy's skull. Pain exploded through his head, and the world went dark once more.

***

The smell of the river filled Jimmy's nostrils as he slowly regained consciousness. His head throbbed, each pulse sending waves of nausea through him. He opened his eyes, and it didn't take him long to figure out he was slung on the floor in the back of the mysterious van, the shadows of figures around them.

Turning his head, he saw Brother Bertie in the same predicament. The van skidded to a stop.

Hoods were thrust over his and his best friend's heads, plunging them into darkness. Hands grabbed their ankles, hauling them backwards out of the van. They were dragged across the ground, every stone and loose brick tearing into them. The cold night air knifed through their clothes. Brother Bertie's shoulder smashed against something solid. A wall maybe. His grunt of pain echoed along with Jimmy's.

'Keep your mouths shut,' a gravelly voice snarled from above.

Jimmy tried to twist free. A boot slammed into his ribs, driving the air from his lungs. The hood trapped his gasps, the fabric sucking against his mouth with each desperate breath. The cloth tasted of oil and something metallic, probably blood.

The Executioner's Steps.

The ancient stone stairs where the tide washed up bodies.

The first step cracked into Brother Bertie's skull, stars exploding behind his eyes. Then another impact, and another. Each edge battered into his spine, his shoulders, his legs. The steps were merciless. Beside him, Jimmy's muffled groans told him his friend was getting the same beating from the stone.

Rough hands yanked them upright, hoisting them onto the old timber wharf piles driven deep into the riverbank. Rope bound and bit into their wrists, tight enough to restrict blood flow. When their hoods were yanked off, the night exploded around them. The vast, dark expanse of the Thames stretched before them, an endless void eager to feed.

The incoming tide surged towards them, a nightmare made real. The wave struck with the force of a sledgehammer, battering into their legs with brutal precision. Then it surged to their waists. The water tortured their flesh with ice-sharp cuts that burned like acid. The stench was revolting, waste and decay gagging them.

'Where is it?' The question came from the shadows above, nearly lost in the roar of the river.

Brother Bertie's teeth chattered violently, his whole body shaking. 'Where is what?' he bellowed back. 'We don't know what you're talking about! Let us go!'

'Who are you?' Jimmy roared into the darkness, straining against his bonds until fresh blood flowed.

Another wave crashed into them, harder this time. The filthy water climbed past their chests, its rotten stench filling their nostrils. Each surge tried to knock them sideways, the current wrapping around them, a python slowly squeezing.

'Tell me where it is,' the voice demanded. 'Or the Thames gets two more secrets tonight.'

Brother Bertie caught Jimmy's eye. In all their years running the streets together, they'd never faced death like this. The freezing water crept higher, past their chests now, stealing their body heat, a deadly numbness creeping through their muscles.

'Last chance! Where is it?'

The black water rose to their necks, ice-cold tendrils seeking their mouths. The foulness of the river kissed their lips. Back and forward, back and forward. This time when it came back, a black wall of death closed over their heads. Brother Bertie's and Jimmy's screams bubbled into watery silence.

They knew they were about to die.

The water receded with agonising slowness. Jimmy and Brother Bertie erupted from beneath the surface, throats raw from screaming, lungs burning while they desperately sucked in air. Violent coughing racked their bodies, river water spewing from their mouths. The taste was vile, like drinking from an open sewer.

Brother Bertie retched, his stomach heaving. His whole body trembled, teeth chattering so hard he thought they might shatter.

'Had enough?' The taunting voice was back with no mercy. 'Where is the fucking car?'

It was Jimmy who made the decision to save them. 'Cut us loose and I'll tell you.' He was quick, he needed to be before the tide rose against them again. This time they might not come back out alive.

Their kidnappers appeared, cut them down and manhandled them up the old stairs to the top. They were shoved to their knees in front of a man cloaked in the shadows. He emerged forward, revealing himself.

'Dad?'

Jimmy couldn't believe his eyes. Terror and disbelief battled inside him. Then again, he should've figured it out because the best entrance to

Executioner's Steps was a back door from the River Rat, his father's dockside HQ.

Danny's features blistered with fury. 'Don't you "Dad" me, you little shit. You could've taken a knife to my heart before I believed it was my boy who'd nabbed that motor.' His released a savage breath that shook the air around them. 'You don't even need to admit it, the guilt is written all over both of you.'

'Mr Steele, I swear we didn't—' Brother Bertie started, but Danny silenced him with a look that could have frozen the Thames.

'I thought I taught you better than that.' Danny's eyes bored into Jimmy, a storm of emotions swirling in their depths. Anger, yes, but also hurt. Disappointment.

Shame gutted Jimmy. He'd let his father down. Let everyone down. The weight of it pressed on his chest, making it hard to breathe. 'I'm sorry, Dad. We didn't know—'

'Didn't know what?' Danny snapped, his voice rising. 'Didn't know it belonged to Commander Reginald Hawthorne, one of the top coppers in town?'

'What?' Both Brother Bertie and Jimmy let out in slack-jawed shock.

Danny studied their gobsmacked faces, his blood beginning to boil. These two brain-dead wankers had actually nicked a motor without having the first fucking clue who it belonged to. His son and that porkpie-hat-wearing tosser had blundered around like a pair of headless chickens, dropping themselves balls-deep in the biggest mess possible.

'For fuck's sake!' Danny erupted, veins bulging in his neck. 'Have I taught you nothing? All these years showing you the ropes and you pull an amateur stunt like this? You're supposed to be my son, my flesh and blood, not some thick-as-doggy-do tea leaf half-inching wheels at random. I raised you better than this, you absolute fucking pair of no-brain bellends!'

Danny sucked back the rest of his words because he didn't trust himself. For a second or two he swallowed shallow punches of air into his lungs, got his head back under control.

When he next spoke he was calm. Too calm. 'Didn't you realise you could have been putting our whole operation at risk?' The men hung their heads at that. 'Did you think you could go behind my back and I wouldn't find out? Nothing happens in this manor without my say-so.'

Danny's voice cracked. 'You've betrayed me, son.'

Jimmy lifted his head. The cold of the river was nothing compared to the killer chill of his father's gaze.

Danny took something from his pocket. The metallic snick of a switchblade pierced the darkness. The steel in his hand caught what little light there was.

Jimmy's heart stopped dead. Hadn't he known it would come to this? His father was honour-bound to meet his betrayal in the rules written in the gangland Life.

'In our world,' Danny started in an awful whisper. 'Betrayal means death. You know that better than anyone, don't you, son?' He turned the blade slowly, letting it dance between his fingers.

Jimmy steeled himself, getting ready. If he was going out he wasn't going to be a snivelling mess. He'd meet it how he'd always lived, with his head held high, with honour.

'It was my fault,' Brother Bertie punched in, trying to save his blood brother. 'I was—'

'Leave it.' It was Jimmy who quietly cut him short. 'This is between a father and a son.'

Danny moved closer. Jimmy's chest seized, his breathing turning ragged. Brother Bertie went rigid beside him. Danny crouched behind him, so close his son could feel hot breath on his neck. The knife's cold edge pressed against Jimmy's wrist. One quick slice was all it would take. Jimmy squeezed his eyes shut, waiting for the blade to bite.

Instead, the rope that bound his wrists snapped apart. His father had cut him free. Danny did the same to Brother Bertie.

And ordered when he was back standing tall, 'Stay put. I want that car back. Now where is it?'

Jimmy hesitated, glancing at Brother Bertie. His friend gave an almost imperceptible shake of his head, loyalty shining in his eyes despite the fear.

'I'm waiting,' Danny growled.

'Dad, please. We've got a fight to get to. If I miss this…'

Danny laughed, a harsh, mirthless sound that echoed in the darkness. 'Fight? You think you're still going to that fight? You're done! Finished! Unless you tell me where that fucking car is stashed.'

'Batters,' Jimmy choked out, the name bitter in his mouth. 'Batters has it.'

The silence that followed was deafening. Danny's face went slack with shock, then twisted into a mask of unbridled fury. 'Batters? You gave it to fucking Batters?'

'We didn't know what else to do,' Jimmy pleaded.

Danny paced back and forth, running a hand through his hair. 'My own son,' he muttered. 'My own flesh and blood, dealing with my worst enemy.'

Finally, he stopped, fixing Jimmy with a look of disgust. 'Get out of my sight. Both of you. And don't think this is over.'

'Dad, I—' Jimmy started, his voice cracking.

'Don't!' Danny snapped, but the fury had drained from his voice, leaving only a bone-deep weariness. 'Just go.'

Jimmy and Brother Bertie stumbled out of the street, soaked to the bone and shivering. The night air bit at their wet skin as they hurried towards the road.

'What time is it?' Jimmy asked, his teeth chattering. 'D'you reckon we can still make it?'

Brother Bertie fumbled with his waterlogged watch. 'Half eight. If we leg it, maybe we've got a chance.'

Jimmy's mind raced. The fight was scheduled for nine-thirty. 'We've got to try. If I miss this chance, my boxing career is over.'

Chapter Fifty-Four

Jimmy and Brother Bertie burst through the back door of the hall, panting and wild-eyed. They'd barely made it, managing to catch a taxi and bomb it the rest of the way. The first thing they saw was the poster on the wall. It was impossible to miss.

The poster screamed for attention in bold, blood-red letters:

CLASH OF THE TITANS!

Beneath the sensational headline, two figures squared off, fists raised. On the left, a stylised rendition of Jimmy, his trademark Southpaw stance captured in stark black ink. His face was a mask of determination, eyes burning with intensity. Opposite him stood Don 'The Destroyer' Dawson, the reigning champ. Dawson's hulking form dominated his side of the poster, muscles rippling, a sneer marring his features.

Between their images, block letters proclaimed:

JIMMY 'SOUTHPAW' STEELE vs. DON 'THE DESTROYER' DAWSON.

The date and venue were splashed across the bottom in eye-searing yellow.

They ran smack into Frankie Foster, the promoter, his face a thundercloud. 'You're late, Steele. Fight's off.'

Breathing heavily, Jimmy squared up to him, towering over the shorter man. 'Come off it, Foster. You know who my old man is, yeah?'

Foster's face paled, but he stood his ground. 'Rules are rules. This is a major league bout, and I can't have you swanning in whenever you fancy. It was clearly stated what time both boxers needed to be in attendance.'

Brother Bertie stepped in, dialling his charm up to ten. 'Look, Mr Foster, it wasn't Jimmy's fault. Blame me, I'm his ride. Got held up, didn't I? Traffic's a right nightmare out there.'

Foster wavered, his eyes darting between them.

Brother Bertie pressed his advantage. 'Think about it. Full house out there. You really want to tell them the main event's cancelled?'

The promoter's resolve crumbled. 'You're on in twenty.'

They hurried to the dressing room. Faded posters of past champions adorned the walls, their glory days immortalised in yellowing paper. An ancient mirror, cracked at one corner, hung above a battered wooden bench.

Jimmy stripped off his clothes and got his boxing shorts on in double-quick time. His hands trembled slightly as he laced up his boots, the reality of the moment finally sinking in. Brother Bertie noticed, resting a firm palm on his shoulder.

'Steady on, mate,' his friend soothed. 'You've got this.'

Jimmy slumped on the wooden bench, his broad shoulders sagging under the enormity of the night's events. The dressing room's harsh lights cast stark shadows across his face, highlighting the worry lines etched deep.

Brother Bertie stood before him, deft fingers working to wrap Jimmy's hands. The familiar ritual should've been calming, but tension crackled in the air like static electricity.

'This is all my fucking fault,' Jimmy muttered, his voice barely above a whisper. 'If I hadn't come up with that stupid, stupid idea to steal a car—'

'Don't start that rubbish,' Bertie cut in, his Jamaican lilt sharp. 'We decided to do it together, remember? Blood brothers and all that.'

Jimmy's silver-grey eyes, usually blazing with determination, now were dull and haunted. 'But it was my idea, wasn't it? And now look where it's got us. My father nearly killed us tonight.'

Bertie's hands stilled for a moment. 'Yeah, well, your dad being Danny effing Steele wasn't exactly something we planned for, was it?'

A bitter laugh escaped Jimmy's lips. 'Christ, when he came out of the dark… I thought I was gonna piss myself.'

'You and me both, bruv.' Bertie resumed his wrapping, the bandages weaving a complex pattern across Jimmy's knuckles. 'But we're here now, ain't we? Made it by the skin of our teeth.'

Jimmy flexed his fingers, testing the wrappings. 'Fat lot of good it'll do if I can't get my head straight. How am I supposed to fight with all this shit swirling around in my head?'

Brother Bertie crouched, forcing Jimmy to meet his gaze. 'Listen to me, you daft fool. This is your shot. Your chance to be more than just Danny Steele's boy. You've worked too hard to let it slip away now.'

'But I gave that car to Batters. And now Dad knows,' Jimmy hissed, the guilt etched across his face. 'I've gone and betrayed my own flesh and blood.'

His friend's eyes flashed. 'You did what you had to do. We both did. And yeah, maybe it wasn't the smartest move, but it's done now. Can't change it.'

Jimmy's jaw clenched, a muscle ticking beneath the skin. 'Dad will never forgive me.'

'Fuck him!' Brother Bertie spat. 'This ain't about him. It's about you. About us. We swore we'd always have each other's backs, didn't we? And I ain't about to let you throw away everything we've worked for because of your father.'

Brother Bertie held the Mexican leather gloves that Jimmy's mum had gifted him. He imagined how his mum had gone without, saving every penny to put towards these gloves.

'Ready?' Brother Bertie asked softly.

Jimmy nodded, unable to speak past the lump in his throat. His friend's gentle hands worked each finger into the first glove. The leather felt butter-soft against his skin. These weren't just boxing gloves. They were his mother's faith in him. Her dreams for her boy.

The door burst open. His mother and Sin rushed in, faces flushed with panic.

'Jimmy!' Sin cried, throwing her arms around him. 'We thought… when you weren't here…'

Iris hugged him tight. 'We feared the worst, love. What happened?'

Jimmy and Brother Bertie exchanged a quick glance. No way were they telling them about Danny's last-minute 'errand' that had made them late.

In a rush, Brother Bertie told them, 'My Morris Minor packed up. We had to leg it to get here.'

No one else noticed how his and Sin's gazes caught each other. The hungry expression in their eyes. She was the first to look away.

Before they could press further, the door swung open again. Danny Steele sauntered in, cool as you please.

Jimmy's jaw dropped in disbelief. 'Dad?'

'Came to wish you luck, didn't I?' Danny boomed, his voice bouncing against the wall.

Jimmy's muscles tensed involuntarily, a knot forming in the pit of his stomach. After everything that had happened, his old man had the nerve to waltz in here like nothing was wrong?

Brother Bertie shifted uncomfortably, glance darting between father and son. The tension in the room was thick enough to choke on.

'Thanks, Dad,' Jimmy managed, his voice carefully neutral.

Inside, his thoughts raced. Less than an hour ago, this man had him hogtied ready to drown him beneath the killing tide of the river.

Danny strode across the room and squeezed Jimmy across his collarbone. 'That's my boy.'

Jimmy flinched slightly at the touch, a movement so subtle most wouldn't have noticed. But Brother Bertie saw, his own fists clenching at his sides.

'Yeah, Dad. I'm ready,' Jimmy replied, struggling to meet his father's gaze.

If Danny noticed his son's reticence, he didn't let on. ''Course you are. The Destroyer isn't gonna know what hit him.'

Brother Bertie cleared his throat. 'Mr Steele, maybe Jimmy needs a moment to focus—'

'Piss off with that!' Danny cut him off, turning his attention to Brother Bertie. 'This is exactly what he needs. Some fatherly advice before the big fight.'

Danny leaned in close, his voice dropping to a conspiratorial whisper. 'Just remember what I taught you, yeah? If you're losing, there's no shame in fighting dirty. Whatever it takes to win.'

Suddenly the terrible truth hit Jimmy. That the timing of his father kidnapping him had been no accident. He'd deliberately chosen when to strike. He'd snatched Jimmy before the biggest fight of his life, when every minute of preparation mattered. His father had done it knowing full well it might not leave Jimmy enough time to reach the fight. Jimmy suddenly understood – his father didn't want him to make it, to be champ. What he wanted was Jimmy to be under his thumb, controlling him, always pulling his strings.

Blood boiling, outraged, Jimmy opened his mouth, ready to confront the man he'd idolized his whole life. But at the last second, Jimmy swallowed the words back down. Years of keeping his head down, of not questioning his father's actions, won out. His jawline tightened, the unspoken accusation burning in his chest.

A sharp knock at the door interrupted them. 'Steele! You're on in two minutes!'

'Make me proud, son,' Danny said, but his smile never met his eyes.

Chapter Fifty-Five

The bell clanged.

Jimmy climbed through the ropes, his muscular frame glistening with sweat under the harsh lights. The hall was a cauldron of noise and tension, the air thick with cigarette smoke and the acrid tang of spilt beer. Punters packed every available space, jostling for a better view, their faces a sea of excitement and bloodlust.

Jimmy's eyes scanned the on-the-edge-of-their-seats crowd. His gaze caught on Sin and Iris, their faces a mix of pride and worry. For a moment, the noise faded, and, in his mind, he saw the faces of his wife and his children, Violet and Robbie. The child who was on their way to join them. He was fighting for them, for their future.

His focus snapped back to the ring. His entire world shrank to the canvas beneath his feet and the mountain of muscle facing him across the ring. Don 'The Destroyer' Dawson prowled the opposite corner, a caged beast ready to do maximum damage. His shaved head gleamed under the lights, face set in a permanent snarl. Jimmy's gut tightened.

He was ready!

The bell clanged.

Jimmy's fists itched for blood, his body coiled and ready for brutal action. He bounced on the balls of his feet, every muscle primed and ready. Dawson charged forward, his massive right fist arcing through the air like a wrecking ball. The punch came from so far out, Jimmy could practically feel the displacement of air whooshing past his ear. He slipped it easily, muscle memory from countless training sessions kicking in. He countered with a lightning-fast Southpaw-left jab to Dawson's solar plexus. The satisfying thud connecting sent a jolt up Jimmy's arm.

'That's it, Jimmy!' Sin's voice soared over the chatter of the crowd. 'Clobber the bloody hell out of him!'

Jimmy pressed his advantage, his stance a fluid dance of controlled aggression. His left hand became a piston, firing off rapid jabs that seemed to materialise out of thin air. One moment, Jimmy's fist was tucked close to his chin; the next, it was snapping Dawson's head back.

Southpaw. That's what they called him, and now Dawson was learning why.

Jimmy's unorthodox stance kept the champ off-balance, unable to find his rhythm. A left hook whistled past Dawson's guard, grazing his cheek. Another slipped through, catching him just under the ribs. Each punch flowed seamlessly into the next, a brutal ballet that left Dawson reeling.

The Destroyer stumbled back, his feet tangling while trying to create distance. For the first time, a flicker of doubt crossed his face. He'd underestimated this upstart from the East End docks, and now he was paying the price.

Jimmy's steely gaze gleamed with predatory focus. He'd found his range, and Dawson knew it. The ring had become Jimmy's hunting ground, and he was closing in for the kill.

But the champ wasn't done. Dawson, a veteran of countless battles, knew how to weather a storm. He planted his feet, narrowed his stance, and waited for his moment. It came when Jimmy, flush with success, overextended a left hook. His opponent ducked under the punch, his massive frame flexing with the know-how of a spring. Jimmy's fist whistled harmlessly over his head, Dawson unleashed a vicious uppercut. The punch started low, gathering momentum travelling upwards, aimed at Jimmy's exposed ribs.

Jimmy saw it coming a split-second too late. He tried to pivot away, but the fist caught him just under the floating rib. Pain exploded in Jimmy's side, radiating outwards with the fierceness of a firework. His breath caught in his throat, lungs momentarily forgetting how to function.

Jimmy's vision swam. The roar of the crowd became distant, replaced by the thunder of his own heartbeat. Gritting his teeth, Jimmy pushed the pain down, shoving it into a corner of his mind. He reset his stance, raised his guard, and met Dawson's predatory gaze with a defiant glare of his own. The message was clear: it would take a lot more than that to keep Jimmy Southpaw down.

Jimmy's mind raced, checking out Dawson's every move. He noticed the champ favoured his right side, leaving a small opening on the left. Jimmy filed the information away, waiting for the perfect moment to exploit it.

Round after round, they traded blows. Jimmy's speed versus Dawson's raw power. The crowd's roars ebbed and flowed with each exchange, the energy in the room electric.

By the fifth, both men were bloodied and bruised. Jimmy's left eye was swelling shut, his ribs screaming in protest with every breath. But Dawson wasn't faring much better. A nasty cut above his right eye streamed blood down his face.

In his corner, Brother Bertie worked frantically between rounds. 'You're doing great, mate. He's tiring. This next round, take his raas down!'

Jimmy nodded, gasping for air. His lungs burned, his arms felt like lead. But he wasn't done. Not by a long shot. He thought of all the early morning runs, the punishing training sessions, the sacrifices he'd made to get here. It all came down to this.

Standing to face the sixth round, his father's words echoed in his head:

'Make me proud, son.'

The memory of his dad's wolfish grin sent a chill down Jimmy's spine. It wasn't encouragement; it was ownership. Jimmy shook his head, trying to clear the doubts creeping in. He couldn't let his father get in his head. Not now.

The sixth round began. Jimmy came out swinging, catching the reigning champ off-guard. He let loose with a flurry of punches, his knuckles feeling his opponent's bones through the limited padding in his smaller gloves, driving the champ back. The crowd roared, the chant building to a fever pitch.

'Southpaw! Southpaw! Southpaw!'

Jimmy's blood sang with the sound of his name. He pressed forward, cutting off the ring, forcing Dawson onto the ropes. Victory was within reach. He saw the gap he'd been waiting for – Dawson's left side exposed.

But as Jimmy wound up for his signature left hook, putting everything he had behind it, his father's voice intruded again:

'Make me proud, son.'

The words seemed to mock him, reminding him of his recent kidnapping, the constant pressure, the impossible expectations.

In that instance of hesitation, Dawson saw his chance. The champ slipped the punch and countered with a monstrous right cross, living up to his nickname, 'The Destroyer'.

The world exploded in a burst of white-hot light. Jimmy's legs turned to jelly. He stumbled, fighting to stay upright. The clamour of the crowd became a distant buzz. Through rapidly blurring vision, he saw Dawson winding up for another blow.

'Jimmy!' Brother Bertie's voice cut through the fog. 'Jimmy!'

He tried to rally, but his body wouldn't respond. Another thunderous punch caught him on the jaw. He felt his body go floppy and limp, all control lost. Falling, he caught a glimpse of his father's face in the crowd. Was that disappointment he saw? Or something worse?

'Make me proud, son.'

The last thing Jimmy saw was the canvas rushing up to meet him.

Then everything went black.

Chapter Fifty-Six

Jimmy slumped on the edge of the bed, his battered body a map of pain and regret. Mini's petite form knelt before him, dabbing his swollen eye.

'Hold still,' she murmured firmly. 'You did your best out there, baby. There'll be other fights.'

Jimmy's laugh was bitter. 'Other fights? I blew it, Mini. My one shot at the big time, gone.'

'Stop talking rubbish,' Mini chided. 'My fella ain't no quitter. Never has been!'

Her unwavering faith made Jimmy's gut churn with guilt. He caught her wrist, stilling her movements. 'Mini, there's something I need to tell you.'

She sat back on her heels, brow furrowed. 'What is it?'

Jimmy took a deep breath, then whispered, 'Christ, Mini, there was a body in the boot of that car.'

Mini's eyes widened, her face paling. 'Bloody hell, Jimmy. What did you do?'

'What could we do? We buried the unfortunate sod,' Jimmy admitted, shame colouring his words. 'But the car was becoming too hot. We didn't know who else to turn to… I went to your old man.'

'My dad?' Mini's stunned questions was barely audible. 'But he hates you.'

'I know, but I didn't have a choice. He took care of it.'

Mini stood abruptly, pacing the room. Her eyes darted to the door; she must be worried about eavesdroppers. 'So my dad, who won't even look at me in the street, helped you out of a jam?'

Jimmy nodded miserably. 'Yeah, and now my dad thinks I've betrayed him. Gone to the enemy. Dad nabbed me and Brother Bertie just before the fight.'

Mini whirled around, her eyes blazing. 'He did WHAT?'

Finally, Jimmy was able to voice his suspicions. 'I'd bet my life he did it on purpose, to put me in danger of missing my chance at the championship.'

Mini's hands flew in the air in maddening frustration. 'That bastard. The sooner we're out from under his roof, the better.'

Jimmy's shoulders sagged. 'Mini, like I said, I had to get rid of the car, so there's no money to buy the house on Molasses Quay.'

To his surprise, Mini let out a small laugh. 'Oh, Jimmy. Is that what you're worried about? A house?'

'But it's your dream,' Jimmy protested. 'To get out of here, have some space of our own.'

Mini knelt before him again, taking his battered hands in hers. 'My dream is YOU, you great lummox. You and our family. We'll find another house. And until then, we'll manage.'

Jimmy felt a lump form in his throat. 'I don't deserve you, Mini.'

''Course you do,' she said firmly. 'Now stop your moping.' Without warning, her eyes lit up. She grabbed his hand and pressed it against her swollen belly. 'Feel that?'

For a moment, Jimmy felt nothing. Then, a flutter against his palm. His breath caught. 'Is that…?'

Mini nodded, her smile radiant. 'That's our baby, Jimmy. Our future.'

For a brief moment, joy pierced through the cloud of despair that had settled over Jimmy. But all too quickly, reality came crashing back.

'What kind of future can I give this kid, Mini?' he asked, distraught. 'I'm a failure in the ring, I've messed things up with both our dads. I'm living in my parents' house, for Chrissakes. I'm a dead loss.'

'Now you listen here, Jimmy Steele,' Mini retorted fiercely. 'You're many things, but a dead loss ain't one of them.'

Jimmy wanted to believe her. God, how he wanted to. But his body aching, his dreams in tatters, all he could feel was an overwhelming sense of inadequacy.

She cupped his face in her hands, forcing him to squarely meet her gaze. 'We'll get through this. Together. You hear me?'

Jimmy nodded, not trusting himself to speak. Mini pulled him close, and he buried his face in her shoulder, inhaling her familiar scent.

A knock at the door made them both jump.

'Everything all right in there?' His mother's concern was plain to hear.

'Fine, Mum,' Jimmy called back, the roughness of his tone in direct opposite to his verbal reassurance. 'We'll be out in a bit.'

Iris' footsteps fading away, Jimmy met Mini's eyes. The love and determination he saw there both comforted and terrified him. He wanted to be the man she believed him to be, the father their child deserved. But even while he held her, feeling their baby move between them, Jimmy couldn't shake the feeling that he was drowning. The walls of their room, in his parents' house, seemed to close in, and the future loomed before him, dark and uncertain.

***

'Brother Bertie's here to see you,' his mum relayed gently on the other side of the bathroom door while Jimmy was shaving the following morning.

He loved his best mate to bits, no doubt about it, but he wasn't in the mood this morning. He was still smarting from losing the fight, and truth be told, every joint and muscle in his body was screaming blue murder.

'What's he want?'

'Didn't say. Besides which, it isn't my business. Best go see, eh?'

He found Brother Bertie in the kitchen, chipper and chirpy. Excitedly, he told Jimmy, 'Got ourselves a plan, haven't we?'

Jimmy's brow furrowed. 'What you on about?'

'Your dad let slip that the car belonged to a top cop.'

'What's that got to do with anything?'

Brother Bertie grinned, a spark of mischief and danger in his eyes. 'We're going to the one place that's going to put me and you back in business.'

Chapter Fifty-Seven

'You must've lost your bloody marbles' Jimmy hissed, his grey gaze wide with disbelief.

Before them stood the East London Police Command Centre. It was a stark monolith of exposed concrete and rigid geometrical forms. Its uncompromising facade seemed to sneer at the surrounding Victorian terraces, a brutal testament to the City's relentless march towards modernity.

'Cool it, bruv,' Brother Bertie said. 'Believe me, this plan is watertight. Remember, we've got one last trick up our sleeve. A trick we never told Batters about. Never told your dad about.'

Jimmy swallowed hard, his throat as dry as sandpaper. With leaden feet, he followed his best mate through the sliding glass doors and into the lion's den.

When they entered, the bustling lobby fell silent, a sea of suspicious faces turning towards them. Jimmy's jaw clenched hard at the poorly disguised sneers and raised eyebrows directed at Brother Bertie. Anger surged up inside him, hot and bitter. These narrow-minded bastards, judging a man by the colour of his skin. He wanted to knock their thick skulls together.

Brother Bertie felt the hostility pressing in from all sides, but he refused to let it rattle him. Instead, he straightened his spine. He remained impassive, a mask of calm dignity in the face of their ignorance. He adjusted the brim of his porkpie hat, a subtle gesture of 'fuck you' defiance. Then, with measured steps, he strode alongside Jimmy towards the desk. Brother Bertie offered a single, courteous nod to the desk sergeant, his very bearing shouting loud and clear that he belonged there as much as anyone else, their petty prejudices beneath his notice.

'State your business,' the desk sergeant snapped.

'We need to speak with Commander Hawthorne,' Brother Bertie answered.

Behind narrowed eyes, the officer asked, 'And why would the commander waste his time on the likes of you?'

Jimmy leaned in, his voice low and urgent. 'Tell him it's about a car.'

Something dark flickered behind the other man's expression. Then he snatched up the phone, murmuring urgently into the receiver. A moment later, he stood. 'This way.'

They were led down a labyrinth of corridors, finally ushered into a small, windowless room. The door clicked shut behind the sergeant with the finality of a coffin lid.

'I don't fancy this.' Jimmy's jittery gaze darted around the bare walls. 'We're sitting ducks in here.'

The door burst open, slamming against the wall with a crash that made Jimmy's teeth rattle. Two men stalked in, their eyes hard and cold. Jimmy didn't need introductions to know who they were.

Detectives Abbot and Long.

'Where's the bleedin' motor?' Abbot got into it straight away, his mouth ruffling with disdain, obviously still pissed to high heaven that Jimmy and Brother Bertie had made mugs of them during the car chase from Piccadilly.

'We ain't here to parley with the hired help,' Jimmy shot back. 'We want Hawthorne.'

Long, wiry and mean as a junkyard dog, was on him in a flash. His fingers dug into Jimmy's throat, slamming him against the wall. 'Listen here, you little prick—'

'Tell Hawthorne we have his package,' Brother Bertie's calm voice cut through the tension like a knife.

The cop's grip loosened, just a fraction. 'What package?'

Jimmy choked through the pressure against his windpipe. 'You'd better pray nothing happens to us in here. 'Cause if it does, every rag in London's gonna be running a certain story come morning.'

The detectives exchanged a loaded glance. Without another word, they stormed out, leaving Jimmy and Brother Bertie alone in the suffocating silence.

'Bloody Nora,' Jimmy breathed, rubbing his throat. 'Thought we were brown bread there for sure.'

Brother Bertie wore a smile of deep satisfaction. He was the one to put two and two together – why would one of the cleanest top cops on the force have a dead body in his car? And not merely dead, but butchered to oblivion with no head, to prevent identification? If this knowledge came out it would cause one hell of a scandal. Hawthorne in disgrace and banged up in prison.

Jimmy caught the glint of steel in his friend's eyes.

'Told you, didn't I?' Bertie said. 'We've got Commander Hawthorne by the balls now.'

***

A prim secretary, her heels clicking a staccato rhythm on the polished floor, led them through more corridors and upstairs. The farther they ascended, the thicker the carpets became, muffling their footsteps and lending an air of hushed importance to their surroundings.

They emerged onto a floor that reeked of power and authority. Dark wood panelling lined the walls, interspersed with framed commendations and stern-faced portraits of long-dead policemen. Jimmy felt very, very uncomfortable indeed.

The secretary rapped softly on a set of imposing oak doors before ushering them inside. The office beyond was large, dominated by floor-to-ceiling windows that offered a commanding view of the city below.

Behind an enormous mahogany desk sat Commander Reginald Hawthorne. His silver hair was impeccably groomed, and he wore a crisp uniform showcasing all the brass of his senior position. He didn't invite them to sit down.

'Gentlemen,' Hawthorne said, his voice surprisingly soft. 'I understand you have something that belongs to me. Where is it?'

'Safe,' Brother Bertie replied, cool as you like. 'And it'll stay that way, long as we all play nice.'

The commander's jawline hardened, a muscle ticking in his cheek. Then the fight drained out of him, and his shoulders sagged. The crushing weight of whatever he'd been carrying etched deep lines into his face, aging him before their eyes.

'You don't understand,' Hawthorne told them, his tone rough and low. 'That package… it's not what you think.'

Jimmy leaned forward, curiosity overriding his nerves. 'Then why don't you explain it to us?'

Gesturing to the chairs, Hawthorne signalled for them to sit.

His troubled gaze drifted to a framed photograph on his desk. From where he sat, Jimmy could just make out the image of a smiling young woman.

'The package was my son-in-law. Gregory Winters,' the older man began, each word seeming to cost him dearly. 'He'd been beating my Margaret. For years.'

A cold knot formed in Jimmy's gut, thinking of his own daughter, Violet.

'I tried to get her to leave.' Hawthorne's fingers laced together, tight and strained on the desk. 'But she was scared. Ashamed. The last time, he put her in hospital. Broken ribs, fractured cheekbone.'

Brother Bertie's usually impassive face twisted in disgust. 'Bloody animal,' he muttered.

'When she got home, he was waiting. Started in on her again.' Hawthorne's hands clenched into fists. 'This time… this time she fought back.'

The silence that followed was deafening. Jimmy could hear his own heartbeat pounding in his ears, feel the enormity of the commander's confession pressing down on them all.

'She called me, hysterical.' Hawthorne's eyes glistened with unshed tears. 'When I got there he was already dead. She'd stabbed him. I've spent my whole life upholding the law, but in that moment… I knew. I knew I had to protect my little girl.'

Brother Bertie leaned forward, his dark eyes intense. 'So you cleaned up her mess.'

Hawthorne nodded, the increasing strain brining out every line on his face. 'I was going to dispose of the body myself, but then the car was stolen. With that wife-beating bastard inside.'

Jimmy's mind raced. This information could destroy one of London's highest cops which meant he was under their total control. The payout he'd give them to keep their mouths shut would be astronomical. Enough to buy that house on Molasses Quay and for Bertie to stop Claudette from destroying his relationship with his little daughter.

But observing Commander Hawthorne, Jimmy experienced a peculiar shift in perspective. The other man's bearing as a police officer, his polished uniform, the medals, the stern authority – it all fell away. Instead, he saw something startlingly familiar: a father driven to desperate lengths to shield his child from harm. The revelation struck him hard. After all, wasn't that exactly why he and Brother Bertie had stolen the commander's car in the first place? Every risk they'd taken, every line they'd crossed, had been about protecting their own children – his Violet and Robbie, Brother Bertie's Precious. In that moment, they weren't cop and criminals in the room.

Just fathers.

Jimmy couldn't milk this man for money. Just couldn't. He glanced at Brother Bertie, saw the same realisation dawning in his friend.

'We'll get rid of the body,' Jimmy heard himself say.

Hope and disbelief warred across Hawthorne's face. 'You will?'

Brother Bertie nodded solemnly. 'We'll take care of it.'

Crippling relief washed over the older man. 'I can pay you. Whatever you want.'

Jimmy shook his head. 'Consider it a favour. If any bastard did that to our girls…' He let the sentence hang, the implication clear.

When they stood to leave, Hawthorne called out, 'Why? Why would you do this for me?'

Brother Bertie held him eye-for-eye. 'Because some debts are worth more than money.'

***

When they got back to Sugar Cane Wharf, they sensed something was off.

'What the fuck?' Jimmy muttered as they turned onto their street.

A crowd had gathered, people spilling out of houses and pubs to gawk at the commotion. Police cars, their lights flashing, were parked haphazardly outside one of Jimmy's dad's warehouses.

Brother Bertie hissed, 'What's going on?'

Jimmy pulled over. 'I'm gonna see what's what.'

He slipped out of Brother Bertie's car, blending into the crowd with practiced ease. He spotted a member of his dad's firm.

'What's the score?'

The other man, features hard and serious, told him, 'Word is, some bigwig copper's car got nicked. Real fancy job, worth a mint. The plod reckon Danny's got it stashed away in a warehouse.' He stared Jimmy in the eye. 'But if that's the same motor we've all been hunting, that got to be bollocks because Danny would've sent word if he'd found it.'

Jimmy was reeling. A cold sweat formed across his hair and oiled the curve of his spine. There was no way his dad could have it. They'd given it to Batters.

Unless…

Chapter Fifty-Eight

Arms folded, Danny stood cool as a cucumber while the police swarmed inside every nook and cranny of his warehouse.

Jimmy and Brother Bertie watched from outside. Jimmy felt sick. This was all his fault. He'd brought this mess to his father's doorstep, and now everything they'd built could come crashing down around them.

'We've got to do something,' Jimmy hissed, starting to move forward.

Brother Bertie grabbed his arm. 'Hold up, mate. Look.'

Jimmy followed his friend's gaze to the other side of the street. His blood ran cold. Batters and his Aunt Chrissie emerged from the shadows, Lucas as expected behind them. Batters had his arm draped possessively across Chrissie's shoulders, a triumphant smirk plastered on his face.

Danny caught sight of them, too. With casual grace, he strolled across the street to meet them.

Batters leaned in close, his voice low and gloating. 'Well, well, Danny-boy. Looks like your luck's finally run out.'

Danny said nothing, his face an impassive mask.

Emboldened by the silence, Batters continued. 'You should've seen your boy, on his knees, begging like a beaten dog.' He chuckled darkly. 'Poor Jimmy, nowhere to turn. Not even to his own father.'

Jimmy's fists clenched at his sides, shame and anger warring in his gut. Brother Bertie put a steadying hand on his shoulder.

'It was almost too easy,' Batters went on, clearly relishing the moment. 'Your Chrissie here's been quite the songbird, telling me all about your business affairs with this new warehouse. Didn't take much to plant that car in your warehouse and tip off the boys in blue.' He winked. ''Course, I made sure they were properly motivated. A little drink goes a long way, eh?'

Throughout Batters' gloating monologue, Danny remained unnaturally still. Then, just as Batters was winding down, Danny did the last thing anyone expected. Tipping his head back, he roared with so much laughter there were tears in his eyes.

Batters' smug expression faltered, confusion creeping into his expression. His uncertainty only grew when a group of visibly frustrated officers emerged from the warehouse.

'Nothing, sir,' one of them reported to their sergeant. 'Place is clean as a whistle.'

'What?' Batters sputtered, his arm falling away from Chrissie. 'That's impossible!'

Chrissie smoothly stepped away from Batters. She sidled up to Danny and wound her arm around his waist.

'Oh, Eric,' she dramatically sighed, using Batters' given name. 'You really are as thick as pig shit, aren't you?'

Batters' face contorted with fury. 'You fucking bi—'

'Now, now,' Danny cut in, his voice silky smooth. 'Is that any way to talk to a lady?'

Chrissie grinned. 'Did you really think I'd turn on my own flesh and blood? For you?' She laughed, the sound sharp and brittle. 'Me and Danny's falling-out was just for show, darling. Had to make it look good, didn't we?'

'You see, Batters,' Danny explained. 'When you took my sister under your wing, you handed me the keys to your kingdom. Every whispered secret, every hidden deal – Chrissie brought it all back to me on a silver platter.'

Batters lunged forward, his face purple with rage, but Lucas caught him, holding him back with his massive arms.

'Let me go!' Batters roared. 'I'll fucking kill them both!'

'Not now, Dad,' Lucas grunted, struggling to contain his father's fury. 'It's over.'

To underscore Lucas' statement, right on cue, Rita sashayed in with her girls into the warehouse, all dolled up in French maid uniforms, carrying silver tea trays. Their rehearsed giggles and fluttering eyelashes were as fake as Rita's smile.

'Evening, gents,' Rita purred to the gathered police, her voice carrying across the street. 'Fancy a cuppa while you're at it? My girls make a lovely brew.'

A few coppers appeared tempted, but their sergeant barked at them to get back to work. Rita just shrugged, a coy smile playing on her painted lips. If Batters had any doubts about being played for a fool, they vanished right then.

Danny and Chrissie turned away, arm in arm, their laughter floating back on the night air.

'We played a blinder, bruv,' Chrissie crowed.

Jimmy and Brother Bertie exchanged stunned glances.

'Fuck me,' Brother Bertie breathed. 'Your old man's something else.'

Jimmy nodded, a complex blend of emotions knotting his stomach. Pride, relief, and a twinge of something darker he couldn't quite name.

They watched Danny approach the lead detective, all charm and easy smiles.

'Sorry for the wild goose chase, boys,' he said, loud enough for everyone to hear. 'Seems like someone's been having a laugh at your expense. And mine.' He shook his head ruefully.

Rita stepped forward, her grin dazzling. 'Why don't you gents retire for some tea on our luxury yacht, The Sing-Song Lady?'

The offer was met with a chorus of approval from the assembled officers. They began to disperse, and Danny's eyes locked on to Jimmy and Brother Bertie. With a subtle jerk of his head, he beckoned them over.

'Come on,' Jimmy muttered, his mouth going dry. 'Time to face the music.'

***

To Jimmy's surprise, his father placed an arm around his shoulder, a display of affection he wasn't expecting.

'Nice work, son,' Danny said quietly. 'You did good, bringing that car to Batters. Played right into my hands.'

Jimmy blinked, confused. 'But you know I didn't mean for—'

Danny cut him short. 'When you told me that Batters had the motor, I knew exactly what the cunt was planning. Just had to get your Aunt Chrissie to confirm.' He chuckled, beside himself with glee. 'Then he goes in for the kill only to figure out too late it's me who'll be doing the murdering.'

'Dad…' Jimmy started.

'Not now, boy,' his dad again interrupted, his voice deceptively soft. 'We'll have our talk. But it's me who will decide when that time will be.'

Jimmy swallowed hard, his nerves feeling like fire. The thought of facing the man he'd looked up to all his life made his palms sweat and the muscles in his windpipe tighten. How could he stare his father in the eye after going behind his back? He was supposed to be the loyal son, for fuck's sake. But another voice piped up from the back of his mind:

Who the hell does Dad think he is? I ain't no snot-nosed kid no more. I'm a grown man with his own family to think about. The defiant voice grew louder, drowning out the fear. Yeah, Dad might be King of the Docks, but he doesn't own me. Not my body, not my mind, and certainly not my future. I've made my choice and will face the fallout like a man. Let the old bastard rage and roar. After all, wasn't that what Dad had always taught me at his knee? To be tough, to take what you wanted? Well, now it's time to show Dad what kind of man he's raised.

Danny's expression suddenly hardened as he studied both his son and Brother Bertie. 'Now, about that car. What I can't figure is why it was so bloody important in the first place. There's something you two aren't telling me.'

Jimmy and Brother Bertie exchanged uneasy glances.

'Out with it,' Danny demanded, his voice low and dangerous. 'And don't even think about feeding me any ole flannel.'

'A body,' Brother Bertie blurted out, wincing as soon as the words left his mouth.

'A dead body,' Jimmy sombrely added.

Danny's eyebrows shot up, his body going rigid. 'You what? Why would Commander Hawthorne have a dead body in his motor?' Suddenly, a calculating gleam lit the fire in his eyes, a crafty, ugly smile spreading across his face. 'We can use that as leverage. Have Commander Hawthorne in our pockets. Do you know what kind of power that could give me… I mean, us?'

Jimmy straightened his shoulders. 'No can do, Dad.'

'What?' The gloating froze on Danny's face.

'The thing is, we gave our word to him that we'd make the body disappear. For good.' He met his father's displeased expression head-on. 'One of the first things you ever taught me about the bizz was once you give your word, that's it. Or you start getting a rep as a double-dealing backstabber. Someone no one can trust.'

His father considered him. 'Can you at least tell me who the body was?'

Brother Bertie remained silent. This tense exchange was between father and son.

Jimmy answered, 'Let's just say some people aren't meant to roam this earth with the rest of us.' He took another step in claiming independence from his father. 'I'm assuming you've got the motor locked up nice and tight somewhere. Well, I'm thinking it's mine and Bertie's. Hawthorne wants shot of it. Me and Bertie see it as his payment to us for keeping his secret.'

Jimmy waited, barely breathing for his dad to slam him down, insist the car was his, that who the hell did he think he was telling the King of the Docks what to do.

Danny shocked him. 'Congratulations, son. I taught you well.'

Typical Danny Steele, another backhanded compliment for his son, but in this instance, Jimmy would swallow it.

His father continued, 'I'm assuming you want to still sell it, so I'll put someone on the case to make it appear sparkling new again.'

Once they were alone, Brother Bertie turned to Jimmy, his eyes wide with elation. 'You know what this means, don't you?'

Jimmy nodded, a wild grin spreading across his face. 'We're back in fucking business. I'll get on the blower to our man in Amsterdam.'

'That house on Molasses Quay,' Brother Bertie started. 'It's all yours and Mini's.'

'And a lawyer for you to make sure Precious has your name,' Jimmy finished. 'We might just fucking pull this off.'

Chapter Fifty-Nine

Brother Bertie fumbled with the key to Candy's flat. His heart was beating hard against his ribs because Sin was sinfully pressed against him, her familiar scent intoxicating and powerful. He couldn't wait to get her inside. Christ, he'd missed her. It felt like forever since they'd been together, the truth being they hadn't seen each other in a few weeks.

That niggling feeling that Brother Bertie had been carrying that something was up crept back. The way her work mates at the hair salon said she wasn't around when he popped in special to see her, although he sensed she was there. The way lately she'd said she was too busy to meet.

Was she avoiding him?

So, being a typical Caribbean man who went by the code of straight talking, he asked her flat out, 'What's going on with you? You've been dodging me like I've got the plague.'

'Nothing's going on.' She wouldn't meet his gaze. 'Just been busy at the salon, that's all.'

'Sin…?'

'For God's sake, can't you just shut up and kiss me?' Her arms urgently wound around his neck. 'Hurry,' she whispered between kisses, thick with desire.

Finally, the lock gave way. They almost fell inside, a tangle of limbs and hungry kisses. Bertie kicked the door shut and hauled Sin close, drinking in the sight of her. Her pixie cut was mussed, her lipstick smudged from their eager lovemaking. She'd never looked more beautiful.

Groaning, Bertie closed his eyes, losing himself in her delicious touch while she caressed him and worked off his shirt. When he opened them again, Sin had shrugged off her blouse.

That's when he saw them. Bruises. Sickly yellow-green marks against her back. Bertie froze, the passion leaving him, replaced by an ice-cold dread. Those marks hadn't been before. They were definitely not there when she was attacked at the party.

'What happened?' he breathed, his heart picking up speed again.

She tried to jerk away, to cover herself, but it was too late. Bertie gently took her wrists, his gaze roving over more bruises. Swiftly, he turned her so that he could inspect her back. What he saw nearly made him lose his shit.

'It's nothing,' Sin muttered.

'Nothing?' Furiously twisted her to face him again. He wanted answers. 'Who did this to you?'

Someone had beaten her black and blue leaving welts on her skin.

'Tell me!' He swallowed back the roughness of his order, conscious that Sin had been hurt enough, he didn't want to add to her pain. Nevertheless, she needed to understand they weren't leaving until he had the truth.

For a moment, Sin remained silent, her eyes downcast. Then, lifting her head up, she explained, 'Someone saw me with you.' She shook her head with such sadness. 'They didn't figure out it was you, but they told Dad they'd seen me with a black man.'

Blood drained from his face, leaving Bertie with the sensation of being encased in a block of ice. Deep down, he'd known this day would come. No matter how careful they'd been, sneaking about in the shadows, meeting in secret spots, they were living on borrowed time. The problem with London was it appeared big and anonymous, but the truth was, it was like a goldfish bowl where this person knew that person who knew this person. Still, he hadn't thought they'd be found out this quickly. Sweet Jesus Christ, not this soon.

His gaze locked on to the brutal purple and yellow bruises mottling Sin's beautiful skin. The woman he loved more than life itself, marked by violence. Rage bubbled up inside him, primitive and murderous.

'Your dad did this to you?' His hands curled into fists so tight his nails cut into his palms.

Sin's response was bitter but guarded. 'Yes and no.'

'What does that mean?' Bertie wiped his hand over his face, trying to clear the buzz in his ears.

'He was behind it.' She wrapped her arms around her belly, like she was trying to hold her broken pieces. Her gaze suddenly became jittery, darting away from him. 'But someone else did the actual beating.'

'That bastard!'

Mouth twisted, Bertie jerked up, making Sin jump. He balled his fist in the air, desperate to pound it into something. The wall. The window. The fucking world. He knew exactly what Sin was telling him. Her father had paid someone to assault her. Probably attacked her on her way from work like she was a dog in the street.

'Which thug did he hire?' His voice dripped venom. 'Because I'm going to hunt that rat-faced filth down—'

'You don't understand.,' she cut over him with a sharp edge. 'Dad would never put the word out to get someone to put the frighteners on me. Not for this.' Her voice dropped low, bitter. 'This is family business. That always stays behind closed doors. This is the East End where family is everything. Always has been, always will be. Family handles family matters. The Steele way.'

'I know that, but…'

The horrific truth exploded in his brain.

'JIMMY!' The name escaped him in a stunned breath.

No! Not Jimmy!

Bertie refused to believe it. His Jimmy? His blood brother? His spar in the ring and outside? The man whom he would lay his life down for without blinking?

But the terrible, stark expression on Sin's face told him the truth. The tear that slid down her cold cheek confirmed his worst fear. The day Jimmy had turned up at Gertie's in a right old state, like the Devil himself was on his tail, came flooding back. Was that the reason for Jimmy's odd behaviour that day? Because he'd done something despicable?

The taste of bile rose thick and sickly in his throat. Rage boiled up, too, threatening to consume him. How could Jimmy do this? His best mate, the man he trusted above all others, had beaten his own sister. And for what? Because she dared to love someone with darker skin?

'I'll kill him,' Bertie growled, already rushing for the door. 'I'll fucking murder him.'

'No!' Sin shot up, grabbing his arm, stopping him in his tracks. Her fingers bit into his flesh, her eyes wide with panic. 'Bertie, please. You can't.'

'Why the hell not?' he harshly cried. 'Look what he did to you!'

'It wasn't his choice,' Sin pleaded. 'Dad made him do it. If Jimmy had refused…' She trailed off, unable to finish the thought.

Bertie's jaw clenched. Of course, Danny Steele, it always came back to him. The bastard had forced his own son to beat his daughter, all to keep his twisted idea of family honour intact. The urge to storm over to the Steele house and confront them both was almost overwhelming.

'They can't get away with this,' Bertie hissed. God, he felt so helpless.

Sin cupped his face in her hands, forcing him to meet her gaze. 'Listen to me. If you go after Jimmy, if you tell anyone what happened, it'll only make things worse. Dad will know for sure it's you I've been seeing. He'll come after you, Bertie. And as for Jimmy,' she softly carried on, 'It might ruin your friendship—'

'I don't care about that. All I care about is you.'

But even as the words left his mouth, that familiar guilt twisted in Bertie's gut. Sneaking around with Sin behind Jimmy's back, it went against everything he stood for. Everything he was. A stand-up guy didn't do his best mate like that. He should've been man enough to front up to Jimmy from the start, take whatever came his way. Should've looked Jimmy in the eye, man to man, and told him straight – he was in love with his sister. Let the chips fall where they may.

Instead, he'd skulked about in the shadows like some spotty youth who didn't know how to handle his cock yet, ashamed of his feelings. Sin deserved better than that. She deserved a man who'd shout his love from the rooftops, proud to call her his lady. Not some coward who hid their relationship like it was dirty.

'Promise me,' Sin begged. 'Promise you won't do anything. That you won't tell anyone, especially Jimmy, that you know.'

Bertie wanted to argue, to insist that he could protect her, protect them both. But the reality of their situation crashed down upon him. They were trapped, caught between family loyalties and a society that saw their love as a sin.

'I promise,' he finally reluctantly agreed, the words tasting like poison in his mouth.

Sin's relief was palpable. She sagged against him, burying her face in his chest. Bertie held her close, his anger giving way to a deep, aching sadness. He stroked her hair, wishing he could somehow make all of this go away.

They stood like that for a long moment, clinging to each other in the dim flat. The passion that had brought them here had evaporated, replaced by a shared sorrow. When Sin finally moved away, Bertie could see the pain etched in every line of her face.

'We can't do this anymore,' she told him in a rushed hush of grief.

The bottom dropped out of his world. 'Sin, no. We can't give up. We'll figure something out.'

'It's too dangerous,' she insisted, her voice breaking. 'For both of us.'

Bertie shook his head vehemently. 'I won't accept that. We've been careful, haven't we? Meeting here, keeping it secret. We can keep doing that.'

'For how long?' Sin asked, her eyes brimming with tears. 'They're already suspicious. Next time, it might not just be a beating. We live in the East End. Dreams don't come true there.'

'Then we'll leave.' He nodded with conviction, the idea forming as he spoke. 'We'll go somewhere they can't find us. Start over.'

'Where? Look what happened in Brighton.'

Bertie drew her close again, desperation clawing at him from all sides. 'Please, Sin. Don't do this. I love you. We can make this work.'

'I love you, too,' she forced out, her voice barely above a breath. 'That's why we have to end this. I couldn't bear it if anything happened to you because of me.'

Openly sobbing, she picked up her blouse and flew at the door.

'Sin, wait—'

But she was already gone, the door wide open after her retreating figure.

Brother Bertie slumped on the edge of the rumpled bed, head buried in his trembling hands. All the warmth from the flat had gone. It suddenly felt cavernous, oppressively empty without Sin's presence. He wanted to scream, to break something, to run after her and beg her to reconsider. Instead, he sat in silence, waves of grief pounding into him.

Sin wasn't like the other women he'd known. Those had been easy come, easy go. Just a bit of fun. But Sin? She'd crawled under his skin, made a home in places he didn't even know existed inside him. Those canny eyes that saw right through his charm, his bullshit. Then there were the quiet moments. Sin curled against him, telling him about her modelling dreams. Her fingers tracing the scars on his knuckles, not judging, just understanding. The way she'd laugh out loud at his outrageous stories.

She was his match. His equal.

Gone.

A sound escaped him, torn from his chest, wild and broken. If he couldn't have Sin, what was the fuckery point of any of this anymore?

Chapter Sixty

Ruddy emerged from Whitechapel station, bone weary. Her feet were killing her something fierce after the hours spent sorting out and supervising one of Lady Pru's legendary afternoon tea gatherings. All she wanted to do was down a glass of Lord Have Mercy Rum Punch and then fall flat on her face on her bed. But the three resident drunks outside the station had other ideas. They rushed her in two seconds flat.

Fuck me! I can do without this lot!

'Ruddy, you need to come, girl. Quick,' Charlie, the one who always did the talking, urged, his voice raspy from years of cheap drink.

The ripe booze fumes coming off him slapped her in the face. Jerking back, Ruddy snapped, her patience wearing thin. 'What do you lot want? I ain't got time for your nonsense.'

They could be a proper trio of nuisances when they put their minds to it, including not above using a sob story to wheedle booze money from you.

Charlie's lined face looked more pale than usual. 'It's The Colonial. You've got to come. Now.'

The mention of the notorious working men's club immediately put Ruddy on her guard. She kept a wide berth of the place, mainly because it didn't take kindly to foreigners within its walls.

'Now why would I want to go there?' If these three were attempting to pull a fast one, trying to pick her pockets…

'Brother Bertie!' Charlie's gaze widened with fear.

Ruddy went cold all over, and her heart plummeted. She didn't even think but took off running, leaving Charlie and the others in her wake. Her mind raced with terrible possibilities as she navigated the narrow, cobbled streets of Whitechapel. The last place her friend should be in was that horrible place.

She burst through the doors to be met with a scene of utter chaos. In the centre of the room, a one-sided fight was unfolding. Brother Bertie, his face already swollen and bloodied, was being restrained by two burly men while a third rained blows upon him. But what shocked Ruddy most was that her Bertie wasn't fighting back, he was making no attempt to defend himself. He hung limply in their grasp, accepting each punch with a sickening thud.

Charlie appeared at Ruddy's side, panting from the exertion of keeping up with her. 'He waltzed in here and started making trouble. Shouting the odds, he was. Like he wanted them to fuck him over.'

Mind reeling, Ruddy tried to make sense of the situation. She knew Brother Bertie was a man who could handle himself in a scrap, but this? This was something entirely different.

Just as she was about to intervene, a powerful and familiar voice rang out from the doorway behind her.

'The Good Book preaches that if your hand causes you to sin, cut it off. Believe you me, the next person to put their cursed hand on my brother, I won't stop at chopping their hand clean off.'

Ruddy spun around to find Gertie standing there, a vision of righteous fury. In her hand, she clutched her brother's wicked machete, its blade glinting menacingly in the dingy light of the club. The room fell silent, all eyes turning to the formidable woman in the doorway.

Gertie stepped inside, her body vibrating with rage. Swinging the cutlass wide, she commanded, 'Now move back, Satan.'

The men beating her brother, eyeing the machete warily, backed away from Brother Bertie, who crumpled to the floor. Ruddy rushed to his side, helping Gertie to lift him to his feet. While Charlie grabbed his porkpie hat off the floor, the women half carried, half dragged him outside.

***

'She doesn't want me anymore,' Brother Bertie rasped, raw with sadness.

He was sitting in his sister's kitchen, the metallic tang of blood on his tongue. The warm, spicy scent of Gertie's fish broth filled the air, a jarring contrast to the pain that consumed him.

His sister tenderly cleaned the cuts and bruises that marred her brother's handsome features. She'd never seen him like this before, so broken and defeated. His usual go-to sparkle and mischievous gleam were gone.

'What happened?' Her question was soft, almost afraid to hear the answer. Although a part of her knew it had to do with that damn girl.

Stare glistening with hurt, he answered, 'It's Sin. Jimmy beat her when he found out she was with a black man.'

Jimmy? That shocked Gertie to the core. That boy didn't have a racist bone in his body. She was convinced there had to be more to this story.

'Did he know—?'

With a strong shake of his head, Brother Bertie urgently jumped in, 'That she was stepping out with me? No.'

Gertie's heart clenched, anger and sorrow knotting her gut. She had warned Sin, hadn't she? Told her that no good could come of this forbidden love. But the girl had been so headstrong, so convinced that love could conquer all. Lord above, the girl was living in some fairy tale.

'Jimmy's got a good heart,' Gertie asserted gently, choosing her words carefully. 'Which is more than I can say for that father of his. That father of his probably pressurised him into doing it.'

An ugly noise from deep within his chest escaped Bertie's lips. 'And that makes it all right, does it?' he demanded. 'If his dad told him to jump off a cliff, would he do it?' His features screwed up. 'I don't understand how he could hurt her like that?'

Gertie sighed, setting aside the bloodied cloth in her hand. 'It doesn't change the fact that you and Sin… it's not possible, Bertram. The world won't allow it.'

'Why won't she fight for us?' Brother Bertie whispered with fierceness. 'Why won't she fight for our love?'

Why am I not enough? That was the real unspoken question which hung heavy in the air, a suffocating weight on his chest.

Gertie's heart broke at the desperation in his tone, the awful pain that emanated from every fibre of his being. Her beloved baby brother was so exposed, so utterly destroyed by heartbreak.

'Is that why you went to The Colonial?' she continued to probe. 'To fight for your love?'

Jaw flexing, balling his hands, he growled, 'I wanted to kill them all. Every last one of those racist bastards. I wanted to make them pay for what happened to Sin. For taking the love out of the world and replacing it with hate.'

Her fingertips touched his arm with soothing care. 'But you weren't fighting back, Bertram. When I found you, you were letting them lick you down.'

'When I got there I wanted to mash them up, but I wanted them to hurt me,' he confessed, his voice trembling. 'I felt so low, so worthless.'

Now it was Gertie's turn to whelm up with rage, but not at the racists but at her brother.

She gripped his shoulders. 'Don't you ever – EVER – say that again, Bertram Watson,' she commanded, fierce and unyielding. 'Don't you ever call yourself worthless.' Her grip eased. 'We are Jamaicans, Bertie. We are proud, strong, and beautiful.'

Gertie pulled him into a tight embrace. His body was rigid with pain, every muscle wound tight enough to snap. With all her heart, Gertie tried to transfer all her strength, all her love.

'Never doubt your worth,' she whispered. 'Never let anyone make you feel less than the magnificent man you are.'

God forgive me, Gertie thought, her heart heavy with guilt and uncertainty. If I did the wrong thing going to see Sin, please, Lord, let me bear the burden, not him.

Aloud, she told him, 'It's for the best, baby brother. I know it hurts now, but in time, you'll see. What about you and Jimmy—?'

'Sin doesn't want me to say anything,' he cut in. 'She wants me to carry on my friendship with him like nothing has gone on.'

'You know Jimmy,' she reasoned with him. 'Know what's really in his heart. If he wasn't under the spell of that Beelzebub-worshipping father of his, he would never have done this. You've lost Sin, don't lose your best friend as well.' Leaning back from him, she searched his ravaged face. 'I know you love this girl, but sometimes, love isn't enough. And I can't bear to see you get hurt again, not like this.'

All of a sudden, her lips curved into a roguish grin. 'You know, there are some lovely sisters at church. Lovely girls. They'd be over the moon to meet a fine, handsome, kind-hearted man like yourself. Especially Hyacinth. Have you tried her macaroni pie? One bite of that, and you'll think you've gone straight to Heaven!'

Brother Bertie couldn't help but chuckle. Gertie joined him, and soon her kitchen was filled with laughter. Then his face crumbled, and he leaned his head into her chest, great hulking sobs racking his body. Gertie rocked him gently, just like she had when he was her little shadow back in Jamaica.

Chapter Sixty-One

'What the holy hell happened to your face?'

In response to Jimmy's question, Brother Bertie touched his bruised jaw, sliding into the passenger seat of his friend's car. They'd been summoned by Danny to meet him at the docks. Jimmy's features were creased with concern.

Brother Bertie had a sudden urge to flatten his friend's face. To slam his fist into it over and over until Jimmy's teeth scattered across the leather seats, until that handsomeness was as battered and broken as he'd left Sin's body. Of course, he did none of that. He'd promised Sin he would let it go, make sure Jimmy never found out that he knew.

But God, it was hard. So hard.

'Got jumped by three blokes down Commercial Road,' Bertie lied, settling into the seat.

Jimmy's whole body went rigid. He twisted in his seat, his blazing eyes as he searched Bertie's features. 'You having a fucking laugh?'

'Nah, mate. But you should see them.' Bertie forced a chuckle that felt like he had a pair of hands strangling his throat. 'Left two of them proper sparked out.'

'Names,' Jimmy insisted, his eyes darkening dangerously. A muscle jumped in his jaw. He gripped the steering wheel hard enough to make the leather creak. 'I want their fucking names.'

'Leave it!'

'Some toerags jump my bruv and you want me to leave it?' Jimmy's voice rose in disbelief. He slammed his palm against the wheel.

The fierce protectiveness in Jimmy's voice made Bertie's chest constrict. This was the Jimmy he knew, the one who'd have his back in a heartbeat, who'd take on an army for him. See, that was the problem Bertie was having. How could this be the same man who'd taken a vicious belt to his own sister?

A terrible image ripped through Bertie's mind. Sin's delicate skin splitting under the leather, her cries echoing off the walls. The memory turned his insides to ice, making him want to retch.

'Beam me up, Brother Bertie,' Jimmy said, using the new catchphrase from the TV show, Star Trek. His troubled gaze squinted with worry. 'You've gone quiet. That ain't like you.'

'Just tired.' Bertie stared out the window. The streets of the East End rolled past

But his best friend wasn't buying it. 'Nah, something's eating at ya.' Jimmy drummed his nails on the wheel. 'Come on, spill.'

The words burned Bertie's throat like acid. Tell me what you did to her. Admit it. Let me hear you say the words.

Instead, he said, careful to keep his tone neutral, 'Got this situation at Gertie's. It's a new lodger. Decent bloke, fell for this girl.'

'Oh yeah?' Jimmy guided the car around a horse and cart, his eyes flicking constantly to Bertie's bruised face.

'Her family found out. Strict Catholics.' Bertie watched Jimmy's reaction from the corner of his eye, searching for any flicker of guilt. 'They locked her away. Beat her. Said she brought shame on the family.'

Jimmy's jaw tightened. His knuckles whitened on the wheel. 'What did her man do?'

'She begged him not to interfere. Said it would only make things worse.' Bertie's fingers dug into his thighs until pain shot through his legs. 'That's what's doing my head in. How can he just stand there? Let the people who hurt her get away with it?'

Jimmy's profile tightened, the veins in his neck standing out. 'Sometimes family business needs to stay in the family.' Tension radiated from every line of his body.

'Even if it means watching someone you love suffer?'

Rage surged a path of fire through Bertie's veins. The memory of the welts across Sin's skin, that's what haunted him worst of all. After they made love, he'd trace kisses down her spine, memorising every perfect inch of her soft skin. It was his way of tenderly worshipping her. Now when he imagined her back, it wasn't his lover's touch he remembered but her brother's brutality.

Bertie fought hard to keep his hands by his sides because they trembled with the need to grab Jimmy by the throat, to make him feel every ounce of pain he'd inflicted on his sister.

'Listen.' Jimmy pulled up at a red light, twisting momentarily to face Bertie fully, before turning back to the road. 'In our world, there's rules. Ways things have to be done.'

'And who decides these rules?' Bertie spat the words out. 'The ones doing the hurting or the ones getting hurt?'

Jimmy shot him a sharp look, his brow furrowing. 'You sure we're still talking about your Gertie's lodger?'

''Course we are.' Bertie forced his features into a mask of innocence. He unclenched his fists slowly, one finger at a time, focusing on the pain of his nails leaving half-moons in his palms. 'It just hits close to home, seeing someone trapped between love and duty.'

'Yeah, well, duty wins every time in my book.' Jimmy swung the car left. 'That's what separates the men from the boys. Knowing where your loyalties lie.'

Where do your loyalties lie, Jimmy?

With your father's belt or your sister's blood?

'Is that what you said when Mini ran off from her old man to be with you?' Bertie threw out.

'What the fuck!' Jimmy exploded. 'What's got into you? Sounds to me like there's something on your mind.'

'Nah.' Bertie's voice was steady, even as his heart thundered with hate. 'We're solid.'

Jimmy suddenly swung the car around, taking Bertie by complete surprise. The tyres squealed on tarmac.

'This isn't the way to the docks,' Bertie said. 'Where are we going?'

Jimmy looked pissed to high heaven. 'Commercial Road. Time to find them fuckers who think they can lay hands on you.'

'I already told you—'

'We're brothers forged through fire and fists, so no one touches you and walks away.' Jimmy's voice dropped to a growl that could chill blood. 'Remember when we first met, back in '63?'

That was a day Brother Bertie would never forget.

'Since that day you've looked after my back and I've looked after yours,' Jimmy said.

Thinking back, Bertie couldn't help chuckling, 'You nearly turned up to your wedding in a fur coat.'

Suddenly, they were both cracking up and laughing their heads off. In that moment, through the laughter, Bertie felt the brotherhood between him and Jimmy. Through shared moments, scraps and schemes, triumphs and disasters, they were blood brothers.

'Stop,' Bertie managed, the laughter dying away. 'Danny will go mental if we're late. Plus, this meeting is about the car.'

The mention of the car sobered Jimmy up. He swung the car back towards Sugar Cane Wharf. 'This isn't over. But I'm settling this. No one hurts my family.'

Bertie nodded, a choking sensation rising in his throat. Even knowing Jimmy would lay down his life for him wasn't enough anymore. Like that belt against Sin's skin, some marks went too deep to heal.

Chapter Sixty-Two

Amidst the shouts and chaos of the docks, three figures stood in silent tension. With hooded eyes, Danny watched the towering crane hoist the sleek Aston Martin that had once belonged to Commander Hawthorne high into the air. Beside him, Jimmy and his sidekick, Brother Bertie, stood rigid. The sun hung low over the River Thames, casting an orange glow across the bustling activity of Sugar Cane Wharf.

The crane creaked and groaned whilst it started lowering the car towards the freighter's deck. It landed with a thud the same time Jan, Jimmy's Dutch buyer, strode over.

Reaching Jimmy, he extended a hand. 'Good doing business with you.'

Jimmy took the proffered hand and shook it hard. 'Likewise. Not quite smooth sailing, yeah?'

The stuffed brown envelope Jan passed over contained the money Jimmy and Brother Bertie had been longing for. The best friends glanced at each other like they couldn't believe it was theirs. Finally.

Danny told his son, 'Funny thing about that car, Jimmy-boy. Once I sussed it was you who had nabbed it, didn't take a genius to figure you'd flip it to Jan here. He's the go-to guy for shifting hot wheels to the continent. Known him for donkey's years, haven't I, Jan?'

The Dutch man nodded, a wry smile playing on his lips. 'What I like about your father is he's a man who knows what's going on.'

Of course, The King of the Docks knew everyone. Once he suspected Jimmy, it hadn't taken Danny long to figure out the rest. So he'd got on the blower to Jan who had confirmed his suspicions.

The Dutch man took out his pipe and pointed it at a metal container discreetly tucked into the side of the ship. 'And I'll make sure that this ends up getting lost in the tide.'

It contained the grisly remains they had discovered in the car. Commander Hawthorne's son-in-law would forever be lost at sea.

Danny steered Jimmy away from the others. Tensing, Jimmy knew what was coming; his father was on the warpath, finally ready to confront him.

Folding his arms across his chest, his father bored his harsh stare into him. 'You've got some bleedin' nerve.' A vein pumped in Danny's temple

Jimmy swallowed hard, fighting the urge to look away. 'Dad, I can explain—'

'Explain?' Danny answered with the force of a grenade, rearing forward, his eyes narrowing. 'You went behind my back, pulled a job on my turf without my say-so.'

Heat rushed to Jimmy's face. Anger and shame warred within him, making his voice shake. 'I wouldn't have done it if you'd given me the sodding loan!'

Danny's eyes flashed with lethal intent. He closed the distance between them, his face inches from Jimmy's. Spittle flew as he snarled, 'You dare blame this on me?'

The furious words cut through the air with the deadly swiftness of a knife. Jimmy's heart hammered against his ribs, but he held his ground. Part of him wanted to back down, to beg forgiveness. But there was a stronger part, the part that was sick and tired of being the obedient son.

'Why didn't you give me the money?' Jimmy's voice rose, matching his father's intensity. 'And don't give me no shit-bollocks-cunty-crap about having to wait till next year.'

'Watch your mouth!' Danny's menacing low growl would've made most run the other way.

Not Jimmy, although he faltered, but only for a moment. He'd come too far to turn tail now. 'Why didn't you give it to me? All me and Mini want is our own place. What's so wrong with that? We've got kids now, another on the way, a family. Don't we deserve our own four walls and roof?'

Lips twisting, Danny stepped back, his face a storm of emotions. For a long moment, he said nothing, just stared out at the churning waters of the Thames. Jimmy could almost see the gears turning in his father's head, weighing up whether to explode or relent.

When Danny finally spoke, his voice was softer, tinged with something Jimmy had rarely heard from his father – vulnerability.

'Truth is, I don't want you to go, son.' Danny's shoulders slumped, the fight draining out of him. He ran a hand over his face, suddenly seeming way older than his years. 'I've still got so much to teach you. Your mum, she loves having her grandbabies underfoot. Now there's a new one on the way. It won't be the same if you're not there.'

The admission hit Jimmy like a sucker punch from one of his opponents in the ring. He'd never seen his dad like this, never imagined the great Danny Steele could appear so lost.

Jimmy choked up. 'We ain't going far, Dad. Still in Sugar Cane Wharf, just down the road in Molasses Quay. You can come round any time, you know that.'

Something flickered across his father's face at the mention of the address, although it was gone in an instant. But Jimmy caught it, a tightening around the eyes, a slight twitch of the lips.

'What is it, Dad?'

Danny could've kicked himself because he should have twigged that the house Jimmy and his missus had their heart set on was the one on Molasses Quay. Well, his son was in for a big-time disappointment, because after their meeting, Danny was going straight to the River Rat where he and Rita had laid on a little surprise for Mortimer Stiffington which would force that stick-up-his-proverbials to sell the house to him.

Deliberately, Danny steered their conversation in a different direction, confiding in Jimmy, 'I've never had a great relationship with my own old man.'

Jimmy scowled with confusion. 'But I thought you'd got on with your stepdad, Ezra.' He remembered him well, a big man, kind-hearted, who'd loved laughing a lot, who had married Dora Green and given her two sons his last name.

'Not Daddy Ezra. I'm talking about that bastard whose blood runs in my veins.'

Jimmy was shocked. 'I thought you didn't know who your old fella was.'

Danny abruptly clammed up, obviously regretting how much he'd revealed. His expression lifted, charming Danny Steele back in place. 'What's done is done. You're my boy. My flesh and blood. We'll work it out.'

Relief claimed Jimmy. 'Thanks, Dad. I mean it. I won't let you down again.'

Danny leaned in close. 'You ever try to pull one over on me again, I'll crush you like a bug. I've built this empire with my bare hands, and I won't have anyone – that includes family – bring it down. Are we clear?'

After Jimmy's sharp nod, his father finished with a chilling warning. 'If you were anyone else, you'd be bloated and floating face-down in the river by now.'

Chapter Sixty-Three

Mortimer Stiffington reluctantly strode into the clamour of East End voices inside the River Rat pub. His gaze darted around, his discomfort palpable. He'd received a message from Lady Henrietta Featherstonehaugh to meet him here. He hadn't heard from her since the meeting of her charity in Soho when he'd turned down flat her request to buy the house on Molasses Quay. His brow furrowed in confusion because this was a very strange venue for her to ask him to meet in. Then again, the pub might be part of the charity work she did.

He finally found Her Ladyship at the bar. His jaw hit the floor. The refined Lady Henrietta he'd met weeks ago had vanished, replaced by a brassy piece of East End rough. Gone was the elegant clothing and pearls. In their place, a psychedelic minidress that barely covered her behind with a neckline so low her tits were practically waving hello. Her face was caked in makeup. Mortimer's world tilted on its axis.

He stiffened as the penny finally dropped.

He'd been had.

This was no member of the aristocracy, and he'd bet his life that all that guff about an East End charity were lies from the start. Face burning with humiliation, he angrily approached her.

'Who are you? And what is the meaning of this?'

Rita's lips curled into a sardonic smile. 'Who I am don't matter, darling. What matters is you're gonna sell that house to a friend of mine.'

'What friend?' Mortimer's eyes narrowed to slits. 'Not that it makes a blind bit of difference. I wouldn't sell to you or your lot if you were the last buyers in London!'

Rita's eyes hardened, cold as ice. She stepped closer, her voice dropping to a menacing purr. 'Oh, but you will, Morty, baby.'

The opening of the pub door caught his attention. Two women entered. Kathleen and Dilly Docherty. The blood drained from his face. He couldn't take his eyes off eighteen-year-old Dilly. Her soft brown eyes held their familiar distant gaze, a haunting reminder of the tragic hit-and-run that had left her with a traumatic brain injury a decade ago.

Her sister clinging to her hand, Kath moved with gushing enthusiasm straight towards Rita. Mortimer was paralysed while she and Rita had a quick, happy exchange. But he barely registered their words, his focus solely on Dilly. Strangely, Dilly watched him right back.

When the sisters left, Rita spun to face Mortimer, supreme triumph blazing all across her face. 'I figured out your secret.'

Mortimer's head snapped towards her, his eyes wide with fear.

'It was you, wasn't it? You're the one who knocked down little Dilly and then drove off like a coward while she's never been the same since.' The disgust she felt towards him was plain. 'And ever since, you've been paying off her family, trying to buy your way out of the guilt.'

Before he could answer, a shadow cast over them. He turned to find a man he'd never met before but he knew all about him. Danny Steele, the so-called King of the Docks. He was not the type of man who Mortimer associated with.

His scarred face split by a grin was all teeth and menace. 'Mortimer, old chum,' Danny purred, extending a hand. 'Danny Steele. I believe you have something I want.'

Ill at ease, Mortimer shook Danny's hand, his own trembling slightly. 'Mr Steele, I'm afraid I don't—'

'The house, Mortimer. Molasses Quay.' Danny's tone was amiable, but his eyes glinted with a hard edge. 'I've got my heart set on it. And word has it, you're the man to talk to.'

Mortimer swallowed hard, but he stood his ground. 'As I was about to tell… erm… this woman, I won't be able to help you.'

Danny's smile didn't waver, but his gaze turned predatory. 'Oh, I think you can. Unless, of course, you want the whole world to know about your little-bitty secret.' The smile disappeared. 'Going around hurting little girls. Well, that isn't something folk like to hear.'

'You wouldn't.'

'Wouldn't I?' Danny settled in close with relish, his breath hot against Mortimer's ear. 'A respectable man like yourself, with a secret like that? It would destroy you. Your reputation, your career, your whole bloody life.' He moved back. 'But it doesn't have to be that way. Get his lordship to sign on the dotted line, and your secret stays safe with me.'

For a moment, Mortimer was the image of a drowning man, desperately seeking a lifeline. But then, something shifted in his expression. A flicker of defiance, a glimmer of resolve.

'I'm afraid that won't be possible, Mr Steele.'

Danny's brow furrowed. 'Come again?'

Mortimer straightened his spine, staring Danny dead in the eye. 'The house. It's been sold. To someone else.'

The silence that followed was deafening. Danny's face contorted with seething disbelief. 'You're bluffing.'

'I assure you, I am not.' Mortimer's voice was steady now, his earlier fear replaced by a quiet determination. 'The contract was signed this morning. The house on Molasses Quay is no longer mine to sell. Not to you, not to anyone.'

Danny's fist slammed onto the bar, making the glasses jump and rattle. 'Who? Who did you sell it to?'

He knew it couldn't be Jimmy because his son had only come into the cash he needed less than half an hour ago.

Mortimer lifted his chin. 'I'm not at liberty to say.'

With as much stiff grace as he could muster, Mortimer turned on his heel and walked out of the River Rat, his step more confident than it had been in years.

***

With a thunderous motion of his arm, Danny swept all the glasses off the bar. The pub fell into a deafening silence.

'Get out,' he roared. 'The lot of ya, get the fuck out.'

The patrons fled, including his men and Rita.

Danny stomped around the bar and yanked down a bottle of Trinidadian rum. The hardcore kind. He unscrewed the lid and knocked it back. The liquor scorched the back of his tongue, searing a blazing trail down his throat, igniting a fierce heat in his gut. Bottle in hand, Danny slammed out of the pub and jumped in his car. He drank as he drove, not giving a shit about the new drink-drive limit and being stopped by the cops with those new breathalyser thingies.

He was on his way to confront the one person who could finally make this pain he'd carried for years go away.

Chapter Sixty-Four

'Mini!' Jimmy called out with breathless excitement, bursting into the hallway. 'Where are you, darlin'?'

Heart pounding, he raced through the house, a bottle of his wife's favourite sweet Spanish red clutched in his hand. He couldn't wait to see her face when he told her the news. He'd finally gone and done it, had the dosh to buy the house. No more living under his old man's roof. They'd have a place to call their own. He knew full well many would turn their nose up at a house near the river on Sugar Cane Wharf, but it would be a start for him and Mini. He could already see them doing it up, turning it from a run-down house into a much-loved home.

He found her at the kitchen table, but it was the sight of her ashen face that stopped him cold.

'What's wrong?' he asked, his voice rough with fear and anger. 'Is it the baby?'

She shook her head. When he took her hands in his, he gasped at how ice-cold they were.

'No, Jimmy, it's…' Her voice trembled as she nodded to the table.

That's when he noticed an open envelope and a letter. Sitting beside Mini, he lifted the letter and read. It was from someone called Mortimer Stiffington, informing a Mr James Steele and Mrs Annabel Steele that they were now the legal owners of 1 Molasses Quay. No wonder Mini seemed frozen in place, she was in shock.

Jimmy blinked, sure he'd misread. He scanned the letter again, the words refusing to change. 'I don't understand,' he murmured. 'I was coming to tell you I'd finally got the money to buy the house, but I haven't done it yet, so how is this possible?'

Mini disbelievingly searched his face. 'You didn't do this?'

'No, I…' Jimmy shook his head, at a loss.

Someone must have made a mistake. Got mixed up because he'd only just sold the car, the money burning a hole in his pocket. There was no way he could have bought the house yet. A thought struck him.

'Could it have been my dad?'

Resentment flashed over Mini's face which she quickly masked. 'You think your old man would do this for us?'

Jimmy bristled. 'He's my dad, Mini. He wants what's best for us.'

Mini's laugh was bitter. 'Best for him, more like. He's never done anything without an angle.' Softening, she touched his cheek with tender love. 'I know you love him, but you've got to see it. He's never going to let you stand on your own two feet.'

Jimmy pulled away, his jawline tightening. He wanted to argue, to defend his father, but doubt nagged at him. None of this business with the car would have happened if his dad had loaned him the money for the house from the off.

The disturbing emotions it stirred up in him were too much to handle, so he shook them off and stood. 'There's only one way to find out what's happening here.'

Jimmy strode to the telephone table in the passage. The black Bakelite phone felt heavy in his hand as he dialled the number on the letter.

'Mortimer Stiffington's office,' a clipped voice answered.

'This is James Steele,' Jimmy said, trying to keep his tone even. 'I'd like to speak to Mr Stiffington.'

'What is it regarding?'

'A house. Number one Molasses Quay. There seems to be some mistake.'

The line crackled, and then another voice came on the line. 'James Steele? This is Mr Stiffington's assistant. He's not available at present, but I am in a position to answer all of your questions.' After he listened to Jimmy, he told him, "I can assure you there's no mistake. The transaction has been completed. The property is now in your and your wife's names. And hands.'

Jimmy's grip tightened on the receiver. 'But I didn't sign no papers. I haven't paid a penny—'

'The buyer wishes to remain anonymous,' Stiffington's assistant interrupted. 'They handled all the necessary paperwork and funds.'

A chill slithered down Jimmy's spine. You learned early in childhood growing up in the East End that there were no freebies in this life. Well, at least not without a price.

'I don't know what game this buyer is playing, but I don't like it. There's always strings attached. Always.'

'Not this time, Mr Steele.' It sounded like the other man was smiling. 'The buyer was quite insistent. This is a gift, freely given, with no obligations or debts. You have their word.'

Jimmy's head spun. A gift? But who would do such a thing? And why? He opened his mouth to demand more answers, but the other man was already speaking again.

'I understand your concerns. But I can only tell you what I've been instructed to. The house is yours. Formal papers will soon follow. What you do with it is up to you.'

The line went dead, leaving Jimmy staring at the receiver in his hand. Slowly, he set it back in the cradle, his mind reeling. He turned to find Mini watching him from the kitchen doorway, her hands cradling the soft swell of her belly. Their unborn child. Their future.

Maybe, just maybe, this was their chance.

He crossed to her, gathering her in his arms. 'It's ours, Mini,' he whispered into her hair. 'The house is really ours.'

Dropping to his knees, he pressed a reverent kiss to her stomach, his heart swelling with love and fierce protectiveness. 'You hear that, little 'un? Your mum and dad are proper homeowners now. I'm gonna give you everything, I swear it.'

But who gifted us your new home, little one? Who was it?

Chapter Sixty-Five

Mortimer saw the solitary figure standing motionless, back turned, gazing out over the murky Thames. With purpose, he strode along the damp cobblestones, his footsteps echoing in the chilly air. The dying rays of the sun cast long shadows across the crumbling facades of 1 and 2 Molasses Quay looming behind them.

These twin Georgian houses, once proud sentinels of Sugar Cane Wharf, now exuded an air of faded elegance and creeping decay. Ivy choked the brickwork, while paint peeled from rotting window frames like diseased skin. Their grimy sash windows stared out blankly, hinting at long-buried secrets within.

'It's done,' Mortimer informed the person, cutting through the eerie silence. 'By now Jimmy should know that the house belongs to him.'

The figure slowly turned.

Iris Steele.

Her fingers nervously gripped the soft leather of her handbag. The tension melted from her face at his news.

'Thank you, Mortimer,' she said softly.

She was the anonymous benefactor who had bought the house for Jimmy and his wife. Originally, Iris had had no intention of stepping in, but when she'd figured out that Danny was after the house, too, she had no choice. The needs of her children always came first, especially above those of her husband.

Mortimer shook his head in the deepest respect. 'Most people would be shocked to know you have the power to do this.'

A tiny smile touched Iris' cold lips. 'There's a lot people don't know about me, Mortimer.'

Indeed there was. To most of the East End, Iris was simply the long-suffering and timid wife of Danny 'King of the Docks' Steele, a meek woman who turned a blind eye to her husband's infidelities and sought solace in the bottle. But there was so much more beneath the surface.

Iris' father had been Alfred Chambers, the well-known and much respected local greengrocer. While not wealthy by any stretch, Alf had been shrewd with his money, putting his family a rung or two above many in their working-class community. What even Danny didn't know was that her father had squirrelled away a tidy sum over the years, leaving Iris a secret trust held in a bank in the City. Her father was a very special and forward-thinking man, going against the trends of many who didn't believe a woman should have their own money.

He'd tell her: ''Listen 'ere, my girl. A clever woman keeps a separate purse, just like I keep a bit extra in the till for them rainy days.'

Iris mused to Mortimer, her gaze distant, 'My father taught me to watch, to listen, to bide my time.'

And she had. Especially to those who mattered the most – her kids. This included the incident with Danny's side piece, Carol Wilson, all those years back during Sunday dinner that had caused all the strife in their family. Danny was telling the truth when he swore blind that it hadn't been him who'd slashed the woman's face to ribbons. Unbeknownst to him it had been Iris. Norma, their neighbour and Danny's lookout, had been more than happy to oblige for a small fee. The husband-stealer had made the mistake of mouthing obscenities in her children's presence. No way could Iris let that stand.

Mess with Iris' children and you messed with her.

'I may be just Danny Steele's wife to most,' she continued, a hint of steel entering her voice. 'But I'm my father's daughter, too. And I'll do anything for my boy, my girl. Anything.'

Mortimer nodded, a shaky breath leaving him, suddenly feeling very emotional. 'I know, Iris. Believe me, I know.'

She turned to him, her silver-grey eyes kind and warm. 'You're thinking about young Dilly, aren't you?'

He swallowed hard. 'Every God-fearing day.'

For all these years, Mortimer had carried the burden of guilt of what had befallen Dilly that fateful day. Iris' bully-boy husband and that venomous Rita thought he was the one behind the wheel.

But it wasn't true. And Iris knew it.

'I'll never forget that night.' Mortimer spoke so quietly, his voice was almost swallowed by the wind. 'When you called me to come to the church and finding Gail hysterical, reeking of wine…'

Iris would never forget that day either. She'd been finishing up cleaning in the church. 'Your wife came stumbling in. Your Gail was in a bad way. Scared out of her wits.'

'She told me what happened,' Mortimer continued. 'How she'd had too much to drink, how the girl came out of nowhere…' He shook his head. 'I was ready to go to the police right then and there.'

'But you didn't,' Iris said gently.

'No,' Mortimer agreed. 'Because of you.'

Gail Stiffington had been a woman haunted by her own tragedy, the death of her own ten-year-old son. Overwhelmed by grief, she'd turned to the numbness of the bottle to see her way through. Calmly, Iris had laid out a plan to a wild-eyed and panicking Mortimer and his sobbing wife. If Dilly passed they'd go to the police. However, if she lived it would be Gail and Mortimer's duty to see that she wanted for nothing. That there would always be money to take care of all her needs.

'You saved us,' Mortimer said, his voice thick with emotion. 'You saved my Gail. I can never repay you for that.'

Iris shook her head. An image of Danny flashed through her mind. 'We all have our crosses to bear. I did what needed to be done.'

'Do you ever regret it?' Mortimer asked. 'Helping us cover it up?'

Iris was silent for a long moment, her gaze drawn back to the looming Georgian houses. 'We can't change the past. We can only try to make things right in the here and now.'

She gestured towards 1 Molasses Quay. 'That's why I'm doing this. For Jimmy, for Mini, for their little ones. A chance at a fresh start.'

Mortimer frowned, a question nagging at him. 'Why was your husband so dead set on getting this particular house? I mean, it's a bit of a state.'

'I learned years ago to stop asking questions about why Danny does what he does.'

However, when Mortimer had gone, after taking a deep swig from the flask she always carried in her bag, Iris answered his question:

'I think something terrible happened to Danny in that house when he was a young lad.'

Chapter Sixty-Six

'I know what you did, you rotten, old bastard.'

Danny's voice came at Lord Xander from the darkness.

Danny was drunk. Off his effing head, pissed out of his loaf. Driving like a maniac from the River Rat, he'd downed the last of the rum before getting out of his car. He'd been lurking in the shadows of the cobbled Soho street waiting for the man who was really his blood father. Long ago, Danny had made it is business to discover the aristocrat's general routine, and this time of night he was to be found between the lush thighs of his mistress. A girl who was half his age and catered to his very individual sexual tastes.

'Whose there?' Lord Xander called out, cautiously stepping back.

Swaying slightly, Danny came out of the shadows, stepping under a streetlight. The harsh glare carved deep shadows across his haggard face, emphasising the red richness of his bloodshot eyes. He was the picture of a haunted man, worn and battered, his usually imposing frame now slumped and unsteady.

'Daniel?' Lord Xander couldn't believe his eyes. 'What on earth are you doing here?'

'You think I don't remember what you did because I was young?' he continued, voice low and trembling, his Cockney accent strong. 'You kept us hidden away in that tunnel in the basement of that house. Like we was something to be ashamed of.'

Xander's brow's flicked up in annoyance. 'Let's not do this now—'

'Fuck! You!' Danny blasted. 'I was only three or four, but I remember. The first years of my life you had us stowed away on the top floor of the that place in Stepney. There was a woman there…Polly – yeah that was her name – who you installed to look after us. Then you knocked Mum up again—'

'I told her there were to be no more children,' Xander spat out.

'DORA,' Danny almost screamed. 'My mother's name was Dora. She never stood a chance when she went to work for your family, did she? Innocent London girl up against your slimy charms – she stood no chance.'

'It wasn't like that.'

'No?' Danny jumped in. 'Then what was it like? Because from where I'm standing, you used her and did your best to suck the life from her.'

Lord Xander tilted his aristocratic chin and nose in the air. He said nothing.

'Your posho family put her out, didn't they,' Danny rushed on. 'Let her go because she had a child on the way. You didn't step forward to your parents to claim the child – me – as yours. Stand up like a man and take the blame.'

'I was young,' his father reasoned. 'I didn't know what to do. My father would have disowned me. I did the best I could.'

Danny drew in a shaking breath. 'When Mum got pregnant again you took us to that house in Molasses Quay.'

Shuddering, Danny momentarily closed his eyes. The flashes of the gut-wrenching memories assaulted him…

Mummy's hand held his tight, clammy and shaking. They were caught in the darkness and shadows of the night. The Mister was here. Danny thought he was his father but his mummy sternly warned him never to say that.

Why was The Mister here?

Whispers hissed, angry and sharp between Mummy and Mister. Little Danny was scared. The Mister dragged them through the house. Outside the house they lived in, in Stepney, the sky started fading. His tummy twisted, like snakes, like knots. Mummy was crying, voice breaking. Now they were in a car that rumbled like a hungry beast.

Another house up ahead. By the river. He shrank back from the bottomless water. The house was filled with shadows, long grasping talons. Stairs, creaking, groaning. Up, Mummy begs. She wants them to go up the stairs, but Mister takes them down. Down, down, into the suffocating blackness. It stank bad, rotten, clinging. Tears, hot, stinging, falling down his ice-cold cheeks. Out of nowhere the tunnel loomed up, gaping wide. He thought he was going to be swallowed whole. He hid in the protection of his mummy's trembling side.

They reached a room. Two small beds, stained, like dirty secrets. Mummy sobbing, shaking. Mister's voice was hard, cold. He told them to stay. They couldn't leave. Someone called Ezra would bring food.

Mister slammed the door. Turned the key. Danny wanted to scream. SCREAM…

Gasping like it was his last breath, Danny hurtled back to the present. He hated going back. Hated it.

'You left us in that dark, nasty room for months. Mum was so scared down there. Sometimes we'd lie huddled together at night, I'd feel the baby kicking in her belly, and all we could hear was the waves of the river. Slapping and slapping against the walls until I thought they were going to burst in and drown us. Sweep us away.'

'I made sure you were looked after.'

'You just left us to rot,' Danny spat, his voice thick with emotion. 'Ezra became our only friend.'

'I wanted to acknowledge you,' Xander insisted. 'Both you and George. But this world… it's not that simple.'

With a fury, Danny rushed up to him. 'You dare mention George. After what you tried to do.'

Smoothing a palm over the front of his jacket, Xander said, 'I have no idea what you're talking about.'

The memories ambushed Danny again. He tried to fight them off, but they wouldn't let him go…

He was tucked in the corner of the room watching Mummy on the bed screaming in pain. A woman missing most of her teeth helped bring something out from between Mummy's legs. The woman smelled sour of drink. He saw the face first. Then the body. Finally the baby slipped into this world. Mister emerged from the dark. Picked up the baby. Said he had to do it. They didn't have a choice. Mummy cried out at him. Please, she begged. Don't throw my child in the river. It was for the best, Mister said. Sobbing, Mummy tried to get up but collapsed back on the bed. Mister took the squalling, wriggling baby, his newborn son, towards the door. Ezra appeared, grabbed the baby. Knocked Mister down. He took them out of that hellhole…

'You were going to kill George,' Danny shouted at him, back in the present.

Xander sneered, 'Well, considering what he became, I would've been doing him a favour.'

Danny knew that if he stayed there a moment longer he was going to kill this despicable man. Twisting around, he strode away. Then his father's voice stopped him in his tracks.

'Me and you are the same, Daniel. We want things from life and aren't afraid to grab them. Those who get in our way, we have to deal with them. We don't have a choice.'

'You're nothing like him,' his mother told Danny time and time again. 'You've got a good heart, my boy. Don't you ever forget that.'

But his mother was so wrong. So wrong. He possessed the same ruthless ambition, the same knack for manipulation. He was rotten to the core.

Calmy, Lord Xander spoke. 'Daniel? I'll see you at your club, as usual next week.'

He should bar him from the Voodoo Lounge. Get rid of him once and for all from his life. But he knew he was lying to himself. Despite everything, all Danny ever wanted was the approval of his father. Still waiting for the day Viscount Blacklock would acknowledge him as his firstborn son.

Not turning, he quietly answered, 'I'll see you there.'

Epilogue

Two Weeks Later

Jimmy Steele and Brother Bertie stood on the roof terrace of Number 1 Molasses Quay, on the banks of the River Thames, before them one of the best views of the river in Sugar Cane Wharf. They shared a bottle of Lord Have Mercy Rum Punch and watched the boats drift past below. The sun caught the water, turning it almost a pretty shade. Almost! Neither man would ever forget that the river had them in its clutches of death.

'Mini's got plans,' Jimmy announced, licking some of the potent rum from his lips. 'Reckons we'll knock through them poky rooms downstairs, make it all open 'n' that. Dead modern.' He gestured expansively. 'The kids can have the whole top floor to themselves.'

Inside, the house told a sadder tale than its grand exterior suggested. It hadn't been loved in a long time. It was riddled with damp and old-style peeling wallpaper. The state of the floorboards was currently a death trap, so they would need attending to urgently. The marble fireplaces were slightly chipped, but he knew a guy who could do them up a treat. Jimmy knew he faced months of hard graft to make it liveable, but he and Mini were prepared to roll their sleeves up and bring back the beauty they knew lurked beneath. The decorative plasterwork ceilings, the elegant staircase, the tall windows with the commanding views of the river.

This would become the family home they'd dreamed of for ages.

Jimmy pointed to a spot on the shore at the edge of the house that bordered on the river. 'I'm thinking about putting a private dock there. Reckon it will come in handy for my line of work.'

His boxing days were over. No point kidding himself anymore. That dream had died with a knockout punch. His line of work was now working full time for his father's gangland empire.

Frowning, he remembered, 'The strangest thing is that tunnel where we hid the car.' He saw a shudder run through his friend. 'It leads to the cellar at the bottom of the house.'

'Bruv, you couldn't pay me enough diamonds to go down there.' Brother Bertie chuckled. 'That place gave me the bloody willies. Rats the size of small dogs!'

Jimmy thought of something else that had puzzled him. 'Mum's been here loads of times, but Dad won't come.'

His mate let out a lengthy sigh. 'Probably still pissed you managed to get this place with no help from him. He'll come around.'

Jimmy wasn't so sure. He could swear every time he motioned the house his dad did a disappearing act. He shrugged. His father would come round in his own good, Danny Steele time.

Brother Bertie grinned, adjusting his porkpie hat against the river breeze. 'Your missus has got taste, bruv. This place is gonna be something else when she's done with it.'

'Too right.' Jimmy's silver-grey eyes sparkled. He passed the bottle over. 'Mini's already turning one of the rooms into a proper place for her to sew.'

'Speaking of family.' Brother Bertie's smile widened. 'That brief I found, says there's no way Claudette can take my name off Precious' birth certificate. She's staying a Watson, blood and paper.'

Jimmy clapped him on the shoulder. 'Good news, mate.'

They fell into comfortable silence, watching a barge laden with cargo navigate the river's bend.

'You know what, Bertie?' Jimmy said softly. 'We done all right, you and me. We done all right.'

Brother Bertie nodded, a warm smile playing across his face. 'That we did, spar. That we did.'

From the corner of his eye, Jimmy studied his closest friend. Something was different about Bertie these days. There was a stiffness in the way he held himself, especially when they were together, a distance that hadn't been there before. If Jimmy didn't know better, he'd swear his blood brother was holding something against him.

Next in the Love and Hate Series

Are you ready for the next two books in the Love and Hate Series?
Available on Amazon and FREE on Kindle Unlimited

Honour and Vengeance
Secrets and Lies

Free Novella

Join Our Exclusive Book Club

If you haven't already, plunge into the gangland world where the Steele and Watson Crime Family Drama started.

Dangerous

A LOVE & HATE SERIES PREQUEL

Fate throws them together. The streets try to tear them apart.

Bertram Watson, aka Brother Bertie, newly arrived from Jamaica, finds himself on the run in London's gritty streets. Jimmy Steele, son of a feared gangster, is bleeding out in a warehouse after a botched heist. Their paths cross in a twist of fate that will change their lives forever.

As Bertie's Jamaican street smarts clash with Jimmy's East End savvy, they form an unlikely alliance. But with rival gangs closing in and dangerous secrets coming to light, their newfound friendship is put to the ultimate test.

In this thrilling novella, loyalties are tested, blood is spilled, and love is pushed to its limits in the unforgiving world of London's underworld.

Visit www.dredamitchell.com

In gangland men reign but it's the women who rule

Big Mo Series

Check out Amazon for all of our books

Dreda Amazon Books UK
Dreda Amazon Books US

Reviews: We write for you!
We adore hearing what you think about our books. Reviews help other readers find books. So do please leave a review.

For news and staying in touch head over to: www.dredamitchell.com including signing up to our newsletter for goodies and free stories.
https://www.facebook.com/dredasaymitchell/
https://www.tiktok.com/@dredaryanauthors?lang=en

All About Dreda & Ryan

Her Majesty Queen Elizabeth awarded Dreda an MBE in her New Year's Honours' List, 2020! She has appeared on Queen Camilla's Reading Room.

Ryan and Dreda are a wife and husband team who write across the crime and mystery genre - psychological thrillers, gritty gangland crime and fast-paced action books.

She scooped the CWA's John Creasey Dagger Award in 2004, the first time a Black British author has received this honour.

Spare Room, their first psychological thriller was a #1 UK and US Amazon Bestseller. Lee Child, named her 2022 novel, Say Her Name his best book of the year so far. She is one of the twelve acclaimed female authors of International Bestselling, Marple, a new reimagined Miss Marple anthology. Dreda is a passionate campaigner and speaker on social issues and the arts. She has appeared on television, including Celebrity Pointless, Celebrity Eggheads, BBC 1 Breakfast, Sunday Morning Live, Newsnight, The Review Show and Front Row Late on BBC 2. She had Fun! Fun! Fun! With Alan Carr on documentary series, Alan's Adventures with Agatha Christie, Channel 4.

Dreda's Black History Month short story about the remarkable Althea McNish was narrated on Amazon's Alexa by Sir Trevor MacDonald. Ryan and Dreda both performed a specially commissioned monologue on the ground-breaking SkyArts50 on Sky TV. She is a judge on the Women's Prize, Discoveries initiative for new writers, 2025.

Dreda has been a guest on many radio shows and presented BBC Radio 4's flagship books programme, Open Book. She has written in a number of leading newspapers including The Guardian and was thrilled to be named one of Britain's 50 Remarkable Women by Lady Geek in association with Nokia. She is a Trustee of The Royal Literary Fund and an ambassador for The Reading Agency.

Some of their books are currently in development as TV and film adaptations.

Dreda's parents are from the beautiful Caribbean island of Grenada. Her name, Dreda, is Irish and pronounced with a long vowel ee sound in the middle!

Printed in Dunstable, United Kingdom

68644502R00298